TANDEM

Liafail:
the third book of Tros of Samothrace

'I build a ship!' cried Tros. 'My friend Caswallon will believe me mad and Orwic will mock me, but the world is round, and I will sail around it!

'Nevertheless you are my friends. I will serve you first and take what comes of it. Caesar offered to make me admiral of his fleet if I would desert Caswallon. He thought me fool enough to believe that he will not close all the ports of Gaul against me and set a big price on my head. The thought never entered the calculating brain of Caesar, that I will go to Rome and there, it may be, break the wheels of his ambition.

'He knows I build a ship, but he does not know how big a ship or how seaworthy, because Caswallon slew his spies. I will sail through the Gates of Hercules, drop anchor in the port of Ostia, proceed to Rome and do there what I can to ruin Caesar's prospect of invading Britain. One way or another, I will break the spokes of Caesar's wheel before I set forth on my own adventure.'

The books of Tros of Samothrace by Talbot Mundy

TROS   Tandem edition 30p
HELMA   Tandem edition 30p
LIAFAIL   Tandem edition 30p
HELENE   Tandem edition 25p

Liafail

Talbot Mundy

TANDEM
14 Gloucester Road, London SW7

First published in Great Britain by Hutchinson & Co.
(Publishers) Ltd, 1934
First published by Universal-Tandem Publishing Co. Ltd,
1971

To
Rose Wilder Lane
with sincere gratitude for her
persistent interest and enthusiasm

Made and printed in Great Britain by
Hunt Barnard Printing Ltd., Aylesbury, Bucks.

'I BUILD A SHIP!'

Whence I came, I know. Whither I go, I know not. I came forth from the womb of Experience. What I know, that I am. What I know not is the limitless measure of what I may become. Life grows, and I see it. And so I grow, because I know it. I will strike such a blow on the anvil of life as shall use to the utmost all I am. Thus, though I know not whither I go nor what I shall be, I shall go to no home of idleness. I shall be no grey ghost lamenting what I might have done but did not.

From the log of Tros of Samothrace

There were ambassadors from half a dozen kings around the fireplace in the great hall in Caswallon's house, and they were dressed in all their finery of jewelled woollen cloth, with golden chains around their necks. Behind them, backs against the long wall, their retainers sat, arms folded – a pattern in half-relief against the shadow that reached to right and left of the door into the gloom of the far-away corners.

Firelight shook the shadows among the ceiling beams and fitfully illuminated shields and weapons, coloured designs on the wall-cloth, faces, shapes of a dozen dogs asleep. Oil sconces by an inner door at one end of the hall and two more on the wall that faced it made halos of light in the smoke from the hearth. A minstrel with a small harp plucked at the strings reflectively, as if searching for music to appeal to many minds in disagreement.

From the vestibule, through the thickness of an oaken door, came thumps of spear-butts and the laughter of men-at-arms, but within the great hall there was hardly any conversation. A man's voice broke too noticeably on the silence for even a king's ambassador to care to voice more than platitudes.

But in a smaller room, by another fireside, there was conference that those ambassadors would have given ears to hear. Tros sat, fist on table, clutching a roll of parchment. Beside him was Sigurdsen.

Fflur faced them, hair in long braids to her waist, her grey eyes watching Tros as if he were the arbiter of destiny. And beside her, Caswallon tugged at his fair moustache, his white skin whiter for the pale-blue figures drawn with fading woad on neck and forearms.

5

Conops sat on the floor, cross-legged, poking at the fire. Orwic lolled at the end of the table, his interest disguised under an air of cultivated boredom.

The room was so hung with coloured draperies as almost to resemble an enormous tent. The door was double-curtained, leather behind embroidered cloth. No sound of what they said could reach the great hall, though they had argued noisily.

'The breadth and length of it is this,' Caswallon said at the end of three hours' hot debate, gripping the edge of the table with a great white hand. 'These lousy cousin-kings* have stirred up the druids against me. Some accused me of ambition to be the king of all Britain; others of cooking an unnecessary war against the Romans. Two of the fools accuse me of befriending Caesar! Mother of my sons, don't interrupt me!

'Only the gods know what will happen to us now Taliesan is dead. He had wisdom. Ere the breath had left his lips we learned that Rome's ambassadors had snatched my wife while my back was turned. Peace, Fflur! I speak. I say, don't interrupt me!

'They slew Helma, wife of my good friend Tros. And here sits Fflur beside me. I have Tros to thank for it.'

'Tros and the luck o' Lud!' said Orwic.

'Tros and the gods and the sorcerer Eough,' said Fflur, 'but I think my Lord Caswallon did his share.'

'Mother of my sons, I would have died for you nine times over like a cat away from home, and have found a tenth life in which to regret you, had I failed! But listen to me! Caesar had no liking to be taken prisoner, though he thought it a great stroke of strategy to sneak my wife away. He feels his dignity is injured. He swore vengeance, pledging himself to invade us with an army and to burn my house. It is war. There is no gainsaying it. Caesar will come.'

'Not if I have my way, he won't,' said Orwic, yawning. 'If half what Tros tells us about the man is true, we need only to send him a woman. She can put poison in his drink or run a bodkin through his heart or –'

Fflur interrupted in a voice as vibrant as that of her father, who was Mygnach the Dwarf. And they said of him that he could ring bells merely by speaking at them.

'If I thought you meant that, Orwic, I would forbid you the house!'

'Nay, nay, I can't spare Orwic,' said Caswallon. 'Let him talk

---

*Not necessarily relatives. The word *cousin* here signifies equals, neighbours, men with similar responsibilities.

as he pleases, so be he plays the man in action. Caesar will come with an army – '

'Not before summer,' Tros put in. 'He will need time to prepare his army and to pin the Gauls down tight before he leaves them in his rear.'

'Worse and worse!' remarked Caswallon. 'If he came before the indignation dies, my men would fight. I might even persuade these craven cousin-kings to lend me ten or fifteen thousand men. But already the kings send word by their envoys that this quarrel with Caesar is of my making, so I must pay for their help if I need it. And if Caesar waits a few months, my men will be saying the same thing. Lud! Lud! Lud's blood!' he exclaimed. 'This kinging, it is a man's task, but there is small reward in it!'

'We talk, we talk,' groaned Orwic. 'What are we going to do?'

'I build a ship!' said Tros, and struck the table with his parchment.

Fflur nodded, her eyes on Tros as if she could see the thought behind his massive forehead. The amber of her ornaments was not more yellow than his eyes. The grey of her eyes suggested no more strength of will than did the line of his jaw, neck, mouth and shoulders. She was Athena to his Poseidon, she quietly wise, he capable of tempests before which cliffs would shatter.

'In the ship, Tros, you will sail away. And then what?' she asked.

'Sigurdsen knows,' he answered, 'and Conops knows. Now I will tell you and I think you will not laugh, although my friend Caswallon will believe me mad and Orwic will mock me at risk of being sat on hot coals on the hearth! The world is round, and I will sail around it!'

Again Fflur nodded.

'You know too much, Tros,' she said quietly. 'And still too little for your own good.'

'Tros knows enough to stand like a true man by his friends,' said Orwic. 'Mad? I like that kind of madman. The world has my permission to be square if it so pleases, and Tros, if he wishes, may call it a triangle. None the less, I sail with him on his adventure.'

'Not you!' Tros retorted. 'I need men who are obedient!'

'Kill me in single combat, or prepare my quarters in the ship,' said Orwic blandly.

Caswallon's face fell, for he loved Tros like a brother. More than that, he counted on his knowledge of the Romans and his passion to wreck Caesar's schemes of conquest. But he knew Tros too well to try to set obstructions in his way, and he knew there was no holding Orwic.

'How soon will the ship be finished?' he asked, trying to mask his disappointment.

'Soon, and for many reasons. A ship's genius is motion,' Tros replied. 'She will rot if she sits still too long – on land or water. My genius, too, consists in action. I am no use at this waiting game. I lose my temper if a dozen popinjays of kinglets strut and claw like poultry clucking for grain that is still in the sack. I would knock those envoys' heads together and send their masters a challenge to provide regiments against Caesar or against me, whichever suits their temper best! That might not be the best course. You can manage your poultry-yard better without me. Nevertheless, you are my friend. I will serve you first and take what comes of it. But I must serve you in my own way, and I must have more men.'

Again he rapped the parchment on the table. He seemed to wish to call attention to it, but the sight of it suggested no solution of the problem to Caswallon's worried brain.

'You forget I am an admiral of Caesar's fleet!'

Caswallon stared and Orwic laughed. Sigurdsen grumbled below his breath, being superstitious about writings in a language he could not read. Fflur leaned back, drumming jewelled fingers on the table.

'Much good a writing will do! There is no seal on it,' said Orwic. 'Caesar will have sent long ago to all the ports to warn them that the parchment is a forgery and – '

There was a small wooden box on the table. Tros struck it with the roll of parchment.

'Perhaps – and let us hope – that Caesar forgets, as you forgot, that when I took his bireme, there was not only his treasure in the well below the cabin, but his seal and a great stack of his private documents. There lies the seal.' He struck the box again. 'A fool maybe I am, but no such fool as Caesar thinks. He smiled when we had him prisoner. He thought he could bribe me, and he knew we would never kill him for fear his own men would retaliate and kill Fflur. He offered to make me admiral of his fleet if I would desert Caswallon. And he smiled again when I made him write me the appointment.

'Caesar was fool enough to think me fool enough to believe that appointment valid without the seal. But I have the seal! He thought me fool enough to believe that he will not close all the ports of Gaul against me and set a big price on my head. He forgot, or else he never knew, that I have his private correspondence,

8

that I know who his friends are in Rome and who are his enemies. The thought never entered the calculating brain of Caesar that I will go to Rome and there, it may be, break the wheels of his ambition!'

'Rome?' Fflur muttered. 'Rome!'

She seemed to be seeing visions.

'If he has any brains at all, he will have written to Rome,' said Orwic.

'Not about me! Not Caesar! I know him. He will count on catching me up to some trick on the coast of Gaul, or possibly in Hispania, at any rate, this side of the Gates of Hercules. In the first place, Caesar's popularity depends on his personal renown. Were it known he was taken prisoner and forced to exchange himself for a British chief's wife, whom he had stolen against all the laws of embassy, there is a man named Cato in Rome who would leap at the opportunity to denounce him before the Senate. Moreover, by appointing me an admiral Caesar usurped the Senate's privilege. He is on the horns of a dilemma. If he will keep the story secret of his having stolen a king's wife by dishonourable trickery and of having returned her in exchange for himself and an appointment that he had no right to make, he must keep silence and watch for me as cats watch mouse-holes. He knows I build a ship, but he does not know how big a ship or how seaworthy, because Caswallon slew his spies. It will never enter Caesar's head that I will go swiftly to Rome.'

'Rome!' Fflur said again. She sat up straight and stared at him.

'Aye, Rome! Where Caesar's masters are and Caesar's enemies. Where the moneylenders live, Crassus, greatest of them all. Where Pompey, Caesar's friend in name, broods jealousy against him. Rome, where Cato lives, who hates usurpers and would rather break a spoke of Caesar's wheel than eat his dinner. I will sail through the Gates of Hercules, drop anchor in the port of Ostia, proceed to Rome and do there what I can to ruin Caesar's prospect of invading Britain. If I were you' – Tros leaned forward, elbow on the table, pointing with the parchment at Caswallon – 'I would tell those kings' ambassadors to go home. I would bid them say to their masters that you prefer to try to save all Britain without their aid, since they ask to be paid to save themselves. That should set them thinking. It should make them more ashamed than if you plead. Then, if my mission fails and Caesar invades Britain later in the year in spite of me, you will be no worse off than you are now, and perhaps they will offer assistance instead of asking to be bought.'

Caswallon shook his head.

'They would plan to weaken me,' he said, 'by waiting until I take the brunt of the invasion. Later, if Caesar should have too much the best of it, they would probably send men. But those same men would force me to pay the bill when they had driven Caesar out of Britain. I would very likely have to abdicate.'

'Cross that river when you reach it,' Tros suggested. 'You gain nothing by promising payment now. You will only whet the edge of the cupidity. The high hand in a bargain is the hand that wins, and the gods love him who plays the man. Be daring!'

Fflur leaned back again, her eyes half closed, her fingers again drumming on the table.

'You – you would dare anything.'

'Except to take me with him!' Orwic interrupted. 'But he shall! I enjoy Tros. He reminds me of the north-east wind.'

'But we,' Fflur went on, 'we have two whole tribes to think of. Caswallon is king of the Trinobantes, and the Cantii pay him tribute. It is they who will suffer unless we can form an alliance with other tribes against Caesar.'

'Suffer!' Tros struck the table with his fist. 'Show me freedom that must not be fought for! Make you ready for the fight and let those kings' ambassadors go home with good proud answers for their kings, who then may find some manhood in themselves before the war begins! They come here to eat and drink your provender, designing tribute from your purse, when they ought to be offering money and men. If they go home and raise no regiments, and if you raise all you can, and if I throw a stick in Caesar's wheel so that he can't invade you, then I think those cousin-kings of yours may have to learn who kings it over them in Britain!

'If Caesar were to beat you he would trample on them, too, wouldn't he? If Caesar were only to weaken you, you say they would rub it in by taxing you for whatever scraps of aid they might have brought in the nick of-time. Well and good. If Caesar doesn't come, but if you have made ready for him, you will be strong. I am no advocate of conquests. I abominate them. But I believe in making my debtor pay whatever bill he owes. If I were in your shoes when that day comes, I would make those cousin-kings pay through the nose for having saved them all from Caesar! There would be no taxes for a while in my domain, but such heavy ones as theirs as should keep them from growing bumptious!'

Fflur smiled and shook her head.

'Caswallon is too easygoing. He is more likely to send them help in famine-time than to remember grudges.'

10

She was not looking at her husband, and when he crashed his great fist on the table, she turned her head away to hide a smile.

'Mother of my sons!' he exploded. 'How often must I tell you that a king of Britain has to steer his course with twoscore councillors pulling him this and that way! The only man of all my council whom I can trust always to vote with me is Orwic. And now Orwic says he sails with Tros! Can't you, won't you see, that if I give these ambassadors a manly answer, my own council will accuse me of hot-headedness and will oppose whatever next I want to do?'

'I see that Tros is right,' Fflur answered. 'And you can get along very well without Orwic.'

Orwic came out of his ostentatious boredom long enough to look surprised.

'Orwic only irritates the council by supporting you whether you are right or wrong, and by being too young to have any right to your confidence. If Orwic goes, there will be rivalry to win your favour and you can swing the council any way you please.'

'I see my end! I surely go with Tros,' said Orwic, hiding chagrin beneath a mask of mannerly good humour. 'No more sitting all day long between fat landholders and listening to speeches that would send a weasel to sleep! No more all-night sittings to decide whether girls without dowries are lawful seisin, or who shall pay for the bridge on Durwhern* road! I visit Rome with Tros. Then what will happen, Tros, if you're wrong and the world turns out to be triangular? When we reach one of the corners, and suppose it sticks up in the air, like that, will the ship go tumbling down the other side, or suppose there isn't any water, what then?'

Caswallon interrupted gloomily:

'I must summon the council – '

'To hear my resignation?' Orwic asked, amused at his own conceit.

' – before I can safely answer these ambassadors. Tros, brother Tros, I think you had better speak before the council. They will resent the intrusion, but it is just possible you might convince them. I know I can't. They wouldn't even vote me an army when Caesar's men stole Fflur. They offered money for Fflur's ransom. They will offer money now, with which to buy protection against Caesar from a company of kings who will make the weather an excuse for breaking bargains when the time comes! Will you speak to them?'

Tros nodded. Fflur drew in her breath.

*The modern Canterbury.

11

'I will be there!' remarked Orwic. 'You could no more sleep through a speech by Tros than you could after a dose of druids' physic! Why not let Tros talk, too, to those ambassadors in the big hall? I would love to listen!'

'If we are not careful,' said Fflur, 'the council will want to inquire into Tros's ship-building. There has been trouble already because he has used so many blacksmiths and has raised the price of food in Lunden by employing so many men in one place. They will want to tax his ship, and they will ask what is to become of all the blacksmiths when the ship is finished. Moreover, when you and Tros came to rescue me in Gaul, you brought nearly two hundred charcoal-burners with you, and they never returned.

'The council blame Tros for the charcoal shortage. They are afraid to go to Tros's shipyard and make trouble there, because of the burning stinkballs that Eough, the sorcerer, taught him how to make, But if Tros appears before the council with too much strong advice, someone is sure to accuse him of sorcery, and of trouble-making and intrigue and what-not else.'

'They accuse him already!' Caswallon laughed. 'But they can't get away from the fact that Taliesan favoured him, and that it was Tros who wrecked Caesar's fleet when Caesar invaded Kent.'

'The druids have lost influence since Taliesan died,' Fflur answered. 'Men are saying Taliesan was the last who knew the Mysteries, and that now the whole company of druids is like sheep without a shepherd. As for Caesar's fleet, there are plenty who say it was not Tros at all but the wind that destroyed it. Several women have told me that their husbands are saying Tros lied.'

Caswallon sat bolt upright.

'Which women? Whose husbands?' he demanded. 'I will deal with those husbands! I will wager they are men who skulked in bed while the rest of us were fighting Romans on the beach! Let me think now. Was one of them – '

'No names!' said Fflur. 'The women will tell me nothing more if I betray their confidences. But I think it will be best if Tros keeps away from the council. Let him finish his ship and sail away and do what he can for us in Rome, leaving us to manage this corner of Britain.'

Tros offered no demurrer. He had faith in Fflur's intuition, even though she had not foreseen that Caesar's messengers would take her prisoner; even though she had not prevented Helma from trying to escape and so being shot by the Roman guards. He knew intuition works by fits and starts. And besides, she proposed what he wanted to do, which was argument enough.

12

'I will finish my ship,' he answered. 'Fflur is right. I will attend to my own business. Purge you those ambassadors and manage your council how you can. Is supper late, or is my belly out of time from too much talking?'

Fflur leaned back again and studied him from under lowered eyelids.

'Out of time, I think,' she said at last. 'Taliesan used to say the proper time at which to do things is as important as the things we do. I think you will not see Rome until – '

'Until I have a crew!' Tros interrupted. 'Men! I need men!'

'Patience! You need patience, until the right time,' Fflur said quietly.

GATHERING CLOUDS

Captains need men's obedience. He is no captain whose commands men disobey. Nor is he fit to be a captain whose heart loveth not rebellion and rebels. For of what is he captain, if not first of his own self? Can he captain himself without rebellion against ten thousand laws, traditions, superstitions, tyrannies, lacks, stupidities, sloth, cravings, ignorance and ten times ten thousand efforts to compel him to obey whatever terror hath a following of fools? He is a rebel, or no captain. In rebellion he learns. His knowledge commands obedience of men in whom growth stirs, but who know not yet what stirs them. It is not obedience they hate, but the indignity of aimless living. Their rebellion is evidence of fitness to be led. Let him look to it whither he leads.

From the log of Tros of Samothrace

Soon – Tros had promised himself. But it was early spring. Britons had a thousand activities that they preferred to hauling choice lumber for him or to letting their wives weave sail-cloth and twist cordage. While winter lasted they were satisfied to have a ready market for almost anything they cared to sell in the way of labour, material or provender. But as soon as the snow melted and the warm wind brought rain that made the tree-buds swell, they began to think of farms, the breeding of cattle and horses, and, not least, the surging in their own veins that made any kind of steady work for someone else unthinkable. So difficulties dogged the heels of unforeseen delay.

Tros's ship, with the ribs of Caesar's broken and dismantled bireme on the mud beside her, still rested in her cradle on the ways, her underbody gleaming like a mirror when the sun shone. Tros had coated her with tin, an innovation daring as it was original, and an extravagance that irritated Britons almost as much as his capture of a whole shipload of the expensive metal had exasperated Caesar. True, the British owners of the tin received their purchase price, because Caesar had had to pay it against a document that bore his signature; but if Tros had plated the whole ship with gold he could have hardly created more jealousy and adverse comment. Tin was wealth, the one sure article of commerce that the Britons always could exchange for foreign goods,

14

the stuff in which ransoms were paid. Ingots of it, shaped like knuckle-bones, were easier to trade than minted money.

It was no use Tros explaining that a smooth, unweeded surface would increase the ship's speed, and that speed meant safety. They bade him stay on land and use the tin for making bronze shields, wheels and weapons; or to buy a farm with half of it and store the rest against an evil day. In vain he showed them pier-piles that had been exposed to tide-water. They retorted that if his ship grew rotten he could build a new one, whereas tin was almost priceless and much harder to obtain than lumber.

Caswallon's council, angry with the king because on Tros's advice he had returned a stiff-necked answer to those other kings' ambassadors, now fanned the flame of irritation by questioning the advisability of permitting Tros to finish a ship that he would certainly use against Caesar, thus providing the Romans with additional excuse for an invasion. Had they not lost enough young men already on the Kentish beach? Was it respectful to the gods, or sane men's policy, to increase the already serious risk of war?

Some said that the gods, and Lud particularly, on the bosom of whose River Thames the great ship would be launched, would certainly resent the barbarous impiety of wasting honest tin below the water level. Floods might follow. Usually pestilence came in the wake of flood. A prevalence of north-east winds might bring successive raids of Northmen. There were a hundred likely ways in which the gods might wreak a vengeance; and there was no longer any Taliesan to whom to go for spiritual succour.

In the end they appealed to the druids, on whom the majority still felt they might depend for light on their perplexity. But the druids had lost their own faith in themselves with astonishing suddenness since Taliesan's great soul departed for another world. They returned evasive answers, of which any man might make his own interpretation, thus increasing doubt without condemning Tros nor yet supporting him.

They hinted that he had cut down far too many oak trees, on which grew the sacred mistletoe, and they made guarded remarks about his misuse of the sacred yew to form springs for his long-range arrow engines, but they declined to interfere in matters that concerned king and council rather than themselves, since, said they, no emergency existed.

The usual gossipers grew busy. The men who, in all ages and in any land, seek always to destroy and to prevent by innuendo without risking their own skins, stirred indignation in the minds of ignorant men who knew nothing of church or state but were

15

easily flattered and easily persuaded that the fate of Britain rested in their hands. There were riots outside the shipyard. Men came by night to set fire to Tros's ship, to the lumber piles, the forge and workshops. Tros had to disperse the mob three times in one week by burning quantities of his stenching chemical. The spluttering stench saved ship and buildings, and after the third demonstration of the stuff's effectiveness there was no more open violence; but the charge of sorcery against Tros became as easy to lay as it was difficult to disprove.

Sorcery meant excommunication by the druids first, and then impeachment before king and council if anyone could be found with courage to take the first step along with the responsibility. Conviction would be tantamount to outlawry, since any man might slay such an offender without risk of punishment.

None did come forward to insist on an impeachment, because of the law that allowed revenge to the accused in the event that he should win a favourable verdict, and because it was known that Caswallon befriended Tros, but mere suspicion of sorcery was enough to cause a boycott of the shipyard; and even Tros's own slaves began to shirk their work as something never destined to be finished.

The Northmen were a superstitious lot, all forty-eight of them. They could gloom like the grey of a Baltic twilight. It had leaked out that Tros had told Sigurdsen the world was round and that he meant to sail around it. Sigurdsen was drunk at Helma's funeral and revealed the secret. They were seamen, who did not mind drunkenness, raiding and looting and the usual concomitants of war. Nor did they pray too often or admire the character of men who did.

But to talk, even in secret, of sailing around the world was altogether too much like blasphemy, even for their strong stomachs. If they could have believed the theory it would have been, in their opinion, irreligious and indecent to discuss it. But to spiritual blasphemy was added temporal danger, since they knew, as everybody always had known, that the world was flat and over its distant rim the sea poured into eternal darkness.

So they spoke of Tros's obsession in gloomy undertones, and at night, when they gathered around the fire in their own snug quarters, they conjectured what would happen when they should reach the world's rim and be caught in the undertow of the eternal waterfall. Could men approach Valhalla by that route? Or would their souls go tumbling for ever downward into dark oblivion? The problem interfered with work and led to grosser superstition.

Some of them had seen the havoc wrought in Caesar's camp by the hot stink-balls. They knew Eough had taught Tros. Eough was a sorcerer. They had seen the mixture burn with its appalling stench when Tros dispersed the rioters. True, they had seen the yellow crystals brought from under the horse-manure below Caswallon's stable, and they knew the rest was sulphur, charcoal, resin and plain sawdust. But it stood to reason no such mixture had any right to explode unless the devils of the underworld had been involved in it. So far, the infernal stuff had only harmed their enemies, but it might just as easily reverse its energy and suffocate themselves.

'With a stink from the caverns of hell he loads the ship, and into hell he proposes to plunge us, ship and all, when we reach the world's edge,' Sigurdsen confided, staring at the embers on the hearth. 'No luck can come of such dark business. Tros had the best of it against the Romans that time, but look you what happened. Was his own wife, Helma, not the first one to be slain, and she expecting child?'

The Britons – rebels, criminals, homeless vagabonds, slaves – hated the sea and everything in or on it, except the fish. Homeless, except for Tros's long labour sheds; hopeless, except for Tros's goodwill; inevitably outlawed, should they dare to run away, and with nothing but Tros between them and a far worse servitude, they dreaded none the less to leave their little corner of the earth and were already homesick at the thought of it.

Glendwyr had changed his mind about serving Tros as a free man, but he had not been taken into confidence. However, he had overheard the Northmen talking, and the secrets that a man learns that way are a lot more mentally disturbing than the facts he truly knows.

He approached Tros, down under the ship one night when Tros was searching with a lantern to make sure no undetected visitor had set some heap of shavings smouldering. There had been a dozen attempts to sneak into the yard at twilight and destroy the wooden ways.

'Lord Tros,' said Glendwyr, speaking manfully, for new-won freedom sat like a god between his shoulder blades, 'I have a thought that would do you no injury if you should listen to it.'

'Speak your mind,' said Tros, 'and if you change mine you shall have the credit.'

But he went on swinging the lantern, poking into corners with a long stick, not suggesting much alacrity of vacillation.

Glendwyr hesitated. It is not so easy to talk confidences to a man whose back is turned, bent forward, hunting danger in the draughty darkness. It was not until a gust of east wind blew the lantern out and Tros had to find the fire-pot and relight it, that Glendwyr's thought took form in words.

'Lord Tros, you have a great ship here, but a crew too small, that will never serve you well unless – '

'Unless I know how to make them, eh? That shall be my task,' said Tros, and the lantern light shone yellow on his stubborn face as he stooped to replace the horn cylinder around the flaxen wick.

'Unless, Lord Tros, their numbers should be increased and they should have work that they understand.'

'Do they understand full bellies, the whip for laziness, freedom for good behaviour?' Tros asked, and he went on poking into corners.

'Lord Tros, they have been told you will sail first to Rome, and they have heard that the Romans will put them into an arena for sport and watch them being torn by wild beasts. It is not easy to encourage men who have that fear in them.'

'I notice you try to discourage me,' Tros answered, but his back was turned. He was noticing the rain, remembering whether all deck openings were covered. 'You have a project of your own. What is it?'

He walked away, and Glendwyr had to follow.

'No project, but a word of advice, Lord Tros.'

Tros climbed the ladder up the ship's side, and stood on the long, wet deck observing that the watchmen had sought shelter from the rain. He ordered Glendwyr to go and rout them out from under the hatch coverings.

'Warn them that if I should catch them skulking there will be whippings! Cuff them about the head, and tell them they are lucky it was you, not I, who walked the rounds!'

He returned down the ladder and examined the magazine where he had stored his chemical. There, presently, young Glendwyr joined him.

'Now, if there were a raid in view, Lord Tros – some chance to prove themselves against a weaker adversary, with the hope of plunder – '

He stopped, because at last Tros turned and faced him, holding up the lantern. Its rays showed slanting rain that blew in squalls between them, dripping from their tarred hoods. Glendwyr's expression began to suggest nervousness, which made him look older than Tros, although he was several years the younger.

'You seek to prove your value,' Tros remarked, moving the lantern the better to see Glendwyr's face. 'But if you know my crew is undependable, be you the stouter-hearted against the day when we must depend on them.'

'Lord Tros, I only sought – '

'To make a pirate of me! To make of me a rogue like Caesar! To persuade me to attack some harmless folk against whom I have neither grudge nor ground, except my own ability to hit and run! Mark this, now. When I need advice, I open up my thought and let the gods pour wisdom in. From you I ask such loyalty as a ship yields to the helm. And mark this, too. Remember it. When a pinch comes, as it will, if the Britons in my crew act shamefully, you will not go blameless, since you are one of them and yet a free man and my officer.'

Tros strode away, swinging the lantern, toward his own snug quarters that had been lonelier than a hermit's cave since Helma died. He had set the slavegirl free who used to wait on his young wife, and the girl had vanished, none knew whither. Conops had resumed old ways, enacting all parts, cook, bed-chamber valet, serving-man, sword-sharpener, factotum, confidant. The hut was all ship-shape and neat, where Helma had kept house with satisfying woman touches that a man does not notice until he has to live again without them.

As Tros entered, standing like a great bear in the doorway, rain dripping from his bearskin coat and from his tarred hood, Conops viewed the wooden floor with pride, for he had scrubbed and sanded it. The heavy woollen carpet Helma laid had been removed. Benches, stools, chests and the arm-chair made from an oaken cask stood in rigidly straight lines against the walls, and even the sticks on the clay hearth were laid with parallel precision.

The expression on Conops' one-eyed face was pertly loyal, asserting what even his privileged lips hardly dared to frame in words:

'You and I, master, are men who need no women to make life soft for us!'

And it was true. Tros knew it. In his heart there was an empty place that he had never known of until Helma filled it, and he had hardly realized it even so until a Roman arrow robbed him of her. Now he understood that she had filled it all too well, and the recluse in him, inherited from his austere old sire, closed such a wall around her memory as not another woman in the world should ever penetrate. He had made his mind up finally on that score.

19

He threw his bearskin off and sat down in the cask arm-chair more resolute than ever, devoid of appetite, although Conops tempted him with beans and venison, not more than sipping at the mug of warm mead, conscious that the memory of Helma fretted him – he could almost feel her presence in the room – and so more careful to control himself. Emotions such as thoughts of Helma carried in their wake he shunned. He must find hard stuff to bite on, and quite suddenly he thought of it.

'Lives Skell?' he asked.

He had forgotten Skell.

'Aye, the red rascal lives,' said Conops. 'His eyes are as red as his beard now, from peeping through the draughty chinks, and because for pity's sake we let him have a fire and there is no hole in the prison roof, so the smoke can't escape any better than he can. He eats as much as ever, and though I don't doubt he has stiffened in his fetters, there are no sores. We let him have fish-oil for wrists and ankles, and he thrives like a fat toad in a hole.'

'Strike off his fetters. Bring him here.' Tros ordered. And then, to please Conops, fell to at the food.

A half-hour later, for they had to find a blacksmith to cut through the fetter rivets, Conops and a guard of Britons brought Skell to the door.

'Bring him in. Dismiss the guard.' Tros ordered, and Skell stood before him, red-eyed, with his red beard tangled into knots, holding his wrists as if a weight still hung from them and reeking of the fish-oil. Skell said nothing, which might or might not prove that he had learned a little wisdom in the solitary darkness of the prison hut.

'You poor trickster, you puzzle me!' Tros remarked when he had stared at him a long time. 'I can understand a whole rogue who acts generously on occasion for the sake of someone else. You, when the gods provide you opportunity to play a man's part, play it with one hand only, using the other against yourself. If you should save my life, I could not trust you not to try to kill me the next minute! Speak.'

'What shall I say?' Skell answered.

'Oho! So that is it! We have learned a little shame, have we? Have fetters done to you what liberality could not? Do you feel like a leper at last, and would like to like yourself?'

'Whatever I say you will not believe,' Skell retorted, and his chin was, it may be, a trifle higher than he used to hold it when a bold man looked him in the face.

Tros crashed his fist down on the table with force enough to drive a nail into the oak.

'Pluto! Who are you to say what I believe or disbelieve? You poor fool! If you knew your own mind half as well as you think you can read another's, I might feel some respect for you!'

'I know my own mind,' Skell said, and his lips closed tight over his teeth. His red-rimmed eyes looked straight at Tros.

'Well, well! Reveal yourself! I listen.'

Tros threw his weight back in the chair and drummed with the fingers of his left hand on a heavy, jewelled sword-hilt.

'I would rather be killed,' said Skell, 'than to continue living, unless my future holds more than the past. I didn't ask to come into the world. Or, if I did, I don't remember it. My mother was a British slave, but my father a free Northman, so, though I was not born free, I was set free before I was old enough to know the difference. You would think a freed man would have equal rights with others. But not so. I was known as Skell the bastard. And I tell you, Lord Tros, I have had to use my wits to come by such small standing as I did have when you first knew me, until I was caught in the Glendwyr rebellion and enslaved and turned over to you like one of the steers men pay to the king in lieu of taxes. Such training as mine was, such self-defence against the Britons' clannishness and such expedients to gain riches as the only way to recognition – birth having been denied me – make a liar of a man. Lord Tros, I dare say you would be a liar if you had had half my difficulties.

'You don't know what it means, Lord Tros, to feel that free men hate or despise you, and slaves regard you as one of themselves by right, only a bit more fortunate! Your equals claim a superiority that carks and galls, and you can't break through the wall they raise. So you turn false, as much from hopelessness as from any other reason. I know I did.

'I lent money, deprived men of their land. I played spy for the Romans long before Caesar ever thought of trying his invasion. I made men fear me whenever I could and however I could, and I betrayed them when it suited me. I would have betrayed those rebels whom I persuaded to rise against Caswallon if I had had time. But I was caught too soon, lost everything, and since then I have been your slave. Slavery did not sweeten my disposition. But of late I have been thinking in the dark.

'Lord Tros, it takes time for a man to change himself. I have a habit, like a fox, of having always one hole in reserve, one back way out of everything. If I see a profit to myself and to another,

21

instinct makes me keep another secret course clear, to which I can turn at a moment's notice in order to wreck that other man. I have learned to trust nobody, because I knew none trusted me.

'But now I have done with all that, and if it is too late I am sorry. But I have done with it. I can't change in a minute or a month. I can't make you believe me, and I won't try. But I have told the truth.'

'By Zeus, I think you have! Is it the first time?' Tros asked.

'No. I told the truth to your wife – who they tell me is dead – here in this house.'

Tros leaned forward, chin on hand, elbow on the table.

'Careful!' he warned. 'If you lie now, your last chance is gone! What said my wife Helma?'

'That if I would prove my good faith she would be my friend.'

'And you, she having said that, knowing of the Roman's plot to carry her to Gaul, said nothing?'

'Yes. I tell you a man cannot change in a moment.'

'And now you ask me – '

'I ask nothing!' Skell interrupted. 'You sent for me. You said to me, "Speak." I have spoken.'

Tros leaned back again, the lids half lowered over his amber eyes.

'I think you have spoken truth,' he said at last. 'And yet one swallow makes no summer. You have been a crafty liar in your day, Skell, and it may be now that you tell truth craftily, with hidden purposes behind that mask of yours. You and I – we are master and slave. What is your thought about that?'

They breathed a dozen breaths before Skell answered:

'It is the law. You own me. But as to the right and wrong of it, though I have owned slaves, I confess I don't know.'

'Then I will tell you,' said Tros. 'The past is like a stream that turned the mill, and there are men who live in the past who float downstream and drown. Such men are slaves. The way to keep from drowning is to swim ashore. The shore is duty. And you are fortunate in that you have but one duty, whereas I have many. There are many men dependent on me, and you have one master to serve. I never sell slaves. I give them freedom when they earn it, but I make them prove to me their right to enjoy freedom, knowing that unless they have it in them to serve me faithfully they will never know enough to serve themselves. I do not bestow freedom as a reward. That is not my province.

'I have not sufficient impudence to try to usurp God's prerogative. But when I see a man, my slave by law, responsible to me, by acts, not mouthing of mock-loyalty, revealing manhood in himself, I know at once that man is fit for freedom. Skell, may my right hand betray me if I rob a man of anything I know is his! When you are fit for freedom you shall go free on the instant.'

He was watching Skell's face, scanning it as, on a poop at sea, he scanned the weather, leaving intuition to interpret what the eye observed. Skell spoke again:

'Lord Tros, it is not easy for a proud man to accept slavery.'

'I know nothing in life worth doing that is easy!' Tros retorted. 'I think when we are dead we rest awhile. Until then – work, with spells of sleep, in which our friends the gods pour into us such wisdom as our work has made us fit to hold!'

'I am persuaded,' Skell said quietly.

'Fool! I seek not to persuade you!' Tros sat up again and laid his great fist on the table. 'You asked the way, like a man who is lost in the dark. I told it. Take or leave it! But as long as you are my slave, I will do my duty and demand obedience. I own your body. Nothing less than your own soul can unlock that barrier to freedom.'

'I am persuaded, nevertheless,' Skell answered.

It annoyed Tros to be told he had persuaded anybody. Adept at persuasion, by the very force of his own passion to decide all issues for himself, he liked to think that other men could judge as definitely as himself, and when they yielded he preferred to think they had seen eye to eye with him unaided.

'Well, take warning. Try not to persuade me!' he retorted. 'It is I who will decide whether you are fit for freedom, if ever that time comes. You are released from prison. Take care lest I have to lock you in again. Conops, give Skell the key of the hut he used to occupy, restore his name to the muster-roll, class him among the Northmen, and put him to work at dawn on rigging the main shrouds. Fall away. Shut the door after you.'

FFLUR PAYS A DEBT

Believing as I do that Dignity is the noblest attainment in this life, I refused a kingdom. I am free to obey my vision and to die pursuing it, in treaty with none, aiding and abetting whom I will. That purple cloak I wear, that angers kings, serves not unhandsomely to keep in mind my vow. And I have sworn no other vow than this, that no king could observe, though a thousand priests should anoint him with all the holy oil on earth:

I will fight for the weak against the strong, and for the lesser tyranny against the greater, until my Soul shall show me wiser wisdom. Without wisdom, dignity is a lying mask. Without courage, wisdom is the solemn vapouring of clowns.

I saw not fit to cozen me a kingdom and be catspaw for the rogues. I see a war worth winning.

From the log of Tros of Samothrace

There was not much Caswallon dared to do to relieve the boycott on the shipyard. Tros was forced to send small boats up-river, two and even three days' journey, to trade for provisions. His hired blacksmiths deserted, and he, with his own hand, had to teach selected slaves the anvil work and such odds and ends of casting as remained to do.

Then there were the huge and complicated catapults to set in place, with double uprights rising thirty feet above the deck, from the top of which ton-weights of lead fell on to basket-work cushions below the waterline, providing force for the projection of the hot stink-balls along a trough that could be moved for elevation and direction.

Last, but not least, there were provisions for a voyage to be accumulated. He would have to start shorthanded, but even so he had a crew of two hundred and fifty men to provide for. There was deer meat to be smoked, and fish; wheat by the ton; turnips, carrots, and dried apples that Fflur showed him how to prepare and that the druids said would help to prevent scurvy; mutton, beef, and hog meat to be salted down; tallow by the hogshead, for a ship needs grease as fire needs fuel; charcoal for the cooking; medicines begged from the druids, who according to their law

24

might not refuse, but who stipulated, nevertheless, that Tros should be gone before midsummer day.

He held out for more than medicines before he struck that bargain with them. As any looker-on with half an eye could see, the druids were fallen from their high estate since the great Lord Druid Taliesan departed to another world. Ambition had developed. There were rival factions for the leadership, some seeking to increase their influence by cautiously intriguing with the kings, some on the other hand plotting to weaken the kings that their own authority might be greater, but all agreed on one point – Tros was dangerous, because he knew too much.

He went to interview their spokesmen in a sun-warmed clearing where great stones stood in a circle far within an oak forest. That interview seemed barren of results, but later they came to see him in the shipyard, secretly at night, lest men should say they were condoning sorcery. They offered medicines and some instructions how to use them, and they smiled when Tros made heavier demands, because they knew he intended to leave Britain in any event.

But Caswallon had advised Tros, and Fflur had seconded, with her usual grey-eyed insight into how to manage men.

'You are going to Rome to seek peace for us Britons,' said Fflur. 'It is fair we should pay for it, but it is not fair that this corner of Britain should pay all the price, or nearly all. The other tribes are just as much concerned as we are.'

'Aye, but whoever can make them pay has genius!' Caswallon snorted.

'The druids have already made them pay,' Fflur answered. 'They, we, all of us have paid the druids ten times over for much more than they will ever do. It was all right when Taliesan lived. He was a true Lord Druid and none grudged the tithe of gold and pearls. Whoever had pearls gave of his own free will the greatest. Whoever had gold gave a tenth. So the druids are rich.'

'And they will pay you to go if you can make them believe you will not go otherwise,' Caswallon commented. But he said it in a low voice, as if afraid of his own words. Himself, he would never have dared to offer an affront to any druid, not even to a druid who he knew was false to the druidic teachings, for he was Celtic to the marrow of his bones, as meek in the presence of spiritual teachers as he was fierce in battle.

So Tros spoke cavalierly to the druids.

'I will not go,' he assured them, 'unless you do your part. Rather I will launch my ship and raid Caesar's ports as it suits me, using British harbours for a base. That will bring Caesar the sooner, so we can have it out with him and learn which way the gods decide the fate of Britain.'

The druids shuddered at the very name of Caesar, knowing well what fate he would impose on them. When spiritual vision wanes and temporal ambition takes the place of it, men flinch from being burned alive in baskets. Compromise creeps into their convictions.

'Pearls!' said Tros. 'You have. Rome covets. I cannot compel Rome, but I can buy Caesar's enemies, I could buy all Rome except perhaps one man, if I had pearls enough.'

'Who told you we have pearls?' a druid asked.

'The same one who told me the world is round! I, I myself! I know it!'

Long into a mystic night in May they argued, seated in the shed where Tros had stored his horrible explosive. Barrels of the stuff were all around them; barrels and great lead balls, as yet unfilled. Their white robes gleamed ghostly in the moonlight streaming through the open door, where Conops sat on guard against intruders. Tros looked like a great black bear among them, growling from the deepest shadow.

'What if we give you pearls? What proof have we how you will use them?'

'None!' he answered. 'Read ye your own hearts. I have read mine for you.'

'If you fail?'

'Then blame the gods, not me! I, Tros, have spoken. I will add no word to it. With pearls' – he pulled off his black tarred cap and held it out toward them – 'this full of pearls, I will go to Rome and try to put a stick in Caesar's wheel. Without pearls I will stay here and let come what may.'

The night after that they brought pearls to him, a dozen huge ones in a small gold casket lined with fleece, and more than a thousand of mixed sizes in a woollen bag. He tossed the treasure into the bronze box that had once been Caesar's money-chest and slammed the lid down, giving them no inkling that, except for those pearls, the chest was now almost empty.

'Let the gods say whether that is price enough,' he commented. 'The gods know what and why you pay. The gods will judge what I do. Now, I would advise you, speed the parting guest! Bid all men aid instead of hindering the launching of my ship!'

So, subtly, the druids began to change the mental atmosphere until Tros actually suffered from embarrassment of riches in the form of unskilled labour and unsuitable supplies.

26

Instead of boycotting, men brought him all the trash they did not need – the mouldy grain, sick oxen to be killed and salted down, old horses for the same ungraceful fate, discouraged-looking slaves devoid of teeth or suffering from ague, who they said would make fine rowers; spoiled honey, hides half full of holes, moth-eaten woollen cloth, and all the odds and ends they had no use for, eagerly demanding money and annoyed when Tros refused it.

There was nearly another riot. Tros was charged with cheating by a noisy mob that refused to take its rubbish home again and called the judges of the land to witness he was liable for damages from rain and theft. Caswallon had to call out all his bodyguard to use spearbutts and to charge into the crowd with chariots that had wooden staves set to the axle-hubs in place of the murderous scythes.

Then, two weeks before the date set for the launching, one last efforty by the powers that impede men's plans – blunt mutiny! Tros's slaves, aware that nothing else could save them from a life at sea, deserted by night in a body, and, before Tros could prevent, some jack-of-anybody's-business-but-his-own had fired the beacons and set bells a-ringing to alarm the countryside. That meant proscription. Every fugitive was outlawed from the moment the desertion became public news, a price by law on each deserter's head, payable by the owner to whoever the captor might be; one-third of the fugitive's market value if brought in alive, or, if dead, one-tenth of it.

So a hunt began, with all the countryside in arms and no hope there would not be bloodshed. Tros did not dare to remove his Northmen from the shipyard without first making some other provision for guarding it. So he mounted horseback, an expedient that with all his sailor's heart he loathed, and rode full-gallop to Caswallon's house on Lud's Hill, falling, as the sun rose, in the mixen of the horseyard when the weary brute came to a halt too suddenly.

Caswallon was up betimes, for he had heard the clamour of the alarm bells, but he proved a sorry comforter, smiling behind his hand while half a dozen grooms removed the stable stuff from Tros's cloak.

'You will get about half of your slaves back, probably – at so much each. I will instruct the judge. He shall assess you lightly. The dead ones won't cost anything to speak of.'

It was Fflur who solved the difficulty. She came to the great front porch where the swallows were all nesting and the men and women already waited who had favours to ask of the king, winding up her long braids and calling to the grooms to bring her chariot.

'Fie!' she called out to Caswallon. 'Laggard! Talking while the ricks burn! Lay a false scent quickly. Then clap your own pack on the right trail!'

'Fflur is always right!' Caswallon muttered. The words had grown into a formula from so much repetition, although he did not always recognize her rightness until after the event.

And then came Glendwyr, riding a mud-bespattered, foaming horse to death, vaulting as the beast fell, finishing the last three hundred yards on foot.

'Lord Tros, they have gone westward. They . . . '

He could not speak for gasping. But no need. Caswallon knew.

'Horns!' he exploded. 'Trumpets! Fifty mounted men! The rally! All directions! Hurry the crowd down-river! Tell them Tros's slaves are making in a body for the woods beyond the Medway!'

Never on earth were finer horsemen than the Britons. Give them leave to show off, and they had four legs beneath them faster than the partridges take wing from stubble fields. The silver horns and trumpets split the morning air as hoofs went thundering through the gate and, fanwise, fifty of Caswallon's gentlemen-at-arms rode belly-to-the-earth to round up groups of searchers and view-hallo them eastward in the wrong direction.

'Runnimede!' Glendwyr panted.

Caswallon nodded. It was a far cry to the swamps by Runnimede where desperate men too frequently outwore the patience of the pursuers. He had already ordered out the chariots. To the summons of a golden bugle more than a hundred bow-and-arrow men turned out, making up the whole force of the standing army. Twenty more breaths, and already four white stallions pawed the air as the king's own chariot came to a plunging halt in front of him. He jumped in, seizing the reins from the charioteer.

'I caught one,' said Glendwyr, recovering his breath at last. 'He had returned to steal an axe. He nearly slew me with it.'

'Lives he?' Tros demanded.

'Aye, you will need him for the oar-work.'

Tros suppressed a smile. He foresaw that he had a good lieutenant in the making. However, too much praise turns willing heads.

'What then?'

'I tripped and tied him. Conops came, put a handful of salt in his mouth, showed him water. He soon told where the rest had gone.'

Fflur's chariot was seesawing behind two red Icenian mares

28

that squealed for exercise, she reining them with one hand as she stood with a foot on the low seat balancing herself, and watched the five-and-twenty war-machines, whose stallions squealed and bit one another, rearing as their drivers formed them into five lines, four men to a chariot.

'Why do we wait?' Caswallon asked.

Tros jumped in. Glendwyr followed. Then Orwic came, driving up-hill from the direction of Lud's Bridge, his handsome face alight with the fun of living at top speed, swinging his chariot on one wheel at the gallop and then backing until, hub by hub, he was in line with Fflur.

'What madness next?' he laughed. 'All Lunden yelps on a stray dog's scent! The roe runs yonder.'

He nodded over-shoulder, roughly westward, up the river.

'Ride!' Caswallon roared, and they were off, all eight-and-twenty chariots in action at the gesture of his arm, before the word could clip the air. He never finished it. It was a vowel cut in half. There was neither shout nor whip-crack, but two hundred hoofs struck earth together and the five lines wheeled into a single stream that poured through the gate behind its leaders, no collisions, no hubs striking, no sound except the bumping of bronze wheels, the squeak of straining basket-work, and the staccato thunder of the hoofs.

Caswallon drove like wind, Fflur keeping pace with him and Orwic not a dozen yards behind. Before a mile had ribboned under-wheel, the leaders were beyond hail and the five-and-twenty let the intervening distance grow, conserving their own horses' strength. Not long, and there was no procession visible, only when Tros listened, he could hear the thump and splash when they who followed plunged into a ford, and now and then he caught a glimpse of them hand-galloping across a crest of rising ground.

So, for an hour, they drove at full-pelt within a furlong of the swamps beside the river, crossing long arms of the forest, skirting the fenced meadows until they reached a hill from whose summit they could see the Thames curved like a silver snake below them. There Caswallon drew rein and let the foaming stallions breathe awhile, his eyes and Fflur's intent on the sunlit view.

Smoke came from fifty homesteads. There were cattle browsing in a hundred fields. Peace lay along the valley like the smile of the Earth Goddess.

'When I tax them for their own protection, they rebel!' Caswallon remarked dryly, his eyes still searching out the details of the landscape.

He was a huntsman born, but Fflur's eyes just as soon as his detected an alertness in the movement of a herd of fallow-deer that grazed, five miles away, on the short, sweet grass, between a copse-edge and the high fence of a homestead. Orwic was the first to speak:

'Men moving – not toward them, but up-wind and rather quietly. There's a road over there beyond the river. It runs between high banks topped with brambles. That's where your runaways are, Tros! They'll be dog-tired and all in a herd – hot-foot – keeping together, lest stragglers get in trouble with the farmers. Where did they cross the river, though?'

Caswallon pointed. Down a vista between tree-tops they could see an abandoned ferry-scow that lay against the far bank of the river, half in water.

'The tide's flowing,' Tros remarked.

'And in an hour,' said Fflur, 'there will be a hundred feet of soft mud there. No good for chariot wheels!'

Caswallon laughed, the quick, short bark he always gave when he could see solutions.

'The fools expect pursuit. There was a second ferry-scow. They've sunk it. I wager they've scuttled the one we can see. If we should cross the river here – it might be done, we could swim the horses – they would scatter. It would take a month of hunting to get half of them. The thing they don't expect is to be headed off. There's a ford at Rhyd-y-Cadgerbydan.'*

'If you get ahead of them and hunt them back toward Lunden, they'll be killed to a man,' Fflur objected. 'Our Lundeners will be in no good humour after having wasted half a morning on a wrong scent.'

'Mother of my sons, I laugh!' Caswallon answered. 'They have been afoot since two hours before dawn. How much farther do you think the fools can run? True, Tros has overfed them, but a man's strength has a limit. When they find us in the way, they will lose all heart and lie down. We will drive them home between the chariots, slowly, like pigs to market!'

Chariot after chariot came galloping and drew rein on the hilltop, breathing the horses, until all five-and-twenty were in line again and all the bow-and-arrow men had gathered beside Caswallon's wheels to receive his orders, leather cases over their shoulders with the arrow ends protruding where they could pluck them with the right hand easily and fast.

Tros felt as resentful as a fisherman whose seine-net has been

*Teddington. The word means battle chariots.

30

torn through his own carelessness. No talking could improve the situation. Advice from him would be impertinence. It was he, not they, who had lost two hundred slaves. They, not he, who must retrieve them for him. It was more than probable that, being in a band and desperate, the runaways had done more mischief than the sinking of one scow. More likely than not, they had murdered lonely farmers and anybody else who might happen to have seen them, their one hope of escape depending chiefly on a long start. They would have done everything possible to prevent the true direction of their flight from being known.

And law was law. The law of Britain as concerned slaves varied very little from that of other countries. For whatever a slave, fugitive or not, might do his owner was responsible. Which was fair enough, considering that an owner was allowed to punish his own slaves as he saw fit, and though he might not kill them he might turn them over to the public executioner, his own unchallengeable accusation being tantamount to sentence by a court of law.

So there would be a bill to pay, none knew how big. For every murder done there would be a dozen or more of the runaways tortured, to discover the real culprits, who would be put to death. And tortured men make poor beginners at the deep-sea oar-work that Tros had in view.

Not least toward the making of the loss disastrous was the point of view of bow-and-arrow men, turned out at a moment's notice and brought full-pelt in pursuit. Such men were hardly likely not to want to flesh an arrow once or twice before accepting slaves' surrender. It appeared to Tros he would be lucky if he only lost a hundred of the fugitives killed, maimed and missing. And he would probably have to reward Caswallon's men at something less than one-third of the market price of each survivor, since not even the king's friendship could offset the law of Britain.

However, Fflur surprised him. Her grey eyes observed the glowering disgust in his.

'Lord Tros,' she laughed, 'you came hot-foot to Gaul to rescue me from Caesar. Watch now how I repay.'

She paused a moment, signing to her husband and to Orwic to be still, then studying the faces of the bowmen. Hot they were, and hard-eyed, leashed hounds, eager to be loosed against the quarry.

'Does any of you love me?' she inquired, and for a moment after that they stared at her, grinning. Then there was a murmur of her name, a rising buzz of protest.

31

She knew, without their saying it, they loved her. All did. Why the question? Two or three men strung their bows – expression of their willingness to fight for her, and die if need be.

'Try us!' said a big man standing close beside her chariot wheel. 'How many shall we slay?'

'You, you at least might have known better!' she answered. 'When the town judge sentenced you to lose a hand for stealing, was it I who had charged you? Or do I remember rightly that I paid the fine, and over and above that, too, the restitution money? Was it I or someone else who begged a place for you in the Lord Caswallon's following? Do you think the maiming of a poor wretch pleases me?'

The man grinned at her sheepishly, leaning his weight on his bow, unstringing it.

'Is there one man here for whom I have not done favours?' Fflur asked, raising her voice. 'Wounds, brawling, and dismissals, wives in child-birth nursed, debts, and the prospect of slavery for debt?'

Murmuring again – another protest of a deep, remembered gratitude from men who were none the less puzzled by her choosing that time and that place for an appeal to their affection.

But Caswallon got down from the chariot to feel his horses' forelegs, satisfied that Fflur could do with men-at-arms what he, their battle-leader, could not.

Orwic looked stolidly bored. The climate, and it may be breeding, had produced in him a distaste for scenes in public that even remotely touched the sentimental. He was for action, first, last, all the time, nor too much talk about it afterward unless by way of humorous, half-cynical review.

'Lud's blood!' he grumbled. 'What now?'

'The Lord Tros helped to rescue me from Gaul,' Fflur went on, using the middle notes of the voice that resembled her father Mygnach's. They did say Mygnach had such magic in him that the birds sat still in the trees to listen when he chanted his orison to the sun. 'The Lord Tros goes to Rome to risk his life and all he has that we in Britain may be saved from Caesar. I would like to treat the Lord Tros gratefully. I think a gift from you, for my sake, if you will, of all those slaves of his, recaptured and unharmed, without the customary price on them, would be an offering the gods would call a manly gift. What say you?'

There was not much that they could say. Some grinned half-shamefacedly, like boys in good time lectured against poaching that they had intended and regretfully refrained from. Many of

32

them nodded, trying to look statesmanly sagacious. All of them watched Tros, expecting he would speak. But Tros sat silent in the chariot, not pleased that he must be recipient of favours. Only he knew how immensely he preferred that others should receive his largesse, rather than he theirs. But also, only he knew that the money he had won from Caesar half a year ago had dwindled almost to the last coin, lavished on the ship, and now he had nothing but the druids' pearls out of which to pay fines and ransoms. He was nearer to disaster than Fflur guessed, and carkingly self-critical.

Tros had the trick of silence; though, as Orwic had asserted, he could blow like a north-easter when he chose with gusts of words that carried all before him. Orwic, like the others, looked at him to speak now and, since Tros continued staring straight in front of him, tried urging.

'Tros, what say you?'

'Fflur is right,' he answered, and sat still. He had an intuition that, though Fflur was right, some other force or set of forces, whether human or superhuman made small difference just then, was gone awry. He ached for action, yet did not dare to show impatience lest the men-at-arms should take that cue to extort a ransom after all. He was trying, with all his self-control, to open his mind and let the gods pour information in, ignoring semblances and listening for the inner voice that seldom failed him. But the only thought that seemed to bubble and repeat itself behind his brain was Skell, Skell!

Caswallon took the reins.

'Are we agreed? Then ride!' he shouted, and they were off once more, down a long lane between sheep pastures where the deer browsed at the forest's edge and awkward fawns loped out of sight behind their dams, to turn and stare when they were gone.

There was no more hesitancy and no speech. Caswallon was in action now, each move fore-calculated, every fraction of the horses' strength considered and expended with the goal in mind.

They thundered down-hill, leaping fallen tree-trunks, so that the chariots were like the slings of catapults and Tros had to cling to the wickerwork side with both hands; taking short cuts that would have scared a squirrel, one wheel over a pit's edge, and nothing but the speed and the weight of a horse's shoulder on the pole to keep the lot from overturning; leaping a ditch without so much as checking, crashing through the farmer's fence beyond it, around three ricks and through the oaken paling on the far side, knocking it down with the bronze-headed chariot pole. They left a swath behind them like the path of a winter's hurricane.

And so to the river by Rhyd-y-Cadgerbydan.

'Where, if Ceasar ever gets this far, I will give him and his legions battle,'* said Caswallon, pausing to let the horses breathe again before they plunged breast-deep into the river.

*Teddington. When Caesar invaded Britain for the second time, this was where Caswallon actually did prepare for his final stand, driving stakes into the ford and holding it with dogged courage until deserted by his men. By preparing this site for a pitched battle he succeeded in decoying Caesar and his legions away from 'Lunden Town', which Caesar never saw or he would surely have mentioned the place in his *De Bello Gallico*.

34

'THE FOOL! LORD ZEUS, WHAT SHALL I DO WITH HIM?'

Justice? Let a captain see he have it. Let him remember that a fellow feeling is the juice of justice. Let him wring out the juice. Let him smite with what is left when the juice is wrung forth and bestowed.

Justice that hath no humour and no mercy is the cloak of fear that hypocrites employ to hide the greed and meanness of their lying hearts.

Aye, let a captain well weigh justice.

From the log of Tros of Samothrace

From the ford to the road the runaways were taking was only a few miles, and the going easy. Caswallon drove full speed.

'To wind the horses well, lest they should neigh and betray us when we set an ambush,' he explained.

He had the lay of all the country in his mind and chose a place where two lanes met in a hollow half filled with elms and brambles. Water and the traffic of the years had cut the lanes so deep that banks on either side of them rose twenty feet high. In the centre of the hollow, near the intersection of the lanes, was a pool of limpid water, brook-fed, with fleecy clouds and branches of the overhanging elms reflected in it, a sure temptation to leg-weary runaways to rest themselves and wait for stragglers.

'For whom they will certainly wait,' Caswallon argued. 'They will not dare to leave lame men along the road, any more than a hunted fox leaves more scent than he can help, but crosses brooks and the bare rock where his scent won't lie. There will be a rearguard, urging on the laggards with sharpened sticks.'

The setting of the ambush was a simple matter. On the theory that perhaps the fugitives had stolen a few horses on their way that might neigh and so give the alarm, Caswallon ordered the chariot teams unyoked and led away to a considerable distance. Then he posted all his men, well hidden, around the rim of the hollow, with orders not to loose one arrow in any event unless he should give them leave by signal.

One bugle blast would mean that they should show themselves; two, that they should be on guard against a rush by the fugitives; three, that they might shoot one flight of arrows to prevent any desperate detachment from breaking through the cordon.

'But you may not shoot to kill,' Caswallon ordered. 'Hit them in the arms and legs.'

Three blasts repeated was to mean that a fight was on in earnest, but that signal would not be given unless it should prove that the runaways had somehow managed to steal weapons and could not be captured without bloodshed.

It looked like a plan that could hardly fail, but Tros was nervous. For a while he lay still beside Orwic, with Glendwyr beside him, admiring the silence that the ambushed Britons kept. So still they were that rabbits came and nibbled the sweet spring grass almost within arm's reach. But a red fox, scouting for a meal, sniffed once, turned swiftly in his tracks and vanished. Birds, busy with their nesting in tree and thicket, sang as if nothing in the world were wrong, but five fallow does with fawns at foot, on their way to the pool in the hollow to drink, sniffed two or three times at the tainted air, listened and then fled as if a pack of hounds were after them.

It was intuition that made Tros restless. The day was one to make the blood race in the veins – all fair spring weather with the leaves a-budding, blue sky overhead, and underfoot the violets and yellow primroses; scent of wet, brown earth, and bird-song in the air. But Tros's skin tingled while his blood ran sluggish, and the constant picture in his mind – he could not blot it out – was of his ship without a crew.

'I go to look,' he whispered, and left Orwic lying prone between two elm trees at one end of the horseshoe ambush. Glendwyr followed him.

He walked a hundred yards and chose a high tree, climbed it with seaman's skill, and from the fork of the highest branches watched the countryside for half an hour. At the end of that time, in the middle distance, he could see his stream of fugitives with half a dozen stolen horses, densely packed together between the hedgerows of the winding lane that threaded its long way toward the hollow where the ambush waited.

So far, good. He could hardly count them, but it looked as if the whole lot were in one herd, heading straight for the net. They were coming with the desperate, determined, silent haste of tired men who have but one hope and no line of retreat. But why so close together? Why no stragglers for the rearguard to prick forward? No scouts in advance or on the flanks? They might have used the horses for the obviously necessary scout work, but instead they had put four men on each horse, and to the eye, at that distance, there was hardly a square yard visible between

36

their serried rank from end to end of the procession.

It was Glendwyr, a branch below Tros, who saw the reason for the dense formation and the grim haste.

'Horsemen!' he said suddenly, and pointed.

Headlong down the hill, beyond the ford, there came a stream of mounted men in hot pursuit, riding like centaurs, scattered, racing to be first to overtake the fugitives – a prize worth spurring for – a third of each slave's value for the captor, and a dozen an easy bag for one armed, mounted man!

'Pluto!'

Tros came down the tree like a bear shot from below, two branches snapping under him as he took all chances. Glendwyr dropped to earth beside him. Tros took him by the throat.

'You were their leader! Go to them! Say you have fled from me and are again their leader! Show them a hiding-place! Lead them to where the ambush waits, and keep them there at all costs!'

'They will kill me,' said Glendwyr. 'They won't believe – '

Tros choked and shook him.

'Do you know what to obey means? Any man can die! That's nothing!'

He let go and Glendwyr ran. Tros, hardly daring to hope that Glendwyr could succeed, or that he would even try to succeed, turned and ran at top speed in the opposite direction, flinging himself breathless on the grass beside Orwic.

'Horses!' he panted. 'To horse!'

Orwic wanted explanations. Tros, recovering his breath, stood leaning against a tree and shouted across the hollow to where Caswallon lay beside Fflur.

'Your Lundeners are coming! Get between them and the runaways, or – '

Caswallon's answering shout clipped off the news midword. There was a stir among the brambles, word passed mouth-to-mouth, and then a long cry, ululating from the ambushed bowmen who lay nearest to where the horses had been hidden. Ten breaths more and the horses were on the way, ridden and led full-gallop by the charioteers. Sooner than Tros could breathe again evenly, the teams were yoked, and eight-and-twenty chariots wheeled clear of the lane toward rising ground, behind which they could make a circuit and arrive unseen behind the rear of the uncoming fugitives.

'They will scatter! I fear they will scatter! How close is the pursuit?' Caswallon asked, leaning forward, fanning the stallions' necks with loose reins.

'On the far side of the Rhyd-y-Cadgerbydan.'

'How close to it? Can we reach the ford first?'

'You can try!' Tros answered grimly, and Caswallon laughed. 'A hundred men can hold that ford against a thousand. If we get there first, I'll spare you half my men to hunt your runaways!'

They ran all risks of being seen and heard, their heads appearing constantly above the shoulder of the rise as Caswallon led the way, forcing his tired stallions to the last strained limit of their strength; Fflur's chariot, lighter than his but with only two mares, close behind him – and keeping pace. It was likely that she could do more than Caswallon could to check the men of Lunden at the ford without having to draw bow against them.

Dense alders, and a heron-haunted swamp between them and the lane, served as a luck-given screen exactly at the moment when they passed the fugitives. Tros, standing in the chariot, heard high-pitched voices that sent the herons winging toward their nests in the near-by elms. It was likely enough that Glendwyr had already reached the fugitives and was in speech with them.

'No need! Never mind the ford!' Tros clutched Caswallon by the shoulder. 'Turn around the swamp and come up from behind them. Herd them all into that hollow and surround them until pursuit comes up!'

'Not I!' Caswallon laughed. 'I'll try the ford. I want to see how many men can hold it against Caesar, if he ever comes!'

He shook the reins again and cried out to the stallions, but Tros still clutched his shoulder, shouting in his ear.

'Then give me one chariot. I'll turn back.'

Caswallon spared him one swift glance and drew rein, recognizing resolution.

'Jump!' he commanded. Then, glancing over-shoulder as the other chariots wheeled right and left to avoid collision, 'Orwic, give Tros the last chariot!'

He was away again almost before Tros's feet were on the ground, Fflur hard at his heels and all the other teams but Orwic's in mid-stride on the instant.

'So!' laughed Orwic, beckoning to Tros to mount beside him. 'Mine is the last chariot! Am I then not obedient? You who are to be my captain aboard ship! At the ford down yonder, if Caswallon gets there first, there will only be a fish-wife argument. I would rather be in at the kill. Let me see you manhandle that runaway mob. I believe you can do it alone. And by the way, Tros' – Orwic's almost unvaryingly bantering voice changed to a more serious note – 'Caswallon rides hard, but he's only a king, and unless, mind you, unless he can reach that ford in time you'll have your work cut out. The pursuers will scatter around him and come howling for the loot like wolves after a flock of sheep!'

There was a din of voices from the lane, where it seemed that Glendwyr or, at any rate, someone or something had halted the fugitives. The din grew to an angry roar and died, then rose again into a tumult as the march resumed; and a minute or two later the herons flew back to the swamp to hunt frogs.

'Follow them?' asked Orwic.

'No. Make the circuit again and be there by the pool when they come.'

The handsome face of Orwic beamed. He foresaw drama, lives of men at stake, his own included; no resource but quick wit and effrontery. He wheeled the team on its haunches, laughed at Tros and then at the charioteei beside him.

Away then, full gallop, toward the tree-surrounded hollow, Tros, eyes studying the approach to it, observing that though men in pursuit of the fugitives might make a wide circuit to outflank Caswallon and win past him, they would nevertheless be obliged to turn into the lane before reaching the hollow in order not to lose time negotiating swamps and thickly wooded, rough ground. There was a neck, where the lane led into the hollow between high banks, through which, inevitably, the pursuit must come.

And, better still, the place looked like a perfect trap from that direction. Bottle-necked, comparatively inaccessible from either flank, it was exactly the sort of spot where hunted fugitives would be likely to offer a forlorn resistance. Men in pursuit, possessed of any martial or hunting skill, would hardly dream of entering that gap between the banks without a pause to reconnoitre. Time would be all in Tros's favour.

He checked Orwic when they reached the narrow entrance; stepped down from the chariot.

'Ride you forward,' he commanded with a gesture of such confident authority that Orwic grinned. 'Ride straight on through the hollow, up the lane on the far side and conceal yourself. There wait. Give me that bugle of yours. So. If I should blow a blast on it, then make as much noise in the bushes as if there were five-and-twenty of you. Shout commands, as if to other chariots, keep out of sight most of the time, but keep moving, showing yourself for a moment at a time, first here, then there.

'It might be well to shoot one arrow, or possible two or three, provided you hit nobody. Remember, they are weary men, easier to herd than cattle provided they are not terrified beyond reason.

When you have thrashed about sufficiently among the bushes, if they should look like making a concerted rush, then show yourself and shout to them they are surrounded but in safety of their lives if they stay still. Make haste now. Hear them. They come running!'

Orwic vanished at full gallop, leaving deep wheel-ruts on soft earth that already had been criss-crossed by the wheels of eight-and-twenty chariots. Tros climbed the bank and hid himself among the trees. The leading fugitives had seen the narrow opening that led to a position they might possibly defend awhile, and now the whole two hundred of them poured along the lane at something better than a jog-trot, breathless.

'I am ashamed!' Tros muttered.

He had seldom seen more miserable-looking men, not even in the labour gangs of Egypt. White skins heightened incongruity. Fed healthiness increased the horror of despair. They were armed with sharpened sticks, scythes stolen from the farms they passed, a few tools such as hammers stolen from the shipyard, and here and there a knife thong-fastened to a pole. They were footsore; nine out of ten of them limped; and because Tros had clothed them all alike in smocks and leather jackets, and none had had hair or beard trimmed since the building of the ship began, they appeared to belong to one drab brotherhood of wild-eyed fear.

'How shall a man make men of them?' Tros wondered. Yet, because they had been well fed and had worked hard, they were stronger than the ordinary run of men. There was no lack there of stature or of muscle.

Glendwyr was in their midst, not bound or hurt, but evidently captive. Four or five inches taller than the men who crowded in on him, alone of them all clothed in a free man's breeches and fur-trimmed coat, he had what they lacked – freedom from within. Obviously he had not succeeded in convincing them that he had left earned freedom to throw in his lot once more with hunted rebels; there were sharp sticks pointed at his back; a scythe swayed too suggestively within an arm's length of his face.

As plain to see as if words told it, they had threatened him with death if his tale should turn out to be false. But he looked like a man in danger, not a hunted slave. His eyes glanced right and left for a sight of Tros, but Tros did not leave his hiding place among the trees until the last man limped into the hollow and he could hear the splashing as they bathed their lame feet in the pool.

'Zeus! But they are beaten men!' he muttered.

They had posted no scouts to give warning of pursuit. Instead of setting men in ambush at the narrow entrance, they were argu-

40

ing, holding a crows' congress by the pool, perhaps condemning Glendwyr. There was angry shouting, but Tros could not catch the words. He began to wonder how to rescue Glendwyr, being minded not to lose a promising lieutenant, but he could think of no way at the moment without adding to Glendwyr's danger and risking a rush by the slaves for the open.

At last he heard Glendwyr's voice in masterful appeal, bold, loud and with a note of mockery:

'What do I care whether I am killed or not? You idiots! Set a guard there at the entrance! If I were the Lord Tros, and caught you maa-ing like sheep that smell wolves, I would hang you for crow meat! You have one hope! Hold this place until the Lord Tros rescues you! Punish you for running? Yes, of course he will, and soundly, or I don't know him! But if I were he, I would whip the slave to death who let himself be caught and ransomed rather than make the best of failure and restore himself to his master without expense! Kill me if you like, you fools! I will die free, which is more than any of you will do! I warn you, the Lord Tros loves a man who loses handsomely. Set a guard there by the entrance and defend yourselves until the Lord Tros comes!'

The answer to that was a babel of long argument, of which Tros could not distinguish anything. The upshot of it was that presently a company of thirty men with knives and sharpened sticks came trudging out of the hollow and sat down in two rows straight across the narrowest neck of the lane, their lines extending up the bank on either side of it. The man in the centre of the front rank had a bow and half a dozen arrows; being better armed, he seemed to have assumed the leadership.

Tros, bugle in his left hand, leaving his right arm free to use his long sword, but not drawing it, retreated from the shelter of the trees and made a circuit, reaching the lane where a bulge in the bank projected just sufficiently to hide him. Very cautiously he peered around the edge of that and watched until the thirty men became engaged in argument, their eyes on one another. Then, in three strides, he was in the middle of the lane, fists on his hips, feet spread apart, his lion's eyes a-laugh and strong teeth showing in a grin that knew fear too well to yield to it at any time. They saw him suddenly, and nine-and-twenty of them froze with fear.

'Put that down!' he ordered.

The man in the midst had drawn bow, arrow to his ear.

'Lay down your weapons! You fools! You know the penalty for slaves in arms!'

He began to stride toward them, conscious of the sword against his left hip, but not moving his right hand toward it; in no hurry, and yet not slowly, aware that the light in the notch of the lane at his back made him a perfect target.

The bowman hesitated. It was the man to his right beside him who struck the bow upward at the moment when he loosed the arrow. It whined in a parabola ten feet in air above Tros's head.

Tros kicked the bow out of his hand, then kicked him hard under the chin and knocked him sprawling; seized a sharpened stick and thrashed him with it until the crimson bruises swelled from head to heel.

Then when the writhing wretch had no more breath to sob with as he bit the muddied turf, Tros strode ten paces farther up the lane and turned to face the others.

'I said lay your weapons down! Lay them down! You are surrounded. You' – he pointed at the nearest man – 'go and tell Glendwyr to come here!'

The man threw down his knife and ran to carry out the order. Tros paused to give him time, then, when he heard him blurting out the news, blew a long blast on the bugle. It was answered instantly by shouts from Orwic and the crashing and plunging of a chariot in the undergrowth on the far side of the hollow. Orwic had divided forces, for his shouts were answered from a distance by the charioteer. There came a noise from beside the pool as if a hundred bee-hives had been overturned, then a cry from one throat:

'Mercy!'

Orwic answered it. Tros had a mental picture of him, standing in his peaked steel cap between two elm trees, laughing as he leaned to peer down at the frightened mob.

'Throw down your weapons! Ho, there, archers! Shoot if they refuse! Wait! Wait! They obey! Throw up your hands! All of you! Archers! Shoot any man who holds a weapon!'

An arrow whined across the hollow and went plunk into a tree.

'Mercy!'

It was a hundred voices this time, followed by Orwic's boyish laugh.

Tros turned to face another problem. There were horsemen coming full pelt up the lane from the direction of the ford by Rhyd-y-Cadgerbydan. As Glendwyr reached his side he turned and strode along the lane to meet them, standing hands on hips exactly where the fellow with the bow had taken aim at him.

'It was the bugle-note that saved me!' Glendwyr laughed. 'They had a noose all tied to hang me by! Some bright one had suggested that if they should hang me they could blame me afterward for having tempted them to run away! They are beaten men, Lord Tros. There is neither fight nor run left in them.'

'Aye, but there is fight in these!' Tros screwed up his eyes to scan the faces of a dozen horsemen who had drawn rein where the lane began to narrow, nearly a hundred yards away, and were discussing the situation. Several of them had dismounted and were examining their horses' legs, scraping the muddy sweat off them with cupped hands. It was a minute or two before they realized who Tros was, because the shadow of the high bank fell across the lane. Then one man shouted to him:

'Hah! Then we are in time, Lord Tros! We hunt your slaves. We rode far on a false scent, but your man Skell rode after us and clapped us on the right one. Skell ought to be rewarded. Caswallon, it seems, wants the slaves to escape! He is blocking the ford against all comers, but we swam the stream. The slaves can't be far ahead. Have you a horse?'

'I have the slaves and five-and-twenty chariots!' Tros answered. 'I thank you for your courtesy, but I need no help.'

The men began to ride up-lane toward him, each clutching his weapon in constrained, ill-omened silence. They had come well equipped for a man-hunt – swords, spears, bows and arrows, rope. They halted again ten yards away, and Glendwyr picked up one of the long knives a slave had dropped. Tros recognized one of the horsemen, Rhys, a member of Caswallon's council.

'I stand by,' Glendwyr remarked in a low voice.

'Lord Tros,' said Rhys, and hesitated, not glancing to the right or left but, as it were, feeling for his men's support. He was red-eyed from exertion – a big lean fellow with a mass of reddish hair, a long nose and high cheek-bones, on a horse whose legs trembled from weariness. 'You shall pay me for this day's effort! We were a-horse before dawn. We have ridden the noon out, all for your sake.'

'Not on my invitation,' Tros retorted, keeping his right hand well away from the projecting sword-hilt. 'Glendwyr, get behind me!' he whispered. 'Keep your weapon out of sight!'

'Lord Tros, that is a lie! Your man Skell came and clapped us on the scent.'

'Not with my authority,' said Tros.

'He is your slave, isn't he? For what he does you answer. It is not our fault if he is ill-trained. You say you have caught your slaves. Where are they?'

'Safe,' said Tros.

'Well, I am a reasonable man.'

The red-haired, thin-nosed nobleman glanced right and left at last. took stock of his companions, and went on:

'Pay me half the proper ransom-money and I will cry quits!'

Tros laughed. He always did laugh when the odds were all against him and demands were made to which he was determined not to yield. Sometimes that volcanic, dry bark bursting from his chest disarmed an adversary's will. Not always.

'Easy to laugh!' said the other, growing truculent. 'I doubt that story of the five-and-twenty chariots! See' – he drew the other man's attention – 'here are the wheelmarks of a score or so proceeding this way, and but one returning. If anybody asked me, I would say those are Caswallon's chariots, and we know where he is.' He turned to the others. 'This looks like a scurvy trick to me. He and his friend Caswallon and Mygnach's daughter Fflur proposed to cheat us of our dues! However, he tries to cheat the wrong man. We will flush that covert and enjoy some profitable hunting after our long ride!'

Rhys jerked the spear free from its sling behind his shoulder and made two or three practice passes with it, with its point in Tros's direction. But Tros still kept his hand away from the projecting sword-hilt. He did not dare to blow the bugle yet, because Orwic might interpret that into a signal to use violence on the slaves. Nor did he propose, if it could be helped, to fight a member of the council. He had a perfect right to protect himself and his human property if he could do it, but the slaves had been proscribed by general alarm as runaways, and the obviously profitable thing for Rhys to do was to chase the slaves into the open, where he could round them up and claim redemption money. Rhys turned to his companions.

'Better make haste,' he remarked. 'There will be others presently. Why share the profit? You four keep his lordship occupied! The rest of us will ride in!'

Tros drew his sword at last, a thing he never did unless he meant to use it. And he said nothing, which was another of his characteristics in extremity. His silence, more than any speech he might have made, gave the opponents pause. Rhys laughed unpleasantly.

'Hold him here, four of you. The rest of you follow me!'

He began to wheel his trembling horse, and Tros made up his mint to retreat to the pool, where the slaves would be all round him, so that afterwards he would be able to assert they were under control and, if he should slay anyone, he would be able to claim he did so in defence of them. But as he took one short step backward he heard a yell behind him. Thunder of hoofs and wheels came, not along the lane but down the bank-side like an avalanche. He and Glendwyr sprang to the opposite bank in the nick of time. Orwic, one foot on the chariot-front, the reins in both hands, made his frantic team leap as they were six feet from the bottom, preserving them from a fall beneath the chariot by a trick of horsemanship so near to magic as to make Tros gasp, wheeled them down the middle of the lane before they could lose impetus, and charged headlong at the twelve who blocked the way.

Down they went, horse and rider, in a shouting, blasphemous confusion, Orwic avalanching through the midst and struggling for fifty yards or more to rein in the frantic team. Before he could turn, some of the riders were on their feet, clustering together, looking the wrong way, expecting another chariot. Three horses were too badly injured to get up, others had bolted. Before the riders had time to collect their wits and scatter Orwic was coming again headlong. A horse's shoulder knocked the Lord Rhys stunned against the bank; the others, leaping right and left, avoided wheels by inches.

'Run!' laughed Orwic. 'Run before I signal!'

He leaned out of the chariot, beckoning to Tros to pass the bugle to him, held it to his lips and filled his lungs. But they did not wait to find out whether a bugle signal would bring reinforcements; they took the threat for granted, cried, 'Hold! Enough!' and ran to catch their horses.

'Home! Home with you!' Orwic shouted. 'Get you home before I name you and lay charges!'

Then he stepped out of the chariot and took the stunned man by the hair, discovered he was conscious, shook him, dragged him to his feet, shook him again and kicked him down the lane toward his friends.

'Better let me forget who you are!' he called after him, and, turning to examine the injured horses, drew his sword across their throats.

'You may have to pay for three horses, brother Tros,' he remarked, wiping his sword as he strolled back. 'That would be an act of generosity that should draw Rhys's teeth. And I wager he won't talk! But if you had killed Rhys or his men, Lud love you! Not even Fflur could have saved you from indemnities that would have cost you half the tin from off your ship.'

Tros stepped into the chariot and they drove slowly to the pool to count the slaves. There were only four men missing, of whom

45

one, they said, was drowned when they crossed the river, and three, losing heart, had returned to the shipyard.

'I will sell those three!' said Tros. 'They are not slaves, they are animals. Nay, I will not even sell them, I will give them in exchange for those three horses that were overthrown just now and injured! Glendwyr, take some men and skin me those three horses. Cut the meat up, have it cooked, and feed these rascals or I'll never get them home!'

He asked no further questions, made no inquiries as to who the ringleaders might be, threatened no punishments, intended none. He and Orwic strolled together, arm-in-arm, beside the pool, Tros praising Orwic's horsemanship and Orwic trying to talk of anything else under the sun because the subject of his own achievements bored him.

'I suppose,' said Orwic, 'you will have to have these poor fools flogged?'

'Not I!' Tros answered with his great full-chested laugh. 'I no more flog a man who has his belly full of grief than you flog a foundered horse. I am rather pleased with them. See how they stuck together! And only three faint-hearted ones among the lot! Those three discovered and all ready to be weeded out before I set sail! Hah! I begin to believe I shall have a fair crew after all.'

'But have you enough yet?'

'No, not by a hundred men. And I have one who will make more trouble for me than the hundred that I lack! Yet I cannot get rid of Skell, for I have promised him a chance to prove himself. Hey! What a fool a man is with his promises! Look you. Skell is nine days out of prison, where I put him for treason as black as the inside of a tar-pot. He inclines now toward honesty, being one of those teetering bastards built like an Antioch scale, with manliness at one end of the balance-arm and false weights at the other. Intending me a good turn, he claps the men of Lunden on the trail of these runaways and all but costs me a fortune. And that's nothing to what he's likely to do when fortune finds him opportunity in some foreign port! What shall I do with the fool? Lord Zeus, what shall I do with him?'

'Send him to Caesar!' said Orwic. 'He might serve as well as a woman to break Caesar's wheels.'

To his surprise, Tros took the suggestion seriously, pacing up and down, both hands behind him now, turning over in his mind the pros and cons of it. He was still meditating, frowning, when Caswallon came with a fresh team he had appropriated somewhere, laughing, confident, Tros's problems out of mind because of a brand new solution or his own.

'Tros, brother Tros!' he shouted. 'I have Caesar by the horns!' Drawing rein, he leaned out of the chariot and took Tros by the shoulder. 'Let him come!' he said, with one of his confident nods. 'That ford by Rhyd-y-Cadgerbydan shall be the battle-ground, for I have seen now how to hold it. I will drive stakes in the river bed. Then we will tempt Caesar inland, away from the coast and reinforcements, harrying his legions all the way with horse and chariot, opposing him enough in front to keep him occupied and out of reach of Lunden until we check him at the ford by Rhyd-y-Cadgerbydan with half his legionaries drowning and our own men charging downhill from his rear to cut off his retreat. Let him come! We have Caesar beaten!'*

*There were stakes in the ford beside Teddington Bridge as recently as thirty years ago. Caswallon's plan succeeded until his own men ran and his allies deserted him. Even so, Caesar only won a 'Pyrrhic' victory and had to retreat to the sea.

A BARGAIN WITH THE DRUIDS

Such wisdom as I have, I think, enables me to recognize a higher wisdom when I meet it. Him who hath it I obey, of my own will in the knowledge that a higher wisdom will demand no more than a lesser can properly do. But when I find clowns in the garb of wise men, masking avarice within the folds of solemn ignorance, by Zeus such hypocrites must buy whatever good for themselves they hope to get from me. For a high price paid in advance I sell to such imposters; and I sell them nothing I would not have given freely had they asked with the decent dignity of honourable men in need. Such men should be made to buy the sunshine.

From the log of Tros of Samothrace

Troubles increased as the day drew near that Tros had set long in advance for the launching. He had hoped, by making that a popular spectacle, to win the public to h's side and, perhaps, to recruit a score or two of free men for his crew by exciting admiration, curiosity and those other emotions that stir men to act on the spur of a moment.

Nothing had he left undone to make the event spectacular, even as he had overlooked no element of danger that could be foreseen. The ways down which the ship must slide had been reinforced and, in places, even shored with masonry. He had anchors buried deep on shore and prodigiously heavy flaxen cables to prevent the ship, when launched, from gliding too far across the river.

To make sure the ship would start when he gave the signal, he had sent a turn-screw in position, by which he could raise the huge balks of timber on which the bow end rested, thus increasing the slant to overcome inertia. And he had greased the ways so thickly with good hog-fat that even his friend Caswallon complained of the extravagance.

The ship rested in a cradle made of elm, so there was no risk that friction would strip off the tin from her undersides. Sigurdsen had spent a whole day taking soundings in the river bed to make sure there were no submerged wrecks or obstructions in the stream. At all strategic points within the yard Tros had secretly placed quantities of his appalling chemical, with instructions to Conops to fire it if the crowd of spectators should unexpectedly turn riotous.

But more than any physical precaution that he took, acceptance by the druids of his invitation to be present and to bless the ship was Tros's chief guarantee of a successful launching. He would have preferred to leave the druids out of it. Having extorted pearls from them, he was conscious of their resentment, and he preferred the ill-will of men less practised than the druids in the art of making thought produce results. He had too much experience of priests in Rome, Alexandria, Jerusalem, and elsewhere not to know that the preliminary steps of decadence destroy all vision and the power to do good, but do not for a while destroy the energy itself or its accumulated impetus. He would have been almost as pleased with the druids' curse, just then, as with their blessing.

But an undiscoverable enemy set rumour stirring. It was whispered, then repeated in the market-place, that Tros intended to perform a human sacrifice before the launching, in order that the ship might have a soul and be superior to other ships. From mouth to mouth the tale waxed circumstantial. He would bind a living slave across the ways and let the ship slide over him, drowning the victim's screams with a fanfare of trumpets and salvo of war-drums. Representations were made to the king and council that the superstitious cruelty should be prevented.

The council in full session sent for Tros, who, arms akimbo, laughing angrily, repudiated any suggestion of sacrifice of any sort whatever.

'Lord Caswallon – noblemen!' he snorted in disgust. 'I hold myself inferior in all things to the meanest of the gods, and I would shudder at the thought of cruelty to win my favour! What then is it likely that the gods would think? I would for ever count myself an exile from the company of all that host of spiritual beings who surround us and employ our manhood, whose very breath is inspiration to the brave. If I should tolerate a human sacrifice, if I should perpetrate it, I would say, "My soul has left me. Henceforth I am no man, a thing!" '

But one member of the council was the Lord Rhys, who smarted from a previous attempt to pull Tros's purse-strings. Rich from impeaching law-breakers and buying up their property when they must sell to pay the heavy fines imposed, he was not to be decoyed by spiritual herrings drawn across a chance to profit by another man's predicament. He already had one issue against Tros. The hope he might be bribed lurked in his cold eyes as he leaned forward and, without rising, pointed an accusing forefinger, used it to knock off a drop from the end of his nose, and then pointed again.

'The Lord Tros speaks with much assurance about gods, of

whom he affects to know a great deal. But we all know that human sacrifice has been made before now at the launching of ships, by men who think more of their own superstitions than of the law and the opinions of decent people. Such men invariably hide their evil practices and deny them after the event. It happens I have seen the ship, which is a monster and not like any ship previously built. Not only is it plated underneath with precious metal of a value greater than a whole year's taxes from my district, but there is a golden serpent having two tails, one of which coils the full length of the ship on either side until they reach the stern, where they are joined together and project into the air. We all know that the use of snakes by anybody but the druids is a blasphemy, and I have this to add . . . '

Rhys paused, stood up, made a gesture toward Caswallon and the council, watched Tros for the space of a dozen breaths with eyes that glittered coldly and resumed:

'That serpent's head curves upward from the ship's bow. It has a long tongue that projects and moves. It has eyes that are made of garnets. It has teeth that were taken from wild boars. And beneath it, at the ship's bow, there is the figure of a woman, carved by Cuchulain the minstrel, of the full size of a woman, painted blue, but with the face pearl-coloured, of crushed oyster-shell, the long hair golden and the head crowned. Unless rumour lies, the hair and the crown are both of solid gold. There are gold rings on the woman's fingers, that are folded on her breast.

'Now I accuse the Lord Tros of intending – mark you, I say, of intending; I do not say he has done so yet, though I reserve my full right to my own convictions – I say, of intending to incorporate a woman's soul into that figure of wood and metal.

'Why else should he tempt Cuchulain the minstrel to commit such sacrilege as to carve a human figure?* Why did he set free Boad, who was serving-maid to his own wife Helma, unless because he wished to sacrifice a free-woman rather than a slave? Where is Boad?'

Rhys sat down, brushing a new drop from his nose-end with his sleeve, and there was a murmur. Men nodded their heads, at which Caswallon on the throne-chair chewed his long moustache. It was true, and all men knew it; Boad had mysteriously vanished.

Tros took two steps forward, so that he faced the semicircle and Caswallon in the midst. He was about to speak when Orwic, at Caswallon's right hand, put a word in.

---

*The Britons made no use of the human form in their designs, which, however, were of a very high artistic standard.

50

'I accuse Rhys himself of having made away with Boad!'

Orwic crossed one leg over the other and leaned back in the carved and painted chair as if he thought the whole discussion a mere nuisance. Before Rhys could spring to his feet indignantly, with a bored air he had tossed another brand into the blaze.

'We all know how Rhys grew rich!'

Rhys stuttered indignation, stood up and sat down again. There fell an awkward silence, broken after a pause by Orwic's lazily amused voice:

'Rhys might fight me, if he dares!'

Then Tros, his face alight with sudden comprehension and assurance:

'Nay! That is my privilege! I know now why a slave came hinting to me that I might do well to go and visit the Lord Rhys by night! The slave, I remember, suggested I should bring no witnesses! So! I will give the Lord Rhys until sunset to produce Boad, my freed woman, alive and unhurt. If he should fail . . . '

But Rhys had left the council hall, slipping out behind his high-backed chair into the shadow and passing through the leather-curtained door into the vestibule where armed men saluted him with grounded spearbutts.

'Noblemen,' said Tros, 'I lost a young wife, through taking your part against Caesar. I have claimed no recompense from you on that account, and as for Caesar, he shall settle his own reckoning. I hired Cuchulain, the minstrel, who was taught in Gaul by Agoras, the Greek, to carve me a true likeness of my young wife for the ship's bow. So, it may be, neither ship nor I will act unworthy of her memory. Now you have heard the whole of it.'

But though they had heard and believed, they were shocked by the idea of a carving of a woman. Rhys sent Boad to the shipyard before evening, but she brought a husband with her, who frowned her into silence, and who was so obviously a spy in Rhys' service that Tros turned both of them out into the rainy night. He might have cancelled the girl's marriage had he chosen. As a freed woman, she was his ward and none might marry her without his leave. But he was heartily glad to be rid of the wench and gave her a sound boxing of the ears for marriage portion. So she went off and lied about him, claiming he had tried to exercise the age-old tyranny – and she already three weeks married.

That brought into play druidic prejudice. Tros went to see the druids to discuss the launching, and a middle-aged Lord Druid, recently promoted from the lower rank in the shuffle that had followed the death of the great Taliesan, took opportunity to lecture him on moral laxity, saying the druids could not countenance such practices or grant official recognition to a man suspected of them.

'For what will become of Britain if we encourage strangers who do such things in our midst?'

But Tros knew he must have the druids at the ceremony or risk disaster. There were too many men who would enjoy the opportunity to start a riot unless the launching should have druidic sanction.

'You shall come!' he retorted. 'You are not such spiritual guides as was your teacher, the great Taliesan, or I would not dare speak to you in these terms. You are not men who possess the vision, or you would know that this woman's tale about me is a lie – as the great Lord Druid Taliesan would certainly have known without my telling him. He had wisdom, but not you! I say to you, you *shall* come!'

'I will curse you!' the greybeard answered. But the threat did not have the same effect on Tros that it would have produced on a native Celt – even on Orwic or Caswallon. Tros smiled and bowed with dignity more gracious than the druid's.

'I have seen curses,' he answered, 'that returned like bad money to the forger! Curse carefully, lord-brother of the dragons! If Taliesan had cursed me, I should be a dead man now. But he blessed. You will come and bless my ship, and for this reason: that if you do not, I will take those pearls and, letting all men know who gave them to me, I will scatter them by the handful into the River Thames as my ship takes water. And I will say, "Lo! These are druids' pearls, a druids' blessing."'

Eyes met, and the druid knew that Tros was wilful enough to carry out that threat.

'Then,' Tros continued, speaking slowly, 'having no pearls, but having returned them to the water whence they came, I would not be under obligations to you. I would suit myself what action I should undertake next.'

Taliesan the Great would have made short work of such a threat. But Tros knew he was dealing with no Taliesan. It was an ambitious, weak-willed hierarchy that had yielded to demands for treasure in the first place. Such were not the men to stand their ground and see wealth wasted – this old rumour-monger, this repeater of slave-girl's accusations, least of all.

'Your heart is bold and bad, Lord Tros,' the druid answered. 'But the evil dig their own pit. It is best we speed your going and soon see the last of you.'

'Taliesan would never have made such a speech in my hearing,' Tros answered.

More than ever he recognized weakness. He had built a ship, had drilled the odds and ends of flotsam of humanity into a crew of sorts, and knew that weakness is no good for a foundation. Unless discarded altogether, weakness must be beaten, pressed, hammered, and backed up until it resists at last, and either breaks or is good for something.

'I am your ally,' he went on, his amber eyes scanning their countenances that were stern but only masked irresolution. 'Ye are willing to make use of me, but not to treat me as your friend. Now Taliesan, had he deigned to make use of me, would have reckoned my well-being as important as his own. He would never have sent me forth without a full crew. He would have manned my ship with kings' sons, had I asked him. Nor would he have prayed to see the last of me. Taliesan would have said one of two things to me. Either, "Thy heart is bad, so get thee hence!" or, "How can I serve thee, thou who servest us?" And I would have asked him for a hundred freemen, ten from each of ten tribes, to increase my crew. Where is the cloak of Taliesan? Who wears it?'

His speech was received in silence. They withdrew into a corner to consult in whispers – nine grey-bearded men possessed of all the outer attributes of dignity, but with its cause lost. They did not know; they thought, they guessed, they were enamoured of their own importance; there were echoes of a wisdom that had flowed through Taliesan but that did not penetrate beneath the crust of their ambition to be powerful.

'We must send to Mona,'* the lord druid said at last. 'Mona is the seat of our authority.'

Tros struck his own breast. 'Mine is in my heart,' he answered. 'So was the Lord Taliesan's. He would have said to me yes or no. He would have given me a crew of druids had he seen fit! And if he had sent a messenger to Mona or any other place, it would have been to say what he had done, not to ask whether it were right for him to do it! Speak ye your own minds. I listen.'

So again they whispered in the corner, shaking heads and glancing at him where he stood in the dim whale-oil lantern-light. Tros realizing more and more, as they delayed to answer him, that something – though he could not guess what – had happened to provide him with an upper hand over them.

'They would like me dead!' he told himself. 'Yet they love their holiness too much to cause me to be slain.'

*The modern Anglesey.

Decaying priesthoods, well he knew, are desperate and justify all evil done to prop up their own despotism. But he knew, too, decadence takes time. Great Taliesan was hardly three months dead; druids would hardly stoop to doing murder or procuring it until a score or so of years should overlie his influence.

'They have news. If I wait and persist, I will learn it,' he assured himself. 'They wish me gone. They are afraid of me. They dare not to offend me too much. Why?' he wondered, and he folded his arms, standing very erect, to await what the gods should bring forth.

'I see destiny in travail,' he reflected.

Presently the new Lord Druid came toward him, fingering the golden sickle at his waist. The lamplight shone on the yellow metal and on the druid's eyes, that were mild enough and not grown worldly, but betrayed doubt where there should have been assurance built on inner strength. But instead of assurance there was arrogance of glance and gesture; and instead of strength there was ambition to appear strong.

'There are mysteries you may not know,' he said, stroking his long beard.

'I can read your heart,' Tros answered, and his hands were still.

He was like a rock, whereas the druid came at him like water feeling for a line of least resistance.

'But if we trust you with a secret – '

'That you will not do,' Tros interrupted. 'You know as well as I that whoever tells a secret cannot expect another man to keep it. Therefore whatever you will tell me you will have decided first is not a real secret, but only something with which to mystify me. Speak. I listen.'

'You remember King Gwenwynwyn of the Ordovici?'

The druid's white hand continued stroking at his beard as he watched Tros's eyes. All Britain knew that Tros and King Gwenwynwyn of the withered arm were enemies. They had quarrelled even in the presence of the mighty Taliesan. The lamp-light showed no change in Tros's expression; his frown dissolved into a fighting smile too slowly to be observed.

'Gwenwynwyn,' said the druid, 'went to Gaul and has returned. Gwenwynwyn spoke with Caesar, who has pledged him friendship. Caesar set a price on your head of three Roman talents, and Gwenwynwyn will offer the third of that to whoever shall kill you and bring your head to him.'

'My head is worth more than three talents to Caesar,' Tros

54

answered with a gruff laugh. 'Gwenwynwyn should have made a better bargain!'

He was studying the druid's face now with all his power of intuition keyed up to the limit of alertness, although on the surface he was perfectly unruffled. It was not the news that puzzled him. To set a big price on his head was Caesar's obvious recourse, and since his first success against Caesar he had expected that. He had been absolutely sure of it since he and Caswallon took Caesar captive and exchanged him against Fflur. But it was beyond his power to guess why the druids should reveal the information to him now.

'What you tell is not news to me. Why do you tell?' he answered.

The druid smiled with an air of superior knowledge – not as the great Taliesan would have smiled, for Taliesan took no delight in knowing more than other men.

'Gwenwynwyn has no army,' he said, fingering the sickle at his waist. 'But he is Caesar's friend, and Caesar has an army.'

Tros let out one of his deep-chested monosyllabic laughs. 'At Verulam,' he said, 'where I met Gwenwynwyn, he accused Caswallon of being Caesar's friend and tried to persuade Taliesan to rebuke Caswallon for it.'

The druid made a gesture of indifference, suggesting that Gwenwynwyn's treacheries were nothing new.

'Gwenwynwyn has no army,' he repeated, 'and he lives afar off in the West. He is afraid if he should cause you to be murdered he would have to meet Caswallon's vengeance, for he knows Caswallon is your friend. It would be hard for Caswallon to march all the width of Britain with an army to attack him, but he knows Caswallon's energy in action just as surely as he knows his carelessness in repose. So he has made a stipulation to which Caesar has agreed.'

The druid paused and eyed Tros curiously. All the other druids gathered nearer, making no sound. They were like disembodied spirits, bearded faces framed in shadow.

'Caesar is to send five hundred Spaniards to Gwenwynwyn's aid! They are to land in Dyvnaint* and to march to Merioneth.† They will be commanded by a Roman, but they are to obey Gwenwynwyn, whom they will defend if you should be slain and Caswallon should try to avenge you.'

The druid paused again, drew in his breath and sighed.

'So you see, Lord Tros, you have brought invasion on us. You

*Cornwall or Devonshire.
†The only county in England or Wales that retains its ancient British name.

have brought on us the curse of foreign soldiers in our midst. Civil war may follow.'

'But?' said Tros. 'I can discern a "but" that lurks – to be discovered presently! What is it? Butt it forth!'

'The Spaniards have not yet started. To send them will cost Caesar money. If either of two events should happen, Caesar might not send those men.'

'Aye,' Tros answered, nodding, 'if I were dead and Caesar knew it, he might not send them. What is the other alternative?'

'If you were gone and Caesar knew it – go soon! Go soon, Lord Tros, and leave us to our own peace!'

Tros threw his head back and laughed.

'Nay, I will not go!' he retorted. 'Nay, nah! Hah!' He began to pace the floor, both hands behind him, knotted fingers clenching and unclenching. 'Five hundred men!' he muttered.

He had the news at last! Suddenly he turned and faced the druids.

'I will bargain with you!'

The Lord Druid appeared horrified. A blunt proposal to drive bargains was an insult to druidic dignity. Not yet, surely not yet, had they descended to such depths that they might not cover bargaining beneath a gloss of condescension. Nevertheless, beneath the horror Tros saw readiness to drive a bargain, should the terms of it appeal.

'We give or we withold,' the druid answered. 'He who wears the golden sickle neither buys nor sells.'

Tros made a gesture of concession. He would not split hairs of definition. He came bluntly to the point.

'I will go, and as soon as may be. I will make no more demands on you. But you shall keep my going secret. You shall tell Gwenwynwyn I will not go. You shall tell him – and no untruth, for you hear me threaten now – that you have heard me boast I will explore the coast of Britain in my ship, until I come to Merioneth where withered-arm Gwenwynwyn kings it in the woods! You shall take no steps to keep those Spaniards from coming. You shall leave that business to me. And meanwhile, you shall guard my life. You shall bless me publicly, that men may know I am not lightly to be murdered.

'You shall lend me countenance by coming to the launching of my ship with ceremonial procession and the minstrels and a choir. And if I send a man to Gaul,' Tros added, with one of those swift afterthoughts that often mean more than the whole of what preceded them, 'you shall give him secret introduction to the Gauls, to the end that they may help him to spy on Caesar. That is all. Now, play the Taliesan for once! Say yes or say no. Say it only like men, that I may count with or without you.'

The druids went again in a conference, whispering together where the darkest shadow fell beyond the heaped-up sacks of grain. Tros paced the floor, no longer thinking of the druids, knowing, because he understood their dread of foreign soldiers, that their answer would be yes.

'Five hundred men!' he muttered. 'And Skell anxious to redeem himself! Hah!'

LIAFAIL

As a man is in his heart the sea reveals him to himself. Be he strong, the sea shall test him. Be he weak, the sea shall discover his weakness. Be he heedless, bold or cunning, or all three, the sea shall find him out and face him with his strength and weakness that he knew not.

From the log of Tros of Samothrace

It was not yet dawn. Tros, sword on the table in front of him, sat by the fireside in darkness except for the flickering fire on the hearth – and, the night being gusty, the room was filled with smoke that spread itself in layers. Conops, squatting by the hearth, baked bread for breakfast. Skell stood and faced Tros, eyes watering in the stinging smoke, and both men coughed at intervals.

'You are a fool,' said Tros, 'and an irksome problem to me. When you were my enemy, I laughed, but now I grieve because a fool is a danger to his friends and deadlier yet to his master.'

'Lord Tros, you sent for me,' Skell answered, shivering, for he was only half clothed. 'I think you did not send for me at this hour to call names or because sleep fails you. I take it you will use my folly. I am willing.'

Tros crashed the table with his fist and made the sword jump.

'Idiot! You cost me three men recently by giving the alarm when all my Britons bolted in the night. I had to swap three in exchange for three slain horses. Another year of your loyalty – and I am beggared!'

'Not so bad as that, Lord Tros! I saved all the stores. It was I who found the fire laid under the pitch-shed floor. I saved you nearly half a mile of hempen rope by – '

'Can you speak the Roman tongue?' Tros interrupted.

'Yes, my lord.'

'And Gaulish?'

'Yes, my lord.'

'Caesar and many of his officers could recognize you?'

'Yes, my lord.'

'Then shave!'

Skell stared, but Conops found a razor and a pair of shears. Before Skell realized it, half his beard was gone.

'There, take the bacon-rind and rub,' said Conops irritably. 'Rub it in well, unless you want your skin to be scraped off with the hair.' Conops shoved to make him turn the unclipped half toward the firelight. 'Spit on the rind! If it's too hard, chew it!'

Tros, in silence, watched the transformation. What had looked like obstinacy through the matted red mask now betrayed itself as a retreating chin accentuated by the big sharp nose. Skell looked ten years younger, and by ten of any measure less a danger to be reckoned with. By some trick of proportion now, his eyes looked much less cunning and more mild. Tros ordered Conops to trim the eyebrows.

'Not too much or he'll look disguised,' he warned. 'Now the hair at the back of the neck. Crop it half short.'

Skell went and washed his face in the great lead bowl in the corner. Luckily he could not see himself, or the last dregs of his self-esteem would have drifted away with the smoke as Conops opened the shutters a trifle to judge what time it might be. Tros had to screw up his own courage before he could trust that weak-chinned specimen with any kind of mission. However, he had none else suited for his purpose. Glendwyr, for instance, knew no Roman.

'At any rate, Caesar won't fear you,' he remarked, as Skell returned to stand in front of him. 'Are you afraid of Caesar?'

'Aye!' said Skell, showing too much of the whites of his eyes.

Tros laughed. 'A month ago you would have boasted that neither Caesar nor any other man could frighten you! Because I am not afraid of Caesar, I will send you to him.'

Skell's jaw fell, increasing the effect of the retreating chin. His red-rimmed eyes grew narrower. Conops, heaping red-hot ashes on a bread-pan, chuckled.

'Aye, I know,' said Tros, nodding. 'When I sent you to Caesar before, you played fast and loose between him and me. He will scourge and crucify you if you are recognized. But you asked me for a chance to act the man, and now you may have it. I am going to give you money, my money, and this from the druids.'

Tros showed him a fragment of parchment, not longer than a thumb-joint either way, inscribed with heavy characters in black ink.

'If Romans should see this they would condemn you to death for possessing it. So swallow it if you are caught. But show it to any Gaul and, if he is a true Gaul, he will help you. You are to discover from which port and when Caesar is sending Spanish troops to Britain. By whatever means present themselves, you are to get exact information to me. Without betraying who you are or even that you know me, you are to start a rumour in Gaul in such a way that it will reach Caesar's ears as soon as possible, that I will remain in Britain all this year in order to help Caswallon against Caesar should he attempt a new invasion.'

'Am I myself to return to you with the information?' Skell asked.

'That is for the gods and your own wit to determine. I need the information more than I need you. You may return by fishing-boat from Gaul or you may attach yourself to the Spanish troops and sail with them. They might need an interpreter, for instance.'

'And how shall I reach Gaul?' Skell asked him.

'By chariot to Pevensey, where you will find a fisherman named Geraint who will take you to the Gaulish coast not far from Seine-mouth. You will only need to show him this druids' writing and he will obey you. Geraint, they tell me, is half Gaul, half Briton. He will remain over there in Gaul among the fisherfolk, and it may be he is the man to bring you back or to bring your news to me if you remain and travel with the troops. But he is not too trustworthy, since he loves the glint of money. I was cautioned by the druids as to that. So, if you use Geraint, he must not understand what he is doing. Nothing in writing. Nothing spoken that he could repeat to the Romans or a Roman spy.'

Conops chuckled again, stirring cow's milk as he warmed it in the embers. Then he cracked six eggs into a frying-pan and threw the shells into the fire with totally unnecessary violence. Tros nodded.

'Eggs,' he said. 'If Geraint or any other man from Gaul should bring me eggs, no Roman could interpret that. If he should say they are eggs of Spanish hens from Seine-mouth or from Caritia or from Caen or from Cariallum,* as the case may be, I would understand that the Spanish troops will sail from whichever port is thus indicated. Let each egg represent a day. Thus, if there were nine eggs, I would understand that the Spaniards will sail on the ninth day after the messenger set forth from Gaul.

'Then you must tell me in how many ships they sail. So, lest the eggs be broken, you will wrap them carefully. If in three packages, then the Spaniards will sail in three ships. If in two, then in two ships. If each egg should be separately wrapped in wool, let that mean that the ships are unarmed merchantmen. But if the wrapping of each egg is of grass or straw, I will understand they sail in warships. But if they should sail in unarmed ships with

*The modern Cherbourg.

warships for an escort, you will place the packages of eggs inside a basket, and that basket inside another one, and so on, to indicate how many warships. The stronger and bigger the baskets, the bigger and better armed I will understand those warships to be. Is all that clear to you?'

Skell nodded. He folded his arms. His delight in intrigue was offsetting the fear that kept his yellow teeth exposed.

'Now as to the Spanish troops' direction. It may be difficult to convey that information, but let us take the harbour of Dertemue† as the place where I will expect them unless there is news to the contrary. If they should sail to the westward of Dertemue, then include a duck's egg in the package. If to the eastward of it, then a dozen or so black hen's feathers. But if there should be two duck's eggs, then I will understand that they sail around the end of Britain to the West Coast. But the Romans are no sailors, so I think that course unlikely. Now, can you remember all that?'

Skell nodded again.

'How shall the messenger find you?' he asked. 'Will you be here?'

'Not I! Nor will I tell you where I will be, since the wind and weather have a part to play. Nor can I spare Conops, for I have a crew of land crabs to be hammered into men with seamen's souls. I will send a man to Hythe, who will await you or your messenger. He will not know where to find me, for there are too many informers on the prowl, but I will find him.'

Conops laid the fried eggs, bacon, hot bread and scalded milk on the table in front of Tros, pushing the sword out of the way and making a great clatter of plates and spoons. Dawn began to peer palely through the chink in the wooden shutters. Tros yawned and fell to at the food.

'Go, eat. Clothe yourself. Be ready in an hour.' he said to Skell, and Skell went out with a stride that alternated between cat-like caution and a swagger.

'Already he thinks he carries eggs!' said Conops, grinning. 'You have chosen a weak agent, master!'

'Aye, and a poisonous bad cook!' Tros spat the bread out of his mouth. 'You dog! You feed me ashes!'

'Wholesome, master! Good for your insides! Ashes – not much, just a little – fell into the dough. I couldn't help it.'

'Ashes? Pluto rot you! It's a charred oak knot. Break my teeth, will you?'

Tros swallowed the hot milk, set down the beaker, took more

†The modern Dartmouth.

of the alleged bread and rammed it into Conops' mouth, holding the Greek's head under his armpit, ramming in more and more with both his thumbs until the gag was solid. Then he buckled on his sword and strode out to the shipyard, where Sigurdsen, in two languages, was bellowing curses at a group of Britons who had knocked out the ratchet of a crane too suddenly and dropped a load of lumber on the ship's deck.

The sun was hardly over the skyline and the mist hung like washed wool over the river, but the whole yard was a-hum already with the orderly excitement of a task now nearly finished. There was a reek of hot pitch and a squeal of cordage as they rigged the tackles to the anchored buoys in mid-stream – sudden squalls of hammer-blows where Northmen in the ship's waist fitted up the berths. For Tros had carried innovation to the limit and provided a dry section of the hold wherein his ablest seamen might sleep comfortably and, aft of that again, an almost sumptuous saloon for his lieutenants. She was a wonder of a ship. She was to have a wonder-name bestowed on her at high noon. For a while, Tros stood admiring her vermilion topsides, which had cost him a fortune in mercury and sulphur for the paint.

Orwic came, dew on his face, leaping along a chariot-pole and standing beside Tros almost before the long-maned stallions could plant their forefeet in the sod and bring the chariot to a clattering halt.

'Men!' he said, agape at the great ship's gleaming splendour, for Tros had made them polish up the tin against the launching. 'Men! Men! Tros, what say you? Let us feed Northmen their own meat! Red rascals! They have raided our coasts since before the memory of man. Let's raid theirs for a change! Cross the North Sea, burn some villages, round up women and hold them until they trade us a man for them apiece! Northmen are better sailors than you'll ever find in Britain.'

'No,' said Tros.

'Why not? Lud's teeth! They've earned reprisals! We'd be doing favours to the gods by raping half a dozen homesteads!'

'I have enough Northmen,' Tros answered. He knew better than to talk to Orwic about the ethics of honest raiding. Orwic would have hunted men as cheerfully as wolves. 'Too many of a kind is worse than too few. I will be captain of my ship.'

Orwic pushed the peaked steel cap back from his forehead, scratched his hair and looked at Tros curiously, as at a man who might be talking nonsense to conceal his thoughts.

'You have nearly two hundred Britons,' he remarked. 'They

are used now to your eight-and-forty Northmen. If a mutiny should start, do you think Britons would take your side?'

Tros looked hard at him.

'When I studied the mysteries,' he said, 'I was taught the properties of triangles. A triangle will carry more weight than a square and, with the weight on it, is not so easy to upset. You understand me?'

'No,' said Orwic.

Tros, refraining from explanations, turned to greet Caswallon, who arrived four-horsed, at full speed, with the morning sun behind him, gleaming on his flowing hair.

'Today? Surely today?' Caswallon asked.

And when Tros nodded he drew him aside by the sleeve.

'I have a thought how you can get more men, but not a word to Orwic! You heard Rhys speak of the taxes from his district? Well, they are in arrear. Orwic is in debt to Rhys, who threatens a suit against him to prevent his sailing with you. If Orwic knew what I intend, he would probably go and kill Rhys, and I have too much trouble on my hands already without that. Listen now. Rhys comes to the launching, and his men will work a mischief to you if it can be managed. Be prepared.'

'I am!' Tros answered, thinking of the chemical and Conops with his torch.

'Be prepared to bag Rhys! Trap him! Seize him!'

'Make a sailor of that raw-bones, that orator, that skin-a-louse?' Tros asked. 'The Sea God would wreck me in fair weather for the insult to his waves!'

'No, no. I need Rhys. He can govern his district. But I need the taxes that he hasn't paid. Catch Rhys and accuse him of anything. Demand from him fifty men. Your Northmen must pounce on his escort, and it won't much matter if they happen to kill a few. I will have some of my bowmen placed where they can keep the public from taking sides. Rhys will appeal to me, of course, and I will refuse to do anything about it until he pays the tribute money.

'But I think – for I know Rhys – that if you should hold him fast, but let him send a messenger, he will attend to it that the tribute money is paid before he appeals to me. I will then demand from him a heavy fine, both for having been slow with his payment and for having started a riot in your shipyard. I will demand a fine that I know he cannot pay. He has too many armed men in his district, so I will let him pay in men instead of money. Those men you shall have for your ship, friend Tros, and I will see to it that they are good ones. Thus we do each other a good turn. But don't tell Orwic. Rhys is threatening to seize his property and hold his person. Orwic would certainly kill him if he knew there was going to be a good opportunity.'

Tros demurred. Like Caswallon, he had too much trouble on his hands without courting more. And besides, he wanted no more Britons in his crew, particularly unwilling ones.

'I am admiral of Caesar's fleet,' he said frowning, but with a smile behind his eyes. 'Lend me a two-horse chariot to send to Pevensey and I will get all the men I need without having to pick bones with Rhys.'

Caswallon stared at him.

'Men from Pevensey?'

'From Gaul! According to my admiral's appointment, written over Caesar's seal, I have full right to levy men, and no Roman may refuse me.'

'Tell me about that later. I need the tribute money,' said Caswallon. 'Catch me this fellow Rhys.'

Tros's eyes grew narrow as he scanned Caswallon's face.

'You are a king,' he answered. 'Kings for ever speak in riddles. But are you and I on such terms? Speak me frankly. Is it likely, think you, I would refuse you an act of friendship, even with my own hands full?'

Caswallon's mouth moved nervously beneath the long moustache, but that was the only sign he gave that there was a deeper intrigue beneath the one he had proposed.

'For you – for your sake I will catch Rhys,' Tros continued, watching him. 'For myself, I have no need of him nor of his men.'

He did not believe for a minute that Orwic would kill Rhys simply because he owed Rhys money. Orwic was wealthy, easily could pay his debts before he sailed.

'King – aye, I am a king,' Caswallon answered wearily, 'I hate the sea, and yet I envy you your ship. Catch Rhys for me. I need him caught. Yes, you shall have the chariot for Pevensey. But why?'

'I send a messenger to Caesar!'

'Are you mad, Tros?'

'I am Caesar's admiral. I need men. I will have them.'

'Rede me that riddle!'

'Rede me yours first,' Tros retorted. 'Aye, I will catch Rhys for you. But why?'

'Leave my shame hidden in my heart, Tros. Pride is a king's one solace for the sweat of ruling people.'

Tros eyed him gravely, hands behind his back, frown slowly changing into a smile.

'I, too, am not without pride,' he retorted. 'I am your friend. I will do as you wish. But would you make a mere blind accomplice of me? Have I ever violated confidence?'

'Lud's teeth! I hate to tell you,' said Caswallon. 'Rhys is a member of my council. He is a lord of Britain, and you are our guest, not only mine. I wish to save Rhys from a crime that would bring shame on all of us.'

'And Orwic is not to know, because he would kill Rhys if he did?'

Tros nodded. He began to comprehend. He had had a dozen opportunities to learn how sacred the Britons held their law of hospitality, and he knew too that, though killing is a simple matter, kingdoms are not preserved by killing. He could understand how Rhys, reduced to impotence, might cease to be a danger to the state, whereas his death might loose such reins of vengeance as should start a civil war. And he understood how shame would devour Caswallon if a member of the council should by any treachery cause disaster to the country's guest.

'I will catch Rhys,' he repeated.

And he held a mental reservation that from Rhys himself he would learn Caswallon's secret, quite confident meanwhile that information would confirm his own guess.

Caswallon drove away to send the chariot for Skell, and Tros made rearrangements in the shipyard, going about it cautiously, because there were already scores of spectators pressing their faces against the picket fence, awaiting admission.

A last look at the ship convinced him there could be no trouble with the launching. A dozen blows to knock the chocks from under her, perhaps a few turns on the great bronze screw to lift her bow end, and she would glide down the ways into her element. He could spare thirty Northmen, and they were freemen entitled to carry arms. None could charge them with crime if they should defend the yard, however desperately, against rioters, whoever those rioters might be.

But he kept the Northmen near the waterfront, concealing them inside a low shed about fifty yards from the ship and nearly midway to the outer fence, warning them what to expect and forbidding them to use sharp-edged weapons unless their first surprise assault with pick-handles and capstan-bars should fail.

'It is worse to be clubbed than to be knifed,' he admitted, 'but it causes less public comment. Let us shed no blood if we can help it.'

Then he laid the trap for Rhys by covering the ways with cloth about ten feet in front of the ship's stern, and so arranging grass beneath the cloth that anyone looking for that might suppose an unconscious human victim had been tied in readiness for the ship to crush to pulp as it slid stern first into the water.

The Lord Rhys came betimes, forcing his way through the crowd at the gate with twenty men behind him and ignoring Conops who bade him wait and give Caswallon precedence. Behind Rhys and his followers the whole crowd flowed into the yard, and if it had not been that Caswallon arrived next, with Fflur and fifty archers, there might have been a riot there and then, because Tros's Britons tried to keep the crowd within the enclosure he had roped off, and freemen resented interference from the slaves. However, the archers solved that problem, extending themselves at intervals outside the rope, stringing their bows suggestively.

Soon nearly all the members of the council came, each with his following of armed retainers. Tros had seats for the principal lords and ladies, and after a great deal of shouting the retainers were all crowded to the rear within easy reach of the secreted chemical that, should Conops touch the torch to it, could reduce them to helpless panic. An hour before high noon there were more than a thousand people in the yard, chattering and staring at the mysterious linen sheet that covered the great ship's figurehead.

Long before the druids came it was evident that Rhys had trouble in his sack and meant to loose it at his own good time. He alone of all the noblemen was truculent, objecting to his seat behind the rope, nervous and argumentative because his men were herded away from him, sarcastic because Caswallon and Fflur had better seats, impatient of delay and rising from time to time to peer as far as he could see around the ship. Tros had placed him carefully. At last, straining his neck, he detected the shape of a human victim shrouded under canvas on the ways.

Instantly he was on his feet and was about to announce his discovery at the top of his lungs, but he checked himself. Blackmailer by profession, he foresaw more profit to himself from crime committed than from its exposure in advance. Instead of saying what he saw he cried out to Tros to come and speak with him, and nothing loth, Tros strode up, looking splendid in his purple cloak trimmed with cloth-of-gold and ermine.

'Lord Tros,' said Rhys, 'there should be proof that no human sacrifice is made today. It is in your interest that somebody should stand near to the ship, some man of repute – myself, for instance –

66

to take oath afterward that there were no black rites performed out of sight of the druids.'

'None better than you, Lord Rhys!' Tros answered. 'Everybody knows you are not my friend. If you can find nothing against me, none can! Come along.'

But Rhys refused to come without his men.

'You mean, don't you, you are not my friend?' he retorted. 'I would not trust myself alone within reach of your engines of destruction.'

'Bring them, then. Bring them, by all means,' said Tros with a laugh and a gesture of lordly carelessness that mightily offended Rhys. But at sight of the gesture Conops pulled a string that warned the Northmen in the shed to hold themselves in readiness.

The interested buzz-note of the crowd changed into a half-roar of excitement as Tros strode beside Rhys to the ship with all of Rhys's men in a double line behind them looking businesslike. There was even jealousy, expressed in catcalls. Was Rhys to have the special honour of a close-up view of the launching? Why? There were Caswallon and a hundred others better entitled to that than Rhys! There was even an effort to follow them down to the ways, and Caswallon's archers had their hands full checking it until a blare of music in the distance announced that the druids were coming downstream in their swan-necked barges. They came very slowly on the slack tide, chanting, and the crowd grew still, spell-bound by the beauty of the scene, for the sun shone on the gilded swans and on the gilded oar-blades. And in the river's bosom there were mirrored white clouds mingled with the limpid blue.

'Lord Rhys,' said Tros, 'I am minded you shall do your spying thoroughly. First look at this.'

He led him to the canvas on the ways and raised it, showing dry grass underneath. Then, before Rhys could recover from that disappointment:

'Let your men look into that shed,' he suggested.

It was a double shed, with a long partition down the middle, and there were no windows, so it was dark inside. Several of the men peered in, reported nothing, but Tros refused to be satisfied.

'Let them examine it,' he insisted. So Rhys, to save his own face, ordered them into the shed, retaining only six to guard himself.

'And while they search within there,' Tros said, 'you and I and these others will search the ship for such victims as you think I immolate. Up that ladder!'

As Rhys turned to look at the ladder Tros shut the shed door quietly and slid the bolt. And as he did that Sigurdsen came glooming up with nine men, all armed with hammers, who placed themselves with their backs to the shed and began a prodigious pounding on a hollow log, breaking it up, and for no reason in the world unless it might be pagan pleasure at the noise. They made such thunder that if there had been a battle royal in the shed, none could have heard it.

'Up you go. That way,' Tros said, pointing.

The ladder was a wide one, resting on a scaffold with a platform at the top that hardly touched the ship's side, so that there was no need to remove it for the launching. Rhys, half suspicious of a trap, began to climb it, hesitated, and continued when he saw Tros standing at the bottom, back turned toward him, seemingly considering the druids, who were anchoring their seven barges in a line across the river nearly a hundred yards below the course the ship would take.

At exactly high noon Rhys stood on the platform, startled by the fanfare of the druids' golden trumpets; that, and the sudden silence by the shed door as the hammer-swinging ceased. Sigurdsen and six men sprang up the ladder. Tros did not wait to watch them hustle Rhys and his six men over the ship's side down into the hold. He ran, four Northmen following, toward the ship's bow, blowing his silver whistle, and while they and the others who were waiting chopped and hammered at the chocks, he pulled the cord that held the sheet in place over the ship's figurehead.

'Oh, *Liafail*!' he cried, and all men heard that wonder name, but the rest of what he said was swallowed by the crack of breaking timber, like explosions, as the ship's weight broke inertia.

There was movement, nigh invisible at first, increasing inch by inch. The crowd roared and the druids' trumpets blared. The sheet fell away from the figurehead, revealing Helma's image, blue, with golden hair and crown, and above that the great glittering serpent's head, whose tongue moved on a gymbal, flashing four ways in the sun.

Slowly, and then with a roar like the sound of an avalanche, to the blare of trumpets and the thunder of a hundred war drums, the ship slid down the ways until she shoved the reeking mud in waves to either side of her, pitched like a horse impatient of the bit, so that her serpent looked like a living dragon with a tongue of fire, rocked into mid-stream and lay rolling to the taut, complaining cables that had ripped the buried anchors ten feet forward through the earth. The druids' barges rocked in obbligato to the big ship's roll, as a hymn swelled forth across the river, praising Lud, the God of the River Thames, whose bosom bears the big ships to the ocean and the storms and deep-sea destiny.

Tros laughed. He could not help but laugh to see his vision launched at last, his dream of dreams, his masterpiece that lay so graceful and enormous on the water – too high yet, for there were the ballast and the stores and water to be loaded; but exactly, to the inch, as he had known she would ride – bow high like a war-horse with a flare to throw off head-seas, and as naturally even on her keel as if the gods had balanced her.

'Oh, *Liafail*! Gods govern you! I am a man at last!' He laughed and clapped his hands together. 'No blood! No man, no beast slain at the launching! Ha!'

Then suddenly he thought him of the shed and went and shot the bolt back from the door. His Northmen came forth one by one, each with his weapon sheathed, but each with a pick-handle or an axe-helve in his hand. He counted them and they were all there, but some limped, and they all looked more or less the worse for what had happened in the dark.

'How many?' he demanded, gesturing toward the shed. He had to ask twice, because the Northmen stared in silent admiration at the great ship they had toiled to build.

'Oh, some are dead and some are tied. They fought. One way or another we did for all of them. I killed two, for they had skulls like eggs,' a Northman answered, then turned his head again to stare and grin at the great ship.

Tros did not enter the shed just then. He was wondering whether the ship was actually launched before the blood flowed.

'Blood!' he muttered. 'Blood is not good at a ship's launching. I should have had a druid cast her horoscope. I should have chosen another hour, another day. But a slack tide at high noon seemed auspicious. Blood!'

He determined not to see the blood just then at any rate. He closed the shed door, turned his back and walked away. A vague uneasiness troubled him, but he steeled his mind to forget this seemingly bad omen.

THE LORD RHYS

I am a mystic. That is why I love action. I know that what I see I can never attain unless I now do what I can and thereon step to something nobler.

I have never known a coward or a scoundrel who did not believe a mystic is a fool of whom he could take advantage. But who has seen the result? Where is it?

From the log of Tros of Samothrace

Caswallon cleared the yard to some extent by leading the way out of it with Fflur. Numbers of the younger people followed Orwic through the same gate, joking with him about his rumoured intention to sail in the monster ship with Tros. But a number remained who defied Caswallon's archers, hanging about the yard in disappointment at the shortness of the spectacle and hoping something else might transpire presently to make the waste of half a day worth while. There were sheds to be peered into, cranes to examine, the splinters to see on the ways where the great ship had slid riverward, scandalous waste of floating grease to be appalled at, and questions to ask of the slaves, who were glad enough to talk if anyone would listen to them.

But Tros blew his whistle three times sharply, and at that signal Conops fired a pound or so of dampened chemical beneath a covering of sawdust. Ominous spluttering, flame, yellow and black smoke, and then the choking stench blew crosswise of the yard, and in a minute it was empty of archers as well as visitors, all racing for the trees beyond the fence. Tros's slaves, now used to the appalling stuff, took refuge to windward, in their own long sheds, whither Tros betook himself to roust out nine of them to make up a boat's crew. Ten minutes later he had climbed the *Liafail's* high stern and stood there for a minute watching Sigurdsen bandage a wound on a Northman's forearm and then put grease on a bruise on the same man's head.

'Blood!' he muttered. 'Blood again. Not good! Where's the Lord Rhys?'

Sigurdsen showed him. Rhys sat fuming in the forepart of the after deckhouse, where the V-shaped slits of openings gave command of a whole broadside to the arrow engines, covered under canvas now. Rhys's wrists were lashed behind him to two rings in the deckhouse wall and his feet were stretched so tightly toward a table leg that he could hardly sit on the narrow bench. His weapons were gone, but he was unharmed – only shaken, ruffled and indignant.

'Where are his men?' Tros asked.

'One's overboard – took a capstan-bar under the chin,' said Sigurdsen. 'The rest are only stunned. They're in the fore-peak under hatches.'

'Loose him.'

Sigurdsen obeyed, and Rhys chafed tingling wrists while Tros kicked at his own scabbard as a hint that he was master of the situation.

'You will pay for this!' Rhys snapped at him, and blew his long nose with his fingers. The effect was exactly as if he had spat, and Tros changed his mind abruptly how to deal with him.

'Pay, shall I?' he retorted. 'Whom?'

'Me!' Rhys answered. 'You will pay me! I am a member of the council!'

Tros rubbed his iron jaw.

'Sit down!' he commanded, for Rhys had risen as if to snap defiant fingers at him. 'Now, I don't know what you ever did, Lord Rhys, to earn the right to live, but you may earn my leave this minute or become a million pieces in the bellies of a million fish!'

'Your – your leave!' Rhys stammered.

He was furious. It had not dawned on his imagination yet that Tros might dare to kill him.

'You would better offer me a price, Lord Tros! You bilked me in the matter of the slaves, but, believe me, this time you shall pay, or I know nothing!'

'Tell what you know. That is the price I set,' Tros answered. 'Come along now. Out with it! The Lord Caswallon begged your life of me, saying you are a member of the council who should be spared if possible. I promised him your life on one condition.'

'You! You will never dare murder me!' Rhys stammered.

It was beginning to dawn at last. Caswallon's name had startled him.

'Dare – yes! But do it – no! Unless you tell me what I wish to know, although I know it – but it will please me to hear it from your lips – you shall fight me, or whichever champion I name. I think I will name Sigurdsen, who hasn't killed a man for weeks and needs the practice. Sigurdsen fights with an axe. Now, which will you?

71

Fight or speak? You may send a message to Caswallon if you wish.'

Rhys grew a whole shade paler. He had counted on appealing to Caswallon. The mere threat of what Caswallon would be forced to do by way of vengeance if a member of his council should be harmed, he had supposed, would be enough to bring Tros to his senses.

'I may send – then you mean – the – the Lord Caswallon is a party to this outrage?'

'He has begged your life,' Tros answered. 'I have named the terms to him – that you must tell me all you know.'

'About what? You have a charge against me?'

'Yes,' said Tros, 'I charge you with plotting to destroy me in league with Gwenwynwyn, king of the Ordovici! Caesar set a price of three Roman talents on my head. Gwenwynwyn will pay a third of that to whoever delivers my head to him. Now, make a clean breast of it or fight!'

'Slay him, Lord Tros!' urged Sigurdsen. 'I would liefer spare a wolf at lambing-time! Here – let me have at him! There are no witnesses.'

'You hear what he says?' grinned Tros. 'You would have had my life. How did you propose to have it?'

Rhys had his doubts of Tros's willingness to kill in cold blood, but no man could have doubted Sigurdsen, who, if necessary, could be made the scapegoat afterwards. That argument stared self-revealed out of his frightened eyes.

'What do you want me to tell?' he demanded. 'What if I tell? What then?'

Tros had not answered when the thump of oars alongside announced the arrival of Caswallon in a boat rowed by his own retainers. He came alone into the deckhouse, eyed Rhys coldly for as long as sixty breaths, said nothing and walked out again, slamming the door behind him.

'The Lord Caswallon has his own fish to skin with you. He wishes to know nothing about mine,' said Tros. 'We will pick mine first. Unfold the plot between you and Gwenwynwyn!'

Rhys capitulated, deathly fear behind his eyes, convinced at last that he was wholly at Tros's mercy. He kept licking his lips as he spoke.

'There is no plot between me and Gwenwynwyn, who is a coward and a fool. It is true that Caesar offered him three talents for your head. but he is afraid to kill you for fear of Caswallon's vengeance, even though Caesar is sending him five hundred soldiers to protect him. So Gwenwynwyn sent his minstrel to me with a promise of one third of the money if I would send him your head in a basket.

'Lord Tros, I believe you to be a public enemy. It is no disgrace to me that I determined there and then for legal cause to have you executed. But why should I share the reward with Gwenwynwyn? I could take your head to Caesar, couldn't I? And I would do no murder. Gods forbid that I should murder any man! But to seize a public enemy and lay a proven charge against him, whether of human sacrifice or what else, to cause him to be executed and to take his head to Caesar to prove he is dead, and thus to remove one of Caesar's excuses for making war on us – that would be a service to my country. Lord Tros, your heart, if you have one, must tell you I am right. There would be no disgrace if I should make a profit for myself by ridding my country of a dangerous alien, such as I hold you to be.'

'No, no!' Tros commented. 'Not you! No, you could not be disgraced that easily! However, you are my prisoner. Your men attacked mine.'

'They did not!' Rhys interrupted, blazingly indignant.

A false charge against himself aroused the uttermost depths of resentment.

'Your men attacked mine in the shed down yonder by the waterside,' Tros continued, making up his story to fit the circumstances, stroking his jaw with his right hand, head a little to one side. 'You planned to have your men seize me. That is why you tried to decoy me on board my ship, you mounting the ladder and turning to tempt me to follow, as all men saw! Caswallon saw it. All the council saw it, and their wives and all the public! Everybody saw your men invade my shed.'

'It is a lie!' Rhys snarled.

'Maybe. Maybe. It is something like what you intended, though it happened I was ready for you and your plan failed.'

'I say it is a lie!'

'I heard you. But it is also a lie that I intended human sacrifice. It is a lie that I am a public enemy. And it is not a lie that you are my prisoner. What do you propose to do about it?'

'I? Nothing! What should I do?'

'No offer you would care to make?'

'You mean money? I – '

'You could offer, for instance, to tell me what arrangements were agreed on between Caesar and Gwenwynwyn, in the event that Caesar should pay those three talents for my head! How many men you will provide to help Caesar against Caswallon when the invasion comes. How many chariots. How many horses. Bah! I know your breed! There are rascals such as you in all lands – liars who can lie within a hair's breadth of the truth, plotters who can plot under a mask of loyalty, law-breakers who can make the law a whip for other men. Lud's blood! If I were king in Britain I would whip your head off faster than a cook kills chickens!'

Tros strode to the door, opened it and nodded to Caswallon, who came in, this time followed by a pair of gentlemen-at-arms.

'Rhys, these are witnesses,' he said. 'I charge you that the tribute money is near two years in arrear. I charge you that you tried to start a riot in the shipyard yonder, where a thousand saw your men invade Tros's shed. I fine you double of the tribute money. And for your lawless conduct in the shipyard you shall pay ten chariots with bronze wheels, a hundred four-year-old horses, a hundred bronze swords, a hundred bronze spear-heads, a hundred shields, a hundred sets of harness, a hundred yew bows, two thousand arrows, bronze-tipped, wild goose feathered, a hundred helmets, two thousand yards of woollen cloth, a thousand ewes, a hundred steers, and ten farms – those that lie nearest Lunden!'

Rhys stared blankly.

'That is all I have!' he said in an awed voice.

'No, not all. Not quite all. But enough to keep you chastened for a while!' Caswallon answered, nodding.

Rhys exploded.

'I appeal! You have no legal right to fine me! This is a monstrous fine for nothing! It is plunder! I defy you! I demand a trial before the council!'

'Shall I leave you to the Lord Tros?' Caswallon asked, raising his eyebrows. 'Rhys, Rhys, I am ashamed! If I were not an easy-going king I would have slain you long ago. I spare you because you rule your district, though you rule it over harshly. But I will not trust you until that fine is paid, because I know you have plotted with Caesar and Gwenwynwyn. Spare me, then, the deeper shame of having to expose you.'

He turned his back to give Rhys time to think. There was no shame on Rhys's face, only calculation of the odds against him and a cold, pragmatic selfishness.

'I will pay,' he said, catching his breath. It hurt him more to say it than a whipping would have done.

'I will see that you do!' Caswallon answered, turning again to face him. 'Tros, I saw Rhys's steward climb the ladder with him. Where is he now?'

'In the fore-peak, unless he was the man who fell overboard.'

'Let the steward be brought. Rhys, you will send your steward, giving orders to him in my presence to bring the doubled tribute money and the fine in full to Lunden. When the whole of it is paid the Lord Tros will release you and as many of your men as have not been killed through your own treachery. Tros, can you keep Rhys safe without fetters?'

Tros nodded.

'Sigurdsen shall nail him into an empty water-cask, and he shall stay in darkness in the ship's hold until you send me word to loose him. As for his men in the shed down yonder – '

'They are yours!' Caswallon interrupted. 'They are not bad fighting men. They are Rhys's best. Bring them here and put a hatch on them until the ship sails.'

Tros demurred.

'They are not slaves,' he objected. 'They will simply run at the first chance, and meanwhile I shall have to handle them with capstan-bars. There'll be trouble enough without – '

'Chain them to the oars!' Caswallon urged.

Tros shook his head. He knew, from long experience of ships in the Levant, the uselessness of that procedure. Men chained to the oars die of heart-break, and the work they do is not worth food and whip. Even the Romans realized it and, except in the case of punished criminals, never chained men at the galley benches.

'Throw them into Lunden gaol,' he answered.

'But I thought you must have men.'

'I must. But I have other men in mind.'

Caswallon strode out of the deckhouse, beckoning Tros to follow.

'Brother Tros,' he said, taking his arm outside the door, 'I cannot put men in Lunden gaol without bringing them to trial, except in cases of high treason and rebellion. Even for high treason or rebellion I must have the council's affirmation.'

'Then let them go,' said Tros.

'*Tchutt!* They would try to rescue Rhys. Rhys is known to be rich. I must reduce Rhys's riches drastically before I can afford to turn those men loose. Bring them abroad the ship.'

Tros laughed.

'I have made no bargain yet with Rhys,' he answered. He returned into the deckhouse, where Rhys sat glowering at Sigurdsen.

'Rhys – '

'I am the Lord Rhys to my enemies!'

'Lord Rhys, I have no notion how many of your men are still alive in yonder shed, but as many as live are my hostages. I will keep them aboard this ship until I am out of reach of your poisoners, your arrows, your informers. If, when you have paid the Lord Caswallon's fine and I have set you free, you do me no annoyance of whatever kind, you shall have those men back, subject to their good behaviour as well as yours. So you would better warn them, even as I will. When I have no further use for them as hostages, say a month from now, or a few days more or less, and provided you have done me not an injury meanwhile, I will set them free somewhere on the coast of Britain, each with his weapon and a little journey money, and they may find their own way back to you. Is that clear?'

Rhys nodded, scowling.

'You understand me? Fully? Very well then. Bring his steward, Sigurdsen. After the steward has received instructions, nail Rhys up in the water-cask and let Northmen stand watch over him in two-hour tricks. Rhys, Lord Rhys, you would better bid your steward make haste. It will be dark there in the hold. A water-cask is big, but not a pleasant place to spend a week in. Fall away, Sigurdsen. I'll watch him while you bring the steward.'

THE LORD RHYS'S TENANTRY

There is a true measure by which to judge any captain's value. Is he fat, and are his led men hungry? Is he at ease, and are they weary? Is he in receipt of dignities, and is their lot humiliation? Does he bribe them to obtain obedience? Is he revengeful; is he afraid to punish, lest worse happen?

From the log of Tros of Samothrace

Stores began coming aboard that afternoon, although the slaves claimed holiday to celebrate the launching. Tros did not dare to waste minutes now. Hours might make the difference between catching Caesar's Spaniards in mid-channel or being obliged to land and fight them somewhere on the British coast. At sea, the odds were in his favour, supposing he could lick that crew of his into anything like shape. On land, five hundred Spaniards under a Roman officer would have it all their own way, as against himself with only eight-and-forty Northmen, Orwic and perhaps a few of his retainers and as many of his British slaves as he might dare to form into a landing party.

Men, men, men! He must have men! That song was singing in his brain while they towed the *Liafail* alongside the light pier he had constructed, and all the rest of that day until midnight. He drove the slave gangs mercilessly. Endless streams of food, stores, water, ammunition, tools, spare sails and cordage poured into their appointed places, and the Northmen laboured at the stowing, each man in charge of one section of the hold.

The risk of fire made Tros's skin creep. He was everywhere, cautioning torchmen, alert and anxious. Glendwyr, with a bucket gang and another gang in readiness to man the great chain-pump, stood watch amidship, and there were boxes of wet sand set wherever there was room for them. Conops in person stowed the leaden balls filled with mixed explosive in the magazines below the four great catapults, and, in other magazines beside those, tons of charcoal, resin, sawdust, sulphur and that other strange ingredient from under the horse manure in the cave below Caswallon's stables.

By midnight, because Tros had foreseen everything, the stores

77

were stowed, the lights were out, the slaves asleep on bunks beside the staggered oar benches, and the hatches, covered with pitched canvas, in position. All lay snug and tight against the rain that drummed on the upper deck. The shrouds were slackened; the ship was again in mid-stream riding to her own bronze anchor with a cowhide parcelling on the warp, and the shipyard deserted. The Northmen – they were Tros's marines, berthed for his protection between his stateroom under the poop and the rows of bunks on which the rest of the crew slept – snored in their own snug quarters. Conops, yawning at the anchor watch, cried, 'All's well!' It was a day's work to be proud of, and a night of nights – the first afloat!

But the more Tros thought, the more he gloried in the great ship's size and her proportions and the novelty and skill of her design, the more he wondered at success, the more the fact oppressed him that he must have men, men, men.

On either side of the ship there were three banks, each for fifty oars. He had less than two hundred Britons. It was just conceivable that his eight-and-forty Northmen were enough to handle, reef, steer and provide the necessary boatswaihs, two lieutenants and two oar captains, one for each side of the ship. But of the Britons, ten were needed for the cooking and such details. Ten more were not more than enough to keep the ship comparatively clean. And though the druids had given him a kegful of pungent-smelling extract that they said would keep the smallpox and the harbour plague away, he knew cleanliness was all-essential. He had seen too many ships rot, crew and all, of their own foulness.

Then the wear and tear aloft would be too prodigious, and would call for constant overhauling, for he had not only three masts, in itself an innovation, but three topmasts, his own bold, original invention, and a corresponding maze of rigging. Under sail he did not doubt he would have speed enough to run from any Roman on the seas, but, failing wind, he would need at least another hundred and fifty oarsmen, to allow for a few sick men and a few reliefs. And even so, there would be no men to spare to man the catapults, the arrow-engines and to stand off boarders.

Men! He must have men swiftly, and at least two hundred. Moreover, they must not be Britons, or the risk of mutiny would be too great. He laughed to think that Caesar should send Spaniards from Gaul exactly at the moment when he needed them. He scowled when he thought of the weakness of his untrained crew.

'The gods,' he told himself, 'enjoy a man's alertness. They are offering me opportunity.'

78

He did not pray to the gods. He knew better. Such prayer as he put forth was will to seize the moment, action, effort and self-watchfulness.

Nor had he qualms about the Spaniards, who were surely not yet slaves. They were men, presumably, who hired themselves to Caesar for his purposes; expecting, in addition to their pay, such loot and opportunities for licence as his victories should provide. In Tros's view of things, that made them his fair prey. He respected no man's liberty unless the man himself respected other people's. A soldier fighting for the freedom of his own land he admired, he loved; a mercenary in the pay of an invader he considered no more than a prostitute to Caesar's will, no more to be treated as a free man with a free man's rights than cattle need be.

But how to get those Spaniards! First, by hook or crook, he must instil enthusiasm into his untrained British oarsmen, and then train them – no small miracle! Thereafter, making out of Thames-mouth for the open sea, he must give his Northmen practice in the handling of the ship before he could dare to engage Caesar's warships, clumsy and ill-handled though the Roman biremes might be. He must cruise along the coast and run in to find Skell's messenger. And if, as was all too likely, Skell should fail him, he must cruise down-channel searching for the Spaniards, trusting to the gods to show them to him.

'Zeus!' he muttered. 'How I'd love a crew of Romans! Give me enough Romans and I'd purge Rome! But they won't follow a man who doesn't believe that Rome is right whatever Rome does.'

If he would go to Rome to plead Caswallon's cause he must have men with him who would regard Rome as their natural enemy, or at least not as their mother city, and who, in consequence, would not desert in the hope of finding easier servitude ashore. He was sure of his Northmen and Britons. He was nearly sure the Spaniards would have had their bellyful of Caesar and would be complacent about changing masters.

He slept not at all that night, but paced the poop with the blustering rain in his face, using himself to the feel of the ship underfoot, to her length and breadth, to her height above the water – absorbing her into his consciousness.

When dawn at last sent shafts of golden light along the river, touching the great serpent's trembling tongue, Tros greeted it, arms folded, on the poop and laughed along the deck to Conops, who came sleepily off watch to urge him to turn in and rest.

'These Britons of ours will tax you, master! Sleep before the trouble starts!'

'It has begun!' Tros answered, glancing at the river. 'Turn out all the Northmen!'

There were twoscore boats already coming up-stream, loaded full of traders and olla-podrida of Thames'-side.

'Watch that no slave goes overboard, and stand those boats off with arrowfire if need be! Let no boats but Orwic's or Caswallon's come alongside.'

It was an ancient game, as old as navigation, to approach a ship about to sail and tempt her crew with promises of shore work and high wages. Her master, then, had the alternative of long delay while he pursued deserters or of putting to sea short-handed, leaving his slaves to become the property of whoever had tempted them ashore.

He began to be angry with Orwic for keeping him waiting; angry with Caswallon because he knew it was Caswallon who had feasted Orwic all night long, and that both of them were probably dead drunk; angry with a longshore crowd that was already looting in the shipyard, breaking up the sheds and carrying off in ox-carts and on men's heads every stick that was removable. But more than all else, he was angry because the boats were there and he must make the first experiments with the oars before an audience of critics who would laugh.

He ate breakfast without appetite, then ordered an anchor out over the stern and let the ship swing down-stream.

'Man the benches!' he commanded, scowling at the onlookers. If he had thought they would accept a reasonable sum he would have paid them all to go away.

First came babbling confusion while the Britons were selected, bench by bench, for reach of arm, known courage or faint-heartedness; and a mark was painted on each man to correspond to the bench on which he was to sit and on the oar he was to use.

The business took two hours, and no one was satisfied. The upper-bank men grumbled at the length and weight of the oar they had to pull; the lower-bank men cried for head room, air, view, noisily asserting fear that waves would enter through the lower oar ports.

'Whip!' Tros thundered. 'Whip for the man who speaks again until I give leave!'

There had not been much whip hitherto in Tros's mixed methods of maintaining discipline. A sudden onslaught by the Northmen leaping along the gang-planks by the benches and the cracking of leather whips on naked shoulders produced more effect than if the Britons had been used to it. There was silence and a long pause. One by one, then, the Northmen showed the rowers what would be expected of them at the signal.

Wand in hand on the poop, Tros stood where the drum and cymbal men could see him. They were stationed forward, under the break of the high bow, protected from the weather, cautioned never, for any reason, to take their eyes off the officer of the watch. Tros gave the signal:

'Ready!'

Drums and cymbals crashed three times, and the oars, after a lot of shouting by the Northmen, moved into position ready for the dip. Again and again Tros repeated the signal, Conops running along the gang-planks, moving and readjusting oar-handles until all the vermilion blades were poised exactly evenly above the water. Then, setting the time slowly for the drums and cymbals, he made them move the oars in air until the rowers caught the rhythm and began to swing in unison. A cymbal-crash began the swing. A drum-beat finished it. Then:

'Dip!' he thundered, and the fun began.

For a while he seemed likely to have to serve out new oars from the spares that were stowed in brackets fastened to the deck-beams overhead, so excitedly the Britons worked, blade hitting blade, oar-handles bumping into backs, the Northmen yelling, and the great ship swaying in the muddied water, straining at her warp. Ten, twenty times Tros signalled, 'Stop!' then started them again. It was two hours, and they were all dead weary, Conops foaming at the mouth and the Northmen growing gloomy with despair, before the rowers had the hang of it and could pull ten strokes without a dozen of them 'catching crabs'.

Then Orwic came, pop-eyed from too much food and drink, seated between Fflur and Caswallon in the state barge, dressed in all his finery of cloth-of-gold and jewellery, with half a dozen boxes full of changes of apparel and sufficient assorted weapons to have armed a company of infantry. With him he brought four fair-haired gentlemen-at-arms, as heavy as himself from too much feasting, looking scared, as if they had made their wills and testaments, not hoping to see home again.

Fflur's eyes were wet with tears. She came up first on to the poop and kissed Tros three times, hugging him.

'Lord Tros, we love you because you have loved us, and we feel we have done too little to befriend you in return.'

Caswallon laughed to hide the quaver in his voice and clapped Tros hard between the shoulder-blades.

'You take my good friend Orwic! Will you leave me my enemy

Rhys in exchange? I sent my archers with that steward to add their own impatience to his zeal. A galloper brings news they are already on the road home with the chariots and the tribute money, driving the cattle in front of them. So loose Rhys. Tros, Tros, look at the sun on the water! Lud laughs to have your great ship on his bosom!'

They all leaned overside to see the ship's reflection, silver and vermilion.

'Rhys's men?' Caswallon asked.

'I have them, all safe under the hatches, except three whose skulls lacked thickness. I will set them ashore when I am out of Rhys's reach. Not, that is, until I see the last of Britain.'

'The last? Nay, nay, Tros. You will come back,' Caswallon answered with an air of prophecy.

Fflur shook her head.

'I fear we see the last of Orwic too,' she said, eyes wet with tears again.

'Not so!' Tros answered. 'I spoke carelessly. This first voyage I make in search of men. If I fail, I will return up-Thames to coax a British crew from you before I sail for Rome. So you must watch Rhys!'

'You will not fail,' Fflur said confidently.

'If I fail not, it would grieve me not to have my friends rejoice,' Tros answered. 'If I win those Spaniards, let us have a feast aboard my ship.'

'Where?'

'Vectis. I will anchor in the lee of Vectis.* Set a watch for me. Whichever way the wind blows, I will anchor on the island's leeward side.'

'That is not my country, and Lud knows I hate the sea, but Fflur and I will come to meet you in a ship from Hythe – which is not in my country either, but they pay me tribute. That is a promise. Let us go now. I hate partings,' said Caswallon.

So Tros had Rhys brought up from the water-cask and bade Sigurdsen return his sword and dagger to him. Rhys went ashore with Caswallon and Fflur in the barge, and Tros grinned as he watched him, looking down his long nose at Caswallon's great white fist that shook to emphasize a torrent of expletive threats.

But it was not the last Tros heard of Rhys. The while he trained the rowers with the ship at anchor, waiting for the tide, teaching them to back oars and to swing together in response to signals, dipping and catching the weight of the ship between the crash

*The Isle of Wight.

and echo of the cymbals, there came three boats alongside from the far bank of the river. They were full of weary-looking men, and a big, shock-headed Briton in the leading boat shouted that he had a message for the Lord Tros. Tros put a hand to his ear, but the man refused to shout his information to the world at large, with all those other boats drifting to and fro within range of voices. So Tros let him come aboard, but kept a Northman handy to throw him overside in case of need.

He was a well-dressed fellow, in a yellow linen smock over woollen breeches, and a big bronze buckle on his belt and a cloak of beaded deerskin. But he was soiled with travel, looked as if he had been out in the rain all night, and his leather-shod feet were smeared thickly with mud. He had a broad nose like a blacka-moor's, with wide nostrils, and an iron-grey moustache like a pair of diminutive horses' tails. He was excited – breathless from excite-ment; anxious brown eyes glittered under shaggy iron-grey brows.

'Lord Tros, I am the Lord Rhys's tenant. I am Eog, son of Louth the blacksmith. Is it true you have the Lord Rhys prisoner?'

Tros did not answer. He waited, watching the man's face. Eog misinterpreted the silence.

'And you sail in your great ship? Then sail away with him! Drown him out there in the sea!'

The fellow glanced to right and left, fearful of being overheard, but there was only the Northman on the poop beside Tros. Orwic and his men had turned in to sleep off last night's drunkenness.

'Lord Tros, he traffics with the Romans! He has sold us to the Romans. He has sold your ship to the Romans! He has promised to let Caesar know by signal on the south coast when your ship sails, if he can't prevent your sailing by having you executed! He is a cruel, hard landlord. We tenants hate him. But he has the council's ear, and men say the Lord Caswallon fears him, so we don't dare appeal against him. Kill him, Lord Tros! Kill him, and earn the blessings of his tenants!'

Tros stroked his chin. 'You are late, my friend. The Lord Rhys left for Lunden in the king's barge.'

Eog's face fell.

'You are undone!' he remarked, shaking his shock of hair over his eyes as he nodded. 'The Lord Caswallon sent his men to Maulden in the night. They seized horses, cows, sheep, chariots, arms, money. The Lord Rhys will beggar us to reimburse himself a little, but what he can wring from us will never satisfy him. He will send to Gaul or go to Gaul. He will betray you to the Romans for a great price! He knows you sent a messenger named Skell to Pevensey, for he sent my brother's son, armed with a sword, on a skewbald stallion to overtake and slay him. We are all undone! We are all undone!'

He wrung his hands. The corners of his mouth drooped. He looked pitifully at the men in the three boats who stared at the great ship as if salvation lay in her.

'Who are they?' Tros asked.

'Tenants and free labourers. Lord Tros, we are all liable for penalties for having left our holdings without leave. We have no right to leave our boundaries except on market days. The Lord Rhys will impose fines that will keep us beggared for ever!'

Tros summoned Orwic, who came sleepily, not pleased to have been routed out of his snug cabin.

'Lud love a fellow, Tros! What ails you? Still at anchor?' His displeasure increased as he recognized Eog. 'Dog!' he remarked. 'I'll wager not a tenant of my own keeps bounds this minute! What do you mean, sirrah, by gadding when your master's back is turned? Are there no fields to till? No cows to milk? No clearing to be done? No fences to repair? Lud's blood! If I were the Lord Rhys I would deprive you of your holding!'

'He will! He will!' said Eog gloomily. 'Already he takes two-thirds – two foals, two calves, two lambs, two pigs out of every three, two bushels out of three of all the wheat, two months' labour out of three to plough his fields and mend his fences. Now he has been fined, and he will wring the fine from us.'

'Lud pity you!' said Orwic. 'But you were born the Lord Rhys's men. I couldn't help you, even if my head weren't splitting so I can't think!'

'Lord Tros, we are not sailors,' Eog said, watching Tros's face. It was plain enough what he intended.

'Where are your women and children?' Tros asked pointedly.

'They are as good as slaves now,' said Eog. 'They will be slaves if we leave them, and the better off!'

Tros shook his head.

'I have some thirty of the Lord Rhys's men aboard my ship this minute,' he said, stroking his chin. 'If I should add you and your companions, the Lord Rhys could indict me as a thief. Nay, nay.'

'Lord Tros – ' said Eog, but Tros interrupted him.

'What say you, Orwic? Can a man take freemen in his service if he finds them wandering outside the jurisdiction of their king?'

Orwic snorted with disgust.

'They forfeit property and holdings if they leave the land,' he answered. 'They are free then to serve anyone they will, but who would employ runaways?'

Tros went into his stateroom underneath the poop and filled a leather purse with minted copper coin, tossing it hand to hand while he debated with himself. Presently he returned to the poop and gave the purse to Eog.

'For your services,' he said. 'Three or four days, maybe a week from now I will drop anchor near the coast of Vectis. If anyone should bring me information of the Lord Rhys's movements, he would find me inclined to be generous. But mind you, no women and children! Leave them on the farms. And if the Lord Rhys's luck is running half as lamely as I guess it is, you might – who knows? – be pleased to return to your wives and your children and your holdings. Eog, son of Louth, the gods are sometimes slow, but if a man has patience, they reward him in the end exactly on his merits. Remember, on whichever side of Vectis happens to be sheltered from the wind! Not later than a week from now!'

And Eog, grinning, wondering, went overside.

MAKE SAIL!

I have listened to much talk of living. A man lives at rare moments and the rest is hope or dread. Too many moments of life, and these carcasses in which we house our ignorance would burn up. I have seen men thrive on vice and grow old in drudgery. But life burns. It is consummation. I have lived thrice: once in a woman's arms, once when I launched my ship, once when I took my ship's helm and let her fill away. Three more such moments might add me to the number of the gods, but for that my time is not yet.

From the log of Tros of Samothrace

That afternoon, on top of the flowing tide, Tros let the *Liafail* drift down-river, cymbals and drums beating a slow measure that the oars might dip sufficiently for steerage way and no more. There were narrow channels between hidden mud-banks, and the *Liafail* had a deeper draught than any vessel that had ever sailed out of the Thames or into it.

Hardly a longshoreman saw the start. Tros, not wanting a crowd of boats around him, had let it be supposed he would remain at anchor until the next day. No villages were visible. Like Lunden Town itself, those were well hidden from the frequent raiders by dense screens of forest that descended to the swampy margin at the edge of tide water. But here and there were clearings, fish-traps and the smoke of homesteads rising half a mile away behind the trees. Whenever they passed such places, crowds came down to the river's edge to watch.

Tros knew the ship looked magnificent, even though the oars moved raggedly. Vermilion top-sides, with a gold-leaf, undulating serpent above where the polished tin began, and the vermilion oar-blades – all were reflected in the water. The three great curved spars were as graceful as swallows' wings; and from the poop he could see the long bronze serpent's tongue that shot forth this and that way, quivering to every motion of the ship.

He knew, too, that there could hardly be a man in Britain who had not heard rumours, at least, of the great ship's building. Judging by the crowd that had come to stare at the ship on the ways – to laugh, sell, steal, obstruct and volunteer the information that a ship with metal on her undersides would never float, he had supposed the spectacle was too familiar in that corner of Britain to cause more than passing comment. He began to receive new education in the workings of the human mind.

At one point where the river curved so sharply around a mud shoal that he had hard work to find and keep the channel, two or three hundred men put out in small boats armed with tridents, spears and all the paraphernalia they used for dispatching stranded whales. Whether it was the gold on the figurehead and the long serpent that they coveted, or whether the sheer beauty and the hugeness of the ship aroused their prejudice against all novelty, he never knew. They quailed before they came within their own short arrow range, and he supposed it was the crash of the drums and cymbals as he called for more speed, and the flickering serpent's tongue that frightened them. At any rate, he left them easily astern.

But at another place, down-river, where the tide flowed swiftly between shoal and shore – the place where, in the bireme won from Caesar, he had caught a Northman longship beam-on and had rammed her to destruction – there was evidence of well-laid plans to wreck the *Liafail* before she could leave the Thames. They had felled great trees and staked them across the narrow channel, leaving a gap through which the tide poured at such an angle as to force any passing ship on the longshore mud.

He backed oars and dropped two anchors overstern. A shower of arrows hummed into the planking of the upper deck. He ordered the port bow catapult into action, lighted the fuse on a leaden stink-ball and sent it crashing into the trees, where it failed to explode but set the woods on fire. It burned with a stench that drifted on the light wind riverward and nearly threw the portside oarsmen into panic.

One stink-ball was plenty; that and the crash and the hum of the catapult with the responding flash and shudder of the serpent's tongue, so that it looked as if the serpent might have spat the burning stench forth. There was no more arrow-fire. No longshore Briton showed himself. Orwic was for landing with the Northmen and imposing penalties for evil manners.

'I know their villages. I will burn them and flog their headmen.' He pulled on his little peaked steel helmet.

But Tros, remembering the Lord Rhys, chose discretion. Delay might bring surprises long prepared by Rhys, who – if it was he who had planned to wreck the ship – would certainly have let fall hints enough to turn out all the countryside in readiness to loot and kill. A wrecked ship was in theory the lawful profit of the king, who owned all river rights, including stranded whale and sturgeon, but in practice it was 'first come, first served', and the wrecker's trade was plied without distinction between friend and foe.

Tros lowered boats and sent two dozen Northmen overside to clear the passage under the protection of his catapults and arrow engines, and it was nearly dark before Sigurdsen reported all clear and the logs adrift. By that time the tide was beginning to change, and it was risky work to navigate uncharted, only half-remembered channels in the gloaming. Tros dropped half a mile or so downstream and, when he found deep water under him where the river began perceptibly to widen into estuary, he dropped anchor for the night, conscious, however, that as night fell he would lose all the advantage against river pirates that the awe-inspiring serpent and the long range of his catapults provided.

One precaution that he took was to bend two warps to the big bronze anchor that he let go from the bow. One warp took up the strain, the other lay slack, sinking below water. Leaving Sigurdsen and Orwic on the poop, he himself took the anchor watch and lay down to sleep with the slackened warp under his neck, and with the port-bow engine aimed so as to discharge twelve arrows straight along the warp at the first touch of the trigger.

Before long Conops awakened him, reporting oar strokes in the dark. There was no moon yet; it was impossible to see as far as twenty feet beyond the ship's bow. All was quiet on the poop, where Sigurdsen was droning Baltic tunes to Orwic. The deck watch, ten men, paced to and fro like shadows, bare feet falling silently; there were no sounds except the tinkle and suck of the water alongside, the slight squeak of the spars, and one other, hardly audible, that might be swish and drip from where the anchor warp met water.

'Shoot!' urged Conops.

But Tros was thrifty; he did not care to loose twelve irrecoverable bronze-tipped arrows without knowing where the target lay. Squanderer of gold leaf and vermilion on the ship, reckless of the price of tin and royally extravagant of linen sails and cordage, it had irked him sadly to have to use one stink-ball more or less at random. To have loosed twelve arrows without due reflection was a sin. He waited, listening – too long.

The loose warp tautened suddenly and hummed. The tight warp slackened, cut through close to the waterline. He pulled the trigger then. The quarrelling arrows whined into the dark and two or three of them hit woodwork. Then a man screamed, like a wounded horse – frightful, sudden – an inhuman sound. A torch shone for a moment somewhere over on the river bank. Then rain that drowned the rising moon and drummed on deck, blotting out all other noises.

Tros did not dare to sound the alarm, unless or until he had work at the oars for the slaves to do. They were unarmed men, as liable to panic in the darkness as so many sheep. Nor did he dare to get up anchor before sunrise except as an absolutely last recourse.

'Turn out all the Northmen!' he commanded. 'Station them along the bulwarks. Go you below, and if the slaves wake, keep them seated on the benches. You may have the two oar captains to help you. Run!'

Conops vanished, and Tros, ears strained, caught the sound of approaching oars. Impatiently, biting his nails, he waited for the Northmen to turn out, and as one of them, axe in hand, came leaning into the rain to take his stand below the break of the bow, he sent him below in a hurry to the magazine to bring up one of the leaden stink-balls. By the time a fire-pot had been brought too, and the oil-soaked fuse inserted, there was no more doubt as to what was coming toward them on the rising tide. The longshore Britons had a barge all fenced about with wickerwork; he could hear the squeaking of the withes as well as the splash of at least a dozen oars.

So he lighted the fuse and held the leaden ball in both hands overhead.

'Man arrow engines!' he commanded, and the Northman ran to pass along the order.

It took time to get the covers off the carefully housed engines; time for the fuse to burn down to the neck of the infernal thing Tros held in both hands. He had time to wonder what rash idiocy Orwic would commit when a general alarm should split the night, and time to curse himself for having started on a voyage without assigning battle quarters to each Northman and inventing a system of signals by which to control all hands in darkness and emergency.

At last, before he thought the enemy was near enough, he had to fling the stink-ball, lest it burst and kill him, aiming at the sound of oars and leaning overside into the rain watching the curved course of the spluttering fuse, shuddering then as a dozen arrows plunked into the woodwork all around him. But there was no splash. He heard the leaden weight fall hard, and instantly there was a burst of flame that threw a whole bargeful of Britons into view, crowded so tightly together behind a screen of willow withes that they could hardly move.

They yelled, and a volley of arrows screamed through the great ship's rigging, but the stink-ball functioned perfectly without exploding. They could not go near it to throw it overboard; the heat melted the lead casing; the blazing chemical spread, setting fire to the barge, and in the reflected flare from that, the golden serpent's head stood forth – an apparition in the night!

Twenty, thirty hastily lighted torches came whirling through the rain on to the *Liafail's* deck, along with lumps of burning fibre, soaked in pitch and tallow, but the rain extinguished those. A terror-stricken Briton yelled that the serpent was moving toward them; and the barge, emitting clouds of yellow, green, and crimson smoke, became a perfect target for the arrow engines.

Volley after volley screamed into the holocaust until Tros blew his whistle shrilly to stop the waste of arrows; blew it to small purpose, because Orwic on the high poop kept on shooting as fast as he could lay the arrows in the grooves and crank the great yew bow.

The men on the barge were jumping overboard; the barge was drifting up-stream with the tide; there was no more danger from that source, and the light from it, mirrored in pools in the river, showed dozens of smaller boats flitting away like phantoms. There was, strangely, little shouting; now and then a swimmer cried to the nearest boat for help, and someone in the distance, who appeared to be controlling the attack, bellowed through a tube of some kind.

'In again! It is only a wooden serpent! Attack from all sides! Cut the cable!'

It was a hollow, haunting voice.

Tros went to the poop, pausing as he passed to rebuke each Northman for an arrow wasted.

He shoved Orwic away from the poop arrow engine and bade Glendwyr cover it again.

'Great sport!' said Orwic, shaking the rain off the rim of his peaked helmet.

'Sport!' Tros came near to exploding with disgust. 'Sport in killing poor fools who obey a rascal? Catch me that bellowing knave who cries the pack on but keeps himself out of harm's reach! To work now! To a man's task! Sigurdsen! Lower a boat. Take axes, eight of your own men, Orwic, and his four. Bring me back that bellower alive!'

The boat went overside, and Tros patrolled the deck, ears strained for warning of another attempt to creep down on him in darkness. He could hear the voices of Conops and two Northmen threatening a thrashing to the slave who should dare to leave his oar bench, and he heard the oar-blades rattle against the ports in readiness to be pushed out the full distance, so he knew he could get instant headway against the tide if the enemy should cut that second warp, though it made him shudder to think of losing a bronze anchor.

But the attack had evidently failed for good. He could see the barge, away up-stream, surrounded by a swarm of boats whose occupants were picking up survivors, keeping well to windward and attempting to steer the gutted hulk into shallow water by shoving it with long poles.

Someone in a boat near the far bank kept on bellowing, but Tros could no longer catch the words, so he supposed the boat had begun to follow the retreat. But the bellowing ceased abruptly, and he heard one long yell mixed of fear and anger. Then silence and, after a while, the steady thump and swish of oars that he knew were his Northmen returning.

He ordered the ladder let down, but Orwic cried out for a rope. Four Northmen climbed the ladder and began hauling on the rope, hand over hand, in great haste, as if there were a hooked fish on the end. The rope shook, and from the darkness overside Orwic's voice half laughed a breathless warning. Suddenly a thing flopped on the deck and struggled, slipping about on the wet planks like a fish. Orwic arrived up the ladder and pounced on it, heaving it upright – a woman! He ripped off the bandage that gagged her, letting loose her wild hair that fell in heavy, rain-wet coils. She threw her head back and howled once like a wolf, then bellowed, 'Help! Help! Rescue!' in the selfsame booming voice that had directed the attack.

Tros clapped a hand on her mouth, and she bit him, drawing blood. He shook the blood off, ordered Sigurdsen to take charge of the ship, and pointed to the after deckhouse – the same place where he had had his interview with Rhys. It took four of the Northmen and Orwic to hustle the woman in there, she screaming and bellowing alternately, but presently they forced her on to the bench where Rhys had sat and lashed her arms to the wall. There, by the light of the whale-oil lamp, Tros looked her over.

'Gwenhwyfar!' he said, coughing up one of his monosyllabic laughs. He shook blood from his hand again. His mind went back to the time when he had first set foot in Britain. Gwenhwyfar, wife

91

of Britomaris, had made love to him, and cursed him for not responding.

'Aye!' she said, using her third voice. It was quite unlike the battle bellow she had sent across the river, or the wolf-howl. It was low and pleasing, though it shook with anger. 'I am Britomaris's wife. And you are Tros, who might have been king of Britain.'

Orwic whistled, grinning, wiping off blood from his handsome face where Gwenhwyfar had gouged him with her nails. Tros leaned against the table, sucking his bitten thumb and laughing silently.

'Where is Britomaris?' he inquired after a long pause.

Gwenhwyfar glared, straining at the cords to test them. She was better than good-looking, even so, all dishevelled, with hate in her eyes. The great amber ornaments heaved on her breast and her thin lower lip flushed crimson where her white teeth clenched it.

'If you have not made Britomaris, who obeys you, king of Britain, how could you have foisted me to that throne?' Tros inquired. 'Is the Lord Rhys the man you favour for the kingship nowadays?'

Gwenhwyfar did not answer. Orwic spoke up.

'She is always looking for a man to ditch Caswallon. Caswallon laughs. I suppose you won't kill her, either. Keep her till morning and watch her swim.'

Tros ignored him.

'Gwenhwyfar, it appears to me the gods have brought you here.'

'Nay, nay! It was I who brought her!' Orwic laughed. 'She clung by the nails to my face, or I might have lost her overside!'

'In the nick of time,' Tros continued. 'Either you shall tell me what you know about the Lord Rhys's plans, or you shall go to Caesar nailed up in a box. Caesar will keep you to walk at his chariot tail when he enters Rome in triumph. After which you will be sold at auction to the highest bidder.'

Gwenhwyfar only glared, and Tros made a mistake.

'In Rome they pay extravagant prices for fair-skinned slave women,' he said, 'and Caesar uses all expedients to fill his purse.'

She did not exactly smile, nor did her eyes soften, but there passed over her a wave of pride that her price would be high. Half Britain knew her as 'Caswallon's scornling'. She burned for even one hour of glory. Tros read her – knew she saw herself glorious, in chains at Caesar's triumph, then on a block at auction, haggled for by all the wealthy men of Rome.

'Nail her in the Lord Rhys's water-cask!' he ordered. There was no use arguing with a woman while she dreamed such dreams as that.

She began to mock him. She used words that made Tros set his teeth and brought the blush to Orwic's cheek. Wharf-rat language would have left them utterly indifferent, but she said things of Tros's dead wife that pierced all sense of decency, as knives cut nerves. And when the Northmen loosed her from the rings in the deck-house wall she fought them like a she-wolf.

'She will never go to Caesar,' Orwic said, when they had carried her below. 'She will sooner kill herself. Gwenhwyfar is no bird that can live in a cage.'

'Has she ever been to sea?' Tros asked, and laughed.

He ordered a mattress laid on the poop, where he lay down to sleep until dawn. He knew what the morning would bring. He proposed to be ready for it.

At daybreak the tide was still making, and there was nothing to be gained by wearying the rowers. Stiff they were from yesterday's short effort, and ill-tempered because there was no milk for breakfast. They could see no sense in cleaning down a ship that still smelt of new paint, and they objected to wet benches, to the herrings and bread served out to them in wooden bowls, to the draught through the oar ports and to being made to fold their blankets. They wanted to sit shivering with the blankets wrapped around them, and above all they insisted they could row no more until the stiffness, that they thought was rheumatism, left their muscles.

So when the tide changed, there was a little whip and a lot of swearing, before the anchor was hauled in at last and the glittering serpent's tongue began to flicker to the awkward oar-swing and the *Liafail* made headway to the sea.

Tros gave the helm to Sigurdsen and spent the first two hours inspecting blocks, sheets, halyards, stays, shrouds, and telling off the Northmen to their stations, while he conned the sky at intervals and hoped for a favouring wind. Not he nor, as far as he knew, any man had sailed a ship with three masts, and he would have liked a day or two to break the oarsmen in and get them used to ship-board before shaking down the furled sails. For he would need all his Northmen then to man the ship, and there would be none to spare to keep the slaves in order.

But he knew that presently he would have to use the sails or else anchor again, and the thought of losing time while Caesar's Spaniards might be on the way moved him to run all risks except such as were unseamanly.

So he set a man to splice the warp Gwenhwyfar's men had cut, told off the rest of the Northmen carefully, assigning each to the work best suited to him, went below for a while to watch Conops moving from bench to bench instructing oarsmen, then stood beside Sigurdsen at the helm to await the inevitable.

First came the wind, a steady, fresh breeze on the starboard quarter, good enough. And presently it heaped the flowing river into regular, smooth waves that swept under the ship and lifted her. Twoscore oarsmen endured that for a while, then ceased to keep time. There was blasphemy below deck because others, finishing their swing, were struck in the back by the oar handles of other men who groaned and vomited. The sick men swore it was the herrings they had had for breakfast. The word poison emerged more than once through the opened hatch.

Then, nearing the bar, where the river banks spread away into the distance and the curious, perplexing currents from the mud flats and mussel shoals went hurrying seaward, there were lumpy waves that changed the easy motion into roll and dip. Oar after oar came in then, resting with its blade just showing through the port, and the din through the open hatch was like the voice of the infernal regions where the souls of unforgiven men lament. Eleven oars still slapped the water in spasmodic jerks, and Conops raised his one inquiring eye above the level of the hatch. He said nothing, but held up his whip at arm's length to draw Tros's attention.

'Cease rowing! Stow oars!'

Tros's voice held laughter that had nothing to do with the slaves' predicament. His ship at last, his wonder ship, should try her wings! It thrilled him as no fight had ever done, nor any sight of woman, nor even the thought of a finish-fight with Caesar!

'All hands make sail!'

The words were Tros's orison to the keepers of his deep-sea destiny, a challenge of his soul to make full use of him and ship and all he had, a greeting to the lords of opportunity. It was a big, bull-throated roar, heart-whole, that shook him as they say great Jove's nod shook Olympus.

Then he took the helm from Sigurdsen, and as the bellying sails were sheeted home he felt the thrill of the contenting sweetness of the ship's response. She steered to a touch, yet steadily. With creaking cordage and a boiling wake, her serpent's tongue aflash in the golden sunlight as she plunged over the lumpy waves, she heeled to the increasing wind and raced for the open sea.

Tros laughed. He had designed her right! His dream had come

94

true, and the seas of all the world were his to conquer and explore!
He wished he had bent on the purple sails with the great vermilion
dragons rampant on them for the first voyage. But thrift had
prevented that. The unbleached linen glistened in the sun like
gulls' wings, and for an omen, as the clean, tin-covered hull gained
speed and he ordered the sheets hauled closer, he beheld a golden
eagle soaring overhead, that circled thrice around the ship and
vanished northward, effortless, climbing and climbing the blue,
windy reaches of the sky.

'I am a man! I live! I laugh!' he said, and with his fist struck
Sigurdsen between the shoulder-blades.

A LETTER TO CAESAR

I know but one worse fault in a commander than to doubt his own intelligence; and that is to doubt his enemy's.

From the log of Tros of Samothrace

One at a time they sorted from between decks Britons who were not so seasick as the rest and put them to the deck work, four to a Northman overseer, trying them out, rope's-ending them a time or two until they learned to jump at the word of command and haul on a sheet all together. That set a few of the Northmen free for Orwic to experiment with. Orwic's genius was battle. He devised swift ways of getting up the ammunition from the magazines and studied how to aim the catapults, allowing for the pitch and roll.

In Orwic was no thrift. He wanted to use the loaded leaden balls for practice, even brought them up on deck and would have fired away a dozen without wondering where new ones could be had. He would have used the catapults without first greasing down the blocks and slides and the ingenious bronze levers that multiplied the speed of the falling weight. But Tros had foreseen that. He had provided stones that weighed almost exactly what the leaden balls did, and he forbade the firing of a catapult three times without regreasing.

So Orwic squandered stones and grease, and for a while, to the crash of the falling weights on basket-work, the sea was spattered with wild shooting, until at last a hit was made on a floating piece of wreckage half a mile away, and the whole deck crew went frantic with delight. Tros inspected the wheels at the top of the thirty-foot uprights, examined the whole mechanism, ordered the wooden box-work greased that guided the falling tons of lead to the basket-work below, observed that the basket cushions took up the concussion without injury, and let them use up all the stones, appointing Orwic his artillery lieutenant and instructing him to choose the steadiest marksmen from among the Northmen.

Then, after a long look at the wind and sun, he went below to where the water-casks were strapped in rows on chocks and, taking a whale-oil lantern, peered through a square hole into the end one, which had not been filled. He heard a groan.

'Have you had enough,. Gwenhwyfar?' he inquired, and knocked on the echoing cask with his sword-hilt. The answer was a curse, choked midway, followed by a louder groan.

'Will you go in this cask to Caesar or will you come out now and tell me what I want to know?'

'Air!' Gwenhwyfar answered. 'Air! I smother!'

Tros chuckled and struck at the cask again, bracing himself against the motion of the ship, not troubled by Gwenhwyfar's cravings. He knew that, though the fire and water torture may not wring confession from a strong-willed prisoner, the motion of the sea will do it always, given time enough. In the dark, when the world goes round and round, all secrets come up with a stomach's contents. All that is needed is patience and a pair of ears.

'You have air enough, unless you propose to speak. But on deck it is very pleasant,' he remarked. 'The sun shines.'

He heard her vomiting. Then:

'Mercy!' she gasped, and, between gulps, 'Tros, pity me! Throw me overboard!'

He laughed.

'I will set you ashore if you tell me what I want to know,' he answered, rapping on the cask again, for it occurred to him that probably the drumming din did not increase her comfort.

The ship was 'talking', as all newly built ships must, each plank and beam complaining of the changing tension. The dark hold was a sea of noises and immeasurable motion.

Gwenhwyfar groaned.

'Are you lying?' she asked.

'Not I. Nor bargaining for lies,' he answered. 'Tell the truth.'

He paused. Her hands clutched the edge of the square hole as she dragged herself upright.

'I will tell! Rhys promised to have Britomaris slain and to make me his own wife if I could wreck your ship. Now let me out! Let me out!' she screamed. 'I have told you.'

'Tell me all,' Tros answered, drumming again on the cask.

'Rhys heard Skell had gone to Pevensey. Let me – oh-h! – Tros, let me out! I can't talk here.'

'You shall come out when you have told all.'

She fell to the floor of the cask and groaned awhile, then presently got on her knees and spoke in great haste, as if to force out the words before her last strength failed:

'Rhys sent a man to overtake Skell, thinking I might fail to wreck you. The man was to bribe Skell to betray you to Caesar. Unless Skell agreed, the messenger was to kill him. Oh-h! Let me out!'

She fell to the floor of the cask. Tros waited.

'Tell me every last word!'

She spoke from the cask floor, her voice booming hollow, like a ghoul's through a hole in a sepulchre.

'The messenger – oh-h! – the messenger was to instruct Skell to find out where Caesar will set a trap for you. Skell was to bring you a false message. There, that is all! Let me out!'

Tros thought a minute, drumming with his fingers on the cask, then pulled a hammer from the rack below the deck beams and knocked the cask-head loose. Then he reached in and lifted Gwenhwyfar by the arms, she groaning, and carried her up the ladder, hanging limp across his shoulder. Presently he had a mattress laid on the floor of the after deckhouse, and placed her on it, locking the door and stationing a Northman on guard.

'Wine!' he commanded.

A slave brought it, but he did not dare to trust a Briton in alone with her, seasick or not.

He went in and knelt beside her, lifting up her head and forcing wine between the pale lips, spilling most of it. He had had no training in the bedside arts. The spilt wine stung her eyes. A mouthful of it choked her. But the strong stuff brought the blood back to her cheeks. She cursed him.

'Gwenhwyfar,' he said, 'you missed greatness by the width of your ambition! I asked you last night, where is Britomaris?'

'He is nothing of yours,' she retorted. But she sipped more wine and presently sat up, holding to the bench and looking scared and dizzy. Catching a glimpse of swaying sky through the deckhouse port, she gasped, lay down again and shut her eyes.

'I think Britomaris is all the husband you are ever likely to have, Gwenhwyfar,' Tros said pleasantly. 'None of us grow younger as the years roll on. Where is he?'

'I don't know,' she answered, burying her face in the mattress.

Tros stood up and paced back and forth a time or two from wall to wall, pausing to glimpse through the after port at the poop and Sigurdsen.

'Rhys,' he said pleasantly, 'might slay Britomaris. He would never make you his wife. More likely he would have you slain too, on a charge of treason, to seal your tongue. Trust me, not Rhys. I am an honest enemy. Rhys is a false friend. Tell me, where is Britomaris?'

98

She stared at him, her eyes red-rimmed and watery, her lower lip protruding, her hair an uncombed chestnut mass.

'Tros,' she said, 'I could have made a king of you!'

He answered:

'Where is Britomaris?'

'Gone!' she answered. 'Gone to the west of Britain to meet Caesar's men. Rhys bribed him. Britomaris is to trick Gwenwyn-wyn of the Ordovici, who is a coward of no account, on whom five hundred soldiers would be wasted. Britomaris is to meet the Spaniards, to persuade their Roman officer and to lead them near to Lunden, where the Lord Rhys will join them with a thousand men and have at Caswallon.'

'Not he!' Tros answered, hands behind him, throwing back his head in one of his discerning grins. 'Rhys may raise a thousand men, but he will play both sides and await the outcome. He will help Caswallon if he thinks Caswallon wins and, after that, de-nounce poor Britomaris and yourself, claiming the half of your heritage for his reward! If he thinks Caswallon loses, he will join the Romans openly, cause Britomaris to be stabbed and presently denounce you as public enemy, because you know too much about him!'

Tros stroked his chin. There was important information he must gain yet. He pondered how to go about it without letting Gwenhwyfar know she had a trump remaining in her hand.

'Gwenhwyfar,' he said presently, 'we were friends once – you, I and Britomaris. I ate your bread when I first set foot in Britain. Shame irks me that I need to see your ruin. I can save your Britomaris. Will you play him fair and be his wife and bide the laws of Britain if I pluck him out of Rhys's net?'

She began to sob, her face between her hands, her body shaking in convulsive sobs. Tros's eyes smiled, but he was sorry for her. Surely he was sorry.

'Speak. Shall I save him?'

She could not speak. He hardly knew whether in truth she nodded or whether the sobs still shook her. He repeated the question.

'Yes! Save him, if you will. Oh, Tros . . . '

She turned with the swift motion of a snake and sat up suddenly to stare at him.

'If I had wrecked your ship and taken you alive last night, there would have been no more talk of Britomaris! It would have been you and I, or death for both of us!'

'As it is, we will save Britomaris,' Tros commented, resuming his stride from wall to wall. He did not choose that she should see his face that minute and each time he reached the wall he turned away from her. 'Where can I reach him?' he asked offhandedly.

'Dertemue,'* she answered, and caught her breath. She realized as well as he did that she had betrayed the secret of where Caesar's men would land. 'Tros!' she said. 'Tros! There is a devil in you!'

There was self-mastery at any rate. His face betrayed no triumph though now he need not trust to Skell! If Skell had accepted a bribe to lead him in the wrong direction, he could nevertheless find Caesar's men. Nothing to do but to sail to Dertemue and await their coming!

'Tros,' she said. She had detected something like a gleam behind the amber eyes. 'You will betray me? You will betray my Britomaris?'

He made one of those strong, slow, confidence-imposing gestures that revealed his character more certainly than words.

'Never,' he answered.

Another thought occurred to him, a blind guess snatched at random as the panorama of the past week's happenings passed swiftly across his mind.

'If you had wrecked me, would you have sent word to Caesar?'

'Yes,' she answered. 'Rhys would have demanded your head to send to Caesar. Lud! But what would Rhys have been to me if I had won you? I would have told Rhys you were drowned. I would have given him your cloak, full of arrow-holes, to send to Caesar, bloodied up from other men's wounds. Rhys has a man in Pevensey who waits all ready to sail to Caritia with your head in a basket.'

'You would have sent the cloak instead?'

She nodded.

'Aye. I love you!'

'I have an old cloak,' said Tros. 'Can you write?'

Gwenhwyfar laughed. The blood began returning to her pale lips and her eyes grew brighter.

'Aye, Tros, I learned that from the druids.'

'Can Rhys write? No? Then I will sign his name! Gwenhwyfar, write to Caesar! We will pin that letter to my old cloak, bloodied up and pierced with arrow-holes.'

She lay back, overcome again by nausea, but she smiled at him nevertheless.

'Tros,' she said, 'Tros, you could have been a king!'

*The modern Dartmouth.

He left her and bolted the door, stationing a Northman to keep watch through one of the arrow ports. Her moods were as sudden as the seas before a veering wind. She would hate him again presently.

He took the helm awhile for the sake of the feel of the ship's response to it, and two or three times he changed the course to give the Northmen practice in trimming the sails. Then, giving charge to Sigurdsen, he went to the hatch and looked down at the rowers, sprawling, vomiting between the benches; went forward to the galley where the cooks were in a like predicament; laughed and returned to his own stateroom underneath the poop, where for a while he studied his water clocks, three bowls with holes in them, that floated in leaden tanks and, slowly filling, sank, the first in four hours, the second in twelve hours and the third in twenty-four.

Presently he pulled out his third-best cloak from a locker underneath the carved oak bunk and, with a wry face, because he hated to see good purple cloth destroyed – he had intended that cloak should be Conops' great reward after he himself had worn it in a few more times – he tossed it into a corner. Then, cutting off a section from a roll of parchment, thoughtfully he wrote a letter, pausing before each word because, though he had great facility with Greek and Latin, he had trouble with the spelling of Gaulish words.

The motion of the ship, as he sat with elbows spread on the oaken table and his legs stretched out in front of him, made it a simple matter to disguise his handwriting. The scrawl looked as if someone half illiterate but with a good command of spoken Gaulish had done it by flickering torchlight.

To Caesar, the Roman, in Gaul, greeting from the Lord Rhys of Maulden in the Isle of Britain, and from the Lady Gwenhwyfar, wife of the Lord Britomaris.

This according to our promise. The great ship built by Tros, the Samothracian, was wrecked on the bank of the Thames by our contriving. There was a great battle by night and many arrows struck Tros. He, fighting furiously, weakened, and his knees gave under him so that he fell headlong and was swallowed by the water, being seen no more. Tide bore his cloak to shore and it was found at daybreak.

Therefore, there is no more the great ship to fear nor any danger to the Spaniards whom the Lord Rhys will await at Dertemue.

We await the proof of Caesar's word. It was three talents for the

head, but it was no more seen and we have sent the cloak as surety
our work is well done.

Now send three talents by a trusted hand to Pevensey, whereafter
all shall be continued as agreed between us.

Tros, after reading the letter a dozen times, signed it 'Rhys
of Maulden', and left a space below that for Gwenhwyfar's signature. Then he took the cloak on deck and ordered Orwic to
shoot arrows through it until it looked as if it had been through
half a dozen battles.

Seasick men were butchering some equally seasick sheep for
dinner on the forward deck. Tros drenched the torn cloak in the
sheep's blood, let the blood dry, then towed the cloak overside
at the end of a line, with a bronze-tipped arrow caught by the
barbs in the lining.

'Caesar,' he said to Orwic, 'is a shrewd lean fox, not easily
deceived, but he will recognize the cloak by the gold braid around
it, concerning the meaning of which he questioned me when I
was his prisoner in Gaul. Now, if Skell should have betrayed me
and should be offering to lead me into Caesar's trap, Caesar may
think I was slain since Skell left Britain, in which case he may
send Skell to Pevensey with a message that the Spaniards are on
their way. So we will go to Pevensey with all haste, but we will
not wait there long.

'And it may be that Caesar will see through this trick. That
nose of his can smell a rat through solid masonry. And it may be
that Gwenhwyfar will yet betray me. But a wise man, Orwic, uses
all expedients and overlooks no opportunity that the gods have
thurst into his hands.'

DISCIPLINE

Show me successful mutiny, and I will show you a commander who
believed his men were as humourless and stupid as himself.
From the log of Tros of Samothrace

Tros had trouble with his top-masts. They were too tall. When he
ordered topsails set that afternoon to take advantage of a steady
breeze, there was too much leverage aloft for the ship's beam and
depth. She steered unhandily, needing two strong men on the
steering oar. And when the breeze freshened, two topmasts
snapped before the Northmen could get sail off or the men at the
helm could bring the ship round into the wind.

So Sigurdsen said, 'I told you so,' which made Tros lose his
temper; and there was other trouble besides. For instance, Orwic
lost his head completely. The slaves below deck heard the sharp
reports of breaking spars and, seasick though they were, began
to storm up the hatch in panic that was increased by the changed
ship's motion as the men at the helm hove her to. Orwic leaped
to the hatch and defended it, drawing his sword, instead of letting
the slaves surge through and find out for themselves that nothing
serious had happened.

It would have been easy enough, on deck, to have laughed them
out of their alarm and that lesson might have done good. But
Orwic wounded three men seriously, driving the rest below and
clapping on the hatch cover. The slaves made up their minds
they were being herded to their death, and there was a riot among
the oar benches that called for all Tros's mastery. They began to
throw the oars out through the ports, there being not much other
mischief they could do, until one bright genius suggested they
could break the deck loose from the beams and force an opening
to freedom.

So the oars that were not yet thrown out through the ports
were turned into battering rams, and a pounding began on the
deck that shook the whole ship. Whip was no use. Conops and
the Northmen oar captains hurled themselves into the confusion,
flailing right and left, but the oar ends made good weapons, and
they were driven backward to the ladder, where Tros opened the

103

hatch in the nick of time and rescued them, bruised and bleeding.

'Stink! Throw the stink into them!' urged Conops.

But Tros wanted oarsmen, not corpses.

'Open all hatches!' he thundered. 'Sigurdsen! Below there with a dozen men, and drive the fools on deck!'

The Northmen plunged into the opening with capstan-bars. The thundering ceased on the deck planking and the Britons began pouring out on deck, where they stormed the two boats, unlashing them from the rings that held them down on the oaken chocks, starting to drag them toward the davits.

Tros, swallowing impatience, stood and showed them how to launch the boats, which, crowded full, were large enough to hold between them about forty men. They got in one another's way – as mad as steers, too mad to know whose voice advised. Tros signalled to the Northmen, who came up red-faced through the forward hatch; they charged down-deck and broke the crowd up into two detachments, leaving a dozen or two frantically labouring at the boats. Once on the run, the Northmen kept the Britons moving, driving them around the deck and herding them up forward. The remainder lowered both boats and swarmed into them, hand over hand down the falls. They had no oars. They had forgotten that. Tros ordered the falls hauled up and two short oars thrown down to each boat.

'Now stay adrift!' he roared. They had neither food nor water, and began to realize it. 'Not a slave returns until you have picked up all the oars you fools threw overboard!'

They were out of sight of shore. Above them the great ship tossed, two topmasts swinging by the stays, the loose sails thundering, the serpent's tongue flashing to right and left. But at last a man in the stern of the row-boat cried:

'Brothers! See the colour of the water! That way lies the river! Row for it! We will pick up long oars as we go!'

'Man the port stern catapult!' Tros thundered. His voice roared clear above the thunder of the sails.

Four Northmen ran and cranked the weight aloft, and every slave in both the boats had seen what the catapults could do.

'Go and find those oars! Look lively now!'

Two short oars to a boat, they began to paddle timidly, afraid of the short waves that pitched and rolled them, more afraid of Tros and his artillery. Tros sent a Northman up to the masthead to shout directions to them, then went forward.

'Get aloft and bring those top-masts down on deck,' he ordered. 'Leave these fools to me!'

The Northmen swarmed aloft, and Tros stood looking at the Britons herded on the bow and on the deck below the bow. A few had armed themselves with odds and ends – belaying pins, capstan-bars, wood from the cookhouse fuel box. They looked ugly enough, but the panic had left them. Some were still miserably seasick; three were wounded; nearly all had bruises, because the Northmen had used capstan-bars to keep them moving. Orwic, and with him Glendwyr, came and stood behind Tros.

'Are ye ashamed?' Tros asked. He stood there, hands on hips, his back against the foremast, looking like a man who knew his own mind perfectly, whereas he was not at all sure how to handle them. 'Six of you, carry those three wounded fools aft!' he commanded.

They obeyed. A dozen made haste to obey, all too glad of a chance to get out of the storm that was coming. Tros had to herd back six of them.

'They're beaten!' Orwic whispered. 'Better thrash them one by one!'

'Is that the way you school a horse?' Tros snorted, turning on him, showing fifty times more anger than he felt. Once more the gods had given him the proper cue! 'Fool!' he thundered. 'These are scarelings. Shall I make them more afraid? Learn to keep that sword in the sheath until it's needed!'

Orwic chewed at his moustache and tried to look like a gentle-man who had not received rebuke.

'Below there! To your benches! Mark this – any more such foolishness and I'll chain you to the seats!'

At the jerk of his thumb the nearest men filed past him to the hatch. The others followed them like sheep, dropping their belay-ing pins and capstan-bars quickly before he should see them. Tros stood conning them, his face a strong enigma. He was making sure that none had been too badly damaged by the Northmen's blows, but he did not let them guess what thought was in his mind. When the last of them had vanished through the hatch he turned to Glendwyr.

'Go below with them,' he ordered. 'Talk to them. Get them good-humoured again. Let them know they are fortunate not to be slaves of a weak and revengeful master. Give them tallow for their bruises. Tell them that any other man than I would hang each tenth fool from the yardarm as example to the rest. Be mother and uncle to them for a while. Then, when they've come to their senses, promise them to try to coax me to let them have mead for their supper. Go!'

Then he turned on Orwic and read riot law, first principles for making panic-stricken scarelings into men.

'Stab, hang, beat. They learn you are afraid of them! You hot-head with your ready sword and dagger! Any fool can stab! That's first instinct. Do you dam the river flood, or do you clear a course for it? Do you stand in the way of a bolted horse? Or do you run alongside of him and get the rein and pull him around in circles until he tires of it? Lud's anguish! I have seen you break a team of horses and not use the whip once. Remember this – a man has more brains than a horse. Out-think him, if you hope to keep control! And take good care that when he thinks, he'll have an unexpected clemency to think about, but never a glimpse of weakness. Justice first, strength always! There is neither strength nor justice in a sword stab at a poor fool afraid for his life.'

'I regret what I did,' Orwic answered, saluting him.

'Go and bury regret and don't do it again!' Tros retorted and turned away from him to watch the Northmen passing down the topmasts to the deck. Not for another five-and-twenty men would he have let Orwic see how satisfied he was. He knew he had accomplished more to discipline his crew than a whole month's uneventful voyage could have brought about. The twenty who were quartering the sea for lost oars would have a long look at the great ship on the water and would return with their minds full of it, to talk about it to the others, beginning to think of the ship with pride instead of as a prison.

But better than that was discovery how well the ship behaved when hove to. He had left the youngest of the Northmen at the helm, a youth not likely to have used much head work if the ship had fallen off the wind and filled away, But all the time that riot lasted and the Northmen laboured up aloft to clear away the broken topmasts, the great serpent's head had curtseyed to the wind, swinging a little this way and then that, but never enough to fill the sails or make the helmsman work. She was a good dry ship, too. Not a gallon of solid water had come overside, although the waves were chopping up before a brisk wind crosswise of the tide. She was a steady ship and weatherly. He judged she had worked to windward just about enough to offset drift.

So when Sigurdsen came down on deck along with the main topmast, grumbling, with a great deal more about his 'told you so' and, stopping to secure the broken spar to the bulwark stanchions, talked back at Tros between his legs, his gloom proved uncontagious.

'Too much newness! Too much untried crazy stuff!' said

106

Sigurdsen. 'You should have listened to me. We laughed at a man on the Baltic who tried new rigs, and we called his wife widow before ever he put to sea. You will lose this ship yet!'

'Aye! Over the edge of the world!' Tros answered, laughing. ' A square world and a Baltic lugger! Rig new topmasts, shorter by two cubits and stayed aft as well as forward.'

'This having three masts is madness!' Sigurdsen went on.

But Tros, with the course in mind, knew fairly well how fast the ship had sailed and, well contented that the damage was no greater, squared his shoulders and went aft to bandage up the wounds of the oarsmen whom Orwic had stabbed. That was a messy business that his heart did not delight in, but the druids had given him pungent stuff that smelt like tar for treating wounds and he attended to the bandaging himself because he could not afford to lose three oarsmen.

That done, he watched the boats come back with the recovered oars, observing that the crews had learned one lesson. They no longer feared the motion of the waves nor troubled when a wave-top lipped over the bow and drenched them. Three of four were bailing leisurely, and some were singing. They reported they had picked up all the oars, and came aboard hand over hand up a rope with their feet against the ship's side, almost with the air of sailors, but not quite.

'Salute the poop, you dogs!' Tros roared. 'You grinning wharf rats! Do you think my ship is a longshore stews that you can swagger into and pay down your money for a drink?'

He made them stand there and salute him ten times running, just to train their memories. Then twice he made them lower away the boats again and haul them up evenly, snatching at the halyards on the run and swinging in the davits handsomely. They went below all grinning at their new-found sea-legs, but Tros stopped the man who had cried from the stern of the boat to the others about the colour of the water and direction of the land. He gave him a red cord to hang around his neck.

'I appoint you first oarsman on the starboard side,' he said.

The fellow grinned, saluted and departed down the hatch. He had expected to be punished. Orwic stared, then exploded.

'You reward him?'

'No. I recognize him. There are seeds of leadership in that man.' He turned to the helmsman. 'Let her fall off – easy now! This is a ship – not a four-horse chariot!'

The Northmen managed the sheets and braces without a word from Tros, keeping their eyes on him, obeying gestured signals.

For a while Tros watched the course, considering the wind, tide, current, then left Sigurdsen in charge and went back to the deckhouse where Gwenhwyfar lay. He found her lying with her face still buried in the mattress, looking like a drowned thing with her hair all matted. But she stirred as he entered.

Tros leaned against the table, fingers rapping his sword-hilt.

'Death, Gwenhwyfar, comes to all of us when we have played our part,' he said. 'The men who know about such things have told me there is a long rest after that and utter happiness before we come again into the world and finish what we left undone. I will start my next life without this one's rotten ropes to splice!'

She raised her head and stared.

'What would you have me do?' she asked. 'You talk like Fflur. You act like destiny! I tremble when you speak. I hate you! What would you have me do?'

'Act nobly!' Tros retorted. 'All of us make errors. Make them bravely, bear the blame and eat the consequences. I will set you free in Pevensey. I have a letter and a cloak full of arrow-holes. Take both. Send them to Caesar or try once more to break me under the wheels of your revenge.'

She sat up, elbows on her knees, head resting on her hands, her chestnut hair a cloud around her shoulders. But between her brown fingers her eyes were watching him.

'You ask me to do you a favour?' she said at last.

'Nay, save yourself, Britomaris, and all Britain. So you and I will square our reckoning and hold no grudge between us when we come to earth another time.'

'I like now better than another time,' she answered. 'Tros, you are too strong. Have you any notion how a scornling feels?'

'Aye. One or twice I have despised myself,' Tros answered. 'But I took care never to repeat the lesson. That is why I will set you free in Pevensey without conditions. I will not have your treachery for which to blame myself. You may be friend or enemy.'

'If I say friend, will you trust me?'

He nodded.

'And if I say enemy, I will set you free nevertheless.'

'Are you a very wise man or a fool?' she asked. 'I know not in my own mind.'

'I speak you fair, Gwenhwyfar.'

'And you bid me send a written lie to Caesar!'

Her lips curled, not exactly scornfully but with a hint of malice. She believed she had him on the quick.

'Lie to Caesar, or betray me and let Caesar's army land in Britain!' he retorted. 'Choose the lesser of two evils or the greater, even as I choose between a fight with Caesar and the chance to run away. I will play the man. Play you the woman.'

'Tros,' she said, 'there is no gainsaying you! Very well, I will send your cloak to Caesar.'

She lay down again, burying her face between her hands and breathing hard.

Tros walked out, fastening the door behind him.

GWENHWYFAR YIELDS

I have heard that a woman scorned is a worse danger than a fire on a ship at sea. But why scorn her? Is it not by scorning fire and tempest that a captain brings a ship home. Though I buy not, need I scorn the would-be seller? Nay, if I show him a better market I may even earn his good will. It is so with women.

From the log of Tros of Samothrace

There was many a delay before they sighted Pevensey, and Tros dropped anchor in the lee of the long sand flat that arose, with coarse grass shaking in the wind, between the harbour and the sea. There was a split sail with a patch on it, due to a Northman's carelessness while Tros slept. A chafed throat-halyard had parted and a falling spar had smashed the cook-house roof. Deck water casks had gone adrift in a three-reef gale, and there was a great gap in the bulwark where a rolling cask had broken through.

But the face of Helma on the figurehead still smiled, and the long, forked serpent's tongue flashed handsomely to every motion of the ship. There was an eye-appealing smartness in the way the sails were clewed up to the spars; and when the oars came out to work up to the anchorage against the tide, they swung together as if a hundred-handed Hercules were prisoned under deck. There was no sound of the whip, no swearing, nothing but the clang of cymbals and the drum-thud as they dipped, vermilion in emerald and white, and swung, Tros with his baton marking time, beside the helmsman on the poop.

He did not choose to enter the port of Pevensey, and there were many reasons. First, the shifting sandbanks with a tortuous course between them where a ship could take the sand bow-on before the lead came up. Secondly, it was late spring. Caesar's biremes might be cruising in the channel. Tros wanted sea-room. Given that, he feared no dozen biremes.

Then, again, he did not care to take his crew into a British port yet. They were too near home. It was a first rule of ship's husbandry to give the crew shore-leave as often as convenient to save them from salt water boils, the scurvy, cramp, and the depression born of oar monotony. But it was also a rule in any seaport to take a toll

110

of all ships' crews, decoying them to hiding-places where they could be caught and re-enslaved in due time, when the ship had sailed away without them. In a foreign port a man dared land his crew, because even a drunken oarsman reasonably treated on his own ship would hardly trust the promises of longshore tavern keepers. But near a home port, where the tavern keepers spoke their language, slaves were safest with a tide-rip hurrying between them and the land.

There was a risk, too, that if he entered Pevensey some fishing-boat might sneak out of the harbour mouth, conceivably by night, and carry word to Caesar that the great ship was afloat and cruising between Gaul and Britain. That would end all prospect of the Spaniards' sailing until Caesar could send a fleet out to destroy the monster ship, of which so many rumours must have reached him. Whereas, at anchor there in the very jaws of the long harbour entrance, although out of sight of Pevensey itself because the coastwise towns of Britain were well hidden from the all too frequent raiders, Tros could see who came and went. Provided the watch were wakeful, even in the night no fishing-boat could pass to sea without his leave.

Last, given a fair wind – and at that season of the year the wind would suit them three days out of seven – the Spaniards could pass from Gaul to Britain at almost any point along the coast between dawn and dawn. If he should hear of them, he would want to waste no time nail-biting at the tide or feeling his way foot by foot to sea, in darkness, between sandbanks.

He had decided he would trust Gwenhwyfar, against Orwic's firm conviction she would play him false. It was against reason, and he knew it. But he had the trick of intuition and had learned, by long experience, that reason is a rut-bedraggled hag, while intuition is a goddess who can see inside the houses, into men's hearts and beyond the hills and trees. Reason reckons yesterdays, but intuition tells about tomorrow.

So the Northmen went to work repairing damage, and the Britons cleaned ship, sanding down the decks, while Tros, with a look-out at all three mast-heads, interviewed Gwenhwyfar for the last time. She was smiling and well pleased with him because he gave her money liberally for the journey home; but he knew no wind changed swifter than her moods, and he was minded, if he could, to say a parting word that should stick barbed into her memory.

'If you can learn in this life to play fair, and to choose between friend and enemy, you might be a queen in the next life,' he said,

111

fixing her with his lion's eyes. He looked like a priest of Isis when he stood that way, still and smooth-browed, with the black hair straight over his forehead.

She did not answer. She stood waiting. British manners offered no alternative, so Tros embraced her, kissing both cheeks. She flung her arms around his neck then, and caught her breath, sobbing, laughing, whispering in his ear:

'I have lost you, Tros, but only this time! I will help you against Caesar, and next time – '

A half-sob choked her speech. She thrust herself away from him, wet-eyed, and she looked older than Tros by ten years, but there was a bravery of youth within her still and something not contemptible in line and gesture.

'Like gods, we live for ever,' Tros answered. 'Do what is right, Gwenhwyfar.'

That came as close to a blessing as he ever gave to anyone in words, for sentimental mouthings nauseated him. He did not know why he should pity and like Gwenhwyfar. He knew he did, as surely as he knew she could never make him captive of her charms.

He sent Orwic ashore with her in the longboat with eight Northmen and ordered up the slaves to line the rail by way of farewell compliment. But as he saw her rowed away, and in his heart knew she would not betray him, but would spare no pains to ruin all her friends this once for sake of him, he wondered whether the gods themselves, in all their infinite and condescending irony, would stoop to use such means.

He blew a great sigh, like a grampus coming up to breathe.

'Well, I am not a god,' he muttered, 'and I think I have hurt her less than she was willing to hurt me.'

NEWS!

*

A good plan is as easy to get as a chestnut from the embers. For one bad one there are ten good. But find me a man who can splice a broken plan and of its two parts build a new one in the crack of a sail's splitting. I will make him free of my quarter-deck.

From the log of Tros of Samothrace

Before the next dawn following the afternoon when Tros dropped anchor off Pevensey, there were five small sailing-boats made fast to the stern of the *Liafail*. Of the five, the first two had essayed to slip past by daylight, keeping to the shallow water on the far side of the channel. But one of the first things Tros had done was to take on a new deckload of flat stones, and to put Orwic to work at the catapult.

Within an hour the catapult crew had all the marks within reach so well ranged that they actually hit one flat stone with another on the edge of the sandy beach. So when two boats sailed by, ignoring signals, one had the mast knocked out of her and the second put her helm up promptly, coming alongside, scandalized, to plead such innocence as only fishermen are guilty of, and none but madmen could believe.

Neither boat carried anything that even looked suspicious, but their five-man crews denied that they knew who Caesar was, denied that they had ever heard of him.

'Then stay here and be deaf a little longer!' was Tros's comment. He put two Northmen into each boat to guard the ends of the ropes with which he tied them to the taffrail.

By night it was not so simple, especially before the moon rose. Lapping of the waves against the ship drowned other noises. It was so dark that from the poop Tros could scarcely see the main-mast. So he showed a light and lowered both boats, filling them with Northmen, who had orders to lie close in-shore on the far side and pounce on all who tried to pass. One by one they brought in three more crews of fishermen, not one grey-bearded innocent of whom had ever heard of Caesar. Nor did they know how many more boats there were in Pevensey, nor who was Skell the North-man, nor Gwenhywfar. They were quite sure they never had heard of Skell – so sure of it that Tros was quite sure they were lying.

'Nevertheless, I think I too would lie if I were in their case,' he reflected, and he lent no ear to Sigurdsen's suggestion of a rope's end, nor to Conops' talk about the virtues of a knife-point thrust between the toenail and the quick. He fed those fishermen and waited.

And a little after dawn there came a sixth boat, rowed by two men with a third man in the stern. And that was followed by a seventh, under sail, that carried, by arrangement with Gwenhwy-far, her own red woollen shawl tied up to the masthead, streaming in the wind. So they let that sailing-boat go by unchallenged, and Tros, superstitious in his own way, laughed to himself to think it was the seventh.

'The sacred number – number of the gods!' he grinned, and waited for the row-boat.

From it stepped and climbed the hanging ladder to the poop, a man whose dull-red beard stuck outward all round his face. He had a basket in his hand as big as those the women carried on their backs to Lunden market. He declared his name was Geraint, but his beady eyes that peered over apple cheeks did not suggest that he expected Tros to believe that or anything else. He set the basket on the deck and stared at Tros and waited.

Tros poked at the basket with his toe a time or two, recalling in his mind the details of the system of communication he had settled on with Skell.

'How many eggs do you bring? When did you leave Gaul?' he asked.

'One egg,' the man replied who said his name was Geraint. 'I left Gaul day before yesterday.'

'One egg! Lord Zeus!'

Tros tore away the basket-lid and pulled out another basket, a third, and then a fourth inside that.

'Four warships? And sailed yesterday?'

The man grinned amiably, as if he admired the way Tros ground his jaws together.

'Too much time wasted! Too late!' Tros muttered, wrenching at the lid of the last basket. It was fastened all round with fibre and not easy to remove. Sigurdsen, Orwic, Conops, and Orwic's four retainers came and watched. Tros pushed the basket towards Conops.

'Use your knife,' he ordered, and Conops slid the blade under the fastenings. Tros had turned away, hands behind him, staring

114

at the open sea, his heavily ringed fingers clenching and unclenching as he ground his teeth.

How should he get men now? The Spaniards probably had landed yesterday in Britain and would be impossible to round up. True, he might catch Caesar's warships on the way back, defeat them and take over the survivors of their crews, but –

A sharp exclamation from Conops made him turn again and stare. His eyes blazed suddenly. In Conops' hand, raised by the hair, was a human head.

'Skell's!' said Conops.

Sigurdsen pounced on the man who had said his name was Geraint, seized his wrists and lashed them tight behind his back. The man offered no resistance.

'Torture!' said Conops, pointing with his right forefinger at the ghastly face. Orwic shuddered. Tros, his eyes changing, stared at the man whom Sigurdsen had pinioned.

'You are not Geraint?' he said.

'No,' the man answered. 'I am Symmachus. I am a Gaul.'

Tros made a gesture of disgust.

'Put that thing back in all four baskets,' he commanded. 'Put a stone in it with it. Sink it in mid-channel.'

He turned on the man who now admitted that his name was Symmachus.

'You have your courage with you,' he remarked.

The man smiled amiably.

'Caesar said you are not a cruel man,' he replied. 'He said, if you should slay me you would do it swiftly. And he paid me well. He gave my two sons money and as much land as two teams of oxen can plough. We had nothing. I am well content.'

'Are you a fisherman?' Tros asked.

The man nodded.

'I lost my boat. My wife died of the hunger.'

The man's comically amiable face, framed in the dull-red whiskers, beamed with satisfaction. He had expected at least a scourging. His story was as frankly told as if he were relating something that was no concern of his at all.

'Geraint brought Skell,' he said. 'Geraint sold him to the Romans, but Skell slew Geraint when he saw he was betrayed. I saw that. The Romans took me for a witness. I saw Skell brought before Caesar. I was within six paces of him, squatting on the ground before the great tent. Caesar said to Skell, "I know you!" But Skell said nothing.

'For a long while Skell was silent, although Caesar asked him

115

many questions. I saw Skell put his hand to his mouth, but the Roman officer who stood beside him saw that too, and smote him in the jaw, and seizing him, gagged him with a sword-hilt, breaking some teeth. He pulled out a piece of parchment from his mouth and offered it to Caesar, who smiled.

'"You are a spy," said Caesar. "You stand convicted." But Skell said nothing.

'"Torture him," said Caesar, "and when he is willing to tell his story, let me know. There is no need to preserve his usefulness," he added. "You may put him to extremity. When we have his story we are done with him".

'So they threw Skell to the ground not far from Caesar's tent, and a black man came up who had a pot of charcoal. Hot irons were put to Skell's feet until he yelled so that Caesar frowned and grew impatient, ordering that Skell be gagged, saying it was impossible to attend to important matters in the midst of so much noise. And after a long time an officer came to Caesar, who said that Skell would now speak.

'So they carried Skell, he begging to be slain, and Caesar, observing him shrewdly, said he would confer that favour provided the truth was told, and all the truth, without prevarication. So Skell told about the eggs he was to send you in a basket to signify when and from which port the Spanish troops were sailing. And he told about this great ship, speaking very swiftly because he wished to die soon and be free from pain. But Caesar made him tell the story three times over. And the secretary wrote it.

'Then Caesar, studying the tablet, made a gesture with his head and with his left thumb. So they dragged Skell away to the camp ditch at the place where the rubbish is burned, and presently they came back carrying his head.

'There was much joking after that, and laughter, Caesar wondering whom he should send to you with that head in a basket in place of the eggs from a Spanish hen. And one said – he was a high officer, he wore a white cloak – "it will not do now to send the Spaniards." But it happened at that moment Caesar's eyes observed me where I still squatted in the dust outside the tent.

'"No," he said, "it will not do now to send the Spaniards. Who is that man?"

'So they told him, and I was made to stand before him in the opening of the tent, he striking his teeth with the thumbnail of his right hand. Suddenly he asked me:

'"Do you speak the Roman tongue or understand it?"

'But I pretended not to understand the question, being fright-

116

ened. I began to beg of him in Gaulish, saying I am poor and have two sons but no more any fishing-boat, having lost mine in the storm when I went to catch good fish for Caesar.

'So he smiled, and when he had thought a while he began to bargain with me, until at last I agreed to carry Skell's head to you in a basket and to take all chances that you might slay me.

'"But I think he will not," said Caesar, "because Tros is afraid for his own soul, and will not take human life if he can help it."

'Then, having agreed how much money and how much land he will give my sons, he tried to catch me, asking suddenly, "Concerning the Spaniards, what will you say when Tros asks you?" But though his words were Gaulish I pretended not to understand his meaning, being fearful he might call the bargain off if I should seem to know too much. I was anxious that my sons should have that money and the land.

'"Did you not hear what Skell told me?" he demanded.

'So I admitted I had heard that. Skell had told his tale in Gaulish. Caesar said:

'"What then will you say to Tros about the Spaniards?"

'And I said "I know nothing of them."

'He thought a long while, chin on hand, and at last he said:

'"If I had ships to spare, I would send those Spaniards and not you. But since I cannot spare ships, I will have my little joke with Tros. It makes no difference what you say about the Spaniards. Say anything you please, since they will not sail. If Tros is still alive when you reach Britain, wait for him in Pevensey and give that head to him, pretending that you bring Skell's message."'

Tros turned his back to hide a grin. He would avenge Skell! The poor knave had done his best to play the man at last. He did not blame him for confessing under torture.

'Shall we put back to the Thames?' asked Orwic. 'No use going any further now.'

'Put that man Symmachus in the Northmen's mess,' Tros answered. 'He has done us a good service. Orwic, bring me Rhys's men from the forepeak.'

Orwic hesitated. He knew his Britons.

'If you let them ashore in Pevensey,' he said, 'they will find Gwenhwyfar, and the next you know she and they will be cooking up a mischief for you. You will have to use British harbours until you get more men and –'

'I will get more men!' Tros answered grimly – 'Spaniards.'

'But we have just heard they are not to leave Gaul.'

'Credulous horseman! Do you think Caesar would have said

117

they will not sail unless they will? If he had said they will sail, I might have doubted it! Bring me those fellows of Rhys's.'

So presently, all blinking at the sunlight, weak-kneed from confinement, filthy from much vomiting in the darkness, Rhys's men were lined up on the deck below the poop, and Tros addressed them arrogantly, standing with his legs apart, a hand on either hip.

'I held you hostages for your master's good behaviour. Since sailing, two attempts were made to wreck my ship, and for both of them the Lord Rhys was responsible. Your lives are forfeit!'

They demurred, very weak and bewildered. They said they knew nothing of Tros's terms with the Lord Rhys, and nothing of his efforts to destroy the ship. They had been locked up in a dark place where food was thrown to them, and they had all been at death's door most of the time, so that they supposed the food was poisoned.

'As hostages, your lives are forfeited to me,' Tros repeated. 'But I will give you one chance for your lives. Can you fight? Are you willing to man my arrow engines against Caesar's fleet if I give you your liberty afterwards?'

They complained they were unfit to fight. They had no special quarrel against Caesar. They were the Lord Rhys's men and needed his permission before they might offer their services elsewhere. Their bellies were all watery with sickness.

'To the oars, then!' Tros commanded. 'Ye shall work as slaves if ye will not fight freely! Shame on you! Your master played a treachery on me and on the Lord Caswallon. He has tried to sell his native land to Caesar. Have ye no honesty, that ye refuse the opportunity to wipe that shame away? Such dogs as you deserve the lower oar bank!'

They replied that they were honest men, trained to use weapons, not oars.

'Honest?' Tros looked them over one by one. 'Orwic, take charge of them. See that they clean themselves on deck where the air can blow the stink away. Feed them. Then give them their choice between the arrow engines or the lower oar bank. If they choose oars, chain them to the benches! Sigurdsen, man the capstan! Haul short! Conops, take those five boats that lie astern of us, set their crews ashore and break a plank from each boat's bottom. We don't want any spy work done for Caesar for a few days! Lars, Harald, Haarfager, masthead men aloft! Oar crews to the benches. Out oars! Ready for slow ahead to come up on the anchor! Cymbals and drums, stand by!'

Of all the certainties on earth Tros knew the surest was that

118

Caesar would be swift. If, as seemed proven, he was planning to throw Britain into discord by sending foreign troops to help one rival king against another, he would send them now, not wait for events to rearrange themselves. Already he had had three days to man the ships since Skell revealed to him the discovery of Gwenwynwyn's and Rhys's plot against Caswallon. He would not be likely to give Caswallon time to oppose the Spaniards' landing.

The arrow-riddled cloak and the letter describing the wreck in the Thames would be in Gaul before night, for the wind was fair, and if the sail-boat men knew anything about the tide they could lay a V-shaped course that would bring them to Caritia at sunset. That news should be enough to make Caesar act in any case, supposing that the Spaniards were not already on the sea.

As he worked the ship seaward under oars, with Conops crying soundings from the chains, his brain was busy with those Spaniards, for he knew what difficulties the Romans had in that for ever turbulent and plundered province. He conjectured the five hundred would be levies who had not exactly mutinied at being brought to Gaul, but who were neither loyal nor safe to be brigaded alongside other troops. All Roman troops, including the Italians themselves, were likelier than not to mutiny if given much encouragement, and it was an old game for a Roman general to transfer disaffected portions of his army to some outlying district where their behaviour toward the inhabitants might lead to trouble and thus provide an excuse for an expedition, loot and easy laurels for the general himself.

'If Caesar thinks me dead, then I will soon have a ship full of good spirited men,' Tros told himself. 'If those Spaniards are such firebrands that Caesar is glad to risk them on any venture, then they're just the lads for me! Better spend time taming good men than waste it coaxing dullards. They'll quarrel with my Britons. Yes, and it'll do the Britons good.'

He began to pace the poop, his eyes sweeping the horizon, then came to a stand again where all could see him.

'Done with the oars!' he roared. 'Make sail! Taut on the port preventer stays! Deckhands to the sheets! Aloft there. Shake her down!'

He watched the big sails sheeted home, felt the ship keel to the wind with a white wake boiling from under her, and laughed.

'Gods, give me but the opportunity!' he prayed. 'I'll use it!'

THE FIGHT OFF DERTEMUE

How few there are who know that victories are not won on the field but in a man's heart.

From the log of Tros of Samothrace

Tros made for Dertemue with all the speed his ship could show, experimenting with the sails, putting the oars to work whenever the wind dropped to less than a strong breeze, making his men sleep by their stations, watching his three water clocks, calculating, fretting and yet letting no man see that he was worried.

He kept well away from the coast of Gaul and anchored for the night under the Isle of Vectis, partly because he feared the tide-race in the dark, but also because he suspected some of Caesar's light ships might be lurking thereabouts, and to have fought them would have taken time, with the added risk that they might escape and carry the news to Caesar that the *Liafail* was not wrecked after all.

Nearly all next day he had to use the oars, for wind failed, but when night fell he carried on with all sail set, considering the coast-wise lights that burned not far above the level of the beach. Sigurd-sen begged him to anchor.

'Wreckers!' he said. 'All Britons ply that trade. They set those lights to tempt raiders on to the reefs, and now and then they catch a merchant ship.'

But Tros believed he saw a system in the lights. They were too bright, spaced at too regular intervals, and did not look innocent enough to be wreckers' decoys. They were signals. He had often seen what care the Roman navigators took, when about to cross uncharted water with a fleet of ships, to send men in advance in the liburnians to build great bonfires, near the headlands as much as possible, but in any case in a long line to guide them to their destination if the fleet should become scattered in the night. They would follow the long string of lights until there were no more of them, and know by that they had reached their port, when they would wait until dawn should show them the harbour entrance.

He did not know how far it was to Dertemue, but he knew the length of the southern coast of Britain more or less, and he was beginning to learn to judge the ship's speed, though it was so much greater under sail than he had ever dared hope it might be that he hardly trusted to his calculations yet. Even without her topsails she would boil along with a following or a beam wind, the clean tin-coated hull reducing friction to a minimum. And she would sail faster and closer into the wind than any ship he had ever known. However, they had toiled a whole day under oars, the half of the time against the tide, so he kept well out to seaward of the long-shore lights, and doubted, when he reached the last one, doubted that really could be Dertemue.

He took a sounding, but the water was too deep, and he laughed at Sigurdsen's suggestion that they should use the oars and work inshore in search of anchorage. Orwic agreed with Sigurdsen.

'If that is Dertemue, we should be ready to enter the river mouth at dawn, and so catch Caesar's Spaniards as they enter.'

'They never shall enter!' said Tros. 'My genius is best at sea, Caesar's on land. I wait here.'

So he shortened sail and hove to; but he did not wait long before the masthead lookout cried that he heard cordage creaking in the dark. Great banks of clouds obscured the moon and there was wind enough to fill the rigging with the sea-wail that deadens hearing. How a Northman could hear cordage creaking through all that sound Tros found it hard to understand; he leaned far over the taffrail, straining eyes and ears.

The Northman warned again, and the man at the helm said something about ghosts in awestruck undertones. But at last Tros's eyes detected blackness blacker than the night, considerably lower on the water than his own great ship, not more than half a cable's length away. There were no lights, nothing but that spot of utter darkness and a mere suggestion of a sound that did not exactly harmonize with the orchestra of sea and wind.

Rhys's men, who had made their choice without much hesitation when the wind had blown the sickness out of them, were sleeping by the midship arrow engines, ready for Orwic to captain them when an engagement should begin. The catapults were useless in the dark, but every Northman had a bow within reach in addition to his axe and dagger. Twelve of the big stink-balls had been set on deck in Conops' charge, the oil-primed fuses ready to insert, a firepot and a torch stowed under cover near by. Below, the drowsy rowers rested on oars indrawn until the blades lay on the ports all ready to be thrust out at a signal.

Tros looked sharply at the shore, and then at the spot of darkness. It was moving very slowly seaward, not toward the coast. It was therefore not a Roman ship. The moon was behind Tros's back as he leaned over the taffrail; clouds obscured it, but the sky was a shade less dark there than in any other direction. Therefore, obviously, since Tros could see the approaching ship, however dimly, whoever was aboard her must have seen the *Liafail*. Yet the ship came on.

'They believe I'm a Roman,' Tros muttered.

He turned to the Northman beside him and ordered:

'Stations! Silence!'

The Northman vanished on the run, with Orwic at his heels, and there was presently a stir below deck where the sleepy oarsmen were awakened, followed by the clanking of the arrow engine cranks. Somewhere forward, Conops rolled a stink-ball closer to the bulwarks.

Hove to, the *Liafail* was drifting gradually seaward, away from the approaching ship, almost bow-on to the stranger, whose captain, likely enough, if he could see three masts, might think there were three ships in the darkness. Suddenly Tros cried aloud in the Roman tongue.

'Ho there! Is yonder port Dertemue?'

The answer came in Celtic:

'Are you Septimus Flaccus, with the Spaniards?'

'I am admiral of Caesar's fleet!' Tros answered. 'Come along.'

Someone on the approaching ship could understand the Roman speech. She changed her course that instant, looking almost ridiculously undersized and awkward as she came near enough for Tros to see her outline. He touched the helm, not taking it, but guiding the Northman's hand.

'Stand by to grapple!' he roared suddenly. 'Out fenders!'

He thought of his new paint even in that crisis, and swore suddenly between his teeth, for as usual, Orwic let go a flight of arrows without waiting for the word. There was tumult aboard the other ship. They put the helm hard over trying to go about, their shrouds missing the great serpent's tongue by inches. It was clumsily done, but it saved them from a second of Orwic's volleys.

'Cease arrow fire!' Tros roared, his hand on the helm again. A second later there was a crash as the bower anchor and a great eight-pronged grappling hook beside went down on to the small ship's deck, splintering the timbers.

'Who are you?' Tros shouted. For as much as sixty breaths there was no answer. Sigurdsen came running aft to report that the grapnel held and that six Northmen were on the small ship's deck to make sure none should cut it loose. Tros bade him take the helm and keep the ship hove to.

'Who are you?' he roared again.

An indignant voice answered him:

'I am Britomaris and a pilot with me. Is it so you treat your friends?'

Tros laughed.

'Come aboard, Britomaris! Come before I sink you.'

He threw a rope-ladder overside, and Britomaris climbed it, standing before Tros, startled and indignant.

'Tros?' he said, bending his head to peer into the darkness.

Tros looked like a big black shadow on the poop.

'You thought me sunk in River Thames, now didn't you!' Tros answered, chuckling. 'Ho, there! Bring a lantern, someone.'

By the light of it he studied Britomaris, wondering that a man so good to see, who stood so upright in his furs and handled a spear so stately, should be such a moral weakling as he knew this man to be.

'You are caught in the act, Britomaris,' he said. 'Do you know of any reason why I should not take you to Caswallon?'

'Do you dare to fight me, Tros?' Britomaris answered. It was his only possible way out. He did not look as if he liked the prospect. Tros laughed,

'You are a prisoner. I don't fight prisoners. Give me that spear. Now the sword, Now the dagger. So.' He threw the weapons on the deck, where a Northman gathered and examined them. 'Do you know of any reason why I should not denounce you to Caswallon?'

Britomaris tugged at his moustache, attempting to look digni- fied, but plainly worried. The Northman who held the lantern grinned.

'No answer? Well, I will tell you a reason. I promised your wife Gwenhwyfar. I have told her I will save you from this infamy.'

'Told *her*?' Britomaris stared at him.

'Aye. She and I have turned friends at last. When do you expect the Romans?'

'Now. I thought you were – '

'Landlubber!' Tros interrupted. 'When saw you a Roman ship like this one? Blind mole! How many ships will the Romans bring?'

'Two, full of Spaniards. Four biremes to protect them.'

'Who said so?'

'Caius Rufus the Roman.'

'When did he come?'

'Since nightfall, post-haste in a liburnian to bid us light the beacons and to have a pilot ready. He said Caesar had moved with his wonted suddenness since learning that Tros is dead.'

'Zeus! But that fellow is swift!' Tros said admiringly. 'Gwenhwyfar's message saying I am dead, with my cloak and a letter to prove it, can hardly have reached Gaul before sunset night before last, and now – aloft there! Use ears and eyes! The wind's against them. The Romans will come rowing!'

'They will come with lights,' said Britomaris.

The man had no resistance in him. He was as plastic in Tros's hands as if the two had been master and man for a generation.

'Caius Rufus said they will burn a lantern at each end of the spar of each ship. Will you battle with them, Tros?'

'You too!' Tros answered. 'You shall boast to Gwenhwyfar that you played the man this once! Forward with you! Into the deckhouse and take Orwic's orders!'

'Orwic?' said Britomaris, and his jaw dropped.

'Aye! Caswallon's nephew Orwic! Fall away!'

So Britomaris let a Northman lead him to the deckhouse, and Tros sent Conops overside to clear away the grapnel. But he took no chances; the smaller ship still might warn the Romans.

'Cut away their rigging! Send their sail up here!'

The Northmen's axes answered. They even chopped the mast away.

'Out oars now, and off home!'

It was an hour before the laboured thumping of the oars died away in the direction of the shore. Another hour before a Northman at the masthead shouted that he saw lights to the southward. Tros himself went to the masthead then. He counted twelve lights, several miles away, scattered in pairs over a considerable breadth of sea. And he studied them for a long time, trying to determine which might be the ships containing Spaniards and which the escort.

The Romans were poor hands at keeping station on the open sea. Likelier than not the ships were all mixed up together, their commanders satisfied to keep within sight of one another, not anticipating an engagement and confident that they would receive ample warning of the presence of an enemy.

No lights showed on the *Liafail*, but her bulk and her three great spars would show up plainly as soon as dawn should begin to steal along the sky. It lacked an hour of dawn yet and the wind had dropped. Glancing shoreward Tros could hardly see the beacons. It seemed to him that their crimson flare was being veiled and was spreading on the veil while it drew dim.

'Fog!' he muttered. He had asked the gods for opportunity!

He returned to the poop and sent for Conops, Sigurdsen and Orwic.

'We will let that fog drift down on us,' he said. 'If it comes not fast enought we will row toward it. When the Romans can no longer see one another's lights they will start their war trumpets a-blaring. They will low like full cows at the milking time. We will pick them off one by one. Their system is to crowd an enemy between the beaks of two or four ships, or to lay alongside and drop their dolphins into her, and to let fall a gangplank with a spike in it. That pins both ships together, and along the plank their boarders come with locked shields.

'Now they cannot use that gangplank, because our deck is higher than theirs. But they can break our oars, and they can use the iron dolphin, since it hangs above the yardarm. Above all, we must avoid their beaks.

'Orwic, their commanders will not stand at the stern, as I will. They will fight their ships from the top of the midship citadel where the sail, which they will keep spread whether there is wind or not, masks them from an enemy, and whence they can shout to the helmsman as well as direct the javelin and arrow fire. So aim first at the citadels and keep those swept with a cross fire from the arrow engines.

'Sigurdsen, take you the helm. See to it that the sails are well clewed up but ready to be sheeted down with all speed if a wind should come and blow the fog away. This fog, which the gods have sent, is better than forty men to us.'

But Sigurdsen was a pessimist.

'It will make the Romans close their ranks, and we will have to fight six ships at once,' he grumbled.

'It sets all Northmen free for the fighting, since neither side can use sails!' Tros retorted.

'Aye, and we under-oared, with a half-trained crew! There are nineteen men so weak from vomiting they can't pull their weight, and if the ship rolls – '

'Clew up the sails!' Tros snapped at him. 'Then come aft and take the helm.'

The giant went forward, grumbling to himself, but Tros had come to understand the pessimism of the man; he liked to set all gloom in a dense formation and then wade into it like a disk into the skittles.

125

'Conops,' he said, 'the catapults are useless until fog and dark-ness lift. You and Glendwyr pick the four best Britons and stand by to serve stink-balls by hand. Let the Britons light the fuses. You and Glendwyr each toss one ball at a time into an enemy's hold, if they come close enough. But no waste, mind! That stuff costs money. Not more than two balls at a time into one ship.'

For a long while after that they lay in silence, rolling leisurely, watching the advancing lights grow pale against the brightening cloudbank to the southward. The big ship drifted very slowly on the changing tide toward the fog that crept toward them from the shore. The first out-reaching wisps of it surrounded them as dawn touched the southerly clouds with gold and turned the edges of the mist to silver. Now they could see four of the Roman ships dis-tinctly. The masthead man reported two more following. Tros bit his nails. The mist was still only in wisps around him. He feared the sun gleaming on the golden serpent might betray his presence too soon.

The four ships in the lead, less than half a mile apart, were armed biremes. According to the masthead man's report, the two-ship convoy trailed a long way in the rear. He must get between the warships and the convoy and engage the biremes one by one, avoiding all collision and yet steering close enough for Conops to lob stink balls into them. Conops and Glendwyr could hardly toss the leaden balls much farther than an oars-length. If he should smash the oars by coming too close, he had plenty of spares ready; but he knew what a panic there would be below decks when the broken oar ends knocked the rowers off the benches. He must avoid that, even at the cost of letting more than half the enemy escape him.

A breath of warm air brought the fog rolling down in clouds at last, and presently Tros heard the warhorns blaring on the Roman ships. The fog moved fast; if it should be one of those narrow, longshore streaks that hug the cost of Britain most days of the year, it might vanish too soon.

'Starboard a little, starboard!' he directed, leaning overside to listen for the horn blare. 'Hold her so.'

Then he took his stand where the drum and cymbal men below the poop could see the wand he held in his right hand. But he made no signal to them until the blare of the nearest horn came from astern, and a Roman, aware of something looming, hailed him through the fog.

Then action, swift and resolute! He signalled to the cymbals, and a crash of brass shook all the oarsmen into life. The water

126

boiled alongside and the ship swung with a lurch as Sigurdsen leaned all his weight against the steering oar, his left foot on the rail and his muscles cracking.

'Stand by all! Ready on the starboard bow there, Conops! Fire when you see them, Orwic!'

He had one bireme by the stern, at any rate. No danger from the dolphin, almost none to the oars if Sigurdsen kept his head. He signalled the cymbals, quickening the oar beat. The man at the masthead yelled incomprehensibly. There was a terror-stricken, flatted chorus from the Roman trumpets, and the bireme loomed up like a ghost.

'Zeus!'

Sigurdsen threw his weight against the helm, or a bank of oars would have gone to splinters. The air twanged as if the devils of the underworld were plucking death's harps, whistled as if death were on the wing – four midship arrow engines – and then Orwic's voice:

'Reload! Lud's blood, what are you waiting for?'

Yells from the bireme, two thuds as the leaden balls struck woodwork, Conops crying, 'Two hits!' and the ghost was gone. Fog, but a glare in the fog and the shouts of men who struggled to extinguish flame but choked in the stench and were forced back by the prodigious heat! Fog, and the blare of horns ahead. Shouts and a thrashing of water where another bireme came about to find out what the matter might be.

'Stop oars!'

The drums and cymbals crashed in sudden unison that checked the oars in mid-swing. Tros let the great ship carry way, and for a minute listened to the Roman oar beats, knowing that his silence would confuse the Romans and that his own man at the masthead, being higher, would see sooner than the Romans could. Astern now, there was a crimson splurge like sunset in the fog, where a bireme burned.

'Right on us! Straight ahead!' The masthead man lapsed into Norse again.

'Beak! Their beak's right into us!' yelled Conops from the bow.

But the Roman helmsman saw the serpent's tongue in air above the bireme's bow and changed course in a panic. The ships struck shoulder on and, in the crash that threw the oarsmen off the benches, none heard the leaden balls thud down the bireme's forward hatch and roll among the rowers. Conops' voice cried:

'Two hits! Back away, master! Back away!'

The arrow engines twanged, and the Romans came back with a

hail of javelins. There was a great splash, for they let the dolphin go and it missed by the width of the roll of both ships as they reeled back from the impact.

Javelins again – *twang, twang*, and shriek of the twelve-arrow flights; a din below decks as the rowers of both ships rioted. The Romans had the better discipline, but there was stenching fire in their hold, whereas Tros's men were only bewildered. Crash of Tros's drums and cymbals signalling for backed oars; the choking, acrid reek of greenish-yellow smoke emerging from the bireme's hatch; response from the oars at last. As the Northmen plied their bows from anywhere on deck, and Orwic's arrow engines, cranking, twanging, screaming, swept the bireme's citadel, the reflection of a crimson glare lit on the serpent's golden tongue. Its agate eyes shone. It appeared to laugh as, curtseying to the swell and the staccato jerk of backed oars, it retired into the fog.

Tros laughed. Two biremes reckoned with! Two crimson splurges in the fog, and only two more ships to find and fight before those Spaniards were his!

But suddenly he swore. The fog was lifting! He could see the shore already, and the burning biremes were in such full view that the crew of the nearest began manning the ballista that was farthest from the flame. An arrow two yards long feathered with burning pitch, hummed overhead, and a second fell short as the backed oars took him out of range.

There were wounded Northmen on the deck, but he had no time to spare for them. In another minute now the hurrying mist would vanish and reveal him to the other biremes and to the ships that carried Spaniards. He ordered:

'Stop!'

And quicker than the echo of the drums and cymbals he was off the poop and down the after hatch, where he stood and roared to the rowers, taking care that laughter, triumph, should beam from his face:

'Good men!' There were half a dozen of them stunned between the benches. 'Two big ships beaten by your steadfastness! When I call for speed, let oars bend! Ye have done well. Now do better!'

In an instant he was on the poop again, his eyes searching the fog's afterguard that still concealed him from four Roman ships.

'Orwic!' he roared, and Orwic's boyish face appeared in the deckhouse door. 'Man the bow catapults! Leave Glendwyr to the arrow engines. Conops! Stand by Orwic!'

Presently, to the sound of grinding, great weights rose between the uprights and the magazine crews rolled the leaden balls into the racks provided. Conops began fitting fuses, soaking them with sulphur and oil of turpentine. Tros ordered Sigurdsen to shake down the great mainsail. He could spare no men for more than that just yet. And as the big sail bellied in the wind the last fog streamers scattered southward, showing all four ships, and him to them.

The apparition of Tros's great vermilion-sided *Liafail*, with three masts and her long-tongued serpent flashing in the sun, struck terror in the Romans. They knew nothing of how dangerously he was under-manned. Two biremes, widely separated from each other and at least two miles away from their crowded convoys, 'bouted helm and ran for it, clapping on all sail to help the oars and striving to get between Tros and the Spaniards.

'Full speed!'

A race began in which Tros was badly handicapped. If he had clapped on more sail he would have had no men to spare to serve the catapults.

Along two legs of a scalene triangle, its apex the slow convoys, Tros and the biremes raced, Tros with the shorter course, but they, with full crews, going nearly two to his one. Around them and about them splashed the stink-balls, as the great weights thumped into the hold, outranging the Roman ballistas easily, but making no hits. Tros ground his teeth at the waste of precious ammunition.

He ordered 'cease fire', ordered the great forward lateen sail sheeted down, thinning out the catapult crews to the point where they were hardly enough to crank the weights, ordered the oar stroke quickened until there was so much splashing that he had to slow it down again. And in spite of all, the biremes gained on him hand-over-hand, until at last, while the leader raced on to tranship the Spaniards from the slower craft and carry them back to Gaul, the other turned and offered fight.

It was the act of a bold captain. No solitary bireme had the slightest chance against that great ship boiling down on him. The terrific speed had tired the Roman's rowers, who had hardly strength enough by now to give force to the iron-shod ram. Tros changed the helm and kept away from him to westward.

'Fire both catapults!'

One missed. The other, laid by Orwic, hurled its lead ball straight against the bireme's citadel, smashing through the woodwork and exploding. Then the Roman captain changed his mind. His ship on fire, he turned in a wide circle and began to race again toward the convoys.

'Try again, Orwic!'

Two more balls whirled on their way, and again one missed, but the second – Conops aimed it – smashed through the bireme's deck, and though it did not burst, the cloud of suffocating smoke increased. The oars collapsed, like the legs of a dying centipede, as the whole crew, marvellously disciplined, went to work to extinguish fire.

'They are mine!' laughed Tros, his eyes fixed on the convoys.

But that other, swifter bireme, lay already beam to beam with the nearest of the transports. They had lowered their spiked gang-plank, and a stream of armed men poured along it to the roof of the bireme's citadel. Before Tros could prevent, both forward catapults went off with a crash and shudder. Two of the leaden stink-balls hit their mark, one into either ship. Orwic, Conops and the whole deck crew went frantic with delight as both exploded. There was an instant blaze too great for Tros's explosive to have caused; one ball had burst into the Roman magazine, where they had stored their own pitch and sulphur, and both ships with their crowd of panic-stricken men were swallowed in a reeking cloud of smoke, shot through with flame.

Tros changed the course to pursue the second convoy. Then he went up forward and took Orwic by the throat.

'Hot-headed horseman!' he swore, forcing him backward against the catapult. 'Those last two shots have cost me tenscore men!'

He shook him, but he could not take the laugh off Orwic's face.

'Look! Lud's teeth, but look!' he exclaimed, and, breaking away from Tros's grip, watched the two locked ships, one mass of flame, sinking.

Tros took no pleasure in the sight. His eye was on one bireme to the northward that had managed to subdue the fire in her hold and was picking up survivors from another bireme nearer shore. The third, a mile this side of them, was losing its fight with the flames.

'Get aft, Orwic!' Then he ordered both the catapults uncranked, and told off men to care for the nine wounded – arrow and javelin wounds, not good to look at and not easy to treat. A Northman screamed and bit the deck beside him as they pulled out a barbed arrow-head and poured hot tar into the wound.

'Conops!' Tros commanded, 'take one stink-ball and stand in the bow. When I lay alongside those Spaniards have the fuse ready, but don't light it until I give the word. If I do, then drop it into their hold to scare them out.'

Again he went down through the hatch to encourage the rowers.

130

Sigurdsen sent a messenger to say they were almost within arrow range of the ship they were pursuing. Then we went up slowly and stood staring over the stern. The capture of the last ship was a foregone certainty. It hardly interested him. It hardly troubled him to see the Romans burn and drown, for they were trouble-hunters with the game reversed on them. But it grieved him to the deep, strong marrow of his being to have lost two hundred and fifty Spaniards.

'Good, spirited, unruly rebels to a man!' he muttered. 'I could have given them their chance. The gods gave me mine, and I let Orwic rob me!'

Sigurdsen nudged him.

'Carry on!' Tros ordered. Then, when they were beam to beam with the slow, helpless ship, he ordered the oars in through the ports and roared to the ship's captain to come about and heave to, setting the example. The man – he was a long-haired Gaul – obeyed. More than two hundred blue-eyed Spaniards, armed with swords, spears, shields, and javelins, crowded the deck.

'Where is your captain?' Tros asked in the Roman tongue. The Gaul laughed dryly.

'They threw him overboard. He did not please them.'

'How so?'

'They are hungry. There was no food.'

'Sigurdsen, lower away the boats!'

When both the boats were in the water Tros gave orders to the Spaniards to throw their weapons into them. A few splashed overside, but presently the boats came back with swords, spears, javelins, shields, and helmets, loaded to the gunwale. Then he ordered a hundred Spaniards brought from ship to ship, which was as many as he dared to have at one time, until he had subdued them properly. Next, he put a small crew of Northmen aboard the Gaulish ship and passed a tow-rope.

'There is one Roman bireme still afloat,' said Orwic, pointing. 'She runs home.'

'Let her! We will have our hands full with these Spaniards. Let the Romans go and tell their tale to Caesar!'

A great Spaniard swaggered up to him.

'Who are you?' he demanded, not exactly insolently. He was curious, and, beyond the ordinary run of mortals, proud.

'I am admiral of Caesar's fleet!' said Tros. 'By right of my appointment I transfer you to my ship. Get forward!'

The Spaniard went to sit and whisper with his friends and watch and wonder.

MEN – MEN – MEN!

In my day I have known eighteen kings, but not one who had enough wisdom to laugh at himself. Caswallon the king came nearest to it. But even he believed his enemies were something other than the goads employed by Destiny to rouse his energy. As a master is, so are his men. I know a people if I know its rulers.

From the log of Tros of Samothrace

It was a long pull back to Vectis, with a favouring wind but one-third of the time, and a heavy, sow-bellied Gaulish freighter in tow. One hundred Spaniards were put to the oars, but they refused work, although they understood oars, were not seasick and, in a blue-eyed opportunist fashion of their own, were not unreasonable.

Tros sent for the man who had first accosted him when captured.

'Who – what are you?' he demanded. The man's muscles stood out like moulded ivory. He smiled with a kind of traditional dignity, as if life were something that his ancestors had borne, and he supposed he too could tolerate it.

'I am Jaun Aksue of Escual-Herria,'* he said in Gaulish. 'There was fighting in my country between us and the Romans. Their proconsul set a trap and caught a thousand of us, of whom he slew one-half. The rest of us he sent to Caesar to help fight Gauls. Caesar armed and drilled us, but we stole his weapons and helped the Gauls in various ways. So Caesar decided to send us to Britain. How are you an admiral of Caesar's fleet and yet attack the Romans?'

'Were you not a Roman soldier and yet helped Gauls?' Tros answered.

'True. I would have helped the Britons, perhaps, or perhaps not. Who knows? We Eskualdenak† are not such fools as Caesar thinks.'

'Then you and I are of one mind,' said Tros. 'It is because I am not such a fool as Caesar thinks that you are my prisoner.'

'We Eskualdenak are not good prisoners. We are worse slaves,' the man answered. 'You have enough slaves on this ship without

*The country of the Basques.
†Basques.

increasing trouble for yourself. What do you propose to do with us, O Admiral?'

Tros, stroking his chin, studied the man.

'Are you these men's leader?'

'In a sense, yes. They elected me to lead them. In all our land all are noblemen. But Caesar's officer degraded me for what he said was insolence. We threw him overboard,' he added casually.

Tros did not propose to cut in halves another opportunity by having to use force where argument would better serve. But he needed the right argument.

'Will you go home?' he asked suddenly.

'Not we! The Roman proconsul, Livius, would crucify us unless we should take to the mountains. We are a sea-faring folk. We hunt whales. But Livius burned our ships.'

'Will you settle in Britain?'

'Who knows? You have a marvel of a ship. We might sail with you if you should make it worth while.'

'Make it worth my while!' Tros answered. 'Of what value is your word?'

The man looked straight into Tros's eyes.

'To you? Why, just the value that you set on it. I never supposed it could have a market price. No more did Livius the Roman, or he would have taxed it a tenth. How should a man sell his word?'

Tros grinned. He liked him.

'Jaun,' he said – and Jaun meant nobleman, a title that all men of that race prefixed to their names; but Tros did not know that, and the word was easy to remember – 'I am the master of this ship. I am obeyed. And I am minded that you Eskualdenak will make a good crew. But I must have your word on it.'

'Whither will you sail?' the man asked.

'Whither I will.'

'How much will you pay us?'

'As much as I see fit, and for the present, nothing except food and clothing. My men prosper as I prosper, sweat and starve too as I sweat and starve, save that I take the master's end of it and sweat the hardest.'

'Are you an equal among equals?'

'By Zeus, no! I am master of this ship!'

'I like you,' said Jaun Aksue. He spoke with dignity, as if he had conferred a boon that were his to refuse, were he minded. 'I will speak about this to my friends. If we agree to serve you, we will serve. You will not sell us to the Romans?'

'I will sooner die,' Tros answered. 'But mark this, and remember it: I will also rather die than not be master of my ship. It is I who confer favours, and the price is full obedience.'

'I will speak to them of that.' Jaun Aksue went down into the hold.

It was an hour before he returned on deck, and then, with Tros's permission, went swarming along the tow-rope, taking his ducking in the bight and climbing on to the Gaulish vessel with a nimbleness that forced unwilling praise from Conops, for Conops disliked to believe that there were seamen half as handy as himself. At the end of another hour he returned in the same way, swung himself up over the poop and stood dripping before Tros.

'We accept,' he said simply. There and then Tros dubbed him Jaun and gave him the rank of a lieutenant under Sigurdsen.

They dropped anchor under the lee of chalk cliffs between the Isle of Vectis and the mainland. All three banks of oars on either side, Britons and Spaniards alternating, had been in full use for a day, and there was a new energy, a new, clean finish, a new majesty to the measured swing and a deep-sea certainty about the plunge of the vermilion blades that made Tros's heart thump.

Orwic espied Caswallon first. He lowered a boat, taking his own four men and some of Tros's slaves, hurrying to meet the clumsy barge that laboured out of harbour under sail and sweeps. Orwic was shouting the news before boat and barge met, so Fflur and Caswallon knew most of it already when they both embraced Tros on the *Liafail's* high poop, Fflur's eyes frankly wet, Caswallon praising the great ship to hide his own emotion.

'Men!' said Tros. 'I have men!'

'Aye, and I peace! Rhys is dead. I slew him! Came Gwenhwyfar, hot-horsed, blurting out the whole of Rhys's plot. Fflur coaxed me to spare the woman, but I slew Rhys. Some said to catch and torture him, but Rhys was of the council. I would almost as soon torture my own son. I sent him warning, and he understood. He took to the forest with twenty men, hoping to reach Gaul, but when I overtook him his men threw down their arms. Rhys, he drew bow but missed me by that much.'

Caswallon measured off the third part of his thumbnail, and Fflur shuddered.

'My arrow went into his heart,' he added, 'so he died in fair fight, and the council was not dishonoured. I found letters on him, written by Caesar's secretary. He and Caesar had it all planned, but I think Caesar will not invade us now Rhys is dead.'

Tros did not answer for the moment. Fflur saw Britomaris standing by the deckhouse door, bow and arrows in his hand as if to advertise the fact that he had fought against the Romans. She drew Caswallon's attention. Eyebrows raised, he questioned Tros.

'A poor fool,' Tros said. 'His wife will tame him. I tamed Gwenhwyfar.'

Caswallon laughed.

'She is as tame as the wind! But we endure the wind. I think you have tamed Caesar. What is it? Four ships sunk?'

'Three. One escaped. Caesar will learn whom he may thank. What of Rhys's men whom I hold hostage?'

'All Rhys's property is mine. I give them to you. Hah! How Caesar will be chewing flints in Gaul! Three biremes and – '

Tros interrupted.

'Caswallon, mend your fences! For love of you and Britain I will go to Rome. I will do my utmost to break Caesar's wheel. If I fail, then, mark you, Caesar will invade Britain as surely as we see each other!'

'We must pray more to the gods,' said Fflur.

'The gods,' he said, 'make opportunities. Prayer consists in seizing opportunities. That is how Caesar prays! I also. I prayed for Spaniards! I have them. Pray you for a stout heart, wisdom, and the men, men, men!'

'PLUTO! SHALL I SET FORTH FULL OF
DREADS AND QUESTIONS?'

Whence I came, I know. Whither I go, I know not. Here I am. I know not why these things are, nor what they shall be. But I discover that if I choose not, I am chosen; and I love the valiance of choosing rather than the vain, unvaliant obedience to ease, which I perceive is slavery.

Unvaliant scud I am not, blown on the gales of circumstance. Valiance, I think, shall not die, though the storm may wreck me and the waves drown.

What is valiance? I know not. But I love it, and it loves me. Let us see whither valiance leads.

From the log of Tros of Samothrace

Farewell to Caswallon was an event. There was something mystic in the air off Vectis. The cry of the gulls that circled around the great ship was the music of far horizons. Tros felt himself an agent of destiny. He wore his purple cloak for the occasion, and his sword in its vermilion scabbard hung from a belt set with jewels. His eyes glowed beneath the gold band that encircled his forehead. The crushing obstinacy of his jaw and chin, the oak-strength of his neck and the masterful lines of mouth and nostril were exposed for whoso would to read. One would oppose him at one's own risk.

'We will see,' he remarked, and the three words told his character.

A druid leaned forward from a seat beside the cabin door, mildly rebuking:

'You will see too much. You are like a bull that breaks the fences. Because you have been told the world is round – '

Tros interrupted. He laughed.

'I will prove it. I will sail around it.'

'At your own risk!' the druid answered. 'We have trusted you. In Britain you have built your ship with Britons' aid, of British oak and sheathed with British tin. Her sails and her ropes are of British flax. Your slaves, more than half of her crew, are all Britons whom the Lord Caswallon gave to you.'

'The Lord Tros earned them,' said Caswallon, gesturing with a blue-stained, white, enormous hand.

Tros smiled, and their eyes met. Those two understood each other far better than either of them understood the druid.

'We gave you pearls out of our treasure,' said the druid. 'Those were for a purpose.'

'Aye,' Tros answered, leaning back against the table, squeezing the edge of it in both hands until knuckles and muscles stood out in knots. A sort of thrifty look was in his eyes now. 'A man cannot keep such a ship as mine on nothing. Wind blows us, but the men eat meat. There is more wear and tear to pay for than a landsman thinks. I will make a profit, but I will not forget to serve you in the making.'

'Not if you turn aside to prove what you have no business to know,' the druid answered. 'Whether the world is round or flat – and, mark you, on that I am silent – your friends, to whom you are beholden, are in peril.'

Caswallon snorted like a warhorse, but Fflur laid a jewelled hand on him and, with her dark-grey eyes, begged silence.

'When I forget my friends, may all the gods forget me,' Tros said solemnly, frowning, not liking that his promise should be called in question. 'I itch, I ache, I yearn to prove the world is round. But I know better than to fare forth on that quest and leave promises unkept behind me. Not while Caesar is free to invade Britain will I reckon myself free to spread sail straight toward the setting sun. In Rome, as I have told you half a hundred times, are Caesar's enemies, his friends and all the riff-raff who will take whichever side is uppermost. One way or another I will break the spokes of Caesar's wheel before I set forth on my own adventure. If I fail in Rome, I will come back to Britain and help you.'

Fflur shook her head.

'You will never return,' she remarked. 'That is why I wish Orwic were not sailing with you.'

Orwic laughed. 'Tros is like the north-east wind. I love him. I will go around the world with him,' he said. 'But I wish he had horses instead of a ship!'

He took up the peaked iron helmet he had laid on the table, turned it bottom upward and began to rock it like a boat.

'However, I overcame the vomiting last voyage when we took the Spaniards. I am a sailor.'

Jaun Aksue shook his head:

'Wait until you have seen the sea! All you have played on yet is this streak of water between Gaul and Britain.'

The druid, watching opportunity, resumed the thread of his remarks, while Aksue and Orwic eyed each other, mutually critical.

'Lord Tros, how will you reach Rome? Ostia lies leagues from Rome. You cannot sail this ship up the Tiber, which is the Roman river. We druids are informed concerning such things.'

'Yes, and you know the world is round!' Tros retorted, grinning at him.

But the druid held to his point.

'How will you go to Rome? Will you dare to leave your ship at Ostia? What is to prevent the Romans from seizing your ship? They will charge you with piracy. Your father held a Roman licence to sail anywhere he pleased; yet how many times have you told us that Caesar charged him with piracy and flogged the crew to death simply because he disapproved of Caesar's policy?'

'Zeus!' Tros exploded, spreading his shoulders and kicking his scabbard. 'I cross bridges when I reach them.'

'There is a bridge to Rome,' the druid answered. 'It is Gades. Go first of all to Gades.'

'I might,' Tros answered. 'I have a friend in Gades who owes me money. The place is a Roman port, but the gods approve a man who seizes danger by the snout.'

'Now listen,' said the druid, 'for you sail soon, and I would not delay you. You are a bold man and a cunning. Danger is only a challenge to your will. But there will be dangers to the left and to the right, before and behind.'

'Pluto! Shall I set forth full of dreads and questions? Had I listened to the yawpings of disaster's friends I should never have set foot in Britain! I should never have sunk Caesar's fleet, never have built my own ship, never have gathered a crew, never have found the stuff to make the hot stink for my catapults! Do you bid me go forth full of fear?'

'Nay, but I bid you beware of risks.'

Tros's amber eyes blazed proudly.

'I am the master of the biggest ship that ever sailed these seas! "Beware of risks!" saith the Lord Druid. Half a thousand souls and all my fortune at the risk of wind and tide, reefs, shoals, gales on the Atlantic, every Roman on the seas my enemy, myself proscribed, three talents on my head, pirates, water and provisions to obtain in harbours that swarm with Caesar's friends – "Be cautious!" saith the Lord Druid!'

'Be bold, Lord Tros!' said Fflur, her grey eyes watching his. But the druid signed to her not to interfere.

'Trust Tros,' laughed Orwic. 'I tell you he is bolder than the north-east wind!'

138

Tros struck a gong and glanced at the three water clocks. A Northman appeared in the doorway.

'Tide?' said Tros.

'Still making. Nearly at the ebb, my lord.'

'Order the blankets stowed below. Wind?'

'Light breeze from the eastward.'

'Mist?'

'All clear, my lord. Sven at the masthead says he can see the coast of Gaul.'

'There,' said Tros, 'is the answer of the gods to all your doubts! A fair wind!'

He began to pace the cabin floor, his hands behind him, kicking at his scabbard as he turned. The druid watched him, alert for an opening into which to drive an admonition. Tros offered him none. The druid had to resume the subject uninvited.

'Lord Tros, those Eskualdenak of yours are Caesar's men. If they should be caught they would be crucified – and you along with them. Yet unless you go to Gades first, it is impossible for you to go to Ostia and Rome. I tell you, in the midst of danger you shall find the keys of safety. But beware of black arts and of violence. There are some who seem untrustworthy whom you may safely trust, and some who may be bought and some not. We druids have read the stars.'

'Rot me all riddles!' Tros answered irritably, but the druid ignored the remark.

'Lord Tros, I could direct you to a man in Gades who would give you information. But I see you are not open-minded. None the less, you are a brave man and your heart is true to friendship, so I will do what may be done for you.'

Tros bowed. He thought more of a druid's blessing than of his material advice. To his mind the druids had lost contact between spiritual thought and the action that a man must take with two feet on the ground.

'I go,' he said, turning to Caswallon, for he felt the ship's changed motion as the anchor-cable slackened and the wind made her dance a little on the ebb.

The druid, Caswallon and Fflur stood up to take their leave of him, and Fflur's grey eyes were moist. Caswallon's face, normally good-humoured and amused, wore a mask of stolidness to hide emotion that he scorned as womanly. Orwic looked bored, since that was his invariable refuge from the spurs of sentiment.

'I go,' Tros repeated, and stood straight before them all, the light through the door on his face, and his lion's eyes glowing against it with the light that blazed up from within. He was minded they should have a bold friend and a brave sight to remember in the dark days coming, when their country should await invasion, and himself afar off. He was minded they should not believe it possible he would neglect to serve them to the last breath and the last ounce of his energy.

'It is thanks to you,' he said, 'that I have my ship that was my heart's desire, and I will not forget you. It may be I will never come again. I am no druid, and I cannot see, like Fflur, with the eyes of destiny. But know ye this: I am a friend in need as in prosperity. Ye may depend on me to worry Caesar's rear until he turns away from Britain. But be ready for invasion, because Caesar certainly intends to try a second time.

'If he should invade, resist him to the last ditch, to the last fence, to the last yard of your realm. And though they tell you I am dead or have betrayed you – for Caesar's favourite weapon is false rumour – know that I persist until the end in trying all means to weaken Caesar from the rear. All means I will try. Truth I will tell to those who will believe it. I will lie, and craftily, to them who deal in lies. Fairly I will deal with honest men. So the gods shall aid me. But believe ye in your own star as well as in my friendship.'

'Goodbye!' Fflur said, choking, and embraced him.

Orwic turned away and strode out through the open door. He hated scenes. His eyes were wet, which would not do at all. He was a British gentleman. Caswallon, muttering 'Lud's blood!' swung Tros toward him by the arms and smote him on the breast a time or two.

'Tros, Tros!' he said, forcing a grin. 'I would rather you would stay here and share Lud's luck with us! It grieves me that you go.'

'Friendship begets grief!' Tros answered, patting the tall, fair-haired chief between the shoulder-blades. 'Grief eats courage, so beware of it. Caswallon, my friend, you and I were not born to mope like vultures over vain regrets. Friendship is a fire that tests both parties to it, so let you and me stand firmer the more circumstances strain. It heartens me to know that you and Fflur have called me friend. I go forth proud of it!'

'Go then!' Caswallon answered, making his voice gruff lest it should tremble. 'Lud's luck go with you! And know this: Come what may – come rumour, and though all the world and Caesar swear you have played us false, we will believe in you!'

'Tide!' That was Sigurdsen's voice from the poop. 'Tide and a fair wind!'

There came a whistle in between decks, where the captains of

140

the oar-banks piped all rowers to the benches; then a clatter as the oar-blades rattled on the ports.

'Haul short!' Sigurdsen again. And then a sing-song and a clanking at the capstan.

Tros led the way on deck. Extravagantly he had ordered the purple sails bent for the occasion. His eyes went aloft to where the Northmen lay on the yards to shake them loose. He turned his back on Orwic, because Fflur wept on the young man's shoulder, and he knew what agonies of shame and nervousness that scene imposed on a British aristocrat. Orwic's funny little peaked helmet had been pushed over one eye, and he was biting his moustache. Caswallon laughed, which brought a curse to Orwic's lips, but Tros leaned overside and shouted at the crew of fishermen who were bringing alongside the barge on which the druid, Caswallon and Fflur were to go ashore.

'Easy! Easy, you lubbers! If you scrape my paint – out fenders there!' He had spent a goodly percentage of Caesar's gold on sulphur and quicksilver to make the ship's sides splendid with vermilion.

There had to be more embracing before Fflur went overside. The British had a sort of ritual of parting. It broke all restraint. But Tros, for the sake of the crew, preserved his air of grandeur.

He stood the whole deck crew at quarters and saluted with a burst of trumpets and a roll of drums as Fflur and Caswallon went down the ladder. Then he turned to face the druid, for the druid waited.

There came a silence on deck and aloft. The druid, with his eyes on Tros, drew out the golden sickle from his girdle. He was mild-eyed, but the eyes were bright with fasting and having contemplated stars and Mysteries.

'In the midst of danger thou shalt find the keys of safety,' he repeated. 'Win Rome in Gades!'

Then the sickle, flashing in the sunlight, moved in mystic circles over Tros's head, severing whatever threads of hidden influence might bind him to the sources of disaster. Upturned, it received, as does the new moon, affluence and wisdom; reversed, it outpoured blessings on his head. Point first, it touched his breast above the heart, invoking honesty and courage; presently it passed in ritual of weaving movements before eyes, ears, nose, lips, hands and feet, arousing all resourcefulness, then tapped each shoulder to confer the final blessing. Then the druid spoke:

'Offspring of Earth, Air, Fire, Water and the Nameless, go forth accoutred. As a sun's ray, go thou forth! A light amid the

141

darkness! A land among the waters! A friend among the friendless, and a serpent*! Be a strength amid the weakness! Be a man amid the elements! Whereso thy foot shall tread, be justice done! Whatso thy tongue shall speak, be truth unveiled! Be strong! Be of the gods who give and guide and not of them who snare and take away! That voice within thee, judge thee! Be thy hand the servant of thy soul!'

Blessing ship and crew with arms upraised, lips moving to the said-to-be-forgotten Word, the druid turned and went, all keeping silence, until, like some white-haired pilot of the years, he had descended to the waiting barge.

'Up anchor!' Tros roared. Then, as the clanking capstan brought the cable in, 'Make sail there! Sheet her home!'

The purple sails spread fluttering and bellied as the ship swung slowly on the tide before the light breeze. On the poop Tros raised his baton. Drums and cymbals crashed. The oars went out in three long banks on either side. Cymbals for the 'ready' and then crash of brass and alternating drum-beat as the water boiled alongside and the great ship leaped ahead, her serpent's tongue a-flicker in the sun.

'I am a man! I live! I laugh!' Tros told himself as he eyed those purple sails and turned to wave his hand toward the barge that danced amid the gulls along the white wake astern.

*The symbol of wisdom.

OFF GADES*

Sent I a fool on my errand? It was I who sent him. Counted I not on his folly? That is my fault. Though he suffer for it, it was I who sent him. It is I who pay, unless I counted on his folly to decoy an adversary, who might have been cautious unless he perceived he had a fool to deal with.

From the log of Tros of Samothrace

How to put into a port controlled by Romans, with part of his crew composed of two hundred and fifty deserters from Caesar's army, and without falling foul of Caesar's letters of proscription, was a problem that Tros left to the gods to clear up for him, although he already had a hint of the solution in his mind. Meanwhile, there was work a-plenty – head winds and off-shore winds, flat calms with a heavy ground-swell that made the bucking rowers grunt, and squally weather in which whales played all around the ship, nearly causing a mutiny because he would not let Jaun Aksue and his Eskauldenak turn aside to hunt them.

'Thus we kill whales. With a spear we slay them. It is easy. We will slay two. You may tow them into Gades, making haste because the sharks will follow, eating at their undersides. The dead whales float, I promise you, and they are worth much money. Romans buy the meat; the traders buy the bone; the Spaniards buy the skin for sandals, shields, mule-harness – '

'Let live,' Tros answered. 'I hunt bigger fish.'

'Aye, but you pay us nothing. Give us a chance to turn the whale meat into money, that we may drink in Gades. I tell you, Lord Tros, we haven't tasted red wine since the sour, thin stuff that Caesar fed to us. We Eskualdenak are noblemen, who like to get drunk now and then.'

But one of the things that Tros had learned in many foreign ports was the difference between a crew mad drunk on its own earned money, and the same crew equally drunk on its master's bounty.

'You shall drink at my expense in Gades,' he remarked, and the tawny-haired soldier of fortune swaggered forward where he discussed with his companions the pros and cons of taking the

*The modern Cadiz.

143

ship away from Tros and hunting whales until she was full of the bone and blubber.

But for three days and three nights waves, tide, current and the wind fought Tros for the mastery. No sight of sun, no stars nor moon, nothing to gauge direction by except the shrieking wind and –nowandthenwhenhedaredit–thunderofthesurfagainsthighcliffs.

But Tros only approached the lee shore twice to find a headland that he recognized, and that was after he had left the dreaded rocks and isles of Finis Terrae* far astern.

Twice – yet he made his landfall. He hove the ship to within sight of Gades Bay in the late afternoon of the eleventh day out from Vectis, sending three men to the mastheads to keep watch for Roman ships. He covered the serpent's head with 'paulin lest the setting sun should glitter on its gold-leaf and attract attention. His ship was notched against the western sky, but her vermilion topsides merged into the sunset splurge, and it was possible her masts might not be seen if none was actually watching for them.

Seated at the table in the cabin, he slipped a piece of parchment from a roll, mixed gum with sepia from cuttlefish, chewed the point of a pen to his liking, and sent for Orwic.

'Lud love me, Tros, but the land smells good!' said Orwic, making himself easy on Tros's bunk.

'Can you speak the Roman tongue?' Tros asked him.

'You know I can't. When I was a boy I learned a few words from a Roman trader who was cast up on the beach. He was killed soon afterwards for taking liberties with women. Even in the battle on the beach last year I couldn't remember a word of it. I wanted to yell the wrong commands to Caesar's men and confuse them until our chariots could ride them down and – '

Tros interrupted, leaning forward with an elbow on the table.

'Gaulish? Can you speak that with a Gaulish accent?'

'Near enough. You know as well as I do that we Britons speak the same tongue as the Gauls. What ails you, Tros? Your eyes look like a madman's. Are you shipsick?'

'Do you dare' – his voice was hoarse with the strain of bellowing his orders to the crew and from the long vigil through the storm – 'do you dare to go ashore tonight, with Conops to guide you, to the house of a friend of mine?'

Orwic barked delightedly.

'Friend Tros, I would swim to Gades just for the feel of good earth!'

'This is a worse risk than a swim. Fail – There is a low hill

*The modern Finisterre and the Isle of Ushant.

behind Gades, outside the city wall, where cross-roads meet. The hill bristles with dead trees that bear ill-smelling fruit. The Romans flog a man before they crucify him, flog him until his intestines hang and – '

'Rot me talk of failure!' Orwic answered. 'Tell me what shall be if I succeed.'

'Tchutt! I must go myself, I need a cautious man.'

'Lud's belly! Tros, you shall not! Listen! Who has better right than I to run a risk for my friends in Britain?'

Orwic leaned across the table. His face flushed. He looked as handsome as Apollo.

'Some man,' Tros said, 'who will take care. No hothead can succeed in this adventure.'

'Tros, I blow cold! I am as crafty as a fox! I forswear horse-manship! I never rode a horse! I never drove a chariot! I am a tortoise! Burn me this great creaking lumber-wain on a tin-bellied boat, and set me on dry land! I am a paragon of caution! Dumb I am, a lurker in shadows, a rap-a-door-and-run-man! Tros, there is none aboard this ship who can do half as well!'

Tros knew it, but he kept the knowledge to himself and let Orwic do all the persuading.

'I need a modest man. The gods love modesty,' he said with the air of a money-lender refusing to do business.

'I am modesty!' said Orwic.

'You!' Tros leaned back in his oaken chair and laughed. 'Modest? Three nights gone I heard you praying that the storm might cease, instead of praising the sea's splendour and returning thanks for guts enough to ride it out!'

'It was the Northmen prayed,' said Orwic.

'Aye. But who bade them? Who paid them? Who gave Skram, the skald,* a gold piece for his pains? I saw you.'

'Tros, you see too much. Our British gods are of field and river. These Northmen are sailors and their gods are – '

'Cripples!' Tros exploded. 'Rot me such a god as likes to see good seamen on their knees! There are gods in Gades, Orwick, but they'll go their own gait. It's for the man who does my work tonight to suit their whimsies, not they his.'

'Well, I will be whimsical,' said Orwic. 'The gods shall like me very well.'

He stooped and scooped up sand out of the box that was kept

---

*A kind of minstrel with peculiar privileges. Like the old-time Scottish Highlanders, who never went on foray without their piper, the Northmen always took their skald on an adventure oversea.

in readiness to put out fire, and heaped six handfuls of the wet stuff on the table. Then he smoothed it out.

'So, draw me Gades. Show me the house I must find.'

'Conops knows the house,' said Tros, but he drew, none the less, with his forefinger, beginning with a circle for the city wall, then marking the five gates and making dots to represent the forum, the Temple of Venus and the gladiators' barracks, with a veritable maze of streets between. 'This is the governor's house. Avoid it as you would death! Now, from the western gate due eastward, do you see? Then this way, to the right, to a point about midway along the street. Turn you back to the west, and forward. The house of Simon the Jew stands nearly at the apex of a triangle that has for base the street between the forum and the gladiators' school.

'It is a house built half of timber, half of mud, smeared with a yellow plaster that will make it look like stone by night. Simon is a rich Jew with the privilege of armed slaves – quite a few of them. There will be dozens of dogs in the street, and the Gades dogs are bad, I warn you. There used to hang a lantern on a chain from the front of Simon's house to the wall opposite. The citizenry have used that chain a time or two to hang night prowlers. None can approach the house unseen because the lamp has several wicks and casts a bright light.'

'I will walk up brazenly,' said Orwic.

'And you will find the brassiest-faced Jews in Europe ready for you! They live in the narrow streets near by, and look to Simon to protect them with his influence. They'll swarm out with stones in their hands at the first bleat from Simon's slaves. But there's worse than they. The city is patrolled by armed slaves who belong to the municipium.* The place is ten times better policed than Rome, and there's a law against being out at night without being able to prove lawful business. It is no light task I set you. I think I had better leave you here and go myself.'

'Tros, I tell you I go! I will be safe enough in a Roman costume. They will take me for some gallant pursuing a love affair.'

'In the Jews' quarter? I think not,' said Tros. 'A man may buy a Jewess in the open market almost anywhere where slaves are sold, but no man in his senses goes philandering near a ghetto after dark! The Jews can fight! And if you beat on Simon's door, his slaves will rush out and cudgel you.'

'Conops shall beat the door,' said Orwic. 'While the slaves beat Conops, I will slip into the house.'

---

*The local government. Gades was not yet, in fact, a municipium. Local officials were appointed and removed at pleasure by the Roman governor.

'Cockerel! I wouldn't lose Conops for his weight in money!'

'Very well. I can wait until dawn ourside the house and – '

'No. By morning Simon must have visited my ship. Now listen! Try to forget you are Caswallon's nephew and a prince of Britain. Only remember you are charged with secret business. If you try to show how smart you are, the gods will raise a wall of circumstance around you that will test your wits to the extremity. Go modestly, and they will modify the odds. Bear that in mind. Now muck me this sand away – so. To the floor with it. Let that Jaun Spaniard clean it up. The rascal rots with laziness. Now I will write the letter.'

He spoke as one who contemplated making magic, and for a while, for the sake of exercising Orwic's patience, he sat listening to the murmur of the short waves overside. Then he wrote swiftly, using Greek, pausing line by line to read aloud and construe it to Orwic:

Tros, the Samothracian, to Simon, son of Tobias, the Jew of Alexandria, in Gades, greeting.

Be the bearer as a son to you. He is Orwic, son of Orwic, a prince of Britain, nephew to the king who rules the Trinobantes and the Cantii, my true friend. Speak him freely.

Knowing I have done you service in the past, whereby we both made profit, and aware you are a man of true heart and long memory, whose zeal for great enterprises is in no wise dulled by the success that has attended many efforts in the past, I urge that you should come to me with all speed, secretly, tonight, for conference concerning matters that may profit both of us.

Lord Orwic will attend you and convey you by the shortest way in safety to my ship.

This is my true word. So fail not.

Tros of Samothrace.

He sanded the letter and passed it to Orwic, who frowned at the thick Greek characters.

'Will he understand you need help? Why not tell him so?' Orwic objected.

'Because I know him!' Tros answered. 'If he thought I needed help, he wouldn't come until he had driven a hard bargain first by daylight. But if he thinks there is a stroke of business I can put his way he will come in a hurry to learn the details of it.'

'Better not tell him anything about your plans then?'

'Tell him all you know of them!' Tros answered dryly, and left the cabin to watch provisions being weighed out to the galley for the evening meal.

VISITORS

Why are they servants, and I master? Not being God, I know not. But I am the master. This is my ship.

They, when they see a danger, fear it, whereas I fear only not to see it.

They, when they see a danger, magnify it and become a danger to themselves. They lend it their wits. I lend not mine to be used against me.

From the log of Tros of Samothrace

The minute the sun dipped below the skyline Tros ordered 'Out oars!' and taking full advantage of the tide, dropped anchor in pitch darkness almost within hail of a spit of land that jutted into the mouth of Gades Bay. The moisture-laden Virazon, the sea breeze that blows all night long between spring and autumn, had not yet broken the dead calm. There was a stench of rotting seaweed from the shore, a croon of short waves on a sandy beach and, except that, silence.

There was no moon yet, but the starlight shone with milky whiteness that revealed the ghost-white city several miles away, rising tier on tier on a peninsula that was almost an island. About half a mile from where he had anchored a beacon light flared in an iron basket, and in the distance, to the northward of the city, was a parellelogram of crimson fires that marked the outline of a Roman camp.

By lantern-light in the after-deckhouse, with the ports well shrouded, Tros watched Conops get into the costume of a Greek slave.

'Now, remember to act slavish!' he instructed. 'Little man, much rests on you this night! To the Lord Orwic be fussily obsequious. See that he treads in no ordure near the gate. Watch that none touches him. Carry a stick to drive the dogs away from him, and use it at the least excuse. Talk Greek to him,* no matter that he doesn't understand. To the gate custodians be insolent. If they ask your master's name and business, tell them they may have it and a whipping in the bargain tomorrow morning for their impudence. In a pinch, use Simon's name, but not if you can help it, because if they learn that you are visiting Simon it might

*There was a large Greek colony in Gades, where the language was as much in use as any other at that time.

occur to them to extort a bribe from Simon by holding you both in the guardhouse until he comes.'

'Trust me, master! I know Gades. There is a place outside the city wall where dancing girls are kept before they ship them for the Asia trade. Too bad we haven't scent of jasmine to make our clothes smell of an afternoon's adventure! Never mind. I'll manage it.'

Then Orwic came, jingling a purse of gold and silver coins that Tros had given him, bending to admire the fashion of a Roman pallium and tunic, loot from Caesar's bireme.

'Walk not like a horseman!' Tros protested. 'A Roman noble walks with a stride that measures out the leagues. Come, try it on deck.'

Tros strode for him. Orwic imitated. Conops ran in front, pretending to drive dogs away and pointing to guide his feet from pools of filth.

'Go. Go now with the gods in mind,' said Tros, and turned to give orders to Sigurdsen, who was to command the longboat.

'You, who were a king, so do, that if others had obeyed you formerly as you obey me now, you would be a king this day! Your weapons are for a last resort. Be silent, crafty, cunning, cautious' – he emphasized each word with his fist on the Northman's breast – 'run rather than resist. If questioned, make no answer. Put one man ashore to follow the Lord Orwic and Conops as far as the city gate. Let him bring word to you when they have passed in. Come back to the ship with the information, taking care to keep the oars well muffled.'

Then one last word to Orwic.

'Cover your long hair with your pallium. One gold piece to the captain of the gate-guard. One piece of silver to each of the others. No more, or you'll merely whet their appetites. Lud's luck!'

The muffled oar-beats thumped away into the dark, and silence fell. The whole crew was aware of mysteries impending. Aloft, the Northmen and some of the Eskualdenak leaned out of the rigging, watching the longboat until its shape was lost in the gloom. There began then a murmur of talking between decks, where the weary rowers sprawled. Jaun Aksue trespassed on the poop without asking permission, and leaned over the rail beside Tros confidently, as if they two were equals.

'Secrecy!' he remarked, grinning. 'My men crave wine and shore leave. We have been eleven days at sea. The Gades girls are famous, and the red wine is the best in all this land.'

149

Tros suppressed his instinct to knock the man down. Friction might ruin the vague plan he had in mind.

'If you're caught in Gades, you'll be crucified,' he answered.

'Maybe. But you have friends ashore, or you wouldn't be here,' said Aksue. 'You can give us shore leave. You can say we're your slaves. We'll act the part, then nobody can interfere with us. We needn't go into the city. There are taverns outside the wall and lots of women. Promise us a day ashore and some money to spend, and we'll keep as quiet as mice till morning. Otherwise, I won't answer for what my men will do.'

Tros found it easy enough now to tolerate the impudence. That those proud Eskualdenak were willing to act the part of slaves solved more than half of the problem that had racked his brain for days and nights on end. He nodded.

'You shall go ashore.'

'And money?'

'I will arrange it. Go and warn your men that if there's any noise tonight, no shore leave!'

For an hour he paced the poop anxiously. There might be Roman guard-ships on the prowl, and he had given hostages to Fortune. He could not desert Orwic and Conops.

At the end of an hour he heard splashing, and thought it was dolphins or porpoises. Then, staring into the darkness, he was nearly sure he saw the outline of a boat.

'Sigurdsen!' he shouted. No answer. It was much too soon to expect Sigurdsen in the longboat.

But the splashing continued. Presently he saw two human heads within a few feet of the ship's side. A voice that he thought was a woman's cried out to him in Greek to throw a rope. He himself went and lowered the rope-ladder, ordering the deck-watch to the other bulwark. A man and a woman climbed up like wet shadows, and stood dripping in the dark in front of him. The woman wore nothing but a Greek chlamys, with the wreck of a wreath of flowers tangled in her wet hair; the man had on a Roman tunic, that clung and revealed a lithe, athletic figure. They were nearly of a size. In the dark they looked like children up to mischief.

'Tros!' said the woman. Tros nearly jumped out of his skin.

Had he been recognized before he even set foot in Gades?

Gesturing with a jerk of the head and arm, he led the way toward the cabin, where he might learn the worst without the deck-watch hearing it.

At the door he paused and let them pass in ahead of him. For a minute he stood, making sure that the deck-watch were not

150

near enough for eavesdropping, wondering how many of them had seen the swimmers come aboard. When he entered the cabin the girl had already clothed herself in his own best purple cloak, that had been hanging on the rail between the bunk and the bulkhead.

'Tros!' she said. 'Tros of Samothrace!' She laughed at him, seeming no worse for her swim, although the man was squatting on the floor and looked exhausted. She curtsied with a rhythm of bare legs. There was no fear in her eyes, nor even challenge, but a confidence expressed in laughter and a gesture of disarming comradeship.

'Lord Tros,' she began again.

'I am not Tros,' he answered sullenly.

Of all the difficulties in the world he dreaded most a complication with women.

'Oh yes, you are!' she answered. 'Horatius Verres saw your ship at sunset notched against the sky. He recognized it instantly. He was in hiding on the roof of Pkauchios's *ergastulum*.* He is a runaway from Gaul. I am Chloe the dancer, Pkauchios's slave. I am the favourite of Gades,' she added, as if she were not particularly proud of it but simply stating fact.

'What do you want?' Tros asked sullenly. That the girl's ivory-white skin shone golden in the whale-oil lantern-light, and that her face was like a cameo against the shadow, only deepened his mistrust. He retired two paces from her and stood with his back against the door.

'Only what I can get!' she answered, and sat on Tros's bunk, arranging his pillows behind her, covering her bare knees with his blanket. 'I could tell Balbus the governor who you are, but I won't if you will bargain fairly.'

Tros glanced at the man on the floor, who was slapping his head to get the water from his ears.

'As prisoners – ' he suggested.

Chloe interrupted, laughing.

'I am a slave who owns slaves. My women know where I am. I have two men-slaves waiting on the beach.'

'Who is this fellow?' Tros asked.

'I told you, Horatius Verres. He had a little difficulty with the Romans and had to run away from Gaul. If what he said is true, he lost his heart to a girl whom Caesar coveted – some young matron, I suppose, or Caesar wouldn't have looked twice at her. Someone, to earn Caesar's favour, accused poor Horatius Verres

*A private prison kept for the punishment of slaves.

151

of accepting bribes, to give Caesar an excuse to send him to Rome in fetters and keep the woman for himself. She found out the plot in time and warned him. So he slew the informer and tried to escape to Britain in one of four biremes that Caesar was sending, along with some Eskualdenak, to invade that country.

'Somebody' – she looked merrily at Tros – 'attacked those biremes, destroyed three of them and captured a lot of Eskualdenak. The fourth bireme escaped to Gaul with Horatius Verres still on board, but he swam away before they reached port and escaped a second time overland. He reached Gades in a dreadful state, but I could see he was a pretty boy under all the rags and whiskers, so I hid him and saved him from Balbus's labour gang, because he had told me his real name and an interesting story. I hid him on the roof of my master's *ergastulum*. Later, when he was rested, I sent him to Simon the Jew, thinking Simon might do something for him, because Simon owes me money and can't pay.'

'Can't pay? You say Simon can't pay what he owes you?'

She nodded.

'You know Simon? He has lent all his money to Caesar and Balbus.'

'Go on,' said Tros, his fingers clutching at his sword-hilt.

He could not have asked a greater favour from the gods than that Simon should be short of money at the moment; but he was afraid of this woman, and still more afraid lest she should realize it.

'Simon was shocked and virtuous,' she continued. 'He would have informed Balbus if I hadn't reminded him of a few little things I know about himself. He agreed to say nothing, but he was afraid to do anything, so Horatius Verres had to return to his hiding-place. I was asleep this afternoon when he sighted your ship from the roof of the *ergastulum*, but he called to me through the window of my cottage in Pkauchios's garden, and said he would be safe if he could reach your ship. so I came with him to help him pass the gate-guards, and then came out here for the fun of it. I wanted to see Tros the Samothracian.'

'And are you satisfied?' Tros asked her.

He knew the reputation of the Gades dancing girls – intrigue, well-educated villainy, greed, ulterior motives. He was sure that this one would not have dared to visit him unless convinced of her own safety. Perhaps she knew Orwic and Conops were ashore, and was counting on them as hostages to prevent her from being carried off to sea before daylight.

She looked at him long and steadily, then nodded with a little uplift of her Grecian nose and a droop of the eyelids that suggested confidence in her own skill to read character.

'Why did you come to Gades?' she asked. 'Balbus, the governor, knows you are a pirate. I have heard him talk of it.'

'I came to see Simon,' Tros answered, and watched her to judge the effect.

By her face, by her manner, by the sudden, puzzled frown with a hint of speculation underlying it, he judged that she did not know about his having sent two messengers ashore. And her next words confirmed the guess.

'Simon has much less influence than my master, Pkauchios, who is an astrologer whom all men fear. If you will hide Horatius Verres on your ship, I will speak for you to Pkauchios. He is almost the only man who dares to go to Balbus at any hour of the night. He would make Balbus afraid to interfere with you by talking about the stars and portents and all that nonsense. Then what do you want to do? You know' – she looked at him keenly and impudently – 'you can buy me. I have much influence in Gades.'

'How much are you worth?' Tros asked her.

'My value in the market? Two hundred thousand sesterces!* You don't believe it? Pkauchios had to pay the tax on that amount. He entered me on the list at much less, but the Roman who had farmed the taxes from Balbus ordered me sold at auction, so Pkauchios had to admit the higher value and pay a tax on the sale in the bargain. But I did not mean you should buy me. I meant you can buy my influence.'

But in a world full of uncertainties, if there was one thing sure, it was that buying dancing women's influence was as unthrifty a proceeding as to throw the money overboard. The only end of it would be the bottom of the thrower's purse. Tros stared at Horatius Verres.

'How did you obtain her influence?' he asked. 'Did you pay for it? The man smiled and troubled himself to rise before he answered.

'Money?' he asked, with a shrug of his shoulders. He had all the gestures of a well-bred man, and he was handsome in a dark way, although his eyes were rather close together. 'I made love to her.'

'I won't enslave you,' said Tros, 'but I won't trust you until I know you better.'†

*About £1,700 – a very high, but not an unheard of, price for a slave who could make enormous profits for her master.

†It would have been quite simple for Tros lawfully to enslave Verres. For instance, on arrival at some other port he could have presented a bill for passage money, and if Verres did not pay that, he could attach his person for debt.

Verres bowed acknowledgement.

'I am grateful,' he said, smiling again with a peculiar boyish uptwist of the mouth.

Tros was about to speak again, but the deck-watch shouted, and a man pounded the cab in door.

'Sigurdsen comes!'

Tros had to go on deck or else summon Sigurdsen into the cabin. He did not want the deck crew in his confidence. He signed to Chloe and Verres to hide themselves in the dark corner, where his clothes hung between bulk and bulkhead.

GADES BY NIGHT

Mastery? Its secret? Hah! Self-mastery! But few believe it; it is so simple that few attempt it. Many who attempt it fail because it is so simple. He who has it blames not failure on the disobedience of others, though he punish and reward. Reward and punishment are for the ignorant, who think that God, or the gods, or unknown powers send disaster. Self-mastery lets in intelligence to disobey the promptings of disaster He who is master of himself, he is also master of events. Disaster shall serve his purpose, and why not? Disaster has neither brains nor heart nor understanding.

From the log of Tros of Samothrace

Orwic jumped on to the seaweed-littered beach, slipped on a heap of the slimy stuff and sprawled among the scampering crabs, where Conops helped him to his feet.

'A bad omen, Lord Orwic. A bad omen!'

But the Britons were not addicted to the vice of reading omens in every accident.

'Go back in the boat, if you're afraid,' he answered. So Conops started to lead the way on the five-mile walk toward the city across a dark, ill-smelling wilderness of sand and scrub where anything might happen. And Sigurdsen sent Skram, the skald, to follow them.

They found a road after a while, with a stinking ditch on either side of it, and before long saw the lights of the drinking-booths, brothels and slaughter-yards outside the wall, where there was neither day nor night, but one long pandemonium of vice and lawlessness. And soon after that the first of the scavenger dogs, prowling in search of stray goats or forgotten offal, winded them and started a yelp that brought the pack.

Thereafter they had to fight their way with knife and stick, not daring to gather stones lest the ferocious brutes should snatch that opportunity to rush them as they stooped. But the noise called no attention from the slums, where a dog-fight in the dark was nothing new, and when Skram, judging he was close enough to the gate, lay down to watch, the dogs devoted all their efforts to attacking him, leaving Orwic and Conops free to approach the gate with a semblance of Roman dignity. There Conops took command.

There was a foot-gate in the midst of one side of the double, iron-strapped wooden one that had been closed at sunset; and in the midst of the small gate was a grilled opening that the guard could look through, and above that a lantern on an iron bracket.

Long before they came into the lantern-light Conops began talking fussily in Greek.

'This way, master! That way! Mind the muck here! Dionysus! But the wine those rascals sell has madness in it! Master, master, try to walk straight!' Anyone who understood Greek could not help but know that a Roman gentleman was coming from an evening's entertainment.

'There, master, give me your purse and lean against that wall while I call the gate-guard!'

Conops set his ugly face against the grill and whistled.

'Quick!' he commanded. 'My master is drunk, and ill-tempered because he has been robbed.'

'Who is he?' a voice asked through the grill.

'None of your business! Be quick, unless the lot of you want to be whipped in the morning!'

'Was he robbed of his purse?'

'Zeus! No. What do you take me for? I keep his purse.'

'Well, you know what it costs. One gold piece from each of you to the man on duty, and then the officer – he makes his own terms.'

'Fool!' Conops roared at him. 'Open! If you knew who waits you'd tremble in your mongrel skin!'

The guard vanished. A moment later Conops heard him reporting through the guard-house window to his officer, and he made haste to improve the passing moment.

'Master, master!' he yelled. 'Don't beat me! I'm doing my best! Order those blackguards in the guard-house beaten for daring to keep you waiting. Ow! Ow! Master, that hurts!'

The captain of the guard came – a Numidian, as coal-black as the shadows, rolling the whites of his eyes in an effort to see through the grill, his breath reeking of garlic.

'Who?' he demanded.

'You'll pay smartly for it if I have to tell you!' Conops answered. 'Hurry up now! Two gold pieces for you to hold your tongue and shut your eyes. Some silver for your men. My master's drunk. I pity you if you keep him waiting!'

A great key jangled on a ring. The lock squeaked. Conops threw his arm around Orwic, whose face was smothered in the folds of his pallium.

'Act very drunk!' he whispered, and hustled him through the narrow opening.

On the far side he pushed him into the darkest shadow, where dim rays from a lantern showed the broad blue border of a Roman tunic and the sandalled legs below it, but nothing else. There was a chink of money. The Numidian signed to half a dozen men to retire into the guard-house.

'Remind him when he's sober that I let him in without a fuss,' he said, grinning. 'Who is he?'

Conops laid a hand on the black man's shoulder and leaned toward him as if to whisper, then apparently thought better of it.

'No,' he said, 'mind your own business. That's wisest. I'll remind him you were civil.' ·

'All right. Don't forget now! I'll remember you, you one-eyed Greek! If I see you and ask a favour some time – '

But Conops was gone, his left arm around Orwic and his right hand closed on something that, it seemed, he valued – possibly the purse. The captain of the gate-guard may have thought so.

'Act drunk – drunk – drunker than that!' he whispered. 'Strike a blow at me!'

It was too early for the streets to be deserted, and the danger was of meeting Romans or some citizen who might imagine he recognized the drunken man and speak to him for the fun of it. But the street was crooked and the upper stories of the houses leaned out overhead until they almost met, creating a tunnel of gloom into which the yellow light of doors and windows streamed at intervals. The moment they were out of sight of the guard-house, Conops advised a change of tactics.

'Now sober! Now walk swiftly, as if we had serious business. Stride, man! Stride out! Remember you're a Roman!'

But the spirit of adventure was in Orwic's veins. It was the first time he had seen a foreign city. Men who stood in doorways, house-fronts, litters of the wealthy merchants borne on the shoulders of slaves – all was new to him and stirred his curiosity. Above all, as they threaded through the maze of narrow streets, the glimpse through certain open doors attracted him. For Gades had not yet been zoned, as Rome was, more or less, and as Lunden did not need to be. There were cavernous, whitewashed cellars visible from mid-street, in which women danced to the jingling strains of strings and castanets.

Naked-bellied women ran from one door, seizing Orwic, trying to drag him in to drink and witness Gadean indecency. One pulled away the pallium that hid the lower portion of his face, and Conops struck at her too late; she glimpsed the long, fair hair that fell to the Briton's shoulders, screamed of it, tried to tug the pallium again.

'*Haie*, girls! A barbarian! A rich barbarian! Let's teach him.'

The owner of the place came out, a bull-necked Syrian who tried to keep Conops at bay while the slave-women struggled to hustle their quarry down steps into the cellar, whence the din of music and the reek of wine emerged. The scuffle drew attention from a guard of the municipium, street-corner lurking, watching for a chance to blackmail somebody. He came on the run and, wise in all the short cuts to extortion, picked on Conops as a slave worth money, worth redeeming from the lock-up.

Too quick for him, Conops stepped into the light that streamed from the cellar doorway, showed him something in the palm of a secretive hand. Whatever it was, the Syrian saw it too, and drove the women down the cellar steps. The guard of the municipium strolled away, the Syrian grew laughingly apologetic. Conops led up-street in haste and around three corners before he paused and let Orwic come abreast.

'What did you show him?' Orwic asked.

'Oh, only a bronze badge I stole from that fool Numidian at the gate.'

They reached the wide street running crosswise of the city – wide, that was, for Gades, where there was no wheeled traffic because of the house-fronts that jutted out promiscuously and the arches and bottle-necked passages – passed a temple of Venus, rawly new, of imported Sicilian marble, where Orwic's British eyes stared scandalized at the enormous figure of the naked goddess, coloured in flesh tints and bathed in the flickering light of torches, and turned due eastward, up an alley between high, blind walls where the air smelt stale and filthy and there was not room for two men to pass without squeezing.

There, in the stinking dark, men slept who had to be stepped over carefully. Some swore when awakened and followed with drawn knives, so that Conops walked backward, his own long knife-blade tapping on the wall to give the nightpads warning he was armed.

And there were high doors in the walls, set in dark and unexpected corners, where men lurked who stepped out suddenly and blocked the way, demanding an alms with no humility. Conops slipped under Orwic's arm and trounced one of them with the handle of his knife, whereafter Orwic called for consultation.

'Tros recommended caution,' he remarked. 'We cannot fight all the thieves in Gades. Yet if we fee one rascal he will call his gang to murder us for the purse. We should be better off in the cellar where the women were; they might have taken our money without killing us, or so it seems to me. Pick me up that rascal. Has he breath left? Can he speak? So. Offer him silver to lead us to the house of Simon and keep other rogues at bay.'

So for a while they went preceded by a man in rags who announced in low growls to fellow-prowlers of the Gades underworld that these were privileged night-passengers who had paid their footing, and none offered to molest them after that, except one leper, who demanded to be paid to keep his filthy sores at a distance. He was of the aristocracy of beggardom and bound by no guild restrictions.

And so into the ghetto, where another sort of night-life teemed in crowded alleyways. Iron-barred windows and a reek of pickled fish; sharp voices raised in argument; song, pitched in minor melancholy with an undertone of triumph; secrecy suggested by the eye-holed shutters; ugliness; no open doors, yet doors that did open secretively as soon as they had passed, to afford a glimpse of the unwelcome strangers.

At the end of a few turns the beggar-guide professed to have lost himself, demanded his money and decamped. Orwic remembered the plan Tros drew in sand on the cabin table, but could not see that it faintly resembled any of these winding alleys. Conops, sailor by profession, had the bearings in his head, but could make nothing of the maze confronting them.

'Let us return to the Temple of Venus and start again,' he suggested. 'There used to be an alley that ran nearly straight from there to Simon's house.'

But Orwic plunged forward at random toward a corner where a dim lamp burned in an iron bracket. Conops warned him they were followed, and struck the blade of his long knife against a doorpost, but Orwic turned and stuck his foot into a door that had opened just sufficiently to give a view of him. Conops, who knew Gades ghetto's reputation, tried to pull him back.

'Caution!' he urged.

But Orwic was already inside. There was a leather screen, and Conops could not see him. He had to follow, and the door slammed at his back. The screen masked the end of a short, narrow passage that turned into a room, where there were voices and a dim light. Conops used up a few seconds lunging in the darkness with his knife to find out who and where the man was who had

159

slammed the door. Then he groped for the door, but failed to find the lock, his fingers running up and down smooth wood. He could hardly even find the crack between door and frame.

'*Oimoi! Olola!* Tros was mad to send a Briton!'

Someone chuckled in the darkness. He lunged with his knife at the sound, but hit nothing, then decided to try the passage and the voices and the light. But first he knocked the screen down, being a Greek strategist. A clear line of retreat, even toward a locked door, seemed better than nothing.

He found Orwic in a room whose walls were higher than its length or breadth. Somewhere in the darkness overhead there was a gallery that creaked, suggesting people up there listening, but the one dim lamp was below the gallery, its flickering light thrown downward by a battered bronze reflector. There was a smell of oil, spice, leather and tallow, but nothing in the room except a leather-covered table and two stools. Orwic leaned against the table. An old Jew sat facing him on one of the stools, his knees under the table and his back against the wall. The Jew wore the robes of his race and a dirty cloth cap, beneath which the oily ringlets coiled on either side of bright black eyes. He was scratching his curled beard as he contemplated Orwic.

'Simon!' said Orwic. 'Simon! Simon!'

The Jew glanced at Conops, who stood sidewise in the door, tapping his knife against the post and swaying himself to see into the shadows.

'Is he drunk?' he asked, speaking Greek. 'My name isn't Simon.'

'Simon, son of Tobias of Alexandria,' said Conops. 'Where is his house? We seek him.'

'Everyone in Gades knows the house of Simon, son of Tobias of Alexandria,' the old Jew answered. 'Why do you break into my house?'

Conops showed him the bronze badge, stolen from the captain of the gate-guard, but that had no effect whatever.

'Such a thing will get you into trouble,' said the Jew. 'You have no right to it. That belongs to a captain of the slaves of the municipium.'

Conops began to be thoroughly frightened. The stealthy sounds in gallery and passage and the confident curiosity of the old Jew assured him he was in a tight place.

'Master, let's go!' he urged in Gaulish.

But Orwic could see no danger, and the Jew smiled, his lower lip protruding as he laid a lean hand on the table.

'A Gaul? Ah! And a Greek slave? Who is your master?' he asked Conops. 'What does he want with Simon ben Tobias of Alexandria? What is a Gaul doing with a Greek slave? You must tell me. Come and stand here.'

He pointed to the floor beside him. Conops obeyed, knife in hand, well satisfied to stand where he could hold the old Jew at his mercy at the first suggestion of attack.

'Put your knife away. Slaves are not allowed to carry weapons,' said the Jew, and again Conops obeyed. He could redraw the knife in a second. 'Who is your master? Why did you come to my house?'

Orwic seemed perfectly undisturbed, although he kept on sniffing at the strange smells.

'Tell him to show us the way to Simon's house,' he said patiently.

'You would never be admitted into Simon's house at this hour,' said the Jew. 'There are always his slaves in the street, and they protect his house unless they know you. Do they know you?'

'Tell him,' said Orwic. 'that we have a letter for Simon.'

But the Jew seemed to understand the Gaulish perfectly.

'Show me!' he remarked, and held out his hand.

'Don't you, master! Don't you!' Conops urged, but Orwic did not understand the Greek. He had supposed the Jew demanded money to show the way.

The Jew's eyes gleamed in the direction of the door. Conops turned instantly. There were three Jews in the passage – confident, young, strong, armed with heavy leather porter's straps, which was a weapon quite as deadly as a knife. They leaned with their backs against the passage wall and gazed through into the room with insolent amusement.

'Simon is my friend,' said the Jew. 'If it is true you have a letter, I will take it to him. You wait here. But I don't believe you have a letter. You are robbers. Who should send strangers with a letter to Simon at this hour of night?'

Conops explained that to Orwic.

'Tell him he may come with us and satisfy himself,' said Orwic, beginning to be piqued at last.

'Which of you has the letter?' the old Jew demanded, and the three young Jews in the passage-way advanced into the room as if they had been signalled.

'I can kill all three of those!' said Conops grimly.

His hand went like lightning to his knife-hilt, but a woman screamed in the gallery and smashed something. Conops and

Orwic glanced up, and in the same second each found himself caught in a rawhide noose, arms pinioned.

They fought like roped catamounts with teeth and feet, but the three young Jews were joined by others, who helped to kneel on them and tie them until they could not move, the old Jew sitting all the while, his back against the wall, as if the whole proceeding were quite usual and did not interest him much.

He said something in a sharp voice, and the men began to search their prisoners.

One of them tossed the purse on to the table. Orwic's short Roman sword followed, then Conops' knife and the bronze badge taken from the gate-guard. At last the letter was discovered, tucked under the belt of Orwic's tunic. The old Jew read it, knitting his brows, sitting sidewise so as to hold it toward the light, his lean lips moving as he spelled the words.

'Eh? Tros of Samothrace! Eh?'

He rolled up the letter and thrust it in the bosom of his robe, then spoke rapidly in Aramaic to the Jews who were squatting beside their prisoners. Presently he opened the purse on the table, counted the money, threw it down, called to the woman, who tossed down a cloak from the gallery, and left the house, shuffling along the passage-way in slippers.

CHLOE – 'QUI SALTAVIT, PLACUIT'

For my own sake I give my slaves freedom. Obedience from a free man is not an insult to my manhood. If I punish free men for disobedience and evil manners, I offend not my own soul. As for other men's slaves, I judge their owners by the slaves' behaviour.

From the log of Tros of Samothrace

Tros and Sigurdsen stood over by the water clocks, the full width of the ship from where Chloe and Horatius Verres sat in hiding. But Sigurdsen's voice was a sailor's and, the Gaulish being foreign to him, he spoke it with peculiar emphasis.

'Skram was badly bitten by the dogs,' said Sigurdsen. 'He saw both men enter the city, and he is afraid now he will go mad from dog-bite. The other men think Skram will bite them. They talk of killing him for a precaution.'

Tros groped in a corner.

'Take this,' he commanded. 'Tell Skram and all those other fools that the druids gave it to me. It'll sting, mind. You'll have to hold him while you rub it on. Tell Skram that if he drinks nothing but water, and eats no meat for three days, he'll recover and the dogs'll die. Tell him I said that. Then put Skram to bed, choose another in his place, and row back to the shore and wait for Orwic, Conops and the man they'll bring with them.'

Sigurdsen departed, and presently Skram's yells announced the application of the pine-oil dressing to sundry tender parts of his anatomy. Being a skald, he had a strong voice trained to out-yell storms and drunken roistering.

Chloe came out of the dark into the whale-oil lantern-light.

'You have sent men ashore?' she asked. 'To get in touch with Simon? At this hour of the night? They'll fail! They'll be caught by Balbus's city guards, or be killed by the Jews.' She thought a minute. 'Better have sent me! Were they slaves?'

'They are friends,' Tros answered. 'Where did you learn Gaulish?'

She laughed.

'Pkauchios sent me to Gaul one time to dance for Caesar.'

'Why did Pkauchios send you to Caesar?'

163

'Pkauchios's business is to know men's secrets. But I failed that time. Caesar is no fool.'

She sat on the bunk again, covering her bare knees with a blanket, and for an hour Tros talked to her, he pacing up and down the cabin floor and she regaling him with all the politics of Gades.

'Balbus bleeds the place,' she told him. 'Balbus pretends to be Caesar's friend, but he is the nominee of Pompey the Great, who has all Hispania for his province but stays in Rome and has men like Balbus send him all the money they can squeeze out of their governorships, not that a good percentage doesn't stick to Balbus's fingers. Balbus intends to rebuild the city. If those men you sent ashore get caught by the city guard, they'll find themselves in the quarries some time tomorrow. Balbus has forbidden the export of male slaves, because he wants to glut the market, so as to buy them cheap for his labour gangs. He sentences all able-bodied vagrants to the quarries. He will crucify you, though, if he catches you, unless – '

'Are there any Roman warships in the harbour?' Tros asked her.

'Only one guard-ship, a trireme, but it's hauled out for repairs. The spring fleet hasn't come yet, and the fleet that wintered here has gone to Gaul with supplies and recruits for Caesar's army.'

'When is the spring fleet expected?'

'Any day. It's overdue. The spring fleet comes with the merchant ships to protect them from the pirates. They say the pirates are getting just as bad as they were before Pompey the Great made war on them; and they say, too, that Pompey is too lazy to go after them again, or else afraid that Caesar's friends might take advantage of his absence. You know, Pompey and Caesar pretend to be great friends, but they're really deadly enemies, and now that Crassus, the richest man in the world, has gone to Syria, people are saying it's only a matter of time before Caesar and Pompey are at each other's throats. Until now they've both been afraid of Crassus' money-bags, which seems silly to me. The winner could kill Crassus – '

'And which side does Balbus take?'

The girl laughed.

'Balbus takes his own side, just like all the rest of us. *Balbus aedificabit.** He hopes to win fame by making Gades a great city. If Caesar should win in the struggle that everybody knows is

*Balbus intends to build.

164

coming – well, Balbus is Caesar's friend. If Pompey wins – Balbus is Pompey's nominee and very faithful to him.'

'What about you?' Tros asked her.

'What do I matter? I am a dancing-girl, a slave – the property of Pkauchios the Egyptian.'

'Which way lie your sympathies?' Tros insisted.

'With me, of course, with Chloe. But Balbus loves me, if that is what you mean. He would buy me, if I weren't so terribly expensive. And he would find some way of freeing me from Pkauchios if Pkauchios weren't so useful to him.'

'How?'

'Pkauchios reads the stars and prophesies. Quite a lot of what he says comes true.'

'Sorcery, eh?'

'Call it that if you like. Pkauchios owns other dancing-girls besides me. We are all of us rather well trained at picking up information.'

'You say you know Caesar. You like him?'

'Who could help it? He's handsome, intelligent – oh, how I hate fools! – he has manners, fascination, courtesy. He can be cruel, he can be magnanimous, he thrills you with his presence, he's extravagant – as reckless as a god with his rewards. Oh, he's wonderful! There isn't any meanness in him, and when he looks at you you simply feel his power. You can't help answering his questions. And then he just looks away – like this.'

Chloe broke into a song that had become current wherever women followed in the wake of Roman arms:

> If my love loves not me,
> May a bear from the mountains hug him.

'So now you love Balbus instead?' Tros suggested.

'Bah! Thirty thousand Balbuses are not worth half of Caesar! I said, Balbus loves *me*. But he is too mean to buy me. What are two hundred thousand sesterces to a man who can tax all Gades and sell judgments and confiscate traitors' property? I myself own more than two hundred thousand sesterces.'

'Then why don't you buy your own freedom?'

'Two good reasons. One is, that I placed my peculium* in Simon the Jew's hands, out of the reach of Pkauchios. And Simon can't repay me at the moment, though he's honest in money mat-

*The private fortune of a slave. Many masters encouraged slaves to purchase their own freedom, since then the master received a high price and retained a valuable 'client', who was still bound to him by various restrictions.

ters, like most of the rich Jews. The other is, that if I buy my freedom I should still be Pkauchios's client. I couldn't leave Gades without his permission.'

'And – ?'

Tros felt himself on the scent of something. He experienced that strange thrill, unexplainable, that precedes a discovery. He shot questions at random.

'Why didn't you deposit your money with the temple priests, as most slaves do?'

'Because the priests hate Pkauchios. They would rob me to spite him. Simon is more honest.'

Possibly she felt in Tros something like that same compelling force that she said had made her answer Caesar's questions. After a moment's pause she added:

'I didn't want my freedom until – ' She glanced at the dark corner where Horatius Verres sat in silence. 'You see, I have more liberty without it. As a slave, there are few things I can't do in Gades.'

'But – ?' Tros insisted.

She shuddered.

'Roman law! If my master should be charged with treason they would have to take evidence under torture. No escape from that. A slave's evidence against her master mayn't be taken any other way. Some of them die under torture. None of them are much good afterwards. They're always lame, and the fire leaves scars.'

Tros whistled softly to himself, pacing the cabin floor, his hands behind him. Suddenly he turned on her.

'You didn't come here just for Horatius Verres's sake! You didn't cross that marshland in the dark for the fun of a swim to a pirate's ship! You called me a pirate just now. You had Verres's word for that. Whose else?'

'Caesar wrote to Balbus to be on the watch for you. I saw the letter. It came by the overland mail three weeks ago.'

'You a slave, and you risk yourself on a pirate's ship?'

'Well, I thought I would make friends with you.'

'Why?'

'Because if Pkauchios gets into difficulties, I might be able to escape to somewhere. Almost anywhere would do.'

Tros, pacing the floor again, turned that over in his mind, reflecting that if she was willing to risk herself in what she supposed were a pirate's hands, she must be in serious danger of the Roman tortures. Pkauchios, her master, must be well into the toils. However, he was not quite sure yet that she was telling the truth.

'You say Balbus loves you and would torture you?' he asked. 'He is the governor, isn't he? He can overrule the court. He would find some excuse –'

'Bah!' she interrupted. 'Balbus would enjoy it! You should see him at the circus. He isn't satisfied unless a dozen horses break their legs under the chariot wheels. See him at the spectacles. He likes the agony prolonged. A month ago he had a woman scourged and then worried by dogs, but he gave her a stick to defend herself, and it took the brutes an hour to kill her. Balbus pretends he does it for the people's sake, but he makes them sick. It is he who likes it!'

Tros grinned pleasantly. The girl was trembling, trying to conceal it. He perceived he might make use of her, but fear, and the more of it the better, though a safe spur, would not provide against her treachery. He must supply hope, practical and definite. However, first another question, to make sure he was not wasting time and wit:

'So after all you have no real influence with Balbus?'

'That I have! I say he loves me! I whisper, and he favours this or that one. But he would get just as much pleasure out of seeing me tortured as he does out of hiring me from Pkauchios to dance before his guests. He would say to the world, "See how just I am. Behold my impartiality. I torture even Chloe, *qui saltavit, placuit*."* Then he would enjoy my writhings! He would enjoy them all the more because he loves me.'

Tros stood staring at her, arms akimbo.

'Do you think, at a word from you, Balbus would admit me into Gades?' he asked.

'That would come better from Pkauchios. Pkauchios can go to him any hour and say he has read portents in the stars,' she answered.

'Can you manage Pkauchios?'

She frowned, then nodded.

'Yes, but he is dangerous. He will try to put you to his own use.' Suddenly she laughed. 'Let Pkauchios go to Balbus and prophesy that Tros the Samothracian will enter the harbour at dawn in his great red ship. It is red, isn't it? So Caesar's letter said.'

'Vermilion, with purple sails!' Tros answered proudly.

'And let Pkauchios say to Balbus that Tros of Samothrace is destined to render him a very great service. At dawn the first

*'Who danced and pleased'. These famous words were a motto on a Roman dancer's tombstone.

167

prophecy will come true. So Balbus will believe the second and will receive you eagerly.'

Tros nodded. He well knew the Roman's superstitious reverence for signs and omens. But he also knew the notorious treachery of the dancing-girls of Gades.

'Do you care for pearls?' he asked her.

She gasped as he took a big one from the pocket in his belt and placed it on the plam of her extended hand.

'You shall have enough of those,' he said, 'to make a necklace.'

'But a slave mayn't wear them.'*

'You shall buy your freedom from your master.'

'But Simon can't give me my money!'

'If all plans fail, you shall escape with me on my ship – you and Horatius Verres.'

'If?' she said, watching him, weighing the pearl in the palm of her hand.

'If you give to me in full, meanwhile, your influence in Gades! If you work for me ten times as faithfully as you have ever served your master! If you fail me in nothing, and lend me all your wit and all your knowledge.

'A bargain! she exclaimed, and held the pearl between her lips a moment. Then suddenly. 'Show me the rest of them! How many pearls?

'You shall have them at the right time. Their number will depend on you.' Tros stepped to the door. He heard the oar-thumps of the longboat. 'How will you go back?

'I will swim.'

He shook his head. 'I will send you ashore. Say nothing to the men. But how will you reach the city? There will be no Horatius Verres this time to fight the dogs off and protect you.'

'I told you I am a slave who owns slaves. I have two men waiting for me on the beach.'

Tros heard the deck-watch challenge and Sigurdsen's answering howl from close at hand.

'There is time yet,' he said, glancing at the water clock. 'Hide there.' He pointed to the dark corner where Horatius Verres sat. 'If this is Simon coming, don't let him see you. Slip out when he enters the cabin and I will order my boatmen to row you to the beach.'

Then he peered at Verres. He could hardly see his outline in the shadow under the row of clothing.

'You,' he said, 'stay where you are, and don't let me hear a sound from you!'

*The Roman law was very strict as to who might wear pearls.

They think they know a thing because they have a familiar word for it. If I say avarice, they think of a craving to have. But do they know the subtle treachery of avarice? It is incapable of honour. But who knows it? Not the avaricious!

Am I over-sudden? Should I threaten? A threat is the snarl of cowardice. A fair warning is no threat, but is treachery entitled to a warning?

A fair warning is an appeal to wisdom as when the clouds warn mariners to furl their sails. Threats are the lies of a coward masking treachery. I smite hard where the threat squeaks. Let the blow be a warning to liars to mend their manners.

From the log of Tros of Samothrace

Tros went to the deck and peered over the bulwark into darkness. There was a half-moon now, but the ship's shadow covered the longboat and he could only vaguely see the shapes of four men sitting in the stern, one of whom was hugely fat, unquestionably Simon.

Sigurdsen climbed to the deck and grumbled, using Norse oaths:

'Helpless! Weights like six men! Have to hoist him!'

'Orwic? Conops?'

'Haven't seen them. Fat man rode horseback to the beach. Asked for you. Others are his servants.'

Sigurdsen ordered a rope rove through a block on the after yardarm and a bight put in the end of it. Tros leaned overside.

'Simon!' he called. 'Simon ben Tobias?'

A hoarse voice answered. Question and answer followed in a mixture of three languages, but Tros could hardly hear what Simon said.

'Ho there!' he exploded. 'Put a parcelling on that rope? Will you cut good Simon's rump in halves? Now steady. That's a nobleman of Gades, not a sack of corn!'

They walked the grunting weight up to the bulwark rail and swung him inboard, where Tros received him in strong arms.

'*Simon, salaam! Salaam aleikum. Marhaba fik!*'

'Peace? Blessing? There is none in Gades!' Simon answered, wheezing with fatness and asthma. 'Curses on this night air. There is death in it! Tros, Tros, I cannot pay the debt I owe you!'

Tros hurried him into the cabin, a slave who had clambered up the ship's side fussily arranging shawls around the old Jew's shoulders. A second slave helped a lean man up over the bulwark, who followed in uninvited.

'Door – door – shut the door!' Simon gasped in Greek, the language he had grown more used to than his native tongue.

The two slaves slammed it and remained outside. Tros helped Simon into a chair beside the table and then turned to face the second man, an old Jew in a cloak and a dirty cloth cap, beneath which long black ringlets curled beside his eyes.

'Who is this?'

Simon, coughing apologetically, answered:

'Herod ben Mordecai.'

It might have been the cough, but it appeared to Tros he did not like the name.

'A friend?'

Simon did not answer – only coughed again, his tongue between his teeth.

Herod ben Mordecai smiled, his lower lip protruding as he thrust his head and shoulders forward to peer into Tros's face.

'Let us hope we are three friends!' he said significantly. 'Shall I sit on that chair or on this one?'

He began to peer about the cabin, his bright eyes appraising everything. Tros sat down in his own oak chair with his back to the stern of the ship, and Simon on his right. Herod ben Mordecai helped himself to the third chair, facing Simon, with his back toward the corner in which Chloe and Horatio Verres crouched in hiding.

'Where are the Lord Orwic and the man I sent with him?' Tros asked, looking straight at Simon.

Simon's face, majestic, heavy-browed and framed in a patriarchal beard, but sallow now from ill-health, wrinkled into a worried frown. Old before his time and physically weak from being too much waited on, he looked too strong-willed to yield to death and yet unable to enjoy the life he clung to. His clothes were wholly Oriental, of embroidered camel hair, and there were far too many of them, making him look even fatter than he was. An Eastern head-dress, bound on with a jewelled forehead band, concealed his baldness and increased his dignity; and he wore heavily jewelled rings on three of the fingers of each of his fat hands. He had kicked off his sandals when he entered, and his fat feet, stockinged in white wool, were tucked up under him and hidden by the bulge of his prodigious stomach.

'I haven't seen them!' he said hoarsely.

'Then how did you get my letter?' Tros asked.

'Herod ben Mordecai brought it.'

Tros stared at Herod. The old Jew's brilliant eyes met his without a quiver.

'How did you obtain my letter?' he demanded.

'My friend,' Herod answered in an unexpectedly firm, business-like voice, 'you are lucky it fell into my hands. I took it straight to Simon, who keeps his house like a castle. There are not so many who could get to Simon at such an hour. and, believe me or not, there are fewer who would not have gone straight to the Romans with the news that Tros of Samothrace is so near Gades!'

'I asked you, how did you get the letter?' Tros insisted.

'I heard you. I didn't answer,' said the Jew.

'Very well,' said Tros, 'you are my prisoner!'

He made no move. He simply kicked his scabbard to throw the sword-hilt forward, and sat still. The Jew looked keenly at him, thrusting out his lower lip again, and for a minute there was silence, only disturbed by Simon's heavy breathing. Then Herod leaned across the table toward Tros, thrusting forward one hand, fingers twitching.

'You should make a friend of me,' he said excitedly, 'for Simon's sake. Let Simon tell it.'

Herod resettled himself, twitching at his curled black beard and showing yellow teeth. Simon sighed heavily.

'Tros!' he gasped suddenly. 'Herod knows too much!'

'What a prisoner knows won't sink the ship!' Tros answered.

Herod leaned forward again, elbows on the table, lower lip protruding, eyes as hard and glittering as jet.

'But it will ruin Simon,' he retorted in a level voice.

Simon blurted out the facts, a list of them, while Herod tapped a finger on the table as if keeping check.

'I am in debt. Caius Julius Caesar owes me three million sesterces, and won't pay. Balbus owes me a million, and I daren't ask him for it. If a word gets out in Gades against my credit, there will be a run on me. I lent my warehouse to conspirators for – '

Tros whistled softly.

'Which faction now?' he asked.

'Oi-yoi! Gades is full of factions!' Herod remarked, rubbing his hands as if washing them. He seemed amused.

' – for the storage of weapons,' Simon went on. 'They paid well. I needed – I need money. I didn't know those bales of merchandise were weapons until Herod spied on me and came and told me.

Now if Balbus learns of it, he will jump at the chance to seize my goods. He will tear up his own promises to pay, Caesar's too, for the sake of Caesar's favour – and crucify me!'

'On a great – big – tree!' said Herod, laying both hands on his knees and smiling cruelly. 'You would better tell Simon why you sent for him and make your proposal, whatever it is, and let us all three consider it. I am a man of business. Offer me business or my young men will be at Balbus's door at dawn. Before he has bathed himself he will have sent his guards to Simon's warehouse, where they will find the weapons in bales and bags and barrels. Then a thousand slaves that Simon owns, and his great house full of curios, and his daughters' children – how many, Simon? How many daughters' children? – will all be sold. And Simon – well, he may escape on this ship. I don't know. But the two who went ashore tonight will remain in Gades, where they will suffer such tortures as only Balbus can imagine – rack, fire, spikes under the nails – '

'Tros!' Simon exclaimed wheezily, his nervousness increasing the effect of asthma. 'We are old friends! You will not – '

'None knows what I won't do!' Tros interrupted, thumping his great fist down on the table. 'My young friend Orwic and my servant Conops went ashore. If a hair of a head of either one is injured, this man' – he scowled and showed his teeth at Herod – 'dies!'

'What if I don't know where they are?' said Herod, shrugging his shoulders impudently.

'So much the worse for you!'

'You heard me. Balbus will ruin Simon!' Herod insisted, thrusting out his lower lip again.

'We will cross the bridge of Simon when we reach it,' Tros said grimly.

Herod showed anxiety at last. His eyes admitted he had over-stepped his reach, grew shifty, glanced from one man to the other, rested at last on Tros's angry face.

'You're a fine friend, to talk of letting your friend Simon be sold up and crucified just for the sake of a Gaul and a Greek slave! Mind you, I can't stop it, not unless I go ashore. My young men know I went to Simon's house. They don't trust him – nah, nah! They don't trust him. They know what to do! Any of Simon's slaves might murder me, mightn't they? Any time. Dead men can't talk. So you see, if I don't return pretty soon from Simon's house, my young men will go straight to Balbus. I tell you, I can't stop it unless – '

'I'll drown you unless my men return!' Tros interrupted. 'You may send a messenger ashore –'

'I'll go!' said Chloe's voice, and even Tros was startled. Simon nearly screamed.

She stepped out from the dark and Simon stared uncomfortably at her, looked like a man caught naked in the bath for all that he wore so many clothes and she so few. Herod ben Mordecai recovered from surprise and found speech first. He became all oily smiles, a mass of them, his very body writhed itself into a smile, and his lower lip grew pendulous like an elephant's.

'Ah, pretty Chloe! Clever Chloe! Who'd have thought of finding Chloe on the ship of Tros of Samothrace! Chloe and I are old friends, aren't we! Often I hired Chloe before she got so famous and so expensive. Many a stroke of business Chloe had a hand in, eh, Chloe? *Yeh-yeh.* Chloe could tell who taught her how to turn a pretty profit now and then, eh, Chloe? Friendship, eh!'

He chuckled, as if remembering old mischief she and he had shared in, dug her in the ribs with his long forefinger, caught the edge of her damp chlamys, trying to pull her closer to him. She broke away, approached Simon from behind and stroked his forehead with her cool hands.

'Poor Simon!' she said merrily. 'And he owes me two hundred thousand sesterces! Am I to lose it, Simon? And you so old! You'll never have time to grow rich again before you die, unless we help you! How shall we do it?'

Tros seemed to know. He reached for pen and ink and set them down in front of Herod. Then he clipped a scrap of parchment from a roll.

'Write!' he commanded. 'To the people you refer to as your young men. Bid them release to Chloe, the slave of Pkauchios, my two men from whom you took that letter. Add that secret business will detain you. They are not to be troubled on your account. They are not to go to Balbus.'

Herod ben Mordecai shrugged his shoulders almost to his ears, then shook his head.

'I won't!' he said. 'Sometimes letters get into the wrong hands. And besides, I can't – I can't write.'

Chloe chuckled. Tros reached into a locker behind his chair, chose a long knife, stuck it point first in the table, bent it back toward him and released it suddenly.

'You have until that stops quivering!' he remarked.

Herod began to write with great facility, using Aramaic characters. He covered both sides of the scrap of parchment and then signed his name. Tros scrutinized the writing carefully, then handed it to Simon for a second censorship before entrusting it to Chloe.

'There, you see, there. I have done exactly what you say,' said Herod. 'I was only bargaining. We all have our own way of bargaining. You had the better of it. Now let's be friendly. I wouldn't have hurt Simon for – '

He wilted into silence under Tros's stare. He looked puzzled – seemed to wonder what mistake he might have made in judging character. Tros turned to Chloe.

'Understand me now, my two friends first! Go bring them here.'

'Too late!' said Chloe. 'I will have to hide them. Remember, I must go to Pkauchios and send him hurrying to Balbus with a reading of the stars!'

Tros nodded, chose a pearl out of the pocket in his belt, held it for a moment between thumb and finger in the lantern-light, and tucked it away again. None but he and Chloe was aware of that sideplay.

'I want an interview with Balbus. Do you think your master could persuade him to come to my ship?'

Chloe shook her head violently.

'There have been too many plots against his life of late,' she answered. 'In some ways he is careless, in others he is like an old fox for caution. If you were an informer, if you had some tale to tell him about new conspiracies – '

Tros grinned. She had touched his genius. His hero was the great Odysseus. He knew the *Odyssey* by heart. He could make up a tale on the spur of a moment to meet almost any contingency.

'Tell Balbus I bring him opportunity to be a greater man than Caesar!' he said confidently. 'Bid your master tell Balbus to trust me, that he may stand in Caesar's shoes.'

She smiled, stared, smiled at him, her eyes astonished.

'Are you a seer?' she asked. 'Those lion's eyes of yours – I – I – '

'Go do my bidding!'

He had aroused her superstition. If superstition might assist the pearls to bind her in his service, he could play that game as well as any man.

He rose from his chair and took Herod ben Mordecai by the neck. The Jew clutched at his wrists and tried to struggle. Tros shook the senses nearly out of him and dragged him out on deck, where he called a Northman.

'Fasten this man in an empty water cask.' Then suddenly he

thought of Horatius Verres and turned to Chloe. 'Fetch your Roman.'

She led out Horatius Verres by the hand. They looked like handsome children in the darkness.

'Verres,' said Tros, 'you may earn my favour. Go below. Stand guard over this Jew. See he doesn't escape from the cask and that none has word with him.'

There was a smile on Verres's face as he followed the Northman. The fellow had the Roman military habit of obedience without remark. Tros decided he liked him. He turned to Sigurdsen.

'Put this woman ashore. Nay,' he said, taking his cloak from her, 'that stays here! You may have a blanket.' He returned to the cabin, took a blanket from his bunk and threw it over her. 'Now I will be in Gades harbour with the morning tide, ready for action. If Balbus is friendly, be you on the beach. If you are not there, I will send a threat to Balbus that unless the Lord Orwic and my man Conops are on board by noon, unharmed, I will burn all Roman shipping. I make no threats that I will not fulfil. For you, in that case, there will be no pearls, no freedom, no Horatius Verres, for I will sail away with him! So use brains and be swift.'

Chloe went overside like a trained athlete, hardly touching the rope-ladder that Sigurdsen hung carefully in place. Tros watched the boat until it vanished in gloom at the edge of the path of moonlight, then returned to Simon in the cabin.

'Simon, old friend,' he said, sitting down beside him, 'in the fires of friendship men learn what they are and are not. I have learned this night that you are not so rich as I believed, nor yet so bold as you pretended. No, nor yet so wise as your repute. Tell me more of this Herod ben Mordecai.'

Simon drooped his massive head in the humility of an Oriental who acknowledges the justice of rebuke, and was silent for as long as sixty laboured breaths. Then, wheezing, he revealed the sharp horns of his own dilemma.

'Tros, that Herod is a professional informer. Now he acts spy for the tax-gatherers, now he betrays a conspiracy, now he plays pander to Balbus. Now he buys debts and enforces payment. Now he lays charges of treason, so that he may buy men's confiscated valuables at the price of trash. And he has found out what is true – that there are weapons in my warehouse!'

Tros thought for a minute, drumming with his fingers on the table.

'Simon,' he said at last, 'you are not such a fool as to have let that happen without your knowledge?'

175

In silence Simon let the accusation go for granted. He stared at the table, avoiding Tros's eyes.

'Tros,' he said presently, hoarsely, 'I am a Jew. I am not like these Romans who open their veins or stab themselves when their sins have found them out. Yet mine have found me out. I let myself be called the friend of Pkauchios, that cursed, black-souled dog of an Egyptian, a sorcerer! *Hey-yeh-yarrh!* It is the fault of all my race that we for ever trust the magicians! We forsake the God of our forefathers. Too late, we find ourselves forsaken. *Adonai!* I am undone!'

'But I not!' Tros retorted. 'I am not a Jew, so your God has no quarrel with me. Tell me more concerning Pkauchios.'

'He has a hold on Balbus through his sorceries. He knows that Balbus owes me a million sesterces. He knows I need the money. He knows Balbus would like to indict me for something or other in order to confiscate my wealth, such as it is – such as it is. I have a thousand slaves I can't sell, some millions I can't collect! Pkauchios plans an insurrection by the Spaniards, who will listen to anyone because they groan under the Roman tyranny. But for ever they plot, do nothing and then accuse one another. I would have nothing to do with it. But Pkauchios knew of nowhere, except in my great warehouse, to conceal his weapons from the Roman spies. He offered me a price – a big, a very big price for the accommodation. And he threatened, if I should refuse, to whisper a false charge against me.'

'And you were weak enough to yield to that?' Tros asked him, wondering.

'I grow old. I needed money. Tros, I have sent much money to Jerusalem for the rebuilding of the Temple. *Aie-yaie*, but will it ever be rebuilt!* Pkauchios swore that when Balbus is slain his debt to me shall be paid at once out of the treasury. I let him use my warehouse. And then Herod's spies! Ach-h-h! Herod came to me tonight with your letter in his hand. He would not say where or how he had obtained it. He said, "What does Tros of Samothrace require of you? Tros is a pirate proscribed by Caesar, as all know. There is a reward of three talents set on the head of Tros of Samothrace." He offered to share the reward with me – two for him and one for me. He said, "Let us tempt this fellow Tros ashore with promises. Let us tempt him into your house, Simon, and then send for Balbus." And he made threats. He said, "Balbus would be interested to learn where those weapons are hidden in barrels and bales and boxes!" So I came with him, bribing the

*It was rebuilt several years later by Herod the Great.

176

guard at the gate. And, Tros, I don't know what to say or what to do!'

Simon bowed his head until it nearly touched the table, then rocked to and fro until the strong oak chair groaned under him. Tros closed his eyes in thought, and for a moment it appeared to him the cabin was repeopled. There were Fflur, Caswallon and the druid bidding him goodbye. He could see Fflur's grey eyes. He could hear her voice – 'Be bold, Lord Tros!' And then the druid – 'In the midst of danger thou shalt find the keys of safety!'

Tros leaned and patted Simon on the shoulder.

'What of Chloe?'

'A slave. A Gades dancing-girl,' said Simon, as if that was the worst that could be said of anyone. 'From earliest infancy they are trained in treachery as well as dancing. That one has been trained by Pkauchios, than whom there is no more black-souled devil out of hell! None in his senses trusts the dancing-girls of Gades. Balbus, so they say, trusts Chloe. He is mad – as mad as I was when I trusted him and Caesar with my money! *Uh-uh!* Trust no dancing girl.'

'She seems to have trusted you with her money,' Tros remarked.

'Aye, and shame is on me. I took her money at interest, even as I took yours. I cannot repay her.'

'But I think you shall!' said Tros, and shut his eyes again to think. 'You shall repay her and you shall repay me.'

For a while there was silence, pulsed by Simon's heavy breathing and the lapping of light waves against the ship's hull.

'Simon!' Tros said at last. 'I need the keys of Rome!'

'God knows I haven't them!' said Simon. 'Until Crassus went to Syria I had a good, rich, powerful friend in Rome, but now no longer.'

'But you have influence with Balbus since he owes you so much money?'

'Influence?' said Simon, sneering. 'He invites me to his banquets, to over-eat and over-drink and watch the naked-bellied women dance. But I asked a favour yesterday – only a little favour – leave to export a few hundred slaves to Rome. If they had been women he would have said yes, but he has placed an embargo on male slaves, to depress the local market so as to have cheap labour to rebuild Gades. He knows I have no female slaves, so it was no use lying to him. He answered he would give permission gladly, only that Tros of Samothrace, the pirate proscribed by Caesar, is at sea and might capture the whole consignment, for which he, Balbus, would be blamed. Bah! So much for my influence! He let Euripides the Greek export a hundred women only last week, and that was since Caesar's letter came. Pirates! What he fears is a rising market! He knows I need money. He knows I have a thousand Lusitanii that I bought for export. At his suggestion too. I bought them at his suggestion! Tros, it costs money to feed a thousand slaves! That dog Balbus waits and smiles and speaks me fair and watches for the day when I must sell those slaves at auction, so that he may buy them dirt cheap for his labour gangs!'

'But you stand well with Caesar,' Tros suggested. 'You say Caesar owes you three million – '

'*Phagh!*' Simon's face grew apoplectically purple. 'Caesar is the greatest robber of them all!'

'But he has brains,' Tros retorted. 'Caius Julius Caesar knows it is wiser to keep an old friend than to be for ever hunting new ones. Why did you lend him the money?'

'Because his creditors were after him and he promised me his influence. Of what use to me now in Gades is Caesar's influence in Gaul? Tell me that! I wrote to him for my money, for a little something on account. No answer! I suppose a secretary read the letter. *Tschch!* With Caesar it is face to face that counts. Nothing matters to him then but the impression he makes on bystanders. Vain! He thinks himself a god! He acts a drama, with himself the hero of it. Approach him, flatter him, ask for what he owes you in the presence of a dozen people and he will pay if it takes the last coin in his treasury. Pay if he has to capture and sell sixty thousand slaves to reimburse himself! That was how he repaid Crassus. Sixty thousand Gauls he sold in one year! *Tschch!* With a smile he will pay, if he has an audience. With a smile and a gesture that calls attention to his magnanimity and modesty and sense of justice! But a letter, opened by his secretary, read to him, perhaps, in a tent at night, when his steward has told him of a nice, young, pretty matron washed and combed and waiting to be brought to him – *Tshay-yeh-yeh!* None but a Jew, but a Jew – would have let him have three million sesterces!'

Tros tried to appear sympathetic. He leaned out of his chair and patted Simon on the shoulder. But the news of Simon's difficulties only strengthened his own confidence. When he was sure that Simon was not looking, he permitted a great grin to spread over his face.

No Roman warships in the harbour, conspiracies ashore, Simon's warehouse full of weapons, between decks two hundred and fifty first-class fighting men, demanding shore leave and agreeable to act the role of slaves for the occasion, Balbus the Roman

178

governor ambitious, greedy, superstitious and in the toils of an Egyptian sorcerer whose slave Chloe, a favourite of Balbus, was in a mood to betray her master – it would be strange, it would be incredible, if the gods could not evolve out of all that mixed material an opportunity for Tros of Samothrace to use his wits!

'Simon,' he said, 'once you did my father a good turn in Alexandria. You did it without bargaining, without a price. I am my father's son. So I will help you, Simon. You shall pay your debts –'

'God send it!' Simon muttered.

'You shall be spared the shame of not repaying Chloe –'

'S-s-sheh-eh!' Simon drew in his breath as if something had stabbed him.

'We will both of us have our will of Balbus –'

'Uh-uh! He is all-powerful in Gades. If they kill him, there will only be a worse one in his place!'

'You shall have your sesterces, and I the key to Rome!'

'God send it! Eh, God send it!' Simon answered hopelessly. 'But I think we shall all be crucified!'

'Not we!' Tros answered. 'I have crucified a plan, that's all. A plan that can't be changed is like a fetter on a man's foot.'

He arose and kicked out right and left by way of illustration that his brain was free to make the most of its opportunity.

THE COTTAGE IN PKAUCHIOS'S GARDEN

If a man insults my dignity by seeking to make me the tool of treachery, let him look to his guard. For if he need it not, that shall be because I lack the skill to turn his treason on himself.

From the log of Tros of Samothrace

Orwic and Conops lay flat on a tiled floor with leather thongs biting their wrists and ankles. The only sound was the quiet breathing of the Jews who squatted with their backs against the wall. Thought was tense, speculative, almost audible, but Conops was the first to speak in a whisper to Orwic:

'Roll toward me. I can move my fingers. Maybe I can untie your –'

A Jew leaned through the dark and struck him on the mouth with the end of a leather strap. After that there was silence again – so still that the rats came, and the slow drip-drip of water somewhere up behind the gallery began to sound like hammer blows on an anvil.

After an interminable time the Jews began to talk in muttered undertones. Then a woman brought food to them. There was a reek of pickled fish and onions that they guzzled in the dark. Orwic took advantage of the noise to try to chafe the thongs that bound his wrists, rubbing them against the floor tiles. But a Jew heard the movement and struck him. After that there was silence again, until one of the Jews fell asleep and snored.

There was no way of judging the time, but no light shone yet through the shutter-chinks when a furious knocking began at the street door. It boomed hollow through the house and brought the Jews to their feet, whispering to each other. One of them leaned over Orwic to examine his thongs, and another kicked Conops in the ribs by way of warning to be still. A woman leaned over the gallery and whispered excitedly. One of the Jews went out into the passage, lighted a lantern after a dozen nervous fumbles with the flint and steel and shouted angrily, but Conops, who knew many languages, could not understand a word he said.

The knocking continued, and grew louder, until the Jew with the lantern began talking to someone through a hole in the street door. He was answered by a woman's voice in Greek. She seemed to have no care for secrecy, and Conops could hear her without the slightest effort.

'I say admit me! Keep me waiting and I'll call the Romans! I tell you I have a letter from Herod ben Mordecai! Open!'

The door opened. Several people entered. There was excited conversation in the passage. Up in the gallery the unseen Jewess fluttered like a frightened hen. The wooden railing creaked as she leaned over it to listen. Then the girl's voice in the passage again, loud and confident, speaking Greek:

'No use telling me lies! I know they're here! You've read Herod's letter, so out of my way!'

'Give me the letter, then!'

'No!'

A scuffle, and then a girl in a damp Greek chlamys, with a thick blue blanket over that – and it surely never came from Hispania – stood in the doorway, holding the Jew's lantern. Over her shoulders two male Numidian slaves peered curiously.

'So there they are! Untie them! If they're hurt I'll speak to Balbus and have him crucify the lot of you!'

Conops cried out to her in Greek:

'Get me my knife, mistress! Then no need to crucify them!'

She laughed.

'I am Chloe,' she said. 'I came from – '

Suddenly she checked herself, remembering the Jews were listening.

'You will do exactly what I say!' she went on. 'No fighting! They shall give you back everything they have taken from you. Then come with me.'

She looked like a princess to Orwic, although the blanket puzzled him. It did not for a second occur to him that she might be someone's slave, although her sandals were covered with filth from the barren land outside the city, and he might have known no woman of position would have walked at that hour of the night. Had she not slaves of her own, who obeyed her orders? Did the Jews not slink away from her like whipped curs? Was her manner not royal, bold, authoritative?

Her Numidians took the weapons off the table – they had none of their own – and cut the thongs that bound wrists and feet.

'Now count your money!' she said, pointing at the purse. So Conops shook out the money on the table.

'Ten gold coins missing!' he remarked, chafing his wrists, rubbing one ankle against the other. If he might not use his knife,

181

he was determined that the Jews should pay in some way for the privilege of having put him and Orwic to indignity. Instantly he wished he had said twenty gold coins.

The woman in the gallery began to scream imprecations in a mixture of Greek, Aramaic and the local dialect, which itself was a blend of two or three tongues. Chloe silenced her with a threat to call the city guards.

'Who will take more than ten gold pieces,' she remarked, 'if I tell them I have authority from Balbus.'

After a few moments, still noisily protesting, the woman threw ten coins down to the floor, one by one, and Conops gathered them, well paid for a night's imprisonment, but grinning at himself because he had not been smarter. Chloe took Orwic's hand and smiled at him, chafing his wrist between her palms.

'Are you ready? Will you come with me?' she asked engagingly in Gaulish.

Orwic would have gone with anyone just then. To go with Chloe, after lying in that smelly room with hands and feet tied, was such incredibly good fortune that he almost rubbed his eyes to find out whether he were dreaming. When she let go his hand he took his Roman sword from one of the Numidians and followed her into the passage; there he drew it to guard her back against the Jews, his head full of all sorts of flaming chivalry. She turned and whispered to him, raising her arms to draw his head close, which, if he had thought of it, a princess hardly would have done on such scant acquaintance.

'You must walk through the streets with an arm around me,' she said, using the Gaulish with a funny foreign accent that thrilled him almost as much as her breath in his ear. 'You must look like a Roman nobleman who has seduced a girl and takes her home with him. We must walk swiftly, and then none will interfere with us.'

She rearranged the blanket, throwing one end of it over her head, as a girl ashamed of prying eyes might do, and led the way into the street where she shrank, as if she needed the protection, into Orwic's left arm, under his pallium.

'To the left!' she said. 'Forward! Quickly!'

The Jews' door slammed behind them, and the procession at once became perfectly regular. Conops understood the game now. He walked in front, just close enough for Chloe to call directions to him, his long knife tapping on the scabbard as a warning to all and sundry to keep their distance. The two Numidians brought up the rear, striding as if they were owned by Balbus himself. Being slaves of a slave, they were much more harmless than they looked.

Orwic's Celtic diffidence prevented him from speaking. He was not exactly shy. He was ashamed of having failed Tros and of having to be rescued by a woman, half inclined to think the gods had personally had a hand in it, so sudden and mysterious the rescue had been, and not a little bewildered, besides thrilled. He hurried along in silence for ten minutes through a maze of winding alleys, thinking furiously before Chloe volunteered some information.

'I sent my two women to Pkauchios to warn him to be up and ready for us.'

But ignorant of who Pkauchios might be, Orwic simply turned that over in his mind. Developments seemed more mysterious than ever. Chloe went on talking:

'Pkauchios may try to scare you with his magic, but remember what I tell you: his magic is all humbug. He gets most of his secret information from us girls.'

'Us girls' did not sound like the words a princess would have used. Orwic's wits were returning.

'Who are you?' he asked, looking down at her, pulling aside a corner of the blanket so as to see her face. It was very dark; he had to bend his head, and at a street corner a drunken Roman stopped his litter to laugh raucously.

'Ho there, Licurgus Quintus!' he roared. 'I recognize you! Where did you find that pretty piece you have under your pallium? Mark me, I'll tell Livia! I'll tell them all about it at the baths to-morrow! Ha-ha-hah! Licurgus Quintus walking, and a girl under his pallium at this hour of the night. Ha-ha-ha-hah!'

Four slaves bore the litter off into the darkness, with its owner's legs protruding through the panel at the side.

'That drunken fool is Numius Severus,' Chloe remarked. 'He offered to buy me last week. Bah! He has nothing but an appetite and debts to feed it with!'

'Who are you?' Orwic asked again.

'Chloe, the slave of Pkauchios of Egypt. I am called the favourite of Gades. Soon you shall see me dance, and you will know why.'

'Oh!' said Orwic.

He relapsed into a state of shame again, his very ears red at the thought of having mistaken a slave girl for a princess. Being British, he had totally un-Roman notions about conduct; it was the fact that he had made the mistake, not that she was a slave, that annoyed him. Chloe misinterpreted the change of mood, that was as perceptible as if he had pushed her away from him.

'I expect to be freed before long,' she remarked.

Suddenly it occurred to Orwic that the best thing he could do would be to head straight for the beach and swim to the ship if there was no longboat waiting.

'Tros – is Tros on the ship?' he demanded.

But Chloe guessed rightly this time, understood that in another second he would be out of her reach, going like wind downhill toward the city gate.

'No,' she lied instantly. 'Tros is with Pkauchios.'

Orwic detected the lie. She realized it.

'Tros came in search of you,' she added.

But by that time Orwic did not believe a word she said. It seemed to him he was escaping from one danger to be trapped a second time.

'How did you learn where I was?' he demanded.

'Tros told me.'

They had halted and were standing in the moonlight face to face where they could see each other. Her clever eyes read his, and she realized she needed more than words to convince him.

'Tros paid me to come and rescue you,' she went on, raising the edge of her chlamys, showing a yard of bare leg as she thrust her fingers into a tiny pocket. 'Look, he gave me that to come and rescue you.'

She showed him a pearl in the palm of her hand, and it was big enough to convince Orwic that it might be one of those pearls that the druids had given to Tros. He decided to let her lead him farther, but his normal mistrust of women, that Tros had encouraged by every possible means, increased tenfold.

'Though you hate me, you must walk as if you love me!' Chloe remarked, and he had to take her underneath his pallium again.

The stars were bright and it lacked at least an hour of dawn when they emerged into a rather wider street that led between extensive villas set in gardens. Trees leaned over the walls on either hand. Toward the end of the street there was a bronze gate set into a high wall over which a grove of cypresses loomed black against the sky; a panel in that gate slid back the moment Chloe whistled; a dark face eyed her through the hole, and instantly the gate swung wide on silent hinges. There was a sound of splashing fountains and an almost overwhelming scent of flowers. Tiles underfoot, but a shadow cast by the cypresses so deep that it was impossible to see a pace ahead.

Fifty yards away among the trees were lights that appeared to emerge between chinks of a shutter, but Chloe took Orwic's hand

and led him in a different direction, through a shadowy maze of shrubs that murmured in the slight sea breeze, until they reached a cottage built of marble, before whose door a lantern hung from a curved bronze bracket.

Two Greek girls came to the door and greeted Chloe deferentially. One of them behaved toward Conops as if he were a handsome Roman officer instead of the ugliest one-eyed, horny-handed Levantine sailor she had ever set eyes on. The Numidian slaves found weapons somewhere – took their stand outside the door on either side of it, with great curved swords unsheathed. Chloe nodded to them as she led the way in.

Orwic followed her because there was light inside and the place did not look like a trap or a prison, although the small square windows were heavily barred. There was a fairly large room, beautifully furnished in a style so strange to his British notions that he felt again as if Chloe must be at least a princess. By the British firesides minstrels had always sung of princes and princesses in disguise who rescued people out of foul dungeons and conveyed them to bowers of beauty, where they married and lived happy ever after; and it is what the child is taught that the grown man thinks of first in strange surroundings. True, British slaves were very often treated like the members of a family, but he had never heard of a slave girl living in such luxury as this.

There was a second room curtained off from the first, and into that Chloe vanished, through curtains of glittering beads that jingled musically. One woman followed, and there were voices, laughter, splashing. Almost before Orwic had had time to let the other woman, on her knees before him, clean his sandals, and before Conops had done staring pop-eyed at the rugs and gilded couch, the little Greek bronze images of half a dozen gods, the curtains from Damascus and the pottery from Crete, Chloe stood rearrayed in front of them, fresh flowers in her hair, in gilded sandals, with a wide gold border on a snow-white chlamys. Over her shoulders was a shawl more beautiful than anything Orwic had ever seen.

'You, a slave?' he said, staring, wishing his own tunic was not soiled from the night's adventure.

Smiling at him merrily, she read and understood the chivalry that stirred him. Suddenly her face turned wistful, but she was careful not to let Conops see the changed expression. Levantines were experts in incredulity.

'Yes,' she said, 'but you can help me to be free. Will you wait here while I find the Lord Tros?'

She was gone before he could answer, closing the door but not locking it, as Orwic was quick to discover. He would have followed her to ask more questions, but the two Numidians prevented him politely enough, but firmly, drawing no particular attention to the great curved swords they held. Staring at them, realizing they were slaves, Orwic decided that he and Conops could quite easily defeat them if necessity arose. Noticing there was no lock on the outside of the door, but only a slide-bolt on the inside, he returned to question the two women.

But they knew no Gaulish. One of them was fussing over Conops, putting up a brave pretence of being thrilled by his advances, which were seamanly, of the harbour-front sort. Conops began to sing a song in Greek that all home-faring sailors heard along the wharves of Antioch, Joppa, Alexandria and wherever else the harpy women waited to deprive them of the coins earned in the teeth of Neptune's gales. It was not a civilized song, though it was old when Homer was a youth in Chios, and its words aimed at the core of primitive emotion.

To keep him entertained, the women danced for him when one of them had brought out wine from the inner room. And because the dance was not the bawdy entertainment of the beach-booths, but a sort of poetry of motion beyond Conops' ken, they kept him half excited and half mystified, thus manageable until Chloe came back, lithe and alert in the doorway, with a look of triumph in her eyes.

'Tros?' Orwic asked her instantly.

'He has gone with Pkauchios to Balbus's house,' she answered.

But it was once more clear to Orwic she was lying. Tros, he knew, would never have gone away without first setting eyes on him, or, at any rate, without first sending a message, if only a word or two of reassurance.

'What did he say?' he demanded.

'He was gone when I got to the house.'

That too was a lie. She had been gone too long not to have talked with somebody; and there was a look of triumph in her eyes that she was trying to conceal but could not.

'I too go to Balbus!' said Orwic. He gestured to Conops to follow, and strode for the door with his left hand on his sword-hilt.

Chloe slammed the door shut and stood defiant with her back against it.

'Prince of Britain!' she said, laughing, but her laugh was challenging and confident. 'Be wise! All Gades would like Chloe

186

for a friend! All Gades fears the name of Pkauchios! You are safe here. I have promised the Lord Tros no harm shall happen to you, and he holds my pledge.'

Orwic sat down on the gilded couch to disarm her alertness. It offended his notions of chivalry to feel obliged to use force to a woman, but the mystery annoyed him more than the dilemma. It had begun to dawn on him that he was dealing with a girl whose instinct for intrigue prevented her from telling stark truth about anything. For a second, observing Conops' antics through the corner of his eye, he even thought of making love to her; but he was too much of an aristocrat for that thought to prevail; he would have felt ashamed to let Conops see him do it.

Above all else he felt stupid and embarrassed in the strange environment, aware that he would be as helpless as a child by day-light in the city streets. He had not even the remotest notion how a Roman would behave himself in Gades, and was sure the crowd would detect his foreign bearing in an instant. His Celtic diffidence and thin-skinned fear of being laughed at so oppressed him that he actually laughed at his own embarrassment.

'That is better!' said Chloe, and sat down beside him.

But he noticed she had shot the door-bolt, and he did not doubt there was some trick to the thing that would baffle anybody in a hurry.

'Why do you keep on lying to me?' he demanded.

'Don't you know all women lie?' she asked him. 'We arrive at the truth by other means than by telling it. Prince of Britain, if I told you naked truth you would believe me mad, and you would act so madly there would be no saving you!'

Conops was becoming rougher and more like an animal every minute. Chloe's two slave-women were having all their work to keep out of his clutches, the one teasing while the other broke away, turn and turn. At last he seized one woman's wrist and twisted it. She screamed.

Chloe sprang to the rescue, broke a jar over Conops' head, and had his knife before he could turn to defend himself. He knew better than to try to snatch the knife back. His practised eye could tell that she could use it.

'Pardon, mistress!' he said civilly. 'I was only playing with the girls.'

Chloe tossed the knife into the air and caught it, noticing that both men wondered at her skill. She said something in Greek, too swift and subtle for Conops' marlin-spike intelligence – more dull than usual just then from the effect of honied wine and an emotion

187

stirred by dancing-girls – then frowned, her mind searching for phrases in Gaulish.

'You can use weapons,' she said, her gesture including both men. 'I too. The Armenian who trained me meant me for a female gladiator. But the aedile* to whom I was offered said it would be bad for Roman morals, so I was sold to Pkauchios. You are male and I female. What else is there that you are and I not?'

Orwic smiled his way into her trap.

'Are you free?' he suggested. 'I am a prince of Britain.' He said it very courteously.

'Now! This morning!' she retorted. 'How about tonight? My father and my mother were free citizens of Athens, if you know where that is. The Roman armies came. I was sold at my mother's breast. She died of lifting grape baskets in a Falerian vineyard, and I was sold to the Armenian, whose trade was the invention of new orgies. But I was not quite like the ordinary run of slave girls, so I was spared a number of indignities for the sake of the high price I might bring. If the Armenian had not set such a high price on me I think the aedile would not have talked so glibly about morals. Today I am a slave. Tonight I think I will be a freed woman; tomorrow, wholly free. And you? Does it occur to you, Prince of Britain, that there is none but I who can keep you from falling into Balbus's hands? Balbus would condemn you as an enemy of Rome. He would put you up at auction to the highest bidder. Why, you might be my slave in a week from now!'

She had his attention at any rate. He laughed, and his hand went to his sword-hilt, but his eyes looked worried. Conops watched her with a gleam in his one steely eye, his muscles tightening for a sudden leap at her; but she understood Conops perfectly and changed the long knife from her left hand to her right with a convincing flicker of the bright Damascus steel.

'You sit there and keep still!' she ordered. 'I am not concerned about you in the least. You may die if you wish! You,' she said, looking at Orwic, 'shall not be harmed if I can help it. You must make up your mind you will trust me, or else – '

'Why did you lie?' Orwic asked her.

She laughed.

'You are here. You are safe. If I had told you the Lord Tros was on his ship, would you have come with me?'

Orwic shrugged his shoulders.

*Aedile. The elected Roman official responsible for the public games and the adornment of the city, which he had to provide largely at his own expense. Aedileship was a stepping-stone to higher office. Aediles ran extravagantly into debt in the hope of reimbursing themselves if elected to a consulship.

'Well, what next?' he asked.

'You must do exactly what I say. Pkauchios knows you are here. He has gone to Balbus to persuade him to let the Lord Tros anchor in the harbour unmolested.'

'Could he prevent that?' Orwic asked, remembering Tros's great catapults and arrow engines.

'And to persuade Balbus to invite Tros ashore for a conference under guarantee of protection. When Pkauchios returns, I will take you to him and leave you with him. I have told Pkauchios, and I will tell him again, that you are a superstitious savage. Remember that. You are to agree to anything that Pkauchios proposes, no matter what it is.'

'And you?'

'I go to Tros, and perhaps also to Balbus. I take Conops with me because Tros, perhaps, might not believe me when I tell him you are unharmed, and I think the Lord Tros is not easy to manage. Also, Conops is a nuisance, who will get drunk presently, and there is no place to lock him up except in the *ergastulum*. And I can take Conops through the streets in daylight because he is a Greek who will arouse no comment.'

'And if I refuse to trust you?' Orwic asked.

'I will have to lock you both in the *ergastulum*. It is not a pleasant place. It is dark in there, and dirty. There are insects. Listen!' she said, obviously making a concession to his prejudices.

A blind man could have guessed it went against the grain in her to lift a corner of the curtain of intrigue.

'You will spoil everything unless you obey me absolutely! Tros wants – I don't know what. But I will get it for him. I go presently to make sure that Balbus's promise of protection shall be worth more than the breath he breathes out when he makes it. Simon the Jew wants his money. Tros, I think, can get it for him. I want my freedom. Pkauchios – well Pkauchios himself will tell you what he wants. Are you still afraid to trust me? Listen then. Tros holds a pledge of mine worth more to me than all the wealth of Gades. He keeps my lover on his ship!'

If Orwic had known more about the reputation of the Gades dancing-girls, he would have mistrusted her the more for that admission. But she would not have made it to a man of more experience. She was as shrewd as he was innocent. Conops, cynically sneering, merely rallied Orwic's inborn chivalry:

'Huh! In Gades they change lovers just as often as the ships come in!'

Whatever she was or was not, Chloe looked virginal in that

Greek chlamys with the plain gold border and the flowers in her hair. And whatever she felt or did not feel, she could act the very subtleties of an emotion instantly. She looked stung, baffled, conscious of the servitude that made her reputation any man's to sneer away, ashamed, albeit modest and aware of inner dignity. She blushed. Her eyes showed anger that she seemed to know was useless. Orwic passionately pitied her.

'You dog!' he snarled disgustedly through set teeth. 'Go with her! Go back to Tros! And when I come, if I learn you have not treated her respectfully, I will have Tros tie you to the mast and flog you – as he did the rowers when they shamed those girls in Vectis!'

'Oh, never mind him,' said Chloe. 'He is only a sailor.'

She hung her head, as Orwic believed, bashfully. But Conops understood right well it was to hide the flash of triumph in her eyes. She had Orwic where she wanted him. But what could a cynical seaman do or say, though he knew all ports and had been tangled in many snares of siren women, to convince a nobleman of Britain that a gesture and a glance were possibly play-acting and not proof of honesty? Conops shrugged his shoulders.

'Very well,' he said. 'I'll go with her to the ship. You stay here and run your own risks!'

GAIUS SUÉTONIUS

My father taught me, and I know that manners are the cloak of dignity, and dignity is man's awareness of his own soul.

But I have yet to learn that peacock people are entitled to the courtesies that manhood commands without asking.

From the log of Tros of Samothrace

The first rule of all crises being that no man behaves according to the law of averages, if there is one, or according to expectation or in keeping with the dignity of great events – which surely calls for a continuous procession of brass bands, torches, incense and acclamation – Tros and Simon slept. They snored, Tros forward on the table, Simon leaning sackwise in the chair. They were fast asleep at dawn when Sigurdsen appeared, enormous in the cabin doorway, to announce the first glimpse of the sun.

'Tide in about an hour, Lord Tros!'

Simon snored on. Tros blew the air out of his lungs, filled them two or three times, felt by instinct for his sword, simultaneously glancing at the water clocks, ran fingers through his long, black hair, looked curiously once or twice at Simon, nodded and knew his mind.

'Serve breakfast. Then out oars! Man arrow engines, clear away the catapults, ammunition ready in the racks, deck crew at quarters. Then haul short. We enter Gades harbour when the tide makes.'

The ship became a thing of ordered tumult, din succeeding din and a smell of hot smoked fish pervading. Simon awoke with a number of grunts and 'ohs' and 'ahs', remembered where he was and fell incontinently into panic.

'Tros! Tros!' he gasped. 'We talked madness!'

'Aye, Simon, aye! The gods love madmen!'

'*Phagh!* You sicken me with talk of many gods! Why not have a row of smirking idols? Worship them! Such talk, such talk, and we looking death in the face!'

'We will see Gades first and then look Balbus in the face!' Tros answered. 'Simon – madder than the gods themselves and than the wind and waves, a man needs be who will risk his neck for friendship! Aye, mad enough to trespass in the porch of wisdom! Rot me reason and religion when the die is cast! Talk yesterday, act now, tomorrow shall say yea or nay to it!'

He laughed and went up on the poop to watch the ship made ready, washed down, cleared for action, and ammunition set in racks and baskets, sand-boxes filled, pumps tested and the trained crews stationed each in its appointed place. Then he ordered one great purple sail spread as a tribute to his own pride, and started the drums and cymbals going to slow measure, that the oars might take up the strain on the anchor-cable.

He gave the helm to Sigurdsen and whistled to himself, striding from side to side of the broad poop to con the harbour entrance, pausing in his stride to listen when the Northman in the chains called out the soundings, memorizing landmarks, feeling as brave and careless as he looked in his gold-edged purple cloak. He wished there might be fifty thousand Romans on the beach to see his ship come in!

But the harbour, splendid with its thirty-mile circumference, looked strangely empty. There was one great trireme hauled out on the beach beside a row of sheds, and six ships that had wintered on the beach lay newly launched, high-sided, all in ballast. One long rakish craft was certainly from Delos, anchored apart from the others – probably a pirate captured by a Roman fleet and kept to be taken to Ostia and sold at auction. Vague objects fastened in her rigging looked suspiciously like the remains of human bodies crucified and picked to pieces by the sea-birds.

Fishing-boats swarmed on the beach and at anchor nearer shore, and there were rows of sheds in straight lines at the seaward end of a narrow road that led from city wall to beach. The city gleamed white in the sun, but its high wall looked dirty and needed repair; outside the wall there were villages of shacks and shambles clustered close against it, and between them a tired-looking grove of palm trees surrounded a cluster of thatched booths.

Between city wall and harbour was a waste of common land, all swamp and rubbish heaps. The shore was piled with seaweed, rotten with the colours of decay and black with flies.

The principal signs of Roman rule were the villas of officials set in gardens near the summit of the slope on which the city stood, and, on a hill to the north of the city, a military camp with regular lines of tents and huts and four straight paved roads leading to it. The lower part of the city was a crowded jumble of mixed Carthaginian, Greek, Roman, and native roofs.

Tros dropped anchor within catapult range of the hauled-out

trireme. That and the store-sheds were at his mercy, although the city itself was beyond reach of his flaming stink-balls. Trembling, gnawing at a hot smoked herring, Simon came to the poop and pointed out the sheds where all the wine was stored for export to Alexandria in exchange for corn and onions.

'We'll save Pompey's people a few headaches by destroying that stuff unless Balbus comes to terms!' said Tros.

But there were already signs of Balbus. A liburnian put out from a wharf near the store-sheds, leisurely rowed by slaves in clean white uniform. It had a bronze standard in the bow with the initials S.P.Q.R., and in the stern under an awning sat a Roman, dressed in the latest military fashion.

Simultaneously, another swifter boat, whose crew were not so neatly dressed nor nearly so in love with dignity, put out from a point much nearer to the ship and speeded at the rate of two to the liburnian's one. It had no awning. Chloe in the stern was plainly visible encouraging the rowers. Conops sat beside her.

The smaller, faster boat bumped alongside, reckless of Tros's vermilion paint, and Chloe came up the rope-ladder like an acrobat, bacchanalian with her wreath awry and her gilded sandals stained with harbour water.

'Lord Tros!' she exclaimed, breathless with excitement, 'your great ship makes a braver spectacle than any Gades ever saw! I love it! We all love it! Look!'

She waved her hand toward the city wall whose summit was already black with people gazing. But Tros took more note of a hundred men who marched behind a mounted officer from the camp to the north of the city toward the shore.

'Orwic?' he demanded.

Conops answered him, climbing the poop steps sullenly with the air of a man expecting punishment:

'He lingers with the dancing-women in a marble palace. Master, he refused to come away with me!'

Chloe seized Tros's arm and began speaking in a hurry with excited emphasis.

'Trust me! Now trust me, Lord Tros! Your prince of Britain is absolutely safe! Look you! In that liburnian sits Gaius Suetonius. He is a youngster whom Caesar sent to Balbus with a recommendation, a wastrel whom Caesar wished to be rid of, but whom we did not care to offend because of his influence in Rome. Balbus makes a lot of him for Caesar's sake, and also because they play into each other's hand to cheat the treasury. He comes with Balbus's permission to you to go ashore and talk with him. Now

193

listen, listen, listen! Gaius Suetonius knows most of Balbus's secrets. Balbus would never dare to let him – '

'I understand,' Tros answered, and strode to the break of the poop to summon men to stand by the ladder and salute the Roman.

He was just in time to provide a flourish of drums and trumpets and to rearrange his own purple cloak becomingly. Chloe vanished into the cabin, and Simon followed.

The Roman approached the poop with the peculiar, half patronizing, noncommittal, but amused air of the aristocratic Roman face to face with something new. The sun shone on his heavily embossed bronze body armour, and his nodding crimson plume was nearly twice the regulation size. He was immaculate down to the tips of his fingernails, much too calculating, insolent and greedy-looking to be handsome, but possessed of strong, regular features and a muscularity not yet much softened by debauch. His richly decorated shield was borne behind him by a Greek slave, the impudence of whose stare was an exaggeration of his master's.

Tros eyed them sourly, but obliged himself to smile a little when the Roman condescendingly acknowledged the salute.

'You are Tros of Samothrace? I am Gaius Suetonius, master of the ceremonies and confidential agent of Lucius Cornelius Balbus Minor, Governor of Gades.'

Tros bowed suitable acknowledgement. The Roman turned himself at leisure to observe the arrow engines and the crews at battle station by the catapults.

'What does this warlike preparation mean?' he asked.

'I am prepared!' Tros answered with a characteristic upward gesture of both hands. His left hand returned to his sword-hilt, whereat the Roman looked as if he had a bad smell under his nose.

'Prepared for what?'

'To receive your message and to answer hot or cold, whichever it calls for.'

'You are insolent.'

'Balbus charged you with something definite to say. I listen.'

'You would have found it wiser to have been courteous to me!' said Gaius Suetonius angrily. 'You will find insolence expensive!'

Tros almost turned his back, which brought him face to face with Conops, standing by the poop rail. He made a gesture, unseen by the Roman. Conops vaulted to the deck and went forward without noticeable haste. The Roman turned as if about to go, and spoke over his shoulder to add visible rudeness to his tone of cold contempt.

'Lucius Cornelius Balbus Minor invites you to the courthouse at the morning session to confer with him. He promises immunity for the occasion.'

'Wait!'

Tros's voice was like a thunderclap. It startled the Roman into facing about – suddenly, indignantly. So he did not notice the dozen Northmen whom Conops was shepherding one by one under the break of the poop. They came unostentatiously, but armed.

'Did Lucius Cornelius Balbus offer a guarantee?' Tros asked.

'You have his promise conveyed by me,' Gaius Suetonius retorted, sneering. But Tros smiled.

'It appears to me he sent you as hostage.'

The Roman's jaw dropped.

'By Bacchus!' he exploded. 'You will suffer for it if you try to make me prisoner! I represent the Senate and the Roman People!'

'Aye, handsomely!' Tros answered, grinning. 'I wouldn't spoil your finery! You and that slave of yours shall have snug quarters for a while, where he may keep your armour bright and you may tell him all about the Senate and the Roman people. Lest he grow weary of listening and try to slay you with that sword, I will keep it well out of his reach!'

Tros held out his hand. The Roman's right hand went to his sword-hilt and his face turned crimson with anger; the slave behind him made haste to pass the shield, but Conops was too quick, struck the slave over the jugular and the shield went clattering to the deck. The Northmen swarmed on to the poop and the Roman saw himself surrounded.

'Dog of a pirate, you shall pay for this!' he snarled. He held his chin high, but he drew his sword and gave it hilt-first into Tros's hand. Tros glanced at Conops.

'Into the forward deckhouse with them! Lock them in. No other restraint as long as they behave themselves. Stand you on guard with as many Northmen as you need.'

Gaius Suetonius strode forward fuming in the midst of his axe-armed escort. Tros could not resist a gibe at him.

'An omen! Lo, the Consul and his lictors! Is the foretaste of a consulship not worth the day's confinement, Gaius Suetonius?'

Tros went into the cabin where Simon sat with his head between his hands refusing to listen to Chloe's optimistic reassurances. And after a short conference with Chloe he wrote a letter in Greek because, though he understood Latin well enough, he could write the Greek more elegantly.

To the most noble and renowned Lucius Cornelius Balbus Minor, Governor of Gades. Greeting from Tros of Samothrace, the Master of the trireme 'Liafail', who cordially thanks you for your invitation to attend you at a session of the court.

Your statesmanlike provision of a hostage in the person of the noble Gaius Suetonius removes all possible objection to my visit, which, therefore, shall be made without delay, the more so since I appreciate the compliment of sending me as hostage one of such rank and so intimate in your secret counsels.

The hostage shall be comfortably housed and safely guarded. He shall be released unharmed, with the dignities due to his rank, immediately after my own safe return on board my ship.

That morning irony was running in Tros's veins. He felt an impulse to be mischievous. To use his own phrase, gods were whispering good jokes into his ear. A glance at Simon, shuddering with nervousness, and at Chloe, all smiles and excitement, confirmed his mood. He opened an iron chest and took from it the seal he had captured along with Caesar's private papers.

It was of glass and of marvellous workmanship, done by a Greek – a portrait of Julius Caesar naked, in the guise of the god Hermes, with an elephant's head below it, by the hand of some other artist who had certainly never seen an elephant.*

Tros melted a mass of wax and affixed the impression of that well-known seal at the foot of the letter, which he placed in a silver tube, and went and tossed it to the men in the boat that had brought out Gaius Suetonius.

'To the Governor of Gades, with all haste!' he commanded.

The boat backed away and made speed for the shore. Tros returned to the cabin and sent for Sigurdsen and Conops.

'In my absence,' he said, touching Sigurdsen's breast. 'you are captain of the ship. The crew obeys you. But you obey Conops, who is my representative. I go ashore, and unless I return before dawn tomorrow you will put to sea after demolishing that trireme on the beach and all the stores and sheds. If I shall have been made prisoner, that hint will probably convince the Romans that they would better release me. So you will keep in sight of the harbour mouth and hold speed with any boat the Romans send out. But

*The elephant's head became the seal of all the Caesars.

196

you are not to surrender that hostage Gaius Suetonius except in exchange for me.'

'Master, let me go with you!' urged Conops.

But there was no need for Chloe's warning frown: Tros had made up his mind.

'I can trust you afloat,' he remarked. 'Ashore you're too ready with your knife and a lot too fond of drink and women! Stand by the ship. You're in charge. Be careful of the prisoners.'

Jaun Aksue came then, none too deferential, demanding information as to when the shore leave might be had.

'We Eskualdenak are fond of seeing promises performed,' he remarked. 'My men are boasting they could swim ashore. Can you suggest to me how to restrain them?'

'Yes,' Tros answered gravely. 'Tell them I go to pay a visit to the Governor of Gades. I will seek permission for my best-behaved men to go roistering. But have you seen those Balearic slingers on the beach? You know their reputation? They can hit a man's head with a slung stone at two hundred paces. None of you have weapons. And mark this: Balbus the Governor needs cheap slaves for his quarry gangs. I will make him a free present of as many of my men as those Balearic slingers stun with their stones and capture!'

'But your promise holds? We are to have shore leave?'

'Certainly,' said Tros; 'but when it suits me and on condition you pretend you are my slaves.'

Chloe listened to that conversation, her eyes intently studying Tros's face. She turned to him and touched his arm when Aksue swaggered forward to explain the situation to his men.

'Lord Tros!' she exclaimed. 'You can make yourself master of Gades! I can show you how! Make use of Pkauchios until the moment when he – then – '

Tros gazed at her, his amber eyes admiring and yet smiling with a comprehension deeper than her own. It baffled her.

'What do you really seek in Gades?' she demanded.

He did not answer her for thirty seconds. Then:

'For a beginning, the Lord Orwic. Where is he?'

'In Pkauchios's house.'

'You shall take me to Pkauchios.'

His eyes did not leave her face. All sorts of probabilities were passing in review before his mind, not least of them that a Gades dancing-girl would hardly carry all her eggs in one chance-offered basket. She would have alternatives that she could switch to at a moment's notice.

'You would better go down in the hold,' he remarked, 'and confer with Horatius Verres. Better ask him whether he won't change his mind and try his luck again ashore.'

It seemed to Tros that Chloe caught her breath, but she was so well trained in self-command that he could not be quite sure.

'I will go to him. I will warn him to stay where he is,' she said, smiling, and was already on her way, but Tros detained her.

'Wait! He goes ashore now to take his chance in Gades unless you tell me who and what he is.'

Chloe stared, at first impudently, then with wavering emotions. Her lips began to move as if in spite of her.

'Tros of Samothrace, you are a strong man, yet you are not a pig. You have not made love to me. I can trust you?'

'Yes,' said Tros.

'If I tell you who Horatius Verres is – '

'I will keep it secret.'

'He is Caesar's spy!'

Tros did not move, although he shaped his lips as if to whistle.

'Caesar spies on Balbus?'

Chloe nodded. Tros began to stroke his chin.

'Horatius Verres has sent his messenger to Gaul,' said Chloe. 'There is nothing further he can do until – '

Tros seized her shoulder.

'Until Caesar himself comes!'

'Hispania is not Caesar's province! Caesar has Gaul. Pompey has Hispania.'

'I know it!'

'When does he come?'

'I don't know! Nobody knows! Horatius Verres doesn't know!'

'And Balbus?'

'No. He doesn't dream of it!'

'By land or sea?'

'None knows! Caesar never tells what he will do.'

'And Horatius Verres waits for him, eh, on my ship?'

'Tros, Lord Tros, you promised – '

'Go and talk to your Verres. Tell him I know he is Caesar's spy. Say I will not interfere with him.'

'I will not! If I admitted I had told you, he would cease to love me. He would say I am a common Gades dancing-girl.'

'Tell him I guessed he is Caesar's spy.'

'He would never believe. He is too keen. He can read me like writing.'

'I have seen writings that deceived the reader,' Tros remarked, and stroked his chin again.

'Listen!' exclaimed Chloe. 'Thus it happened: Caesar sent a thousand Gauls to Gades to be shipped to Rome for sale for his private account. Balbus put them in the quarries, where the most part died, for he did not feed them properly and there was a fever.* Caesar, receiving no word of the arrival of the slaves in Ostia, sent Horatius Verres to find out about it. He spied and he discovered that Pkauchios, pretending to have read the stars, told Balbus he might safely keep the slaves because Caesar will presently die.'

'How did Verres discover that?' Tros asked.

'I told him! Pkauchios makes prophecies come true. You understand me? He sent his own men to Gaul to murder Caesar. I knew all about it. I told Horatius Verres because he said he loves me, and I know that is the truth just as I know when an egg is fresh, just as I know I can trust you, Tros of Samothrace. But then I had to tell more, just as a witness has to when the torturers go to work. One piece of information led quite simply to the next. I told Horatius Verres how Pkauchios grew afraid that when Caesar is slain Balbus might turn on him and have him crucified for the sake of appearances. There are always plots on foot in Gades, so Pkauchios joined a conspiracy to murder Balbus. He began by merely listening and giving his advice, but now he leads it. And I am afraid! I am afraid Balbus may discover everything and put me to the torture. That is why I want my freedom quickly, quickly; why I want to get away from Gades!'

'And Horatius Verres lies in hiding while all this is afoot?'

'He hides from Pkauchios. Somebody, I don't know who, warned Pkauchios, who put a dozen men to look for him and kill him. But he was hiding in the midst of danger, on the roof of the *ergastulum*.'

'Hasn't he tried to warn Balbus?'

'He daren't. Besides, what does he care about Balbus? He is Caesar's man.'

'What do you mean by "he daren't?"'

'Balbus would order his head cut off or have him stabbed or crucify him. As soon as Pkauchios learned there was a spy of Caesar's in Gades, he pretended to read the stars and went to Balbus, saying there would come a Roman with a tale about conspiracies, but that the tale would be a lie and that the man's real purpose would be to get Balbus into difficulties with the Roman Senate.'

*Gades was always one of the unhealthiest places in Europe.

'And Balbus believed that?' Tros whistled softly to himself. 'And the Lord Orwic is with Pkauchios? And why waits Pkauchios?' he demanded. 'Why hasn't he slain Balbus?'

'He likes others to do that work,' Chloe answered. 'And the others are hard to bring up to the point. They are half mistrustful, and they fear the soldiers. It is always so in Gades – talk, talk, talk, and then someone at last dares it or else somebody betrays. There has been one betrayal already. Balbus has made some unimportant prisoners. But I think this time Pkauchios has his plans well laid and merely waits for the news of Caesar's death. Then he will strike swiftly, and he thinks all Hispania and Gaul will rise together and throw off the Roman yoke.'

Tros laughed.

'Your Pkauchios can dream!' he said with irony. 'When Gaul joins Hispania against the Romans we may look for the Greek Kalends! Divide – *divide et imperal** Go and talk to Horatius Verres in the hold. Reassure him and be swift about it. You shall take me to the courthouse to see Balbus, and thereafter to the house of Pkauchios.'

She hesitated. There was indecision, terror in her eyes. Her muscles twitched at the thought of the Roman tortures. Tros' nodded to her confidently.

'You shall have your freedom and your pearls and your Horatius Verres before tomorrow's dawn!'

Chloe stared into his amber eyes, nodded to herself and went down into the hold to do his bidding.

---

*'Divide and rule,' the motto of the Roman Empire and the secret of its mastery.

PKAUCHIOS THE ASTROLOGER

It has been my destiny to speak with wise men, of whom there are
more in the world than fools imagine. Though I comprehend not wisdom, I respect it; to salute it stirs in me no shame, whatever else. My
sword and my whole heart are at wisdom's bidding, if I find it. But the
wise are wisely quiet. They forbid not, neither do they bid me to go
storming after virtue, that being the impulse to which I yield because I
know no better.

Aye, I have met wise men. I have yet to meet one who dealt in treachery, or counselled treason, or pretended to know what he knew not.

From the log of Tros of Samothrace

Chloe had pushed Orwic into a room in a marvellous marble house
and left him face to face with Pkauchios, closing the curtains
behind him on their noisy rings and rod. Orwic stared at the
Egyptian, wondering at the severely splendid furnishings and at
the quiet that was accented by lute strings strummed slowly in
another room, suggesting the procession of the aeons and the
utter insignificance of days – months – years.

Pkauchios was dressed as an astrologer – a tall old man, immensely dignified, in flowing black robes and head-dress, with the
asp of Egypt on his brow, to which Tros would have at once known
he was not entitled. But Orwic knew nothing about Egypt. He had
an hypnotic presence, and used his large eyes as a swordsman
should, directing his gaze not at the pupils of the man in front of
him but a fraction of an inch lower, so producing the effect of an
indomitable stare without wearying himself or giving his op-
ponent a chance to retaliate.

He possessed almost the majesty of a Lord Druid, but that only
served to remind Orwic of the druids' warnings about magic. He
had been educated by the druids, and whatever else they taught,
they were succinct and vehement in their instruction as to the
danger of any contact with the black arts.

Bridling at the calculated silence, Orwic broke it, asking curt,
blunt questions:

'You are Pkauchios? I am Orwic of Britain. You sent for me?
You wish to speak to me? What do you wish to say?'

There was no answer, no acknowledgement. Sweet-scented

incense of lign-aloes burned on a tripod-table, and its blue smoke curled around the Egyptian until, where he stood in shadow, he began to look unearthly, and the human skull on another table near his right hand appeared to make grimaces, mocking the short-lived dreams of men.

Orwic shrugged his shoulders and strolled to the open window. Down a vista between well-tended garden shrubbery he could see Tros's ship at anchor, miles away. The sight encouraged him; he began to think of jumping through the window, measuring with his eyes the height of the wall at the end of the garden and calculating the distance to the beach. But the Egyptian spoke at last:

'Orwic, prince of Britain, fortune favours you!'

The voice was resonant, arresting, but the Gaulish words were ill-pronounced. Orwic remembered druids who had spoken in much the same terms more gently, and yet with infinitely greater majesty.

'I was born lucky,' he answered over his shoulder, and then resumed his gaze out of the window.

'Look at me. Look into my eyes,' said Pkauchios.

'I admire the view,' said Orwic, and continued to admire it.

Pkauchios ignored the snub and went on speaking as if Orwic had obeyed him. He badly mispronounced the Gaulish, but his voice compelled attention, and he was fluent.

'I, who nightly read the stars, have read your destiny! I fore-warned Balbus of the great ship with the golden serpent at her bow. The stars in their conjunction said that ship should – shall – must enter Gades harbour, and from out of her shall step one in whose hand is the destiny of Hispania and Gaul. I said, because the constellations indicated, that the man will be a prince from a far country, bold in war, young, handsome, destined to be lost in Gades but to be recovered by a stranger. Last night I told Balbus that the prince in the ship with the purple sails will arrive before dawn.'

'Well. Here I am, but it is not my ship,' said Orwic, and began to whistle softly to himself. When he was a little boy the druids told him that was the simplest means of avoiding a magician's snares.

But magicians are not easily rebuffed. The business of snaring men in nets made of imagination implies a thick skin and persistence, along with an immeasurable, cynical contempt for the prospective victim's powers of resistance.

'You are indeed the man the stars foretold,' said Pkauchios with admiration in his voice. 'Indifferent to flattery, not stirred by

202

rumour, iron-willed! It is of such men that the gods make weapons when the tyrannies shall fall! I see your aura – purple as the sails of yonder ship!'

He struck a bronze gong and the music in the next room ceased. The sound of the gong startled Orwic, for it resembled the clash of weapons. He turned suddenly to face the Egyptian, who was no longer standing but seated on a sort of throne, whose arms were the gilded tusks of elephants. There was a canopy above the throne that threw that corner into deeper shadow, and the Egyptian's eyes appeared to blaze as if there were fire in them. In his lap he held a crystal ball, which he raised in both hands when he was sure that Orwic's gaze was fixed on him.

'Approach me!' he commanded. 'Nay, not too close, or your shadow dims the astral light!'

He was staring at the crystal, frowning heavily, brows raised, lips parted, eyes glaring. The effort he was making seemed to tax his powers almost beyond endurance.

'You are the man!' he said at last, and sighing, set the crystal down on the table where the skull stood. His eyes had lost their frenzy suddenly. He leaned back, looking deathly weary, all the lines and wrinkles on his dark face emphasized by pallor.

'You, who listen, never know what we, who look into the unseen, suffer for your sakes,' he said.

Even his voice was aged. Orwic began to feel pity for him, and something akin to shame for his former rudeness.

Pkauchios left the throne and, walking forward wearily, took Orwic by the arm. His manner was of age that leaned on youth with perfect confidence.

'So, help me to that seat and sit beside me.'

They sat down on a bench of carved ebony, and Pkauchios leaned his back against the wall.

'Youth! Youth!' he said. 'With all the world before you! Age must serve youth. We who have struggled and are old may justify ourselves if we can guide youth through the dangers. Age and responsibility! If I should guide you wrongly, what responsibility were mine! I will say nothing. It is wiser. I will not foreshadow destiny.'

Now that was something like the druids' way of viewing interference with a man's own privilege of living as he sees fit. Orwic began to feel a vague respect for the Egyptian and to wonder whether he had not misjudged him. He might after all be a seer. It has hardly reasonable to suppose that all the prophets were in Britain. However, Orwic was still cautious.

'I don't believe in magic,' he remarked.

'Rightly! Rightly so!' said Pkauchios. 'It is destruction. It will destroy the Romans. It has ruined nations without number. Fools, who know no better, call me a magician. When I tell the truth to them, they weary me with their demands for untruth. It is restful to meet you. Honest unbelief is sweeter to me than the dark credulity of those who seek nothing but their selfish ends. Your incredulity will melt. Their superstition toughens as it feeds on vice. But I must crave your pardon. I am a laggard host, forgetting the body's needs in the absorption of a spiritual moment. You are hungry, I have no doubt.'

He clapped his hands, and almost on the instant two slave girls appeared bearing trays heaped with refreshment. One of them washed Orwic's hands and combed his hair; the other spread before him milk, fruit, nuts, three sorts of bread, butter, honey, and preserves, whose very scent excited appetite.

'I will return when you have refreshed yourself,' said Pkauchios. 'We who commune with the stars eat little earthly food.'

He left the room, but the slave girls stayed and converted Orwic's first meal on foreign soil into an experience that melted his reserve.

He began by being half ashamed to eat while the Egyptian fasted, remembering that the druids hardly ate at all during their periods of spiritual commune with the universe. He began to be almost sure that fasting was a sign of the Egyptian's purity of purpose. It was incredible that such food as the slave girls set before him should not tempt a man with worldly motives – such as Orwic's own, for instance.

He began to confess to himself that he was having a glorious time, and he hoped Tros would not come for him too soon. Deeply though he admired Tros, loyal though he felt toward him, he dreaded Tros's abrupt way of dispersing dreams and scattering side issues. He could imagine Tros's contempt, for instance, for the slave girls. Orwic liked them.

Used to slaves and serving-women in his own land, he had never dreamed of such attentions as these two dark-haired women lavished on him. They were beautiful, smiling, silent, exquisitely trained, but that was not the half of it. In Britain guests were made to feel that their comfort was the host's one sole consideration, and the servants vied with one another to that end. But those two slave girls made man feel that he owned them, that their very souls were his, that they would think his thoughts if he would only deign to half express them, and be overjoyed to be the mothers of his sons.

204

It was bewildering at first, embarrassing; then gradually rather pleasant; presently as natural as if all other forms of hospitality were crude, uncivilized, and no part of a nobleman's experience. This was the way to live. It was no wonder that foreigners regarded Britons as barbarians, with their crude ideas of courtesy and the servants' air of being members of the family instead of servants in the true sense of the word.

One of the girls was on his knee when Pkauchios returned. She was wiping his mouth and moustache with a napkin. She removed herself in no haste, unembarrassed, curtseying to her master, helping the other girl at once to carry out the tray and dishes. Pkauchios took no notice of either of them, which seemed to Orwic to prove that the man was an aristocrat, if nothing else.

'You are right, you are right,' said Pkauchios, taking a seat beside him. 'You should have nothing to do with magic. It is safer to avoid true revelation than to listen to the false. But tell me why you came to Gades.'

Orwic told him all of it; told him the whole story of how Caesar had invaded Britain and had been repulsed; and how Tros of Samothrace, for friendship and because his ship was built in Britain, had undertaken to go to Rome and by any means that should present themselves to deter Caesar from invading a second time.

'Wonderful! Wonderful!' said Pkauchios when the tale was done and Orwic has finished his eulogiums of Tros. 'All this and more I have seen written in the stars. You are a man of destiny. And yet – '

He leaned into the corner, frowning. It appeared that the decision between right and wrong, between his own high standard of integrity and a convenient alternative, was forming in his brain.

' – if I should tell you what else I have seen – '

'Oh, you may as well tell me,' Orwic interrupted. 'I am not a child. And besides, I will do nothing without consulting Tros.'

'Do you not see,' said Pkauchios, 'that if Hispania were to rebel against the Romans, Caesar's army would be needed to prevent the Gauls from rising too?'

'Yes, that seems obvious,' said Orwic. He was devoting at least half his attention to wondering where those slave girls were. The scent from the one who had sat on his knee still clung to his tunic. No British girls that he had known had ever smelled like that.

'And if Caesar were to die,' said Pkauchios.

205

He paused, aware that Orwic was only partly listening to him.

'And if Caesar were to die,' he repeated solemnly, then suddenly he gripped Orwic's arm and leaning forward, fixing him with penetrating gaze, almost hissed the words:

'Do you not see that you and Tros of Samothrace, with Hispania in red rebellion, north, south, east and west, could lead the insurrection into Gaul and stir the Gauls until they too rise against the Romans?'

He sat back again and sighed.

'All this,' he said, 'and more, I have seen written in the stars. Sight must be given us that we may see. And yet – '

'Such a deed would save Britain,' remarked Orwic. He was thinking now.

He was still aware of the faint, delicious woman smell, but its effect on him was changing. There were thoughts of women whom a sword could win, quite other thoughts than Orwic was accustomed to, thoughts not exactly chivalrous but blended in with chivalry, suggesting that the rescue of the Gauls from Roman rule might lead to a delightful destiny. He began to wonder what Tros would have to say to the proposal, and whether Tros too, secretly, in the recesses of his heart, would not rather like the prospect of – well, of whatever victory might provide.

'I should not be surprised at anything,' he said after a moment's pause. 'When I left Britain it was to face my destiny, whatever it might be. Now that girl Chloe – is it true she is your slave?'

Pkauchios' answer was startling:

'Do you covet her? Shall I give her to you?'

It was almost too startling; it rearoused suspicion. Orwic eyed the Egyptian narrowly, turning over in his mind vague notions as to how much Chloe might be worth. He was not so stupid as to believe that offer genuine.

'If you should do what the stars indicate you safely may do,' Pkauchios said mysteriously, 'then by tomorrow's dawn you will be all-powerful in Gades. I shall need your friendship then. To flaming youth in the hour of victory, what gift could be more suitable than Chloe? I am an old man. Her beauty means nothing to me.'

Orwic's veins began to boil, so, being British, he proceeded to look preternaturally wise.

'What is all this about destiny? What did you read in the stars?' he demanded.

'You would better not let me influence you,' Pkauchios suggested. 'I have never yet made one mistake in reading other's destiny, but I have no right!'

'Oh, nonsense! Out with it!' said Orwic. 'If you can read my destiny, you have no right not to tell me.'

'I must have your definite permission.'

'You have it.'

'Know then, that the stars have indicated for a month that this is the night when Balbus, Governor of Gades, dies! On this night too dies Caesar, imperator of the Roman troops in Gaul! But the conjunction of the stars is such that, if the Governor of Gades dies by the hand of a common murderer, as may be, then anarchy will follow and no good come of it. But should he die by the hand of the prince who stepped out of the red ship and was lost in Gades, then the prince shall wear a red cloak and shall rule a province.'

'Strange!' said Orwic. 'Strange! I have had peculiar dreams of late.'

'And how many men have you on board that ship?' asked Pkauchios. 'If I should show you how to smuggle them ashore and where to hide them, and how to reach Balbus's house unseen at midnight, and should tell you that in Balbus's treasury is money enough with which to recompense those men of yours and to pay others and to raise an army – '

'I am not a murderer. I am not a thief,' said Orwic, his sense of self-restraint returning.

'Did you slay no Romans when they invaded Britain?' Pkauchios asked. 'Did the Romans slay none of your friends? According to the stars, that prince who steps out of the red ship is to be an avenger and shall drive the Romans out of Gaul!'

'Ah, now you are trying to persuade me!' Orwic commented.

'Not I! But I will give you Chloe if you seize your opportunity. She is the richest prize in Gades. She is worth two hundred thousand sesterces.'

Orwic had not the slightest notion how much money that was so he magnified it in his own mind, and the result rearoused suspicion. He got up and began to pace the floor, to discover whether or not Pkauchios was proposing to detain him forcibly. But Pkauchios made no move; simply leaned against a corner of the wall and watched him. Orwic decided to probe deeper; he desired to justify temptation by proving to himself that Pkauchios was friend, not enemy. He drew back the curtains at the doorway by which he had entered the room. There was nobody there. He passed into a hall lined with statuary, entered rooms that opened to the right and left of it, found nobody, and tried the house door.

It was unlocked; doves were cooing in the garden; fountains splashed; there were no lurkers; only a few old Egyptian slaves who dipped out water from a well a hundred yards away.

Plainly, then, he was not a prisoner. And as he breathed the incense smoke out of his lungs, refilling them with blossom-scented air, he felt the challenge of his youth and strength.

'Off Vectis, the Lord Druid said,' he muttered to himself, 'there is a man in Gades to whom he could have sent Tros, only that Tros's mind was closed against him. This Pkauchios is probably the man!'

Musing to himself, his hands behind him, he returned along the hall toward the room where he had left the old Egyptian. Chloe had said he should agree to anything the Egyptian should propose. It might do no harm to pretend to agree. But he wondered how he should explain away his rudeness, how he should accept the man's proffered aid now without cheapening his own position, and above all, how he should explain to Tros.

'You must help me to convince the Lord Tros,' he began, re-entering the room.

But Pkauchios was gone. There was no trace of him nor any answer, though he called his name a dozen times.

BALBUS QUI MURUM AEDIFICABIT

I believe it is true that people have the rulers they deserve. The very wise have said so. Nothing that I have seen has made me think the contrary.

Therefore, when I observe those rulers, is it insolence in me to hope that these, whom I rule, are a little worthier than some?

From the log of Tros of Samothrace

Pondering the situation in all its bearings, Tros called Chloe back into the cabin while the deck crew lowered Simon into the long-boat.

'Your Horatius Verres waits for Caesar and is Caesar's man. You have befriended Verres. Therefore Caesar will befriend you. Why, then, should you be in haste to flee from Gades?'

'Torture!' she said, and shuddered. 'Horatius Verres sent a messenger who may reach Caesar in time to warn him. But if Balbus dies and Caesar comes, then Caesar will investigate – '

'This is not his province. He has no authority in Hispania.'

'He is Caesar,' Chloe answered. 'And I shall be tortured, be-cause Pkauchios will certainly be found out and they will need my evidence against him.'

'So, unless we save Balbus's life – '

Chloe looked into Tros's eyes. She laid the palms of her hands against his breast, her lip quivering for a second – on the verge of tears, but struggling to regain her self-control.

'Lord Tros,' she said, 'there isn't a slave in Gades but knows Caesar would jump at an excuse to invade Pompey's province. Pompey and Caesar pretend to be friends. They're as friendly as two lovers of one woman! Balbus is Pompey's nominee, and he is willing to win Gaul for Pompey or to betray Hispania into Caesar's hands, whichever of the two he thinks is stronger. All men know there will be war before long, and none can guess whether Pompey or Caesar will win. Pompey is lazy, proud, rich, popular, Caesar is energetic, loved, feared, hated, deep in debt.'

'Wager your peculium on Caesar!' Tros advised.

'Nay, on Horatius Verres! Have you ever loved a woman?' she asked.

Tros did not answer. He stroked his chin, watching her eyes. She asked him another question.

'Do you think it possible for me to tell the truth?'

He nodded. He expected a prodigious lie was coming. Her eyes were melting, soft, abrim with tears, held bravely back. The stage was all set for Gadean trickery. But she surprised him.

'I would die for Horatius Verres! I would submit to torture for him. But not for you, Pkauchios, Simon, Balbus, Caesar, nor any other man!'

'Pearls?' Tros asked her, studying her face.

She reached for the hem of her chlamys and produced the one pearl he had already given her, holding it out in the palm of her hand.

'You may keep them! Simon may keep my money unless you find a way of freeing me tonight! I will sing no more. I will dance no more and please none but myself. For they shall bury me where the other dead slaves' bodies rot if I lose Horatius Verres. Tros of Samothrace, if you have never loved a woman – '

'Come,' said Tros.

The longboat set them on the seaweed-littered beach, where an officer of Balearic slingers, aping Roman airs and very splendid in his clanking bronze, signed to Tros to pass on, but demanded to be told by what right Simon the Jew paid visits to a foreign ship in harbour. A party of Simon's slaves, with his great, unwieldy, panelled litter in their midst had been detained some distance off, a detachment of slingers guarding them.

Simon began to argue excitedly, gesticulating, gasping as the nervousness increased his asthma. Chloe interrupted.

'Do you know me?' she asked.

'I pass you, exquisite Chloe!' the officer answered in Latin with an atrocious Balearic accent.

'I pass Simon!' she retorted. 'Do you dare to prevent me?'

'But, Chloe – '

'Bring me Simon's slaves or count me your enemy!' she interrupted.

With a half-humorous grimace the officer beckoned to his men to let Simon's slaves advance.

'Remember me, O favourite of Fortune!' he said to Chloe. 'My name is Metellus.'

'I will mention you to Balbus. I will lie to him about your good looks and your loyalty,' she promised, and motioned to Simon to climb into his litter.

'Be your memory as nimble as your wits and feet!' Metellus

answered, shrugging his shoulders and signing to his men to let the party pass.

Those Balearic slingers lined along the beach were a godsend from Tros's point of view. There was a crowd of hucksters, pimps, idlers and loose women noisily protesting because the soldiers would not let them approach the shore. In the distance, where the fishing-boats were anchored, three liburnians patrolled the water-front and kept small boats from putting out. There was no chance of communication with the ship, no risk of the crew getting drunk or of Jaun Aksue and his Eskualdenak escaping.

All the way to the city gate the road was lined with idlers who had come to stare and touts who heralded the fame of Gades, brothels. They praised Tros's purple cloak, admired his bulk and strength, flattered, coaxed and tried to tempt him with descriptions of alleged delights, pawing at him, pulling, fighting one another, spitting and cursing at Simon's slaves for thrusting the litter through their ranks. They offered horses, donkeys, mules, drink, women, and at last a litter.

Tros hired the litter and bade Chloe climb into it and ride with him. But she refused.

'There are some things I cannot do. Once I bought a litter. But it is against the law for a slave or even for freed women. The Romans' wives threatened to have me whipped. So I walk, and those women envy me my health, if nothing else!'

They were stared at by the gate-guards and by the crowd that swarmed there, but not in any way molested. There was no wheeled traffic, but the narrow street was choked with burdened slaves! mules, oxen and leisured pedestrians who flowed in a colourfu hot stream between the lines of stalls and booths that backed against the houses. There was a din of chaffering and a drone of flies where the fruit and meat and fish shops made splurges of raw colour; and there was a stench of overcrowded tenements that made Tros cough and gasp.

But people were less curious inside the city, and Chloe's presence had more effect. She walked ahead with one of Simon's slaves on either side of her, and the crowd made way, occasionally cheering, calling compliments, addressing her by name as if she were a free celebrity. One man, forcing his way through the crowd, presented her with flowers and begged her to ride in his chariot if he should win next month's quadriga race in the arena.

She nodded gaily and led on along the winding street until it widened suddenly and approached an irregular square with trees along one side of it and a statue of Balbus, the governor, in the midst. On the left hand of the street, with its front toward the square, was a great white building with small, iron-barred windows, and the legend S.P.Q.R. in enormous letters amid scroll work all along the coping. From the windows issued shrill, spasmodic, tortured woman's screams, increasing and increasing, until the street crowd set its teeth and some laughed nervously. It ceased abruptly, only to begin again.

There was no passing at that point. The crowd jammed the street. Even Chloe was helpless to force a way through, and while she pushed, coaxed, pleaded, argued, a girl younger than herself rushed out of a doorway fighting frantically with the crowd that interfered with her and, falling to her knees, seized Chloe's legs.

Her face was half hidden in a shawl; Chloe pulled it back and recognized her. The girl sobbed, and as the screams from the window rose to a shrill, broken summit of inflicted agony, she burst into a torrent of stuttering words all choked with sobs, her fingers clutching Chloe's knees.

Tros rolled out of the litter, for it was useless to try to force that eight-manned object through the crowd. He touched Chloe's shoulder.

'Her mother!' she whispered. 'Some informer has told Balbus of a plot. He takes her mother's testimony.'

She stooped and kissed the girl, then broke away from her and, beckoning to Tros to follow, began using violence and Balbus's name to force her way through, the crowd gradually yielding.

Around the corner, on the side of the building that faced the trees, eight Roman soldiers under a decurion leaned on spears beside the stone steps that led to a wide arched entrance. Beyond them, in the shadow of the wall, eight more legionaries stood guard over a group of miserable prisoners, gibing at them when they shuddered at the screams that could be heard there even more distinctly than in the street because the stone arch of the entrance magnified the noise. Held back by a rope between the steps and the trees at the back of the square was a crowd of Romans, Spaniards, Greeks, Moors, Jews, slaves and freemen, their voices making a sea of sound that paused regularly when the screams increased.

Chloe led Tros to the steps and whispered Balbus's name to the decurion in charge, who stared at Tros but nodded leave to enter. They fought their way into a crowded lobby, where men and women stood on tiptoe trying to see through the open courtroom door over the shoulders of two legionaries whose spears and broad backs blocked the way. There was hardly breathing room. A

212

woman in a corner had fainted and a man was pouring water on her from a lion's-mouth drinking fountain built into the wall.

Chloe kicked, shoved, imprecated, cried out Balbus's name and worked her way at last, with Tros behind her, until she touched the spears held horizontally across the room and Tros could see over her shoulder into the crowded courtroom.

The screams for the moment had ceased. On a sort of throne on a raised daïs, with a chair on either side of it on which the secretaries sat, was Balbus, governor of Gades, exquisitely groomed, pale, clocking at his front teeth with a thumbnail. He was handsome, but much darker than the average Roman;* there were rings under his eyes, that had a bored look, as if he found it difficult to concentrate on a subject that vaguely irritated him. His crisp black hair was turning grey, although he was a comparatively young man. He looked decidedly unhealthy.

Presently he sat bolt upright and the crowded courtroom grew utterly still. When he spoke his well-trained voice had the suggestion of a sneer, and his frown was a tyrant's, impatient, exacting, final – like the corners of his mouth that tightened when his lips moved.

'I have considered the advocate's argument. It is true, it is a principle of Roman law that no injustice shall be done; but this woman is not a Roman citizen, nor is she the mother of more than one child, so she has no rights that are involved in this instance. Treason has been charged against the Senate and the Roman People, a most serious issue. This woman has refused to answer truthfully the questions put to her, although she has been accused of knowing the conspirators' names. Let the torturers continue. Apply fire.'

He leaned forward, elbow on his knee, and again the awful screams began to fill the stone-roofed hall. A scream from the street re-echoed them. The crowd on the wooden benches reached and craned to get a better view, and the sentries in the doorway stood on tiptoe; all that Tros could see over their shoulders was a glimpse of the men who held the levers of a rack and the red glow of a charcoal brazier. There began to be a stench of burning flesh.

Chloe stepped under the spears of the sentries; one of them reached out an arm, but recognized her as she turned to threaten him, grinned and nodded to her to go wherever she pleased. She disappeared into the crowd that stood in the aisle between the benches. The next Tros saw of her she was in front of the daïs, looking up at Balbus, who sat motionless, chin on hand, elbow

*Balbus was born in Africa.

213

on knee, apparently not listening. The tortured woman's screams made whatever Chloe said inaudible to anyone but Balbus, and, perhaps, his secretaries, who, however, were at pains to appear busy with their tablets.

Balbus suddenly sat upright, raising his right hand.

'Cease!' he exclaimed in a bored voice. 'There will be a short recession. Remove the witness. Let the doctor see to her. After the recession I will examine the other witnesses in turn. It is possible we may not need this one's testimony.'

The witness's screams died to a sobbing moan, and there was a murmur in the courtroom. Someone cried out, 'Favouritism!' At the rear of the room there were audible snickers. Ushers and sentries roared for silence and, as two men carried the victim out on a stretcher through a side door, Balbus spoke with a metallic snarl:

'I will clear the court if there are further demonstrations! This is not a spectacle, but a judicial process. A courtroom is not an arena. Let decency attend the acts of justice. The next spectator who betrays disrespect for the dignity of Roman justice shall be soundly flogged!'

He arose and left the courtroom by a door at the rear of the daïs, nodding to Chloe as he went. She seized a court official by the arm and the crowd in the aisle made way in front of them. The official, lemon-faced, his skin a mass of wrinkles, sly-eyed from experience of litigation and his long nose looking capable of infinite suspicion, beckoned to Tros. The sentries let him through, and the crowd in the courtroom turned to stare as he swaggered up the aisle, his sea-legs giving him a roll that showed off his purple cloak and his great bulk to advantage. With his sword in its purple scabbard and the broad gold band that bound his heavy coils of black hair, he looked like a king on a visit of state, and, what was more to his purpose, he knew it. They passed the torture implements, where a Sicilian slave on his knees blew at a charcoal brazier in preparation for the next unwilling witness; the long-nosed official opened the door at the rear of the daïs and Chloe, all smiles and excitement, led the way in.

'The renowned and noble Tros of Samothrace!' she exclaimed, and shut the door behind her, leaning her back against it.

Balbus looked up. He was sitting by the window of a square room lined with racks of parchments, holding toward the light a tablet, which he appeared to find immensely interesting. Tros approached him and bowed, hand on hilt.

'So you are that pirate?' said Balbus, looking keenly at him.

'That is Caesar's view of it,' Tros answered. 'I had the great Pompeius' leave to come and go and to use all Roman ports, but Caesar stole my father's ship and slew him.'

'Why do you come to Gades?'

'To find a friend who shall make it safe for me to take my ship to Ostia, and there to leave the ship at anchor while I go to Rome.'

'For what purpose?'

'To stir Caesar's enemies against him; or, it may be, to persuade his friends of the unwisdom of his course. I hope to keep him from invading Britain.'

'Who is this friend whom you propose to find in Gades?'

'Yourself, for all I know,' said Tros, spreading his shoulders and smiling. 'I offer *quid pro quo*. A friend of mine may count on me for friendship.'

Balbus was silent for a long time, appearing to be studying Tros's face, but there was a look behind his eyes as if he were revolving a dozen issues in his mind.

'You took a hostage from me!' he said suddenly.

'Aye, and a good-looking one!' Tros answered. 'I was fortunate. You shall have him back when I leave Gades. I am told he knows your secrets.'

'What if I hold you against him?' Balbus sneered; but he could not keep his eyes from glancing at Tros's sword.

Tros smiled at him.

'Why, in that case, my lieutenant would take my ship to Ostia. And I wonder whether that hostage, whom he will there surrender to the Romans, will keep your secrets as stoutly as the woman in the court just now kept hers!'

Balbus glared angrily, but Tros smiled back at him, his hand remaining on his sword-hilt.

'However, why do we talk of reprisals?' Tros went on after an awkward pause. 'Balbus, son of Balbus, is it wisdom to reject a friendship that the gods have brought you on a western wind?'

Balbus looked startled, but tried to conceal it. Chloe, her back to the door, took courage in her teeth and interrupted in a strained voice:

'What said Pkauchios? A red ship with a purple sail? A bold man in a purple cloak?'

'Peace, thou!' commanded Balbus, but in another second he was smiling at her. 'Chloe,' he said, 'you dance for me tonight?'

She nodded.

'As long as Pkauchios owns me.'

Balbus stared at her, frowning:

'Pkauchios will never manumit you!' he said. 'You know too many secrets.'

Chloe bit her lip, as if she regretted having spoken, but her eyes were on Tros's face, and appeared to be urging him to follow the cue she had given.

'Balbus, what if I should save your life?' Tros asked. 'What then? Or shall I sail away and leave you?'

Again Chloe interrupted:

'Balbus, what said Pkauchios? What said the auguries? "Death stalks you in the streets of Gades unless Fortune intervenes!"'

Balbus stared at Tros again.

'How come you to know about conspiracies in Gades?' he demanded.

'I too consult the auguries,' said Tros. 'For my ship's sake I read the stars as some men read a woman's eyes. The stars have blinked me into Gades. The very whales have beckoned me! My dreams for nine nights past in storms at sea have been of Gades and a man's life I shall save.'

Balbus's lips opened a little and his lower jaw came slowly forward. He used his left hand for a shield against the sunlight streaming through the window and, leaning sidewise, peered at Tros again.

'You look like a blunt, honest seaman,' he remarked, 'save that you are dressed too handsomely and overbold!'

'My father was a prince of Samothrace,' Tros answered; whereat Balbus shrugged his shoulders. It was no part of the policy of Roman governors to appear much thrilled by foreign titles of nobility.

Now Tros was utterly perplexed what course to take, for which reason he was careful to look confident. He knew the information he had from Chloe might be a network of lies. There might be no truth whatever, for instance, in her statement that Caesar was on his way to Gades; on the other hand, it might be true, and Balbus might be perfectly aware of it. Examining Balbus's eyes, he became sure of one thing – Balbus was no idealist; a mere suggestion of an altruistic aim would merely stir the man's suspicion.

'I come to fish in troubled waters,' Tros remarked. 'I seek advantage in your disadvantage.'

Suddenly, as if some friendly god had whispered in his ear, he thought of the Balearic slingers on the beach and how readily their officer had yielded to Chloe's arrogant support of Simon.

He remembered that shrug of the shoulders when she promised to praise him to Balbus.

'Are your troops dependable?' he asked, knowing that mutiny was as perennial as the seasons wherever Roman troops were kept too long in idleness. He began to wonder whether, perhaps, Balbus had not sent for Caesar to help him out of an emergency. Secretaries, slaves might have spread such a rumour. Chloe might have magnified it and distorted it for reasons of her own; the Gades dancing-girls, he knew, were capable of any intrigue. For that matter Horatius Verres might be Balbus's spy, not Caesar's.

But Balbus's startled stare was more or less convincing. And it dawned on Tros that a Roman governor who felt entirely sure of his own authority would not yield so complacently to that hostage trick; a man with his nerve unshaken would have countered promptly by arresting Tros himself. Balbus was worried, nervous, trying to conceal the fact. Subduing irritation, he ignored Tros's question and retorted with another.

'You used Caesar's seal! What do you know of Caesar's movements?'

'None except Caesar can guess what he will do next,' Tros said, trying to suggest by his expression that he knew more than he proposed to tell.

'Word came,' said Balbus, 'that you fought a battle with his biremes. I have heard that the druids of Gaul report to you all Caesar's moves in advance. Can you tell me where he is now? If you tell the truth, I will do you any favour within my power.'

The pupils of Tros's amber eyes contracted suddenly. His head jerked slightly in Chloe's direction, and Balbus took the hint.

'Chloe,' he said, 'go you to that woman who was tortured. Help to bandage her. Condole with her. Try to persuade her to confess to you the names of the conspirators who are plotting against my life. Tell her that if she confesses she shall not be tortured any more, and she may save others from the rack.'

Chloe left the room, and Tros did not care to turn his head to see what effect the dismissal had on her.

'Now what do you know of Caesar?' Balbus asked.

Tros smiled. He was determined not to answer until sure of where the forks of Balbus's own dilemma pricked. And the longer Tros hesitated the more confident Balbus grew that Tros knew more than he would tell without persuasion.

'You are Caesar's enemy?' he asked.

Tros nodded.

217

'I am of the party of Pompeius Magnus,' Balbus remarked, narrowing his eyes.

Tros nodded again.

'It would not offend Pompeius Magnus if – ah – if death should overtake Caesar,' Balbus remarked, and looked the other way.

'So I should imagine,' Tros said, watching him.

Balbus stroked his chin. It had been beautifully shaven. Tros kept silence. Balbus had to resume the conversation:

'If Caesar should visit Gades and should die, all Rome would sigh with relief; but the Senate would assert its own dignity by crucifying any Roman who had killed him. You understand me?'

Again Tros nodded. He was having hard work to suppress excitement, but his breath came regularly, slowly. Even his hand on the jewelled sword-hilt rested easily. Balbus appeared irritated at his calmness. He spoke sharply:

'But if an enemy of Caesar slew him – ' Tros passed a hand over his mouth to hide a smile – 'that man would have a thousand friends in Rome!' Balbus went on. Then, after a moment's pause, his eyes on Tros, 'Caesar's corpse would harm no friends of yours in Britain!'

For as long as thirty breaths Tros and Balbus eyed each other. Then:

'Spies have informed me,' said Balbus, 'of a rumour that Caesar intends to come here. What else than that news brought you into Gades? Did you not come to waylay and kill him?'

Tros assumed the slyest possible expression.

'I should need such guarantees of safety and immunity as even Balbus might find it hard to give,' he remarked.

'We can discuss that later on,' said Balbus. 'Caesar moves swiftly and secretly, but I know where he was three days ago. He cannot be here for four or five days yet. We have time.'

However, Tros remembered his friend Simon – probably already home by now and in abject terror awaiting news of the interview. Also he thought of Chloe. Those were two whose loyalty he needed to bind to himself, by all means and as soon as possible.

'I will make a first condition now,' he said abruptly. 'Simon the Jew owes money, but cannot pay. He says you owe him money and will not pay. Will you settle with Simon?'

Balbus looked exasperated.

'Bacchus!' he swore under his breath.

It needed small imagination to explain what situation he was in. Like any other Rome governor, he had been forced to send enormous sums to Rome to defray his own debts and to bribe the professional blackmailers who lived by accusing absentees before the Senate. He had not been long enough in Gades to accumulate reserves of extorted coin.

Tros understood the situation perfectly. He also knew how men in debt snatch eagerly at temporary respite.

'There is no haste for the money,' he remarked. 'Let Simon write an order on your treasury which you accept for payment, say, in six months' time.'

Balbus nodded.

'That would be an unusual concession,' he said, 'from a man in my position. But I see no serious objection.'

'Would anyone in Gades dare to refuse to accept such a document in payment of a debt?' Tros asked him.

Balbus stiffened, instantly assertive of his dignity.

'Some men will dare almost anything – once!' he remarked. 'It would be a dangerous indiscretion!'

'Even if it were the price of the manumission of a slave?'

'Even so.'

'Very well,' said Tros. 'There is a female slave in Gades whom I covet. Can you order the sale of that slave to me?'

'Not so,' said Balbus. 'But I can order the slave manumitted at the price at which the owner has declared that slave for taxation purposes, and provided the slave pays the manumission tax of ten per cent on her market value.'

'I am at the age when a woman means more to me than money,' Tros remarked.

Balbus nodded. That was no new thing. The dry smile on his face revealed that he thought he had Tros in the hollow of his hand.

'But how did you make the acquaintance of this slave in Gades?' he asked curiously.

Tros could lie on the spur of a moment as adroitly as he could change the ship's helm to defeat the freaks of an Atlantic wind.

'She was sold under my eyes in Greece two years ago. I was outbidden,' he answered promptly. 'I learned she was brought to Gades and, if you must know, that is why I risked coming here. She is extremely beautiful. I saw her just now in the street.'

'Do you know who owns her?'

'I will find out.'

'Well,' said Balbus, 'make your inquiries cautiously, or her owner may grow suspicious and spirit her out of sight. You would better get her name and legal description, her owner's name and her taxable value, have the document drawn and bring it to me to sign before the owner learns anything about it.'

'When? Where?' Tros asked him.

Balbus turned in his chair suddenly and looked straight into Tros's face, staring long and keenly at him.

'At my house. Tonight,' he said deliberately, using the words with emphasis, as a man might who was naming an enormous stake in a game of chance. 'I bid you to my house to supper at one hour after sunset. There is an Egyptian named Pkauchios in Gades, an astrologer of great ability in the prediction of events. For two months he has predicted daily that Caesar will die very soon by violence. Last night, between midnight and the dawn, he came to me predicting your arrival after sunrise. He prophesied that you shall serve me in a matter of life and death. I am thinking, if it should be my life and the death of Caesar . . .'

'I must consult this Pkauchios!' said Tros, and Balbus nodded. 'I will send you to him.'

'No,' said Tros, 'for then he will know I come from you. And if he has lied to you, he will lie to me. But if I may go alone I may get the truth from him. I will not slay Caesar unless I know the elements are all propitious.'

'Go to him then,' Balbus answered. 'Make yourself as inconspicuous in Gades as you can. Bring me an exact account tonight of all that Pkauchios has said to you. I will sign the order for Simon's money and for the manumission of that slave girl just to let you feel my generosity. Thereafter we will discuss the terms on which you shall – ah – shall – ah – act as the instrument of Fate.'

CONSPIRACY

Money? Aye, I need it. But has money brains, heart, virtue, intelligence, courage, faith, hope, vision? He who sets his course by money sees a false star. He who measures by it is deceived, and his measure is false wherewith he measures all else.

From the log of Tros of Samothrace

The litter Tros had hired had vanished when he left the courtroom. In its place was a sumptuous thing with gilded pomegranates at the corners of the curtained awning, borne by eight slaves in clean white uniform. An Alexandrian eunuch, who seemed to have enough authority to keep the crowd at bay, came forward, staff in hand, to greet Tros at the courthouse steps.

'My master, the noble Pkauchios, invites you,' he said, bowing, gesturing toward the littler.

'Where is my own litter?' Tros demanded.

The eunuch smiled, bowing even more profoundly.

'My master would be ashamed that you should ride in such a hired thing to his house. I took the liberty in his name of dismissing it and paying the trifling charges.'

Tros hesitated. He would have preferred to go first to Simon's house, supposing that the Jew had hurried home to wait for him, but as he glanced to left and right in search of Simon's litter the eunuch interpreted that thought.

'Simon the Jew is also my master's guest,' he announced.

Tros disbelieved that. It was incredible that Simon should accept hospitality from a man whom he had so recently described as a vile magician. But the decurion in charge of the soldiers at the courthouse entrance nodded confirmation.

'Simon went to have his fatness charmed away,' he suggested with a grin. 'Pkauchios has a name for working miracles.'

Reflecting that in any event he had better see Orwic as soon as possible, Tros rolled into the splendid litter. There was no sign of Chloe, and he did not care to arouse comment by asking for her. He was borne away in haste, the soldiers shouting to the crowd to make way for the litter, and, after a long ride through well-swept but fetid-smelling streets, he was set down at Pkauchios's front

221

gate, where the eunuch ushered him into the marble house, not announcing him, not entering the incense-smelling room with him, but drawing back the clashing curtains, motioning him through and closing them behind him.

He was greeted by Orwic's boyish laugh and by a gasp from Simon. The two were seated face to face on couches near the window, unable to converse since Simon knew hardly any Gaulish, and both of them as pleased to see Tros as if he were a meal produced by a miracle for hungry men. Orwic ran to greet him, threw an arm around him, trying to say everything at once in an excited whisper.

'A great wizard. This must be the man our Lord Druid might have sent you to if you had only listened – made me a proposal – slip the Eskualdenak ashore – he says he knows how to manage that – hide them in a place he'll show me – kill Balbus tonight – lead an uprising against the Romans – carry the rebellion into Gaul – no need then to go to Rome – we'll keep the Romans' hands too full to invade Britain!'

Tros snorted. One sniff was enough. There was a woman smell on Orwic's clothes.

'Magic works many ways,' he remarked, and then thought of the curtains behind him. 'We will consider the proposal,' he added in a somewhat louder voice.

He approached Simon, who appeared too exhausted to rise from the couch and, glimpsing through the open window his great ship at anchor in the distance, he paused a moment, thrilled by the sight, before he spoke in Aramaic, his lips hardly moving, in an undertone that Orwic hardly caught:

'Out of the teeth of danger we will snatch success, but you must trust me. We speak now for an unseen audience.'

He could feel the espionage, although there was no sign of it. He leaned through the open window, but no eavesdroppers lurked within earshot. He strode back to the curtains through which he had entered, jerked them back suddenly and found the hall empty. There was another door a few feet from the throne with the arms of gilded ivory. He jerked back its curtains too, and found the next room vacant, silent, beautifully furnished, but affording no hiding-place. There was a lute left lying by a gilded chair and the same smell of scented women that he had noticed on Orwic's clothes, but the wearers of the scent had vanished.

Nevertheless, he was convinced he was being spied on. He could feel the nervous tension that an unseen eye produces, and he suspected the wall at the back of the ivory throne might be hollow; the corner behind the throne was not square but built out, forming two angles and a short, flat wall. The canopy over the throne cast shadow, and there was a deal of decoration there that might conceal a peep-hole. He signed to Orwic to sit down by the window and, standing so that his voice might carry straight toward that corner wall, himself full in the sunlight, stroking his chin with an air of great deliberation, he spoke in Gaulish:

'It is good we may speak among ourselves before the Egyptian comes. What kind of man is he?'

'A nobleman!' said Orwic. 'A good hater of the Romans! It was his slaves who rescued me from some ruffians in a mean street. He is not a false magician but a true one. He had prophesied the coming of your ship, and my landing by night and being lost in Gades. He has read our destiny in the stars and he refused, like a true magician, to say a word about it until I almost forced it out of him.'

Tros nodded gravely.

'Then he made me that proposal. And I tell you, Tros, you would do well to consider it.'

'I am an opportunist,' Tros said. 'I will do whatever Fortune indicates.'

'I objected to murdering Balbus,' Orwic went on. 'But the Romans invaded Britain. They killed our men. And he said Balbus is doomed anyhow, but, according to his reading of the stars, if he should be killed by the prince from a far country who steps out of the ship with the purple sails, it will mean the end of Roman rule in all Hispania and Gaul. Whereas, if he is killed by a common murderer, no good will come of it.'

Tros frowned. No trace of incredulity betrayed itself as he answered solemnly:

'Few men can read the stars with such precision.'

'That is exactly my opinion,' Orwic agreed. 'He speaks like a Lord Druid.'

Simon had made very little of the conversation, but he was watching Tros's face with a sort of blank expression on his own, as if his intuition rather than his ordinary faculties were working. He had suppressed his noisy breathing.

'Get me my money, Tros! Get me my money!' he gasped suddenly, noisily, in Aramaic.

But his expression had changed and his eyes were brighter; Tros interpreted the remark to mean that Simon could see light at last. He answered him in Greek, speaking very proudly.

'I will put the illustrious Pkauchios to a test, as a man throws dice to solve a difficult decision. For I think that in such ways the gods are willing to indicate a proper course to us in our perplexity. If he shall grant me the first favour that I ask, and faithfully perform it, then I will let him guide me in this matter. But if he shall quibble with me or refuse, or, having promised, fail to do what I shall ask, then no. So let the gods decide!'

He made a gesture as of throwing dice and turned his back to the window, striding the length of the room with measured steps. He had paced the room three times before he saw Pkauchios standing in the doorway, not the doorway near the throne – the other one.

'I welcome you. Peace to you!' said Pkauchios in Greek. 'But I foresee that you must snatch peace from the fangs of war!'

'I thank you for your courtesy,' Tros answered, bowing.

He did not bow so deeply that his eyes left Pkauchios' face. He hated the man instantly, and hid the hatred under a mask of eager curiosity.

The magician's dark eyes seemed to be trying to read into his very soul, but Tros knew nothing better than that men of genuine spiritual power are careful never to display the outward signs of it, and, above all, never to distress strangers with a penetrating stare. The astrologer's robes and the air of superhuman wisdom were convincing, but not of what Pkauchios intended. The Egyptian spoke again pleasantly, with the air of a wise man condescending:

'I regret I should have kept you waiting, but I observed the flight of birds, from which much may be foretold by those who understand natural symbology. Why do you come to Gades?'

'You are a magician. You should know why I came,' Tros answered.

'And indeed I do know. But I see there is a question in your mind,' said Pkauchios.

The pupils of the Egyptian's eyes contracted into bright dots. He made a gesture with his hand before his eyes, brushing away veils of immaterial obscurity.

'Doubt? Or desire? One blended with the other, or so it seems. You have a request to make,' he went on. 'Speak then, while the vision holds me.'

He had not moved. He was standing before the curtains like a dignified attendant at the door of a mystery.

'There is a slave,' said Tros, 'who at great risk brought me information. Speak for me to Balbus that he manumit that slave.'

224

'I will,' said Pkauchios, without a second's hesitation. 'Whose is the slave?'

'Do you or do you not see that the slave should be set free?' Tros countered.

'I see it is just and can be accomplished. But how shall I urge Balbus unless I know the slave's name and his master's?' Pkauchios answered.

'Speak to him thus,' said Tros. ' "It would be well if you should order manumitted whichever slave Tros the Samothracian indicates." '

'It shall be done,' said Pkauchios. But he did not quite retain his self-command. There was a twitching of the face muscles, a discernible effort to conceal chagrin.

Tros did not dare to glance at Simon or at Orwic. He was so sure now that the Egyptian had been spying through an eye-hole in the wall behind the throne that he would have burst out laughing if he had not bowed again and backed away, biting his lower lip until the blood came. That gave him an excuse to break the tension.

'Blood?' he exclaimed, frowning, wiping his mouth with the back of his hand and examining it.

'Aye, blood!' said Pkauchios in a hollow voice, and walked in front of him to near where Orwic sat.

By the window he turned and, after greeting Simon with a stare and a gesture of condescension, spoke again:

'Blood! Mars with Saturn in conjunction! And a red ship on the morning tide! The blood must flow in riverfuls! But whose?'

He stared at Simon balefully until the Jew in nervous resentment gaped at him and tried to force himself to speak, but failed because the asthma gripped his throat.

'I know your danger!' Pkauchios remarked. 'There are weapons in your warehouse – '

'Yours!' Simon interrupted, pointing a fat finger at him. 'You – ' The Egyptian cut him short.

'Jew! Have a care! You come to me for help, not for recrimination. At a word from me you would be tortured with the rack and charcoal. Rob not opportunity!'

Tros kept staring through the window at his great ship in the distance. She summoned to the surface all the mysticism in him, and he muttered lines from Homer as he gazed. The blind poet who once dwelt on rocky Chios, when he stamped on to the racial memory that character of crafty, bold Odysseus, hymned a hero

225

after Tros's own heart. The Egyptian seemed to read the tenor of his thought.

'Tros of Samothrace,' he said, turning his back on Simon, 'you have impelled yourself into a vortex of events. You – your ship – your friends – your crew – are all in danger. Win or lose all! Forward lies the only road to safety!'

'It appears you have a plan,' said Tros. 'Unfold it.'

The Egyptian nodded.

'We are few who can interpret destiny, but to us is always given means with which to guide events. I have awaited you these many days.'

'I am here,' said Tros.

'And you have men with you! You will sup tonight with Balbus; that I know, for I advised him to invite you. Listen. There is a quarry close to Balbus's house where you can hide your men. There is a wall between the quarry and the house, where no guards are ever posted. It is easy to scale that wall from the side of the quarry. It is simple to bring unarmed slaves into the city. It is easy to bribe Balearic slingers to see and to say nothing after darkness has set in. There are weapons in Simon's warehouse. There is only a small guard at Balbus's house at night – not more than twenty or thirty men. You have, I think, two hundred and fifty men who could hide in the quarry and at a signal overwhelm the guard.'

Simon was growing restless, trying to catch Tros's eye and warn him against being caught in any such network of intrigue, but Tros trod on his foot to signal to him to keep still. Orwic, who knew no Greek, was walking about the room examining strange ornaments. The Egyptian, after a pause, continued:

'Balbus, who envies Caesar, has sent emissaries into Gaul to murder him! Hourly he awaits the news of Caesar's death! The stars, whose symbolism never lies, inform me that Caesar is already dead, and the news will reach Gades tonight! But if Balbus lives, he will blame others for the murdering of Caesar. Therefore Balbus shall die too!'

Tros nodded. Not a gesture, not a line of his face suggested that he knew it was the Egyptian himself who had sent slaves to murder Caesar. His lion's eyes were glowing with what might have been enthusiasm. He stood, hands clenched behind him, making no audible comment.

'It is expedient that Balbus shall die tonight,' said Pkauchios. 'He has received word of a conspiracy against him. Sooner or later a witness in the agony of torture will reveal names. The conspirators are fearful; they lack leadership. But if Balbus were slain, the whole city would rise in rebellion! I have a plan that at the proper moment will draw away the legionaries from the camp outside the city.'

He paused, and then dramatically raised his voice:

'By morning messengers will have gone forth summoning all Hispania to rise. Good leadership – and I, Pkauchios, will guide you, Tros of Samothrace – good, ruthless leadership. Hispania and Gaul will throw off Roman rule!'

Tros grinned. He had made up his mind, which is a difficult thing to do in the teeth of an expert in personal magnetism. He succeeded in convincing even Simon.

'Well and good,' he said, folding his arms. 'But I will not kill Balbus until he has set that slave free and has repaid Simon what he owes.'

'Those two preliminaries granted?' said the Egyptian.

He seemed quite sure that Tros had committed himself.

'Orwic shall smuggle my men into the city if you show him how,' said Tros, 'and at the proper signal. But who shall give the signal?' he asked.

He was wary of definite lying. Any promises he made he liked to keep. But he had to objection to the Egyptian's deceiving himself.

'I will give the signal,' Pkauchios answered. 'Let brazen trumpets peal the death of Balbus! Six trumpets shall clamour a fanfare on the porch. Then plunge your dagger in!'

'Where will you be?' Tros asked him.

'At the banquet. Where else? Behold me. I rise from the banqueting couch. I stand thus to announce an augury. My servant, squatting by the door, will watch me, and when I raise my right hand thus, he will pass out to the porch where the trumpeters will be waiting who are to make music for the midnight dance Chloe has invented. The fanfare resounds. Your men come swarming over the quarry wall. Your dagger does its work – and – and you may help yourself, if you wish, from Balbus's treasury!'

Tros acted so immensely pleased that Orwic came and wondered at him. Simon hove himself off the couch at last and clutched Tros's arm.

'Tros, Tros!' he gasped. 'Don't do this dog's work! Don't! You will ruin all of us!'

Scowling, Pkauchios opened his thin lips to rebuke and threaten the Jew, but checked himself as he saw the expression on Tros's face. Tros took Simon by the arms, driving his fingers into the fat biceps, the only signal that he dared give that his words need not be taken at face value.

'Simon!' he exclaimed, in a voice of stern reproach. 'You owe me money! Yet you dare to keep me from this golden opportunity? Fie on you, Simon!'

Simon wrung his hands. Tros turned to Orwic.

'Go you to the ship,' he said. 'Our friend here, the Egyptian, will provide you a guide to the beach. Talk with Jaun Aksue. Tell him all the Eskualdenak shall come ashore tonight under your leadership, and do a little business of mine before I turn them loose to amuse themselves. Say they shall be well paid. Make them understand they must be sober until midnight. I will come to the ship later and explain the details of the plan. Go swiftly.'

THE COMMITTEE OF NINETEEN

I am not wise, I seek wisdom. But I know this: tyranny is never slain
by slaying tyrants. Let valiance first slay tyranny in its victims' hearts.
Tyrants then will die of being laughed at, quicker than any hangman
could make an end of them.

But a man must begin at beginnings. I have not yet learned to laugh
at tyranny. I hate it.

From the log of Tros of Samothrace

It approached high noon. Simon had left an hour ago in a sort of
wet-hen flutter of indignant misery, with a threat from the Egyptian in his ear:

'Jew, Balbus owes you money! He would welcome excuse to
proscribe you and seize your property! One word from me – '

Thereafter, Pkauchios held Tros in conversation, seeking to
make sure of him, promising him riches should the night's attempt
succeed, and more than riches, 'power, which is the rightful
perquisite of honest men!' Too shrewd to threaten, he nevertheless
dropped hints of what might happen if Tros should fail him.

'You are not the first. Man after man I have tested. One fool
tried to betray me, and was crucified. My word with Balbus out-
weighed his! Another thought he could do without me, after I
had made all ready for him. Those he would have led to insurrection burned his house and threw him back into the flames as he
ran forth in his night-clothes. No, no, you are not the first!'

'I am the last!' Tros answered grimly, and Pkauchios's dark
eyes took on a look of satisfaction. Then Tros tried to find out
where Chloe was without arousing Pkauchios's suspicion.

'Who was that woman,' he asked, 'who came out to my ship?'

'Oh, a mischievous Greek slave. A very clever dancer who will
perform tonight for Balbus.'

'Trustworthy?' Tros suggested.

'No Gades dancing-girls are trustworthy. Theirs is the very
religion of intrigue.'

'*Ergastulum?*' Tros suggested.

'No. She sleeps to be ready for tonight.'

However, there was plainly a mask over Pkauchios's thought.

Tros was quite sure he was lying, equally sure he was worried. All sorts of fears presented themselves that Tros was hard put to it to keep from showing on his face. Chloe might have disappeared, turned traitress. He decided he was a fool to have left Horatius Verres at large on the ship. If Chloe loved that spy of Caesar's – or was he Balbus's spy, pretending to be Caesar's – then she would quite likely do whatever Verres told her and perhaps betray everyone, Pkauchios included.

Yet he decided not to return to the ship until he had spoken alone with Simon. The old Jew was possibly the weakest link in the intrigue. In terror he might run to Balbus and betray the whole plot. Before all else he must reassure Simon.

Pkauchios ordered out the litter, with the eunuch in attendance and the eight white-liveried slaves. Tros saw him whisper to the eunuch, but pretended not to see. He had contrived to look entirely confident when the Egyptian walked with him to the garden gate.

'After sunset,' said Pkauchios, 'there will go a messenger to the gate-guards, who will bid them admit two hundred and fifty slaves on the excuse that they are needed as torch-bearers for the midnight pageant in Balbus's garden. They will be shown a writing to that effect which the fools will think is genuine. Another messenger will go to the Balearic guards who line the beach. And he will take money with him, a considerable bribe. At sunset a great barge will be rowed alongside your ship. Put your men into that. They shall be led to Simon's warehouse where they may help themselves to weapons. And the same guide will lead them afterwards to the quarry outside Balbus's garden. He will lead them by roundabout ways so as not to attract attention.'

Tros rolled into the litter and allowed the eunuch to lead as if his first objective were the ship. But he had no intention of being spied on by that eunuch, and when the litter halted at a narrow passage in the street to let three laden mules go by he rolled out of it again.

'Wait for me by the city gate.' he commanded.

The eunuch demurred, tried persuasion, offered to carry him anywhere, and at last grew impudent.

'You insult my master's hospitality!'

A crowd began to gather, marvelling at Tros's purple cloak and at the broad gold band across his forehead. The eunuch tried to drive them away, fussily indignant, prodding with his staff at those who seemed least likely to retaliate, but the crowd increased. Tros felt a tug at his cloak and, glancing swiftly, caught his breath. He saw Conops slip out of the crowd and go sauntering along the street! His red cap was at a reckless angle and his bandy legs suggested the idle, erratic, goalless meandering of a sailor in a half-familiar port.

Tros climbed back into the litter promptly as the best means of escaping from the crowd. Conops, faithful little rascal, would never have left the ship without good reason. Clearly he expected to be followed. The eunuch contrived to clear the way and the crowd dispersed about its business, which was mainly to sit in doorway shadows. As the litter began to overtake Conops he increased his pace until, where five streets met, he turned up an alley and turned about to watch. He made no signal.

Making sure that Conops was not following the litter downhill toward the city gate, Tros vaulted to the ground and had made his way to the alley mouth before the eunuch, walking rapidly ahead to clear the way, realized what was happening.

'This way, master – swiftly!'

Conops opened a door ten paces down the alley and Tros followed through it. The door slammed behind him, and in stifling gloom he was greeted by a laugh he thought he recognized. It was nearly a minute before definite objects began to evolve out of shadows. He could hear a rasping cough that seemed familiar, and there were other noises that suggested the presence of armed men, but the sunlight had been dazzling on the whitewashed walls and there were no open windows in the place in which he found himself. It took time for eyesight to readjust itself. The first shape to evolve out of the darkness was a stairhead, leading downward; then, down the stairs a leather curtain of the rich old-golden hue peculiar to Hispania. Above the curtain, on a panel of the wall the stairway pierced, was a painted picture of a bull's head; and there was something strange about its eyes. After a moment's stare Tros decided there were human eyes watching him through slits in the painted ones. There was a murmur of voices from behind the curtain and, every moment or two, that sound of laboured breathing and a cough that resembled Simon's.

Conops was in no haste to explain. He slunk behind Tros in the darkness, and a man stepped between them in response to a thundering on the street door. He opened a peephole and spoke through it to Pkauchios's eunuch; Tros could see him clearly as the light through the hole shone on his face – a lean, intelligent, distinguished-looking man. He assured the eunuch in good Greek that he was mistaken. None had entered the house recently. Perhaps the next house or the one over the way. Finally, he advised the eunuch to wait patiently.

'People who vanish usually reappear unless the guards have seized them. Private business, or perhaps a woman, who knows? At any rate, I will trouble you not to disturb a peaceful household. Go away!'

He closed the peephole, and in the darkness Tros could sense rather than see that he bowed with peculiar dignity.

'Do me the favour to come this way,' he murmured, using the Roman language in as gentle a voice as Tros had ever heard.

He led down the dark stairs as if they were not quite familiar to him.

Tros groped for Conops, seized him by the neck and swung him face to face.

'Well?' he demanded.

Conops answered in a hurried whisper:

'That fellow Horatius Verres came out of the hold and said, "If you value your master's freedom, follow me!" Then he jumped overboard and swam. I followed to the beach in a boat. All the way to this place he kept a few paces ahead of me. Then he said, "Find your master and bring him here, or he'll be dead by midnight!" I was on my way to Pkauchios's house when –'

'Go ahead of me!' Tros ordered.

He loosed his sword in the scabbard and trod quietly, hoping Conops' heavier step would be mistaken for his own in the event of ambush, so leaving himself free to fight. But the curtain was drawn aside, only to reveal a dim lamp and another curtain. The sound of men's voices increased; there was now laughter and a smell of wine. Beyond the second curtain was a third with figures on it in blue and white. Someone pulled the third curtain aside and revealed a great square room whose heavy beams were set below the level of the street. The walls were of stone, irregularly dressed. There was a tiled floor covered with goat-hair matting, and a small table near one end of the room, at which a man sat with his back to a closed door. Around the other walls were benches occupied by men in Roman and Greek costume, although none of them apparently was Roman, and by no means all were Greeks. There were two Jews, for instance, of whom one was Simon. All except Simon rose as Tros entered. Simon seemed exhausted, and was sweating freely from the heat of the bronze illuminating lamps.

'The noble Tros of Samothrace!' said the man with the gentle voice who had led the way downstairs.

Tros glared around him, splendid in his purple cloak against the golden leather curtain, and the man at the table bowed. Simon coughed and made movements with his hands, suggesting helplessness. He who had led the way downstairs produced a chair made of wood and whaleskin, and with the air of a courtier offered it to Tros to sit on, but he pretended not to notice it.

'Illustrious Tros of Samothrace, we invite you to be seated.' said the man at the table.

He looked almost like Balbus, except that his face was harder and not wearied from debauch of the emotions. He had humour in his dark eyes, and every gesture, every curve of him suggested confidence and good breeding.

Tros noticed that Horatius Verres was seated in the darkest corner of the room, that Conops' knife-blade was a good two inches out of the sheath, that his own sword was at the proper angle to be drawn instantly, and that the men nearest to him looked neither murderous nor capable of preventing his escape past the curtain.

'Illustrious Tros of Samothrace,' said the man at the table, 'we have learned that you will lend your dagger to the cause of Gades.'

'Who are you?' Tros retorted bluntly.

'We are a committee of public safety, self-appointed and here gathered, unknown to our Roman rulers, for the purpose of conspiracy in the name of freedom,' he at the table answered. 'My own name is Quintilian.'

Tros heard a noise behind the curtain, was aware of armed men on the stairs. By the half-smile on the chairman's face he realized he was in a trap from which there was no chance of escape without a miracle of swordsmanship or else a shift of luck. He stared very hard at Simon, who seemed to avoid his gaze.

'We wish to assure ourselves,' said the man who had called himself Quintilian, 'that we have not been misinformed.'

'There are two who might have told you,' Tros answered. 'One is Simon, the other Chloe, a Greek slave. I will say nothing unless you tell me which of them betrayed me.'

Quintilian smiled. His dark, amused eyes glanced around the room, resting at last on Simon's face.

'Your friend Simon,' he said, 'has refused to answer questions. We are pleased that your arrival on the scene may save him from that application to his person of inducements to speak which we had in contemplation.'

Tros blew a sigh out of his lungs, half of admiration for his old

233

friend Simon, half of contempt for himself for having trusted Chloe. Then he glared at Horatius Verres over in the corner.

'How came I to trust you?' he wondered aloud.

'I don't know,' the Roman answered, smiling. 'I myself marvelled at it. I am greatly in your debt, illustrious Tros. You gave me the opportunity to hold a long conversation with Herod ben Mordecai down in the dark, in the hold of your ship. And you left me free to watch for signals from the shore. You knew that Chloe loves me. I am sure you are much too wise to suppose that a woman in love would neglect to signal to her lover.' The voice was mocking, confident, cynical.

Tros tossed his head as if about to speak, staring straight at the man at the table to conceal his intention of charging up the stairs and fighting his way to the street. Up anchor and away from Gades – there was nothing else to do! The only thing that made him hesitate was wondering how to rescue Simon.

'You are in no danger at present. Be seated,' said Quintilian courteously. 'We wish to hear from your lips confirmation of a plot that interests us deeply. We also are conspirators.'

Tros closed his mouth grimly.

He did not sit down, but laid his left hand on the chair-back, intending to use the chair as a shield when he judged the moment ripe for fighting his way to the street.

'Ah, you have not understood us properly,' said Quintilian. 'Trouble yourself to observe that we are not warlike men, not even armed with anything but daggers. We are students of philosophy, of music, of the sacred sciences. Our purpose is, that Gades shall become a centre of the arts, a city dedicated to the Muses. We have heard that Pkauchios the Egyptian plans an uprising which you will lead by slaying Balbus, for whom none of us has any particular admiration. In the interests of Gades we propose to discover in what way we can be of assistance to you.'

Tros let a laugh explode in one gruff bark of irony.

'I am no friend of Balbus. I am the enemy of Caesar and of Rome,' he answered. 'But if I were so far to forget my manhood as to cut a throat like a common murderer, it would be the throat of Pkauchios! You fools!'

'Not so foolish, possibly, as weak!' Quintilian answered with a suave smile. 'But as the poet Homer says, "The strength even of weak men when united avails much"!'

The mention of the poet Homer mollified Tros instantly. He began to feel a sort of friendly condescension. There were harmless, poet-loving people after all. They might be saved from indiscretion.

234

'Fools, I said! But I too have been foolish. I thought to pluck my own advantage from the whirlpool of this city's frenzy! Murder never overthrew a tyranny. Ye are like dogs who bite the stick that whips them instead of fighting foot and fang against the tyranny itself! Slay Balbus, and a tyrant ten times worse will take advantage of the crime to chain a new yoke on your necks!'

There was a murmer of surprise. Quintilian raised his eyebrows and, leaning both elbows on the table, answered:

'But we know for a fact you have agreed with Pkauchios to stab Balbus in his house at the supper – tonight.'

'Chloe told you. Well, I too was fool enough to trust her, but not altogether,' Tros said grimly. 'I would not trust Pkauchios if I had him tied and gagged! My plan was nothing but to rescue Balbus, to protect him and so win his gratitude! I seek a favour from him. Bah! Do you think I would lend my men for a purpose that would bring disaster on a city against which I have no grudge? *Plaugh!* Murder your own despots, if you will, but count me out of it! Look you – '

He drew his sword and shook the cloak back from his shoulder. Behind him he heard the click of Conops' knife emerging from the sheath.

'I go!' He took a stride toward the door, but as none moved to prevent him he paused and faced Quintilian again. He decided to test them to the utmost. If he had to fight his way out he proposed to know it. 'Simon may come if he will. I have two words of advice for you: Kill me if you can before I gut your men who guard the stairs, because I go to Balbus! I will warn him, for the sake of Gades! Fools! If you must murder someone, make it Pkauchios! If that dark trickster has his way, all Hispania and Gaul will run blood! You have let the Romans in and now you must endure the Romans! Make no worse evil for yourselves than is imposed already!'

He beckoned to Simon, but Quintilian rose and bowed with such dignity and obvious good will that Tros paused again.

'Illustrious Tros,' Quintilian said, 'if you could favour us with any sort of guarantee that those are your genuine sentiments, we would even let you go to Balbus! It is just Balbus's death that we hope to prevent!'

Smiling, his dark eyes alight with amusement and with something strong and generous behind that, he struck the table sharply with the flat of his hand. There was a sudden sound behind Tros's back; the inner curtain had been drawn; in the opening stood two men armed with javelins, and there was a third behind them with a bow and arrows.

'You may live, and we will turn you loose if you will convince us,' remarked Quintilian. 'Time presses. Won't you do us the favour to be seated?'

But Tros refused to sit.

'It is you who must convince me!' he retorted.

With his cloak, his sword, the whaleskin chair and Conops to create diversions, he knew himself able to defeat javelins and bow and arrow, but he was interested to discover whether there were any more armed men in hiding. Quintilian, however, gave him no enlightenment on that point beyond continuing to smile with utmost confidence.

'You see,' he said, 'none of us can go to Balbus, who is altogether too suspicious. He would have us crucified for knowing anything about conspiracies. Yet we have suffered so much in pocket and peace and dignity from former abortive risings that we ventured to take liberties with you in order to nip a new one in the bud, or rather, to prevent its budding. Balbus and his troops would nip!'

'Then his troops aren't mutinous?' Tros asked.

Quintilian smiled.

'They are always mutinous. Just now they talk of marching to join Caesar in Gaul. But a chance to loot the city would restore them to sweet reasonableness, as Balbus perfectly understands. Illustrious Tros, perhaps we might not feel so determined if we liked Pkauchios or if we thought the city were united. We believe ourselves sufficiently intelligent to take advantage of the disaffection in the Roman camp. The moment might be ripe for insurrection but for one important fact: We have learned that Julius Caesar is coming!'

He glanced at Horatius Verres, who smiled at Tros and nodded with the same air of amused confidence that he had displayed from the beginning.

'Speak to him,' said Quintilian. So Horatius Verres stood up, arms folded, and in a very pleasant voice explained how he came to be there.

'Illustrious Tros,' he said, 'I am in a worse predicament than you, I being Caesar's man, and you your own. I obey Caesar because I love him. While I live I serve him at my own risk, whereas you are free to follow inclination. I discovered a plot to murder Caesar. It was launched in Gades, and I sent him warning as soon as I knew.

236

'I received a reply that he will come here. But though he is Caesar, he cannot be here for several days, whether he come by land or water. I cannot warn Balbus, who is touchy about being spied on and would have my head cut off to keep me from telling Caesar things I know. But it is not Caesar's desire that Balbus should meet death, there being virtues, of a sort which Balbus imitates, that might serve Caesar's ends to great advantage.

'From Herod the Jew, in the darkness of the hold of your ship, I learned of these distinguished Gadeans, who call themselves a committee of public safety. So I risked my life by coming to them, and I risked yours equally by persuading your man Conops to summon you, believing you to be a man who might see humour in the situation and take the right way out of it.'

He sat down again.

'May the gods behold your impudence!' said Tros. But he could not help liking the man.

'We know,' said Quintilian, 'that Pkauchios has ruffians ready to attack Balbus's house at midnight. We also know that he has bribed some of the bodyguard, and we suppose he will make some of the others drunk with drugged wine. We imagine he has offered you inducements to bring a few hundred men ashore – '

'You had that from Chloe,' said Tros, but Quintilian took no notice of the interruption.

' – to give backbone, as it were, to the mob that might otherwise flinch. And we know there are weapons in Simon's warehouse, some of which we presume are to be supplied to your men. We ourselves might kill Pkauchios, but Balbus has a great regard for him and, strange though it may appear, though public-spirited, we prefer not to be tortured and we object to having our possessions confiscated. Nevertheless, we will not permit Balbus to be slain, and if you are willing to protect him for the sake of Gades – '

He paused, and Tros waited almost breathlessly. In his mind he made a bargain, named the terms of it by which he would abide for good or ill – a final test of these men's honesty.

'We will offer you our silent gratitude,' Quintilian went on, 'and we will take a pledge from you not to reveal our names or our identity to Balbus.'

It was a tactful way of saying they would not murder him if he succeeded and provided he should keep his mouth shut. Tros laughed.

'If you had offered me a price,' he said, 'I would have spat on you.'

'As it is, are you willing to betray Pkauchios to Balbus?'

Quintilian asked. 'You could do it without risk, whereas we – '

Tros snorted.

Quintilian smiled with a peculiar, alert, attractive wrinkling of his face and glanced around the room. Men nodded to him one by one.

'Had you agreed to betray Pkauchios, we would have known you would betray us!' he said. 'Illustrious Tros, what help can we afford you? We are nineteen men.'

'See that Caesar doesn't catch me when he comes!' Tros announced. 'Keep me informed of the news of his movements.' He looked hard at Horatius Verres. 'You,' he said, 'will you keep me informed? Your Caesar is my enemy, but I befriended you.'

'I know no more than I have told you,' Verres answered.

Once again Tros hesitated. Impulse, sense of danger, urged him to escape while it was possible. It would be easy to make these men believe he would go forward with the plan, then to return to his ship ostensibly to instruct his own men for the night's adventure. Orwic was on board. He could sail away and leave Gades to stew in its own intrigues.

But obstinacy urged the other way. He hated to withdraw from anything he had set his hand to before the goal was reached. And again he remembered the Lord Druid's admonition, 'Out of the midst of danger thou shalt snatch the keys of safety!'

While he hesitated, the door behind Quintilian opened. He recognized the hand before the woman came through, knew it was Chloe without looking at her, looked, and knew she held the keys of the whole situation. There was triumph in her eyes, although she drooped them modestly and stood beside Quintilian's table with hands clasped in an attitude of reverence for the august assembly.

'Speak!' Quintilian commanded, and she looked at Tros, her eyes alight with impudence.

'Lord Tros,' she said, 'would you have come here of your own accord? Would you have come had I invited you? Would you not have sailed away if you had known these noblemen would kill you rather than permit you to kill Balbus? And do you think I propose to lose those pearls you promised me, or my freedom?'

She nodded and smiled.

'Do you think I intend to be tortured?'

There was a long pause, during which everybody in the room, Quintilian included, looked uncomfortable. Then she answered the thought that was making Tros's amber eyes look puzzled:

'These noblemen don't kill me because they know there are others who know where I am, who would go straight to Balbus and

238

name names. It would deeply interest Balbus to learn of a committee of nineteen who propose to direct the destiny of Gades unbeknown to him! It was not I who told these nobles of your plot with Pkauchios. There is one of this committee – illustrious Quintilian, shall I name him?'

Quintilian shook his head.

'There is one in this room who pretends to be Pkauchios's friend and whom Pkauchios trusts. It was he who told. To save your life I signalled to the ship, and when Horatius Verres hurried through the streets I whispered to him so that he knew where to come.'

'Who told him to persuade Conops to come?' Tros demanded, not more than half believing her. But Verres himself answered that question:

'Caesar does not select agents who are wholly without wits,' he remarked in his amused voice. 'Chloe signalled, which she would not have done if all went well. Suspecting that you might be causing her trouble, I proposed to myself to bring a hostage with me, whose danger might bring you to reason. I had observed that you value your man Conops. So I hinted to him that your life was in danger, and of course he followed me, being a good, faithful dog. Chloe reached this place ahead of us, and when she whispered to me again through the hole in the door, I sent Conops to find you. Is the mystery explained?'

'You are a very shrewd man,' Tros answered. 'But why did you tell these noblemen that Caesar is on the way?'

'To confirm them in their resolution not to let Balbus be slain. It might not suit Caesar to find Gades in rebellion. You see, this is not his province, and it is not certain what the troops would do. If he should assume command here, it might stir Pompey to go before the Senate and demand Caesar's indictment and recall to Rome.'

All the while Verres was speaking Chloe whispered to Quintilian. Her hand was on his arm and she was urging him. Suddenly Quintilian sat upright and rapped with his hand on the table.

'Time presses,' he said. 'Comrades, we must come to a decision. Shall we trust the illustrious Tros and take a pledge from him?'

There was a murmur of assent.

'A pledge?' said Tros. 'From me?'

'Why, yes!' said Chloe. 'We think you are an honourable man, but at a word from you to Balbus we might all be crucified!'

The men in the doorway behind Tros rattled their weapons.

'We all risk our lives if we give you liberty,' Quintilian remarked. 'You are a stranger to us.'

Tros began to turn over in his mind what pledge he could deposit with them. There was no alternative except to fight his way out to the street, and he suspected now that there were more than three men on the stairs. Quintilian enlightened him:

'You would have seven men to fight, besides ourselves. But why fight? Why not leave your faithful follower with us?'

Conops drew breath sharply. Tros turned his head to glance at him.

'Little man,' he said, 'shall we fight?'

'Nay, there are too many,' Conops answered.

For a fraction of a second Conops' face wore the reproachful look of a deserted dog's. But he saw Tros's eyes and recognized the resolution in them. Never, in all their long experience together, had Tros looked like that at him and failed.

'You are not such a fool as you look!' Conops sneered, staring straight at Quintilian. 'My master would lose his own life rather than desert a faithful servant. Harm me if you dare, and see what happens!'

At a sign from Quintilian everybody in the room rose, making a rutching of feet and a squeal of moved benches. Only Tros heard Conops' whisper:

'Now they will trust you. It was I who led you into this trap. Leave me and sail away. The worst they'll do is kill me.'

For an answer Tros grinned at him, grinned and nodded, clapped him on the back.

AT SIMON'S HOUSE

What money is, I know not. But concerning its lending, I know this: that if I lend not with it courage, sympathy and vision, I but burden a man already burdened with his own need.

Give, then, and forget. Or else lend heart and money—aye, money and a gale of good will to blow it to good use.

From the log of Tros of Samothrace

Tros watched Conops led away through the door by which Chloe had entered, and then beckoned to Horatius Verres.

'Roman,' he said, 'you have risked my life for Caesar's sake. Now the wind shifts. Lean the other way and serve me or, by all the gods, you shall not live to mock my downfall!'

'I serve Caesar!' Verres answered.

'I also, by the irony of Fate!'

Tros took him by the shoulder.

'My father Perseus, Prince of Samothrace, tortured to his death by Caesar's executioners, told me with his dying breath that I should live to serve that robber of men's liberties, whose enemy I am! I see I must.'

'Serve well!' said Verres. 'Caesar values good will higher than the deed.'

'I bear him ill will, but I will not be his murderer,' Tros answered. 'In fair fight, yes. In treachery I have no willing hand.'

'I believe you,' said Verres, and nodded.

'Then tell me, when is Caesar coming?'

'I don't know,' Verres answered. 'If I did know, I might lie to you. Since I don't know, I tell you the plain truth.'

'You know that Pkauchios has prophesied the death of Caesar. Do you know that he expects the news of Caesar's death tonight?' Tros asked him.

Verres nodded.

'Do you know by what means he expects the news?'

'By a slave, I suppose. He sent murderers to Gaul. Doubtless he has reckoned up the days, hours, minutes, and awaits a messenger.'

Tros gripped him again by the shoulder.

'Get you a disguise,' he said. 'Tonight, near midnight, creep into Balbus's garden and send word to Pkauchios by one of Balbus's slaves that a messenger has come from Gaul who wishes word with him. When Pkauchios comes to you, whisper to him from the darkness, "Caesar is dead!" Then Pkauchios will return into the house and make the signal to me to slay Balbus. But instead, when the trumpets sound, my men will rush into the house and protect him against Pkauchios's rabble.'

'There will be more than rabble,' Verres answered. 'Pkauchios has bribed some of the Roman guard. I know that, for I know where some of them have spent the money, and I have heard that they boast how they will excuse themselves by saying that Balbus plotted against Rome. I think you will have a hard time to save Balbus's life. Yet if you warn him, he will only suspect you and throw you in prison. Caesar understands good will. Balbus only understands a fact that he can see with his two eyes, feel with his two hands, bite with his teeth and then turn promptly into an advantage for himself. I think that even should you save his life he will turn on you afterwards.'

'I will cross that bridge when the time comes,' Tros replied. 'Will you whisper that word to Pkauchios?'

'Yes. I can lie to him circumstantially. I know the names of the murderers he sent to Gaul.'

Tros wasted no more time on him, knew he must trust him whether he wished to or not, dismissed him with a gesture, beckoned Chloe. She laughed in his face confidently, yet not without wistfulness.

'Now we are all committed,' she said, 'and all depends on you! We die unless you win for us all tonight!'

It was her action that restored Tros's trust in her. She slipped a phial into his hand, a tiny thing not bigger than a joint of her own finger.

'Three drops from that are enough,' she remarked. 'It is swifter than crucifixion or being butchered at the games!'

'I go to Simon's house,' Tros answered, pocketing the phial. He understood enough of the Samothracian teachings to despise the thought of suicide, but he did not propose to chill her friendliness by refusing such proof of it. 'Go you to Pkauchios's eunuch. Lie to him as to where I am. Invent your own tale. Bid him look for me at Simon's house. Then go back to your master Pkauchios and tell a likely tale to him.'

She nodded and vanished through the same door through which they had taken Conops.

'Simon, old friend, we squander time like men asleep!' said Tros. 'Where waits your litter? Will it hold the two of us?'

Simon rose to his feet, but he was numb, dumb, stupid with the fear that made him tremble and contracted all the muscles of his throat until his breath came like the rasping of a sawmill. He gestured helplessly, but no words passed his lips, though he tried as he leaned on Tros's shoulder. Quintilian approached to reassure them both:

'We nineteen and the few we keep in our employ are not ingrates,' he said. 'Balbus tortured one of our people all day yesterday. He betrayed no one. We will protect you in all ways possible.'

Quintilian led Tros and Simon out by tunnels and devious passages to a walled yard where Simon's litter waited; there he told off four men to follow the litter secretly as far as Simon's house, where they approached by a back street so as not to be seen by Pkauchios's eunuch.

It was an almost typically Eastern house – all squalor on the outside, with windowless walls and doors a foot thick, fit to be defended against anything less than Roman battering-rams. The plaster on the walls was peeling off; there was no paint, nothing except size to offset the appearance of mean shabbiness. But within was splendour.

The door in the wall of the back street opened on a tiled court, with a fountain and exotic trees in carved stone Grecian pots. A Jewish major domo marshalled half a dozen slaves, who set chairs and a table beneath potted palms. More slaves brought cooling drinks and light refreshment. Simon in the guise of host began to throw off some of the paralysis of fear; in his own house he was master, and the evidence of wealth around him counteracted the terror of debt and the anguish of unsecured loans made to powerful, slow-paying creditors.

'Write two bills on Balbus's treasury,' said Tros, 'one for two hundred and twenty thousand sesterces, the other for whatever balance Balbus owes you.'

Simon wrote, his hand trembling, and, signing, gave the bills to Tros.

'Tros! Tros,' he said, 'I rue the day I ever came to Gades! It was bad enough in Alexandria, where Ptolemy the Piper borrowed from the Romans and taxed us Alexandrians to death to pay the interest. But Ptolemy was human and knew men must live. We all lived well in Alexandria. *Yey!* These Balbuses and Caesars think of nothing but themselves and their ambition!'

243

Tros clapped him on the back, his mind on pearls he had on board the ship. There was market for enough of them in Gades to relieve all Simon's difficulties. Yet the druids had not given them to him to provide relief for slave-trading Jews. It was bad enough to have to give a dozen of them to a dancing-girl. Simon, his mind groping for new hope, detected something masked under Tros's air of reckless reassurance.

'Tros,' he said, 'haven't you a cargo on your ship, some tin or something with which we two could turn a profit? Better that than running risks with Balbus! *Stchnyarrh!* That Roman would kill us both for having talked with the committee of nineteen rather than pay those orders on his treasury! Any excuse would serve him! Spies may have seen us. Safer to go to him straight away, denounce Pkauchios and beg a trading favour from him as reward! That's it! That's it! Beg leave to take a shipload of my slaves to Ostia! Then I can draw money against them here in Gades – '

Tros interrupted with another shoulder slap. That panic mood of Simon's had to be cured at all costs, druids or no druids. But he was cautious.

'Simon, I have assets in reserve. If I should fail tonight to coax your money out of Balbus for you, I will loan you enough to tide you over.'

'Ah! But that Roman wolf is crafty! What if Balbus learns of this conspiracy too soon and sets a trap for you, accuses you of a plot to murder him and – '

Tros touched his sword-hilt.

'Simon, I have two hundred and fifty fighting men. It will be a sorry pass if I can't cut my way to the beach.'

'And me? What of me?'

'I will take you with me. Since you are so fearful, hide yourself tonight on my ship – '

'No,' said Simon, 'no! Those beach guards would arrest me!'

'Very well, then hide by the city gate. Watch the street from an upper window. Keep two or three men near you whom you can trust. Then, if you see anything of Roman soldiers entering the city after dark, you can send me warning – your messenger can pretend he brings me news about the safety of my ship. Balbus's servants may admit him, but if not, they will at least announce a messenger and I will understand. If it comes to a fight, Simon, I will pick you up by the city gate and carry you away with me. But I hold a hostage on my ship – one Gaius Suetonius. Balbus will search all Gades until he finds Conops to exchange against Gaius Suetonius.'

'*O-o-o-hey!* But my household goods!' groaned Simon. 'My daughters and my daughters' children!'

He put his head between his hands and leaned his elbows on the table. Tros stared at him, scratching the back of his head, wondering what argument to use next. He did not dare to leave the man in that state of panic, nor did he dare to threaten him. Fear is no antidote for fear. Somehow he must make him hope and give him courage.

'Simon,' he said suddenly, 'it is not too late for me to turn back. I will go to that committee of nineteen, tell them I have thought better of the risk and reclaim Conops. They will return him to me if I promise to leave Gades straight away!'

Simon sat up and for a moment stared at him with frightened eyes.

'You mean – you mean – ?'

'I will sail away. I will forgive you what you owe me. I will let Gades rot in its own conspiracies.'

'Tros! Tros! You can't! You promised! You can't back out of it now you have gone this far!' Simon clutched his wrist, and Tros gave him time to feel the full force of a new emotion, staring at him coldly, looking resolute in his determination to have no more to do with Gades and its dancing-girl conspiracies. 'Tros, I am an old man, you a young one! We are friends, your father was my friend. You – Tros!'

Tros shook off his hand.

'Farewell, Simon!'

'Tros! You will leave me to be crucified?'

'You have frightened me with your fears and your forebodings,' Tros answered. 'No man can succeed with such a lack of confidence as yours to make the skin creep up his back.'

Simon staggered to his feet and, almost tottering, took hold of Tros by either arm.

'You – are you your father's son? You turn back? You?' His hoarse breath came in snores. 'You leave us all at Chloe's mercy? Tros, do you know what it means to be at the mercy of a dancing-girl of Gades? She knows everything. She will betray us all to save her own skin. Tros, if you leave us in the lurch now, may God – '

Tros drew Chloe's phial out of the pocket in his cloak. He offered it to Simon.

'Three drops,' he remarked.

'*Stchnrarrh!* You! To that, what would your father have said? Tros, I will sooner endure the torture!'

Tros poised the phial in his hand.

'Simon, is it yes or no? Do we burn our bridge and see this matter through to a conclusion, or – '

He offered the phial again on his open palm. Simon took it, held it in his clenched fist, set his teeth – then suddenly dashed the phial to the tiles and smashed it into fragments. A cat came and sniffed at the liquid.

'Then we are agreed? You will be brave? You will see this through?' Tros asked.

His eye was on the cat; he was beginning to feel nearly sure of Simon.

'Go!' said Simon hoarsely. 'Yes, I see this through. God give you wisdom, skill, cunning, and make Balbus blind! May God protect us all.'

'Amen!' said Tros.

He was watching the cat. It had lapped up nearly all the poison and seemed none the worse for it.

'Watch Chloe!' Simon urged. 'She is as fickle – as fickle as quicksilver! She will betray you for the very sake of cleverness at the last second if she can see a way of doing it!'

Tros nodded. The cat had selected a sunny, warm place in a palm pot and was licking its fur contentedly.

'She will play on your emotions, she will win your confidence, she will put herself into your power, but remember, she loves nothing except slavery! Her wits are sharp. She loves to be outwitted! She is clever enough to govern Gades by whispering to Pkauchios and Balbus. And with her whole soul she craves to be governed by someone clever than herself! Watch her, Tros!'

Tros watched the cat, which was watching a bird, its tail twitching with the inborn instinct of a destroyer. He kicked the fragments of the phial.

'Better have those gathered, Simon! Now I go marshal my men for tonight. I have a golden bugle that the Britons gave me, and if anything goes wrong at Balbus's supper I will wind a blast on it to summon Orwic and my men. So be waiting by the city gate with your daughters and your daughters' children if you wish, in case that I have to fight my way out of Balbus's clutches.'

'Have you only that Briton and those Eskualdenak?' asked Simon.

'Aye,' Tros answered. 'I must leave my Northmen on the ship, and to man the longboat and the barge.'

'Take care! Take care!' urged Simon. 'Chloe will turn that Briton and your Eskualdenak against you if she sees advantage in it!'

'She will have shot her bolt and earned her pay,' Tros answered 'if she has persuaded Pkauchios that I went from his house straight to yours. I will see that the eunuch has no chance to carry tales. Those Balearic slingers on the beach shall guard him and the litter bearers until I need them again to carry me to Balbus's house. Now, swiftly, write me out an order for the manumission of a slave and leave a space blank for the slave's name and plenty of room at the bottom for Balbus's seal and signature.'

IN BALBUS'S DINING-HALL

The Jews have a proverb that says, 'Give strong drink unto him that
is ready to perish.' And the Romans say, 'Wine tells truth.' But how
often is not such truth shameful?

As for me, I will not perish. I cannot imagine that beyond death
there is less than this life. Nay, nay, death is an awakening. But to some
it may resemble waking after too much wine in evil company.

From the log of Tros of Samothrace

In the litter belonging to Pkauchios, borne by eight slaves and preceded by a sulkily insolent eunuch, Tros presented himself at the
guardhouse by the arched front gate of Balbus's palace one hour
after sunset. An officer of the gate-guard peered into the litter;
the eunuch sneered to him in an audible falsetto whisper about the
incredible grossness of barbarians who did not give self-respecting
servants time to change their uniform; the legionary clanked a
shield against his breastplate as a signal to proceed, and Tros was
carried up a winding, broad path, in the shadow of imported
Italian cypresses, into the glare of lamplight at the marble-
columned porch.

There was a veritable herd of well-trained slaves in waiting. Two
laid a mat for Tros to tread on as he rolled out of the litter. Two
more held his cloak, lest it should inconvenience him as he moved.
Two others spread a roll of carpet across the porch into the house,
covering the three-headed dog done in coloured mosaic and its
legend, *Cave Canem*. Two splendidly dressed slaves preceded him
into the house between two lines of bowing menials and led him
into a small room to the left of the hallway, where three slaves
dusted off his sandals. A household official offered to take charge
of his sword, but Tros refused, which caused some snickering
among the slaves.

'Tell Balbus, your master, that to me this sword is as his toga
to himself. As he receives no guest without his toga, so I enter no
man's house without my symbol of independence!'

The official, shrugging his shoulders, smirking, went away to
bear that message, and Tros sat down on a bench to wait. The
slaves seemed amused that he should give himself such airs, yet

have no personal attendants of his own; they whispered jibes about him in a language they thought he did not understand; but their snickering among themselves did not prevent Tros from hearing fragments of another conversation.

Close to the bench on which he sat were curtains concealing a doorway into another small room. He heard Chloe's voice distinctly:

'Pkauchios, it is a long time since you have dared to whip me! Come to your senses! I am Chloe, not one of the slaves who knows nothing about you!'

Pkauchios's answer was indistinct, a mere murmur of anger forced through set teeth. Then Chloe again:

'Pkauchios!'

The Egyptian spoke louder, with bitter emphasis:

'I have endured your impudence too long! One disobedience tonight or one mistake, and I will have all your peculium confiscated!* I know where you put it out of my reach! I will demand it of Simon, who can't pay! Simon is one of many who will feel the weight of my hand when tomorrow's sun rises! So remember, it is your own fault you have had no sleep. Dance and sing so well that Balbus is beside himself, or take the consequences and be whipped, reduced to beggary and sold tomorrow morning!'

The curtains parted and Pkauchios came through, frowning, stately, black-robed, with the asp of Egypt on his brow. He checked an expression of surprise at sight of Tros, but Tros managed to convince him he had heard nothing, by avoiding the obvious mistake of trying to convince him. He merely appeared glad to see him, showed him ostentatious deference for the benefit of the watchful slaves, and in a low voice spoke of the main issue:

'My men came ashore with your man, though the barge was hardly big enough to hold them. They are warned to keep silence in the quarry and to expect a midnight signal. Are your Gades rioters ready?'

Pkauchios nodded.

'They gather. Balbus's guard has been well bribed and will not interfere when a crowd surrounds the wall. When your men lead, mine will follow. Near midnight a small town twenty miles away will be set on fire, and the legionaries will be summoned to keep order and to help put out the flames.'

'In what mood is Balbus?' Tros asked him.

---

*A slave's master had the right to do this, but the force of public opinion was against it. The usual practice was to manumit the slave in exchange for a lion's share of the money, and thus retain a valuable 'client', plus more than the price of a substitute.

'He glooms. He has tortured witnesses all day and to no purpose. He even tried to read an augury in the entrails of a woman who was gored by a bull in the streets as he came homeward. I have assured him you bring fortune.'

'Go to him again, then. Tell him I must be allowed to wear my sword and cloak.'

'He will never permit it,' said Pkauchios, shaking his head.

'Then I go away now!' Tros answered, and began to stride toward the door.

His cloak was quite as necessary as the sword because it concealed the golden bugle.

Pkauchios detained him, clutching his arm violently; nervousness robbed him that second of all his hierophantic calm.

'I will try. But ask not too much, or you spoil all.'

However, Tros knew how to deal with Romans, also with Egyptian sorcerers.

'All or nothing! Cloak and sword, or he may sup without me, and you may manage your own murders!' he added in a deep-growled undertone. Then, 'Warn him he must make concessions if he hopes for help from me.'

The Egyptian's face looked livid with resentment, but he vanished through the curtains and presently returned with Balbus's head steward, a freed man, ruddy from high living and exuding tact as well as dignity. He bowed, offering a wreath of bay leaves.

'Illustrious guest of my noble master,' he said, 'you are asked to pardon the indiscretion of the officious fool who first received you. He shall be soundly whipped. The noble Balbus naturally makes allowances for the customs of his guests and feels outraged that indignity was offered you. That handsome cloak and sword will ornament the simple style we keep, as truly as your presence will confer an honour. Pray permit me.'

He adjusted the chaplet of bay leaves and, again bowing, led the way across a fountained courtyard into Balbus's presence, in a room whose walls were painted with pictures of Roman legendry, but done in the Egyptian style by an artist who was evidently trained in Greece. There were six other Romans in the room, two of them military tribunes in crimson tunics. All rose to their feet as Tros entered; all eyed him curiously, each in turn acknowledging his stately bow, but not one of them taking the trouble to return Pkauchios's ravenly solemn greeting. Pkauchios stood back against the wall, and Balbus in a rather tired voice broke the awkward silence:

'Welcome! Be whatever gods you worship kind to us all!'

He presented Tros to all the other guests, explaining nothing, merely saying he was Tros of Samothrace whose ship lay in the harbour. They asked Tros whether he had had a pleasant voyage, and one or two of them marvelled loudly at his good health.

'Most sailors come ashore so sick they can hardly walk,' said a tribune, admiring Tros's bulk and stature.

'Aye,' said another, 'and they all get drunk in Gades, where the fever enters as the fumes of wine depart. When Balbus rebuilds the city he will have enough sailors' bones to mix all the mortar, if he pleases!'

Ushering six slaves in front of him, the steward brought in sharply flavoured wine, and Tros noticed that Balbus hardly took time to spill the usual libation to the gods before he drank deep and let the slave refill his goblet. He had drunk three times and appeared to feel the effect of it, for his eye was brighter when he gestured very condescendingly to Tros to walk beside him, and led the way across the fountained court toward the dining-hall.

'You shall sit at my right hand,' he said, as if offering the greatest favour in his gift.

The room in which the supper had been prepared was too large for the house, too grandiose, a foretaste, possibly, of Balbus's plans for a new city. It was overloaded with extravagant decoration. Two rows of columns divided the room into three equal sections, in the middle one of which was the supper-table with the couches set, ends toward it.

At the host's end of the table was a daïs hung with curtains, furnished with two gilded couches almost like long thrones. The daïs was approached by three steps, and behind it were three more steps leading to a platform beneath a gallery. They had entered by a side door facing the kitchen and scullery; the main door of the room opened on that platform under the gallery at the rear of the daïs.

Facing the daïs, twenty feet beyond the table's lower end, was a wooden stage for the entertainers, with a flight of steps leading to the tiled floor of the room, and smaller, narrower stages on either side for the musicians, who greeted the guests with a noisy burst of string-music – a jarring twangle of very skilfully manipulated chords.

'I dread draughts,' said Balbus, explaining the crimson and blue curtains that hung from the canopy above the daïs. 'These stone buildings are cold when the night wind comes in from the sea. It is an ill wind, that sea wind. It moans. It makes me shudder.'

He tossed off a great gobletful of red wine that the steward handed to him, then reclined on the couch and signed to Tros to take the other one. The remaining guests were ushered to the places on either side of the table by obsequious attendants, and Pkauchios strode gloomily to what was evidently his usual place at the table's lower end, with his back to the stage. A procession of slaves brought jars of wine, offering each guest his choice of half a dozen vintages, and the guests began drinking at once, ignoring Pkauchios, pledging Balbus and one another amid jokes and laughter.

Balbus acknowledged the toasts with a nod, but was silent for a long time, now and then glancing at Tros while he toyed with the food – all sorts of food, fish, eggs, whale-meat, peacock, sow's udders, venison, birds of a dozen varieties. Tros ate sparingly and drank less, but Balbus ate hardly at all, though he drank continually. There was almost no conversation up there on the daïs until entertainment commenced on the stage, and most of the guests readjusted their positions so as to watch more comfortably a performer on a slack-wire, who went through diabolical contortions with a naked knife in either hand.

The contortions seemed to suggest unpleasant memories to Balbus. He drank deep and leaned toward Tros.

'Now,' he said, 'we can talk.'

Tros glanced at the curtains behind the daïs, and hinted to Balbus that he was ready to talk secrets. Balbus jerked the curtains apart, revealing the great carved cypress door at the rear of the platform behind them. The door was slightly ajar, but it was fifteen feet or more away from the daïs, and there was nobody there except one of Pkauchios's slaves squatting beside a basket.

'What do you do there?' Balbus asked him.

'I wait to summon the midnight dancers.'

'Wait outside!' commanded Balbus, and closed the curtains on their noisy rings and rod with an impatient jerk. The wirewalker had vanished from the stage. There were nine girls dancing bawdily to dreamy music in a greenish light amid incense smoke, and the guests were giving full attention to the stage.

'I understand you wish for influence in Rome,' said Balbus. 'Caesar has denounced you as a pirate. There is a way open to you to become the friend of all Caesar's enemies.'

'Are you his enemy?' Tros asked, and Balbus pouted, frowning.

'No. But the great Pompeius is my patron. A man in my position falls between two stools if he tries to serve two masters. If Caesar should trespass into Hispania, which is Pompeius's and not Caesar's province, he would do so at his own risk. My information is that he will be here within a few days.'

Tros pretended to think awhile and to drink cup for cup with Balbus, but at the foot of his couch near the corner of the curtains there was a very large Greek vase containing flowers, into which it was not particularly difficult to empty a wine-goblet unobserved.

'If Caesar died,' Tros said at last, 'Pompeius would be practically owner of the world. He would reward you.'

Balbus nodded and drank deep again.

'Nothing for nothing!' Tros said abruptly. 'I have brought with me the documents of which we spoke.'

He drew the parchments from the pocket in his cloak.

'Presently, not now,' said Balbus, showing irritation. 'We will discuss those later. Watch this.'

'There is nothing to discuss,' Tros answered. 'You have said you will sign these. Thereafter –'

But Chloe was on the stage, dancing and singing, and now Balbus had eyes and ears for nothing except her.

'Wonderful!' he muttered. 'Wonderful!'

It was her wistfulness that pleased. Beneath the laughter and the daring was a hint of tragedy. She was arrayed in white, a wreath of roses in her hair – a picture of youth, innocence, mirth, modesty. But with an art beyond all fathoming she made it evident that modesty and innocence did not protect her. Not a gesture of indecency, no hint of the vulgarity the other dancers had displayed marred rhythm, voice or harmony of sound and motion. *Saltavit placuit.*

But she pleased by being at the mercy of the men who watched, not posing as a victim that had been debauched, which is a blown rose, but as a bud just opening, aware of life, outbreathing from herself the fragrance of its essence, yet not hoping to be spared the pain of being plucked and trampled underfoot.

The words of the song she sang were Latin, but the mood was Greek, the tune a mere street melody imported by the legionaries from the wineshops in the slums of Rome, cynically mocking its own plaintiveness.

> Lover, trust the night. Day's beams shall burn again.
>   Dreams, trust the dawn; night's shadow shall return.
> Blossom blow! Wind shall bring the warm rain.
>   Fruit fall! Sleep! Again a summer sun shall burn.
> Vineyard, thy plunder sparkles in the red wine!
>   Wind among the sedges, ripples on the shore,
> Laugh to me of glory in the passing. Oh my lover,
>   Is it only love whose ashes live no more?

There were tears in Balbus's eyes. He had reached an almost

253

maudlin stage of drunkenness. When Chloe's dance was done and the noisy guests pledged her in refilled goblets of Falernian, he leaned over toward Tros again and murmured:

'I will buy that girl, though she cost me a senator's ransom! That dog of an Egyptian sorcerer shall find himself surprised for once! He may be able to read the skies, but in Gades I am governor!'

Tros laughed, his mind on opportunity.

'For luck's sake, noble Balbus, sign these first and pledge me to your service!'

He thrust the parchments forward.

'What were they; I forget,' said Balbus, passing a hand before his tired eyes. 'Oh yes, Simon and a manumitted slave. Yes, I will presently be drunk. Yes, I will sign them.'

He called for his secretary, who came with pen and ink-pot, kneeling on the daïs beside Balbus's couch. The secretary read the documents.

'Are they correct?' asked Balbus.

'Simon's account is correct, and he has charged no interest, although he grants six months' time, but – '

'He may be dead in six months, or an outlaw!' Balbus commented. The secretary smiled.

' – but the name of the slave to be manumitted is not written. The master's is – '

Balbus pushed him away; he nearly fell over backward. Chloe was coming down the steps from the stage amid shouts of greeting from the guests. 'Dance, Chloe! Dance down here among us!'

Balbus beckoned to her.

'Bring my seal!' he snapped at the secretary. 'Get me this business over with!'

Chloe came up to the daïs and Balbus seized her round the waist, dragging her down beside him on the couch. To Tros it seemed her wistfulness was due to weariness as much as anything, but Balbus was too far gone in drink to make discrimination of that sort.

'Chloe!' he murmured sentimentally. 'Chloe! Divine Chloe! What shall I do for you? That old Egyptian holds you at a price that – '

He kissed her and she let him cling to her lips, hugging her. The secretary came and pinched her leg. She glanced at him.

'Noble Balbus,' she said, 'documents to sign! Oh, who would be a governor of Gades! La-la!'

She broke away and knelt beside the secretary, exchanging one swift glance with Tros as she rubbed at her mouth with the back of her hand. Balbus had crushed her lips against her teeth.

'Swiftly now and be gone with you!' said Balbus, and the secretary put the seal on all three documents, thereafter holding them for Balbus to attach his signature. Having signed, Balbus snatched them and gave them to Tros. Chloe laughed excitedly in a way that made Balbus stare.

'Your pen,' said Tros, and the secretary brought it to him.

Tros wrote the name of Chloe in the space provided and the secretary, leaning, watching him, laughed aloud, throwing up his hand in a salute to Chloe. Her eyes blazed answer, and it was that that made Balbus turn and stare at Tros.

'What is that? What have you written?' he demanded.

'I will read,' Tros answered, and stood up.

There was dancing on the stage that had been set with branches to suggest a forest, through which satyrs pursued wood nymphs; but it was dull stuff after Chloe's entertainment. All eyes turned to Tros, and the musicians dimmed the clamour of their instruments.

'An order for the manumission of a slave,' Tros read, his great voice booming through the hall. 'In the name of the Senate and the Roman People, I, Lucius Cornelius Balbus Minor, Governor of Gades, in conformance with the law and with the powers vested in me, hereby manumit one Chloe, formerly a slave of Pkauchios the Egyptian, and do accord to her the status of freed woman with all rights and immunities thereunto pertaining, she having paid in full her value of two hundred thousand sesterces to Pkauchios and thereto in addition, into the public treasury, the manumission of tax of ten per cent.'

Pkauchios sprang to his feet, indignant, staggered, his jaws working as he chewed on solid anger.

'But she hasn't paid it!' he exclaimed, his voice broken with excitement.

Tros gave a parchment to the secretary.

'Take it to him!'

The secretary, smiling with stored-up malice, descended to the floor and gave Pkauchios one of Simon's six months' bills on the treasury. He appeared to believe that Balbus had contrived the entire high-handed business, so proceeded at once to lend a hand in it.

'Noble Balbus!' he cried from the end of the table, where Pkauchios stood staring at the parchment, 'this order is for two hundred and twenty thousand sesterces, whereas the price was but

255

two hundred thousand. The tax has been included in the payment made to Pkauchios.'

The Egyptian lost his self-control. He shook the parchment in the faces of the grinning guests.

'This!' he exclaimed. 'This is no payment! This is a mere promise – '

There was too much fume of wine in Balbus's head for him to let that speech pass. Tros had watched him hesitating angrily between repudiation of the documents on the score of trickery and the alternative of making a hard bargain in exchange. Now he turned the full force of his insulted dignity on Pkauchios:

'You speak of my promise as – what?' he demanded, rising from the couch. His legs were steady, but Tros stepped close to him and offered his arm, which he leaned on with relief. 'Do you question my signature? Do you dare to insult me in the presence of my guests?'

'But this is an unheard-of thing,' Pkauchios stammered, struggling to speak calmly.

'You question my authority?' demanded Balbus.

The Egyptian regained his self-control with a prodigious effort, drawing himself to his full height, breathing deeply, then folded the parchment and stuffed it into a pocket at his breast. His mouth was bitter, his eyes malignant.

'I was taken by surprise. I regret my improper exclamation. I accept the order,' he remarked and sat down, rising again promptly because Balbus was still on his feet.

Tros's lips were close to Balbus's ear.

'You will never have to pay that bill,' he whispered.

'He will sell it on the market,' Balbus answered irritably.

Suddenly, under the pressure of personal interest, his brain cleared.

'Yes, yes, the tax!' he said, gesturing with his left hand to the secretary. 'Hold that order on the treasury until Pkauchios pays the twenty thousand sesterces in coin. Otherwise the tax-farmers will accuse me of irregularities.'

He remained standing until Pkauchios had returned the parchment to the secretary, then sat down and drank from the silver winecup that Chloe held for him.

'Divine Chloe, now you are a freed woman, but I have offended Pkauchios,' he said, and kissed her. 'No more will he read the omens for me.'

Most of the guests were growing very drunk, and the girls who had been dancing on the stage came down to sprawl on the

256

couches beside them. One of the two military tribunes noisily demanded that Pkauchios should deliver an augury. The Egyptian glared at him with concentrated scorn, but Balbus heard the repeated demand for an augury and approved.

'Pkauchios!' he shouted. 'Prove to us you are a true seer and no caviller at Fortune!'

Pkauchios rose, glaring balefully at the drunken men and nearly naked women sprawling on the couches. It was nearly a minute before his eyes sought Balbus's face.

'I see fire!' he said then in a harsh voice. 'I see a whole town burning and a thousand men fighting the flames!'

'Thank the gods, not Gades!' Balbus muttered. 'If it were Gades it would be twenty thousand men!'

'I will read the stars!' said Pkauchios, and with a bow of angry dignity began to stride toward the daïs in order to leave the room by the big door behind Balbus.

It was Chloe who intercepted him. She broke away from Balbus's arms and ran to meet him midway of the room, putting both hands on his shoulders. Pkauchios stepped back from her.

'Ingrate!' he growled between set teeth. The coiled asp on his forehead was a perfect complement to the hatred in his eyes. Chloe began whispering to him rapidly, but Pkauchios's face was like a wall against her words.

There began a noise of shouting in the court. The door behind Balbus swung open and a centurion entered breathless. Balbus jerked back the curtains.

'Well? What?' he demanded.

'Fire!' said the centurion. 'A town is burning about twenty miles away. We think it is Porta Valleculae. The tribune Publius Columella has marched all available men to extinguish the flames. He requests you to make arrangements on behalf of those whose homes are burned.'

'They shall have work in the quarries!' Balbus answered. 'Bid him bring the destitute to Gades!'

The centurion saluted and withdrew. Balbus closed the curtains with a shudder at the draught, then stared at Pkauchios who was still scowling at Chloe; but it was now Pkauchios who was whispering. His lips moved slowly, as if he were measuring threats between his teeth.

'A marvel of a man!' said Balbus. 'Did you hear him just now say he could see fire? Fire and a thousand men?'

Chloe had moved so that she could catch Tros's eye; it seemed to him that she was trying to signal to him almost imperceptibly. He touched Balbus's elbow.

'It is too early yet to read the stars. He should read them nearer midnight.'

Balbus glanced at Tros impatiently.

'It was he,' he said, 'who prophesied your coming and Caesar's death.'

'Near midnight is the time,' Tros answered. 'I am a seaman. I know.'

Suddenly Chloe screamed so shrilly that she startled all the amorously drunken guests and brought them sitting upright, staring at her. She clapped both hands to her eyes and ran toward the daïs, stumbling up the steps and flinging herself on her knees by Tros's couch, sobbing.

'Stop him!' she whispered. 'Stop him!'

Then, as if realizing she had come to the wrong couch, still sobbing with her hands before her eyes, she rose again and staggered into Balbus's arms.

'He cursed me!' she moaned. 'He cursed me!'

Balbus began to try to comfort her, patting her between the shoulders, burying his own face in her hair, which gave her an opportunity to catch Tros's eye again. She made a grimace at him and jerked her head in the direction of the stage, then resumed her sobbing. Pkauchios strode solemnly toward the door. Balbus, distracted by Chloe's grief, took no notice of him.

'Music!' Tros suggested, nudging Balbus's elbow. 'Who is in charge of the entertainers? It is music that – '

Balbus laid Chloe sobbing on the couch. She was crying. 'He cursed me! Oh, he cursed me!'

'Pkauchios!' he thundered, and the Egyptian turned to face him. 'Never was such a miserable farce in my house as this night's entertainment! Where are the singers? Why has the music ceased? You promised me such song and dancing for tonight as should – '

'You bade me read the stars,' Pkauchios retorted angrily.

'No insolence!' said Balbus. 'To your duty! Read me the stars at midnight.'

Pkauchios turned back toward the stage and gave his orders to a wizened man with painted cheeks, who disappeared behind the stage. The orchestra began a brilliant, eccentric tune; the kitchen slaves came hurrying with a dozen dishes heaped with steaming food, and the wine-bearers went the rounds. Laughter and conversation began again as a dozen girls writhed on to the stage to perform one of the dances that had made Gades infamous. Chloe ceased her sobbing. Balbus drank deep. Chloe begged leave from him to go and wash her face before she danced again. The slaves filled up the wine-cups, and Balbus, refusing food, leaned over toward Tros, his drunken brain leaping from one passionate emotion to another.

'We were speaking of Caesar. I must have no official knowledge. Do what you will suddenly, at the first chance that presents itself. Then go to Rome and I will send letters overland recommending you to the favour of Pompeius, who will be absolute master of Rome as soon as Caesar is out of the way.'

'Do you wish me to kill him in your house?' Tros asked.

'Kill him anywhere, so be you do it!'

The women on the stage danced in a delirium of orgy, parodying Nature, blaspheming art, ideals, decency. Red light and incense smoke distorted the infernal scene; low drum-beats throbbed through it. One of the military tribunes stood and began singing drunkenly a song that had been outlawed by the Roman aediles. Balbus lay chin on hands, staring at the stage. Tros felt a hand on his back, heard a whisper. Chloe had crept back between the curtains.

'Simon sends word there are soldiers coming through the city gate!'

She slipped away and knelt beside Balbus, who threw an arm around her, but went on staring at the stage. Tros did not move. He was watching Pkauchios, who was listening to the whisperings of a slave. The Egyptian's face was a picture of emotions stirring beneath a mask worn very thin.

There began to be a creeping up Tros's spine. He felt the crisis had arrived too soon. Something, he could not guess what, was happening to upset calculations. He glanced at Balbus, who was almost sleeping; Chloe with subtly caressing fingers was stroking the back of his head and his temples. She smiled and nodded, her eyes shining with excitement. Plainly she knew what was happening. Tros drew out a little bag of pearls, poured them into the palm of his hand, showed them to her and put them away again. She nodded, but he knew her delight in intrigue had run away with her. She would let the pearls go for the thrill of a dramatic climax.

The girls on the stage writhed naked in infernal symbolism. The stringed instruments and muted drums tortured imagination. Pkauchios got up and left the room by the door close to the stage, and Balbus, staring at the dancers, did not notice him. Tros felt for the bugle underneath his cloak, wondering whether Orwic and the Eskualdenak were ready. It was not yet nearly midnight. Possibly

259

some spy had seen them in the quarry; perhaps the soldiers coming through the city gate were on their way to surround them in the dark. But if so, why had nobody warned Balbus?

The suspense became intolerable. He made up his mind to wind a signal on the golden bugle. Better to summon his men and run for it than to run the risk of having them made prisoners. But as he clutched at the bugle. Pkauchios returned and stood with his back to the stage, both hands raised, eyes ablaze, his body trembling with excitement.

'Balbus!' he shouted. 'Caesar is dead! The news has come from Gaul!'

Balbus sat up suddenly and stared. The music stopped, Chloe slipped away from him and stood at the edge of the daïs. The dancers ceased their writhing. Pkauchios signalled to Tros with a gesture like a dagger thrust, then threw up his right hand and shouted:

'Let the trumpets peal the verdict of the sky!'

Tros clutched his sword. He thought he heard the tramp of armed men, but it was drowned by a flourish of trumpets. There was a clang of shields on armour. He leaped to his feet as the door behind the curtain opened suddenly. A hand wrenched back the curtains of the daïs and revealed Julius Caesar with an armoured Roman veteran on either side of him!

Caesar was in white, unhelmeted, a wreath of laurel on his brow, his scarlet cloak thrown back over his shoulder and his lean face smiling like a god's, inscrutable, alert, amused, as calm as marble.

The centurion at his right hand raised a richly decorated shield and shouted:

'Caius Julius Caesar, imperator, proconsul and commander of the Roman troops in Gaul!'

Aye, measure. Milestones; beacons-distance from a headland to a headland; time; the price of onions and sailcloth; speed; angle of heel of a ship in a gale of wind. A ship is built by measure.

But the measure by which one man is greater than another, show it to me! I have seen a pox slay thousands. Is a pox, then, greater than the wisely gentle whom it slew with its foulness?

Blow ye your boasts! I have a sail and the sun and stars to steer by toward open sea.

From the log of Tros of Samothrace

The dancers vanished. The women sprawling on the couches fled. Balbus and his guests staggered to their feet.

'Caesar!' said Balbus.

Caesar smiled genially. If he had noticed Tros yet, he gave no sign of it.

'No, no, Balbus! Pray be seated. Pray don't disturb yourself.'

His voice, a shade ironical, was reassuring. There was no hint in it of violence. But behind him were more armed men than Tros could count from where he stood. They were formed up in a solid phalanx in the hall.

'Don't let me interrupt your gaiety,' said Caesar. 'I have already had my supper.'

'There came news of your death!' Balbus stammered.

'I overheard it. Does it seem true to you?' asked Caesar, smiling again.

His eyes began to scrutinize the guests, who saluted as he noticed them, but he ignored Tros at the corner of the daïs. He appeared to Tros to be deliberately giving Balbus time to recover his wits. Tros, the golden bugle in his left, kept his right hand on his sword-hilt, listening, trying to discover how many armed men Caesar had with him. None noticed Pkauchios, until suddenly Chloe screamed as the Egyptian sprang at the daïs from behind Tros – mad, foaming at the mouth.

'Slay!' he screamed, striking at Tros with his left hand, trying to push him forward toward Balbus, then rushing at Caesar.

Tros tripped him. He fell on his back on the daïs, striking with a wave-edged dagger at the air.

'Dog of a Samothracian!' he yelled. Frenzied, he leaped to his feet with the energy of an old ape at bay and sprang at Tros, who knocked him down again. A legionary stepped out of the ranks at Caesar's back and calmly drew a sword across his throat.

'Now I am no longer a freed woman. I am free!' said Chloe. 'And Balbus, you need never pay that debt!'

Caesar looked bored by the interruption. Slaves came and dragged away Pkauchios's body, Balbus's steward superintending, making himself very inconspicuous. A wine-bearer poured choice Falernian over the blood on the daïs carpet, and another slave mopped it up with his own long loin-cloth, running naked from the room. The steward threw salt on the carpet and covered the spot with a service napkin of blue linen.

Chloe stepped straight up to Caesar and knelt smiling up at him with all the charm she could contrive.

'Imperator,' she said, 'I am Chloe, who danced for you in Gaul – she whom Horatius Verres trusted.'

Horatius Verres stepped out from behind the ranks of legionaries and stood between Tros and Caesar, watching with a quiet smile on his handsome face. He was dressed as a slave in a drab-coloured tunic of coarse cloth.

'Tut-tut!' said Caesar. 'Go and clothe yourself!'

Horatius Verres made a humorous, helpless gesture. Balbus's steward touched him from behind and beckoned. He shrugged his shoulders and went with the steward to be rearrayed in borrowed finery. Tros made up his mind there were not so many men at Caesar's back; he raised the bugle to his lips and Caesar noticed him at last.

'Your men are here already,' he said. 'They are behind me!'

As if in answer to his words there began a roar of fighting. A centurion barked an order. About half of Caesar's own men faced about and vanished toward the front of the house, but Caesar took no notice whatever of the disturbance.

'Balbus,' he said, 'a noble enemy is preferable to any faithless friend. The story goes you sent men into Gaul to murder me.'

Chloe was still kneeling. She caught her breath and glanced sharply at Balbus's face. Balbus, deathly white, threw up his right hand.

'Caesar, by the immortal gods I swear – '

Something choked Balbus. He coughed. He had become aware

that Tros was staring at him. He drew three breaths before he found his voice again:

'That sorcerer, now dead, that Egyptian Pkauchios – and – '

He turned and looked straight at Tros, began to raise his arm to point at him. Tros drew his sword.

'Balbus,' said Caesar, 'you have been well served! Well for you that Tros of Samothrace put into Gades!'

Balbus gasped. Tros stood with drawn sword watching Caesar's face. A centurion came pushing past the legionaries and whispered to Caesar from behind him. Horatius Verres re-entered the room, handsome, smiling, splendid in a Roman tunic with a broad blue border, and stood close to Tros again, glancing at the drawn sword with a humorous expression.

Balbus's brain was wavering between surrender to the fumes of wine and a sort of half-hysterical recovery. Tros's mind was on Orwic and his men, but he could not fight his way past Caesar's legionaries. Caesar fascinated him. The man's cool self-command, his manners, daring and superb contempt for any genius less comprehensive that his own stirred grudging admiration.

Chloe broke the silence:

'Imperator – '

But Caesar checked her with a gesture of his left hand. He was listening. Tros, too, caught the sound of footsteps surging over the porch into the house.

'Orwic!' he shouted.

There came an answering yell, and half the legionaries behind Caesar faced about.

'Orwic, hold your men!' Tros roared in Gaulish. Then, watching Caesar's face, 'Let none escape! Let a hundred of your men surround the house and guard all exits!'

He laughed. He heard Orwic's boyish voice repeating the order to the Eskualdenak.

'Caesar,' he said, 'I have more than five men to your one! The camp is empty, the Roman legion went to a burning village – '

'Yes,' said Caesar, 'but that was not your doing, Tros, so you must not boast of it.'

'Caesar!' said Balbus suddenly, recovering his wits, 'this is not your province!'

He glanced at Tros, a fever of excitement in his eyes. The legionaries behind Caesar moved alertly to protect him.

'The illustrious Tros and I are enemies,' said Caesar, 'whose activities are not confined to provinces or marred by malice. We use common sense. I have not interfered with your government,

263

Balbus. You must pardon me if I have interrupted even your' – he glanced at the stage – 'amusement.'

Tros's brain was speculating furiously. There were only two things Caesar could be doing. Either he had surprises up his sleeve and was talking to gain time, or else he was deliberately trying to bring Balbus to his senses with a view of getting his gratitude and making use of him. In either event, time was all-important.

'Caesar,' said Tros, 'why did you come to Gades? What do you want?'

'Yes, Caesar, what do you want?' demanded Balbus.

Caesar smiled.

'For one thing, courtesy!' he answered. 'Balbus, I consider you a churlish host! You offer me no seat, no welcome. You oppose me guiltily, as if I caught you in the act of treachery. Whereas I came for your sake.'

But Balbus was too drunk to take a hint.

'You came uninvited!' he said, sneering.

Caesar smiled again and glanced at Tros.

'I think we both did! Tros, for what reason did you come to Gades?'

'To prevent you from invading Britain, Caesar!'

'Imperator, that is the truth!' said Chloe, and she would have said more, but Caesar silenced her with a frown.

'Are you a slave?' he asked.

'No, Caesar, I am free!'

'Then go to Horatius Verres and keep still.'

Chloe sprang gaily to Verres' side and threw her arms around him, kissed him, or else whispered in his ear. Tros suspected the latter. Orwic was having trouble with the Eskualdenak, who were anxious to begin looting Balbus's treasures. In the outer hall his voice kept rising sharply. There were hot answers in almost incomprehensible Gaulish, and every once in a while a Roman centurion added his staccato warning to the noise. Horatius Verres spoke at last.

'Imperator,' he said quietly, 'I had the honour to report to you that Tros refused to murder Balbus, and you saw that when Pkauchios rushed at you, it was Tros who prevented. Now Chloe tells me that while Tros and Balbus supped together they discussed – '

'Silence!' snapped Balbus angrily. 'Caesar, will you take the word of a dancing-girl against me?'

Caesar eyed him with amused contempt.

'If she should testify for you, should I accept her evidence then?' he asked. Then after a pause, 'Let Horatius Verres speak.'

'Tros even left a pledge with the committee of nineteen to guarantee that he would not kill Balbus.'

Balbus snorted.

'A committee of nineteen? I never heard of them!'

'You shall know them well,' said Caesar. 'Continue, Verres.'

'And while Tros and Balbus supped together they discussed –'

'Stop!' commanded Balbus, almost choking. 'Caesar, this is not your province! You have no authority to –'

Caesar raised his right hand with a gesture so magnificent that Balbus checked a word midway and stared at him open-mouthed. Chloe was whispering again in Verres' ear. Caesar nodded to Verres.

'They discussed what Tros had previously said to me before the committee of nineteen – how that his father, dying, prophesied he should eventually render Caesar a great service.'

Balbus breathed heavily and felt for something to lean against. His steward stepped up to the daïs and, lifting his arm, placed it on his own shoulder.

'My noble master has so burdened himself with public duties that he faints,' he said, beckoning to a slave to bring wine.

'I suggest he has had wine enough,' said Caesar. 'You may continue, Verres.'

Chloe was watching Tros out of the corner of her eye. Her breast fluttered with excitement. Verres spoke:

'While Balbus and Tros supped together, they discussed whether it were true that you invaded Britain for the sake of pearls.'

'I invaded Britain,' said Caesar, smiling slightly with the corners of his eyes as he saw Tros glare at Chloe, 'because the Britons intrigued with the Gauls against me, despite all warnings. But I confess the thought of pearls did interest me. I have in mind to make a breastplate of them for the statue of the Venus Genetrix in Rome, from whose immortal womb I trace descent,' he added pompously. It was his first hint of vulgarity, his first betrayal of a streak of weakness. 'What else, Horatius Verres?'

'Tros, who promised thirty pearls to Chloe to procure for him the interview with Balbus, discussed with Balbus at the supper-table how he might offer three hundred pearls to yourself, Imperator, as an inducement to you to bury enmity!'

The lie slid off his handsome lips as smoothly as the passing moment. Balbus, his steward urging with a whisper, leaped at opportunity at last.

'I told him he should offer at least a thousand pearls,' he blustered, avoiding Tros's eyes. 'Caesar, the words had hardly left my lips when you burst in on us!'

Horatius Verres, hand to his mouth, stepped back a pace.

'I told you I serve Caesar!' he whispered to Tros.

'Have you the pearls?' asked Caesar, and Tros saw light at last, knew he must make a sacrifice, but saw he held the situation in the hollow of his hand.

'I have them on my ship,' he answered, standing forth and facing Caesar.

But his eyes were busily numbering the men at Caesar's back. Beyond the legionaries, in the gloom of the fountained courtyard, he could dimly make out Orwic and the Eskualdenak crowding the Romans.

'I have here five men to your one, Caesar, and I care nothing for your friendship.'

'Have I offered it?' asked Caesar, adjusting his wreath with one forefinger. 'Let us have no brawling, Tros. The place smells like a tavern' – he sniffed disgustedly – 'but' – he bowed with mock politeness – 'perhaps our host Balbus will excuse us if we act like sober men!'

'Caesar, I could have slain you when you entered. I could slay you now,' Tros answered. 'I would hold my own life cheap at the price of saving Gaul and Hispania, but the gods have laid no such task on me. Ten tyrants might replace you if I slew the one. I came here for my own sake. I will pay three hundred pearls for what I want. Agree with me or – '

He raised the golden bugle to his lips. Orwic began shouting to him:

'Tros! Tros! What is happening?'

'Await my bugle blast,' Tros answered. 'Caesar, is it yes or no?'

The legionaries raised their shields an inch or two, but Caesar spread both arms out to restrain them.

'Better to die a thousand times than to live in fear of death,' he said, 'but I see, Tros, that you know that. Since neither you nor I fear death, we may stand on common ground. What is it you require of me?'

'You named me pirate.' Tros growled at him.

'I withdraw that gladly, though you sunk my ships. You have served Rome by saving Gades from the mob. I will write it,' said Caesar.

'You owe my friend Simon of Gades three million sesterces,' said Tros.

266

'If that were only all!' said Caesar, smiling with an air of mock humility. 'Debts, Tros, seem as necessary to a statesman as is the appetite that makes us eat. Your friend Simon shall be paid.'

'How? When?' Tros asked him.

A flash of humour blazed in Caesar's eyes. He looked at Balbus long and keenly.

'Balbus – how? When?' he asked calmly.

Balbus bit his lip.

'Come now, Balbus. Tros saved your life, and it is easier for me to act against you than to threaten you. How shall Simon be paid? That legion that went to Porta Valleculae is on its way back, Balbus, shouting. "Caesar is imperator!" – No, no, Tros, there is a truce between us. Stay! I merely wish that Balbus should choose his allegiance – of your free will, Balbus – of your free will! You are under no distraint. As you wisely remarked, I have no authority in Gades, even though the committee of nineteen has begged me, on my way between the harbour and your house, to add Hispania to my province and appoint my own officials. They amused me, but it might amuse me more to – '

'Caesar, I beg you to permit me to assume the debt!' said Balbus.

'I am afraid it will keep you poor and out of mischief for a long time,' Caesar remarked. 'If I consent to allow to escape my mind irregularities that I have heard of, would it be agreeable to you to confer in future with that committee of nineteen with respect to all local issues?'

Balbus nodded sulkily.

'And to remember, Balbus, that they have my individual protection? If the world were my province – then would you wish to rebuild Gades?'

'Caesar, I yield,' said Balbus. 'When the day comes that you strike at Pompey, I am with you.'

'Tut-tut!' remarked Caesar. 'Who spoke of striking at Pompey? But I see Tros grows impatient. He is thinking of that legion on its way back from Porta Valleculae. Tros, you are a greater man than I believed you. A mere pirate would have plundered Gades with the opportunity you have had. Had you been a rash fool, you would have tried to kill me. You might even have succeeded and the world would have been the worse for it. So the world owes you a reward, Tros.'

'Reward my men!' Tros answered. The Eskualdenak were growing noisier every minute, and Orwic's voice was hoarse from trying to restrain them.

'Balbus shall pay them handsomely,' said Caesar. 'They have saved his life. The world is richer for our noble Balbus, although he personally will be poorer for a long time! Yes, Tros, I will accept your gift of pearls for the breastplate of the Venus Genetrix, be it understood – a very amiable goddess, my immortal ancestress.'

He strode forward to a couch and sat with grace and dignity, letting the scarlet cloak fall carefully to hide his knees.

'You are in haste, I don't doubt. Yes, of course, that legion is returning. Yes, yes. Balbus, may your secretary bring me ink and parchment? I carry my own pen. Tros, I believe you have my seal. Will you return it to me? Balbus, will you kindly see that Tros's men are handsomely paid? They were my men until Tros ran off with them, hah-hah! Very clever of you, Tros, but beware next time we meet! There was three months' pay at that time owing to each man. So I suggest it would be very handsome of you, Balbus, to give each man three months' full pay of a Roman soldier. It might encourage them not to loot the house! Then, will someone go for Simon and for the committee of nineteen? Balbus, I would like to introduce them to you and to recommend them personally to your generous consideration. By the way, Tros, where are those pearls?'

'On the ship,' Tros answered.

Chloe came and stood in front of him and smiled. She held out her hand. Tros counted thirty pearls into her palm, holding his sword under his armpit.

'Caesar!' she said excitedly. 'Imperator! Grant me permission to wear pearls!'

Glancing up from the parchment he was writing, Caesar frowned. Horatius Verres put in a word:

'Imperator, no permission will be needed. She will be a Roman's wife!'

'Very well. Why interrupt?' said Caesar, and went on writing. 'Balbus,' he jerked over his shoulder, 'are Tros's men being paid?'

'My treasurer is paying them.'

'Has Simon been sent for? Very well. Be good enough to sign this undertaking to pay to Simon three million sesterces in equal payments of three hundred thousand sesterces every three months. You understand, of course, this payment is not taxable. He must receive the whole of it. Tros – '

He stood up, holding out a parchment.

'This confers on you authority to go anywhere you please, including Ostia and Rome. It specifically withdraws the charge of piracy against you and names you the friend of the Roman people. You will find the committee of nineteen on the porch. They will return your one-eyed hostage to you. If you should remove the other eye, he might see his way into trouble less easily.

'However, that is for you to decide. You will meet your friend Simon on your way toward the city gate. Be good enough to take him with you to your ship and to give him those pearls, which he may bring to me and I will give him this liquidation of his debt in exchange for them. I understand you have a hostage on your ship, one Gaius Suetonius. Release him, please. Not that he has any virtue, but for the sake of his beautiful armour. Have you any other prisoners?'

'Herod the Jew,' Tros answered.

'That scoundrel?' Caesar nodded. 'Send him to me in charge of Gaius Suetonius! Be good enough to avoid collision with the little ship on which I came. It is anchored rather close to yours. You will go to Rome now?'

'Aye!' Tros answered, accepting the parchment.

'Hah! You will try to prevent me from invading Britain! You will find the Romans less reasonable than myself. When you have failed, come and make your peace with me. I will receive you! Thanks for the pearls for the –'

'For the wives of the Roman senators!' said Tros, and bowing first to Caesar, then to Balbus, marched out straight through the ranks of Caesar's bodyguard. He was greeted by a roar from the Eskualdenak:

'Wine! Women! Wine!'

His answering roar, bull-bellowed, cowed them into silence.

'To the ship! Behind me, march! Or I will give the lot of you to Caesar! Ho there, Conops! Run ahead of me and keep a bright lookout for Simon.'

Then he strode under the gloomy cypresses to Balbus's front gate, and Orwic fell in step beside him full of eagerness to know exactly what had happened.

'Happened?' he said. 'I have promised druids' pearls to Caesar's lights-o'-love, and I have served Caesar, though I had the best of him. Rot me all death-bed prophecies. They dull men's wits!'

'What next?' asked Orwic.

'Oar and sail for Ostia, before Caesar has time to set a trap for us in Rome!'

Occult and the Unusual in Tandem editions

ESP Your Sixth Sense   Brad Steiger 17½p

Astrology   Glyn Truly 17½p

Witchcraft in the World Today   C. H. Wallace 25p

Voices from Beyond   Brad Steiger 17½p

The Mind Travellers   Brad Steiger..   ..   ..   ..   17½p

Real Ghosts, Restless Spirits and Haunted Minds   Brad
   Steiger 25p

Satanism and Witchcraft   Jules Michelet 30p

Witches and their Craft   Ronald Seth 30p

Reincarnation   Hans Stefan Santesson 25p

The Burning Court   John Dickson Carr 25p

Bring Out the Magic in Your Mind   Al Koran 30p

Guide to the Supernatural   Raymond Buckland   ..   25p

The Vampire   Ornella Volta 25p

The Accursed   Claude Seignolle 25p

U.F.O.s in Tandem editions

New U.F.O. Breakthrough (Allende Letters) Brad
   Steiger and Joan Whritenour 17½p

Flying Saucers from Outer Space   Donald E. Keyhoe   ..   30p

Flying Saucers are Hostile   Brad Steiger and Joan
   Whritenour 25p

Strangers from the Skies   Brad Steiger 25p

The Sky People   Brinsley Le Poer Trench 25p

Name ....

Address ....

Titles required................................

....

--- --- --- --- --- --- --- --- --- --- --- --- ---

The publishers hope that you enjoyed this book and invite you to write for the full list of Tandem titles which is available free of charge.

If you find any difficulty in obtaining these books from your usual retailer we shall be pleased to supply the titles of your choice—packing and postage 5p—upon receipt of your remittance.

WRITE NOW TO:
     Universal-Tandem Publishing Co. Ltd.,
     14 Gloucester Road,
     London SW7